We hope you enjoy this book. Please return or renew it by the due date.

You can renew it at www.norfolk.gov.uk/libraries or by using our free library app.

Otherwise you can phone 0344 800 8020 - please have your library card and PIN ready.

You can sign up for email reminders too.

17 | 8 | 19

28. FEB 20.

NORFOLK COUNTY LIBRARY
WITHDRAWN FOR SALE

KU-750-675

Also available in Arrow by Georgette Heyer

A Civil Contract

Georgette Heyer

arrow books

Published by Arrow Books in 2005

16

Copyright © Georgette Heyer, 1961
Initial lettering copyright © Stephen Raw, 2004

Georgette Heyer has asserted her right under the Copyright, Designs
and Patents Act, 1988 to be identified as the author of this work

First published in the United Kingdom in 1961 by William Heinemann Ltd

Arrow Books
The Random House Group Limited
20 Vauxhall Bridge Road, London, SW1V 2SA

www.penguin.co.uk

Addresses for companies within The Random House Group Limited can be found at:
www.randomhouse.co.uk/offices.htm

The Random House Group Limited Reg. No 954009

A CIP catalogue record for this book
is available from the British Library

ISBN 9780099474449

Penguin Random House is committed to a sustainable future for
our business, our readers and our planet. This book is made from
Forest Stewardship Council® certified paper.

Printed and bound in Great Britain by Clays Ltd, St Ives plc

Typeset by SX Composing DTP, Rayleigh, Essex

To Pat Wallace with Love

One

The library at Fontley Priory, like most of the principal apartments in the sprawling building, looked to the south-east, commanding a prospect of informal gardens and a plantation of poplars, which acted as a wind-break and screened from view the monotony of the fen beyond. On an afternoon in March the sunlight did not penetrate the Gothic windows, and the room seemed dim, the carpet, the hangings, and the tooled leather backs of the books in the carved shelves as faded as the uniform of the man who sat motionless at the desk, his hands lying clasped on a sheaf of papers, his gaze fixed on a clump of daffodils, nodding in the wind that soughed round the angles of the house, and passed like a shadow over the unscythed lawn.

The uniform showed the buff facings and silver lace of the 52nd Regiment; it was as threadbare as the carpet, but for all its shabbiness it seemed incongruous: as out of place in this quiet room as the man who wore it felt himself to be.

He should not have done so: the Priory was his birthplace, and he owned it; but his adult years had been spent in very different scenes from the placid fens and wolds of Lincolnshire, and his transition from the grandeur of the Pyrenees had been too sudden, and attended by circumstances of too much horror to make it seem to him anything other than a bad dream from which he would presently be awakened by a call to arms, or by a stampeding mule brought down by the guy-ropes of his tent, or by the mere bustle of a camp at first light.

The letters from England had reached him on the last day of January. He had first read his mother's, written in the agitation of her bereavement, and conveying to him in a barely legible series of crossed and recrossed lines the news that his father was dead. He had been more shocked than grieved, never having enjoyed more than a casual acquaintance with the late Viscount. Lord Lynton, while bluff and good-natured when confronted with any of his offspring, had not been blessed with domestic virtues. A close friend of the Prince Regent, he had so much preferred the Prince's society to that of his family that very little of his time had been spent in his home, and none at all in considering what might be the hopes or characteristics of one surviving son and two daughters.

He had been killed on the hunting-field, in the first burst, taking a double at the fly: not a surprising end for an intrepid and frequently reckless horseman. What did surprise his son was to discover that contrary to advice and entreaty he had been riding a green and headstrong young horse, never before tried in the field. Lord Lynton was a bruising rider, but not a fool; his heir, knowing the wild hurly-burly of a first burst with the Quorn or the Belvoir, concluded that he had ridden his young 'un for a wager, and passed on to a maternal command to sell out instantly, and return to England, where his presence was most urgently needed.

The new Lord Lynton (but it was to be many weeks before he answered readily to any other title than Captain Deveril) could not find in his mother's letter any reason why he should pursue a course so repugnant to himself. The letter from Lord Lynton's man of business was less impassioned but more explicit.

He read it twice before his brain was able to grasp its horrifying intelligence, and many times before he laid it before his Colonel.

No one could have been kinder; to no one else, indeed, could Adam Deveril have borne to have disclosed that letter. Colonel Colborne had read it, his countenance unmoved, and he had offered no unwanted sympathy. 'You must go,' he had said. 'I'll grant you furlough immediately, to expedite the business, but you'll sell out, of course.' Then, guessing the thoughts hidden behind Adam's rigid countenance, he had added: 'A year ago there might have been doubts which way your duty should have led you, but there are none now. We shall soon have Soult on the run in good earnest. I shan't say you won't be missed: you will be – damnably! – but your absence won't affect the issue *here*. There's no question about it, you know: you must go home to England.'

He had known it, of course, and had argued neither with his Colonel nor his own conscience. He had sailed on the first available transport, and, after a brief halt in London, had posted on to Lincolnshire, leaving his man of business to discover the extent of his liabilities, and his tailor to deliver with all possible expedition raiment suited to a civilian gentleman in deep mourning.

This had not yet arrived, but the news that his Regiment had distinguished itself at the Battle of Orthes had reached Fontley, making him at once exultant and wretched; and Mr Wimmering had presented himself at Fontley on the previous day. He had spent the night at the Priory; but the younger Miss Deveril was of the opinion that he could not have enjoyed more than two or three hours of sleep, since he had remained closeted with her brother until dawn. He was very civil to the ladies, so it was unkind of her to liken him to a bird of ill-omen. He was very civil to the new Viscount too, and very patient, answering all his questions without betraying that he found him lamentably ignorant.

Adam said, with a smile in his tired gray eyes: 'You must think me a fool to ask you so many stupid questions. I'm a Johnny Raw, you see. I've never dealt with such matters as these. I don't understand them, and I must.'

No, Mr Wimmering did not think his lordship a fool, but deeply did he regret that the late Viscount had not seen fit to admit him to his confidence. But the late Viscount had not seen fit to admit even his man of business wholly into his confidence: there had been transactions on the Stock Exchange in which

3

agents unknown to Wimmering had been employed. He said mournfully: 'I could not have advised his lordship to invest his money as he sometimes did. But his nature was sanguine – and I must acknowledge that on several occasions he was fortunate in ventures which I, as a man of affairs, could not have recommended to him.' He refreshed himself with a pinch of snuff taken from the battered silver box which he had been tapping with the tip of one desiccated finger, and added: 'I was well-acquainted with your honoured parent, my lord, and have for long been persuaded that it was his hope to have restored to its former prosperity the inheritance to which he succeeded, and which, he knew, must in the course of nature presently fall into your hands. The speculative, and, alas, unlucky enterprise upon which he entered shortly before his untimely demise –' He broke off, transferring his gaze from Adam's face to the line of swaying tree-tops beyond the gardens. To them he apparently addressed the rest of his speech, saying: 'It should never be forgotten that his late lordship's nature was, as I have remarked, sanguine. Dear me, yes! If I had a hundred pounds for every occasion on which his lordship suffered reverses on 'Change without the least diminution of his optimism I should be a wealthy man, I assure you, sir!'

No answer was vouchsafed to this. Adam, instead of seeking further reassurance, said in an even tone: 'In plain words, Wimmering, how do my affairs stand?'

Plain words, in situations of the utmost delicacy, were obnoxious to Wimmering, but, impelled by some quality in that quiet voice, he replied with unaccustomed bluntness: 'Badly, my lord.'

Adam nodded. 'How badly?'

Mr Wimmering set his fingertips exactly together, and replied evasively: 'It is in the highest degree unfortunate that your lordship's grandfather should have deceased before the coming of age of his late lordship. It was his intention to have resettled the estates. At that time, as I need not remind your lordship, my own revered parent stood in the same relation to the Fourth Viscount as I have stood in to the Fifth, and – if I may be permitted to express the wish – as I hope to stand in to your lordship. When you, my lord, attained your majority, it was my earnest desire to have induced his late lordship to repair an omission rendered inevitable by the inscrutable workings of Providence. His lordship, however, did not consider the moment opportune for the prosecution of a design which, I assure you, he had very much at heart. *Your* presence, my lord, must have been essential: I can have no need to recall to your mind the circumstances which would have made it hard indeed for you to have applied for furlough just then. The Combat of the Coa! It seems but yesterday that we were eagerly perusing the account of that engagement, with the words of commendation bestowed by Lord Wellington on the officers and the men of your lordship's Regiment!'

'The estates, I collect, were even then encumbered?' interpolated his lordship.

Mr Wimmering bowed his head in sorrowful assent, but raised it again to offer a palliative. 'But her ladyship's jointure was secured to her.'

'And my sisters' portions?'

Wimmering sighed. After a pause, Adam said: 'The case seems to be desperate. What must I do?'

'Serious, my lord, but not desperate, we must trust.' He raised his hand, as Adam made a gesture towards the mass of papers on his desk. 'Let me beg of you not to refine too much upon demands which were, under the circumstances, inevitable! None are immediately pressing. A certain degree of alarm in the creditors was to be expected, and to allay that must be – indeed, *has* been – my first concern. I do not by any means despair of composing all these matters.'

'I have no great head for figures,' Adam replied, 'but I think the debts total a larger amount than my disposable assets.' He picked up a paper, and studied it. 'You have set no value on the racing-stables, I observe. Those, I think, should be sold at once, and also the town house.'

'Upon no account!' interrupted Wimmering earnestly. 'Such

an action, my lord, would prove fatal, believe me! Let me repeat that my care has been to allay anxiety: until we see our way more clearly that is most necessary.'

Adam laid the paper down. 'It is already clear to me. I am facing ruin, am I not?'

'Your lordship takes too despondent a view. The shock has overset you! But we need not despair.'

'No, if I had time enough, and the means, perhaps I could restore our fortunes. Surely Fontley was prosperous in my grandfather's day? Since I came home I have been going all about with our bailiff, trying to learn from him in a week the things I ought to have learned when I was a boy. Instead –' he smiled rather painfully – 'I was army-mad. One doesn't realize, or foresee – But repining won't help me out of my difficulties. The land here is as rich as any in Lincolnshire, but so much needs to be done! And if I had the means to do it I should wish above all things to redeem the mortgages, and that I certainly have not the means to do.'

'My lord, not all your lands are mortgaged! Do not, I beg of you –'

'Mercifully, not all. The house, and the demesne-lands are unencumbered. Can you tell me what price we should set on them? Both have been neglected, but the Priory is generally thought to be beautiful, and has, besides, historic interest.'

'Sell Fontley?' exclaimed Wimmering, aghast. 'Your lordship cannot be serious! You are speaking in jest, of course!'

'No, I am not speaking in jest,' Adam replied quietly. 'I don't think I ever felt less like jesting in my life. If you could show me how to pay off this load of debt, how to provide for my sisters, without selling Fontley – but you can't, can you?'

'My lord,' said Wimmering, recovering his countenance, 'I trust I may be able to do so. It might not be an easy task, but it has occurred to me – if I may speak frankly on a subject of an intimate nature?'

Adam looked surprised, but nodded.

'Such unhappy situations as this are not of such rare

6

occurrence as one could wish, my lord,' said Mr Wimmering, intently scrutinizing his fingers. 'I could tell you of cases within my own experience where the sadly fallen fortunes of a noble house have been resuscitated by a judicious alliance.'

'Good God, are you suggesting that I should marry an heiress?' Adam demanded.

'It has frequently been done, my lord.'

'I daresay it has, but you mustn't expect me to do it, I'm afraid,' returned Adam. 'I don't think I'm acquainted with any heiresses, and I'm sure I shouldn't be regarded as an eligible suitor.'

'On the contrary, my lord! Your lineage is distinguished; you are the holder of a title; the owner of very considerable estates, and of a seat – as you have said yourself – of historic interest.'

'I never suspected that you had a turn for nonsense!' Adam interrupted. 'These possessions of mine are very fine-sounding until you tap them, when they have a hollow ring. In any event, I don't contemplate putting myself up for sale.'

There was a note of finality in his voice, and Wimmering bowed to it, content for the present to have instilled the idea into his brain. He might recoil from it, but Wimmering had formed a favourable opinion of his good sense, and he hoped that when he had recovered from the shock of finding himself on the brink of ruin he would perceive the advantages of what was, in his adviser's view, a very simple way out of his difficulties. It was fortunate that he was unattached – if he *was* unattached. Wimmering knew that a year previously he had fancied himself in love with Lord Oversley's daughter; but no notice of an engagement had ever appeared, and the connection had not met with the Fifth Viscount's approbation. The Fifth Viscount had been quite as anxious as Wimmering that his son should marry money; and from what he knew of Lord Oversley's circumstances Wimmering could not suppose that he either regarded with enthusiasm such an alliance. Miss Julia was an accredited Beauty; and if any man could have made an accurate guess at the extent of Lord Lynton's embarrassments it must have been his old friend Oversley. No, Wimmering was inclined to think that his late lordship had been right when he had dismissed the affair as mere calf-love.

('And now there's that cub of mine fancying himself in love with Oversley's girl!' had said his lordship, in one of his moments of exasperation. 'All humdudgeon! never looked twice at the chit till he was sent home with a ball in his hip! He's been living in the girl's pocket ever since he could hobble round to Mount Street. A couple of green 'uns! I shan't lose any sleep over such fiddle-faddling nonsense!')

Wimmering would lose no sleep either. The new Viscount had repudiated with distaste the suggestion that he should hang out for a likely heiress, but he had given no indication that his affections were already engaged. It was not wonderful that he should have alleviated the pain and the weariness of the months he had spent in and out of the surgeons' hands with a flirtation with the lovely Miss Oversley; still less wonderful that a romantic girl should have encouraged the gallantry of a hero of Salamanca. In Wimmering's opinion, it would be more wonderful if so youthful an affair had survived separation.

As for his lordship's doubt of his acceptability, Wimmering did not share it. Lord Oversley might not welcome the alliance, but it was not of such parents as Oversley that Wimmering was thinking. It had plainly not occurred to the Viscount that he should seek a wife in the ranks of the rich merchants: probably he would dislike that idea at first, but he seemed to be a sensible young man, and one who would probably go to almost any length to preserve the place which had for generations been the home of the Deverils. There would be nothing unusual in such a match: no need at all for his lordship to marry a vulgar mushroom's heiress. Mr Wimmering could call to mind a dozen very gentlemanly persons engaged in trade who were anxious to thrust their offspring up the social ladder; but, on the whole, he was inclined to think that the ideal bride should be sought in one or other of the great banking-houses. That would be quite unexceptionable. The chances were, too, that unless the girl was very hard to please she would take a fancy to his lordship. He was a good-looking young man, though not handsome in his father's slightly flamboyant style. His was a thin, sensitive countenance, rendered charming by his smile, which was of peculiar sweetness. He looked older than his twenty-six years, his face being a little lined through constant puckering of his eyes against a scorching sun, and his skin rather weather-beaten. He was of average height, well-built, but lacking his father's magnificent physique: indeed, had it not been for a certain tautness in his carriage, betraying the muscles in his spare frame, it might have been suspected that he was delicate, so thin was he. When he walked it was with a slight halt, but that legacy from Salamanca did not seem to discommode him much. He was lucky not to have had his leg amputated, though it was doubtful if he had thought so at the time. Wimmering did not know how many agonizing operations he had been obliged to undergo before the surgeons succeeded in extracting the ball and all the splinters of bone, but he thought that those weeks had set their ineradicable mark on his lordship's face.

He did not again mention the marriage-scheme, but devoted himself instead to the task of guiding the Viscount through the tangled maze of his father's affairs. He was genuinely grieved to see the look of care deepen in the young man's fine eyes, but he did not try to minimize the gravity of his predicament: the more fully my lord realized this the more likely would he be to overcome his reluctance to marry for the sake of a fortune. When Wimmering left the Priory it was in a hopeful mood, for his opinion of his new patron's good sense had mounted considerably. He had taken the shocking news well, not railing against fate, or uttering any word of bitterness. If he blamed his father it was silently: he seemed more inclined to blame himself. He was undoubtedly a little stunned; but when he had recovered he would think it over calmly, and, in his search for a solution to his troubles, remember the suggestion that had been made to him, and perhaps think that over too.

Mr Wimmering was not a very warmhearted man, but when

he took leave of Adam he was conscious of a purely human desire to help him. He was behaving beautifully: much better than his father had behaved in moments of sudden stress. When he saw Wimmering off in one of his own carriages, which would convey Wimmering to Market Deeping, on the first stage of his journey back to London, he said, with his delightful smile: 'You will be jolted to bits, I'm afraid! The road is as bad as any in Portugal. Thank you for undertaking such a tiresome journey: I am very much obliged to you! I shall be in town within a few days – as soon as I have settled some few matters here, and consulted with my mother.'

He shook hands, and waited to see the carriage in motion before going back to the library.

He sat down again at the desk, with the intention of arranging in some sort of order the litter of papers on it, but when he had gathered into a formidable pile the tradesmen's bills, he sat quite still for a long time, looking through the window at the daffodils, but not seeing them.

He was recalled from this abstraction by the sound of an opening door, and looked round to see that his younger sister was peeping into the room.

'Has he gone?' she asked, in conspiratorial accents. 'May I come in?'

His eyes lit with amusement, but he replied with due gravity: 'Yes, but take care you are unobserved!'

She twinkled responsively. 'I like you the best of all my family,' she confided, coming across the room to the chair lately occupied by Wimmering.

'Thank you!'

'Not that that's saying much,' she added reflectively, 'for I don't count aunts and uncles and cousins. So there are now only four of us. And to tell you the truth, Adam, I only loved Papa in a dutiful way, and Stephen not at all! Of course, I might have loved Maria, if she hadn't died before I was born, but I don't think I should have, because from what Mama tells us she was the most odious child!'

'Lydia, Mama never said such a thing!' protested Adam.

'No, exactly the reverse! She says Maria was too good for this world, so you see what I mean, don't you?'

He could not deny it, but suggested, with a quivering lip, that Maria, had she been spared beyond her sixth year, might have outgrown her oppressive virtue. Lydia agreed to this, though doubtfully, observing that Charlotte was very virtuous too. 'And I am most sincerely attached to Charlotte,' she assured him.

'To Mama also, surely!'

'Of course: that is obligatory!' she answered, with dignity.

He was taken aback, but after eyeing her for a moment he prudently refrained from comment. He was not very well-acquainted with her, for she was nine years younger than he; and although, during his weary convalescence, she had frequently diverted him with her youthful opinions, her visits to his sick-bed had been restricted by the exigencies of education. Miss Keckwick, a governess of uncertain age and severe aspect, had rarely failed to summon Lydia from her brother's room at the end of half-an-hour, either for an Italian lesson, or for an hour's practice on the harp. The fruits of her painstaking diligence had not so far been made apparent to Adam, for although there was a good deal of intelligence in his sister's lively face she had as yet vouchsafed no sign of the erudition to be expected in one educated by so highly qualified a preceptress as Miss Keckwick.

He was wondering why she was so much more taking than her elder, and far more beautiful, sister, when she emerged from some undisclosed reverie, and disconcerted him by demanding: 'Are we ruined, Adam?'

'Oh, I trust it won't be as bad as that!'

'I had better tell you at once,' interrupted Lydia, 'that although I have always set my face resolutely against Education, which I very soon perceived would be of no use to me whatsoever, I am not at all stupid! Why, even Charlotte has known that we stood on the brink of disaster for *years*, and no one could say that her understanding is superior! And also, Adam, I am turned seventeen, besides having a great deal of worldly

11

knowledge, and I mean to help you, if I can, so pray don't speak in that *nothing-to-do-with-you* voice!'

'I beg pardon!' he apologized hastily.

'*Is* it ruin?'

'Something uncomfortably like it, I'm afraid.'

'I thought so. Mama has been saying for weeks that she expects at any moment to find herself without a roof over her head.'

'It won't be as bad as that,' he assured her. 'She will have her jointure – do you know what that is?'

'Yes, but she says it is a paltry sum, and that we shall be obliged to subsist on black-puddings – and that, Adam, will *never* do for Mama!'

'She exaggerates. I hope she will be able to live in tolerable comfort. She will have about eight hundred pounds a year – not a fortune, but at least an independence. With a little economy –'

'Mama,' stated Lydia, 'has never studied economy.'

He smiled. 'Have you?'

'Only Political Economy, and that's of no use! I may not know a great deal about it, but I do know that it has to do with the distribution of wealth, which is why I decided not to tease myself with it, on account of not having any wealth to distribute.'

'Didn't the learned Miss Keckwick teach you household economy?'

'No: her mind was of an elevated order. Besides, everyone knows what *that* means! It's having only one course for dinner, and not enough footmen, and making up one's own dresses, which is perfectly useless, because if you have no money to pay for anything it's the most idiotish waste of time to be learning how to save it! Mama won't – but I wasn't thinking of her: I was thinking of you, and Fontley.' She bent a serious gaze upon him. 'Mama says Fontley will be lost to us. Is it true? Please tell me, Adam!' She read the answer in his face, and lowered her gaze. After carefully pleating her muslin gown across her knees, she said: 'I find that a truly *detestable* thought.'

'So do I,' he agreed sadly. 'Too detestable to be talked of, until

I've grown more accustomed to it.'

She looked up. 'I know it is much worse for you, and I don't mean to talk of it in a repining way. The thing is that I'm persuaded we ought to make a push to save it. I have been thinking about it a great deal, and I perceive that it is now my duty to contract a Brilliant Alliance. Do you think I could, if I set my mind to it?'

'No, certainly not! My dear Lydia –'

'Well, I do,' she said decidedly. 'I can see, of course, that there may be one or two little rubs in the way, particularly the circumstance of my not yet being out. Mama had meant to present me this season, you know, but she can't do so while we are in black gloves, and I see that if I don't go into society –'

'Who put this nonsense into your head?' interrupted Adam.

She looked surprised. 'It isn't nonsense! Why, don't you know how hopeful Mama was that Charlotte would contract a Brilliant Alliance? She very nearly did, too, but she wouldn't accept the offer, on account of Lambert Ryde. And I must say that that put me quite out of charity with her! Anyone but a wet-goose would have known what would come of it, and it *did*! For *weeks* Mama talked of nothing but Maria, and how *she* would never have been so unmindful of her duty as poor Charlotte!'

'Ryde?' said Adam, ignoring the latter, and very improper, part of this speech.

'Yes, don't you remember him?'

'Of course I do, but I haven't seen him since I came home, and –'

'Oh, no! he's away. He had to go off to Edinburgh, because one of his Scotch aunts died, and he was a trustee, or some such thing. Adam, *you* won't forbid Charlotte to marry him, will you?'

'Good God, I've nothing to say in the matter! Do they still wish it?'

'Yes, and you have got something to say! Charlotte isn't of age yet, and I know you are our guardian.'

'Yes, but –'

'If you are thinking it wouldn't be proper to permit anything

Papa disliked I can tell you that it wasn't he, but Mama,' disclosed Lydia helpfully. 'He said that she must settle as she liked, but for his part he didn't care a rush.' She added, after a thoughtful moment: 'I shouldn't wonder at it if you are able to bring Mama round to the notion, now that we are ruined. She won't like it above half, of course – and I must own that it does seem shockingly wasteful of Charlotte to be squandering herself on Lambert Ryde! However, there's no need to despair! I'm not acquainted with many *young* gentlemen, but I do know that I take very well with the old ones, because whenever Papa entertained any of his friends here I went along with them famously! And, from all I can discover, it is the *old* gentlemen who have the largest fortunes. And I do *not* see what I have said to make you laugh!'

'No, of course you don't – pray forgive me!' begged Adam. 'I think you must have been talking to Wimmering?'

'No! Why?' she asked, surprised.

'It is precisely the advice he gave me: to contract a Brilliant Alliance!'

'Oh!' she said, subjecting this to profound thought. She shook her head. 'No, not you. Charlotte says that when one has formed a connection the very thought of marriage to Another is repugnant.'

Adam, making the discovery that his young sister could be as embarrassing as she was amusing, replied with creditable coolness: 'Does she? Well, I expect she must know better than I do, so I shan't dispute the matter.'

'Did you see Julia when you were in London?' enquired Lydia, impervious to snubs. 'The Oversleys removed from Beckenhurst at the beginning of the month, you know.' She observed the slight stiffening of his countenance, and said anxiously: 'Ought I not to have mentioned it? But she told me about it herself!'

Realizing that only frankness would serve him, he said: 'I don't know what she may have told you, Lydia, but you'll oblige me by forgetting it. We did form an attachment, but we were never betrothed. I haven't yet called in Mount Street, but I must of course do so, when I return to town, and – well, that's all there is to be said!'

'Do you mean that Lord Oversley won't let Julia marry you now that you're ruined?' she demanded.

'He would be a very bad father if he did,' he answered, as cheerfully as he could.

'Well, I think it is wickedly unjust!' she declared. 'First you are obliged to settle Papa's debts, which are no concern of yours, and now you must abandon Julia! Everything falls on you, and you are less to blame than any of us! Mama thinks she is the one to be pitied, but that's fudge – and you may look as disapproving as you choose, Adam, but it *is* fudge! In fact, you are the only one of us to be pitied in the least! Mama will have her jointure, Charlotte will marry Lambert, and I have now quite made up my mind to marry a man of fortune!' She smiled warmly at him. 'Naturally it would be most disagreeable for you or Charlotte to be obliged to do it, but I shan't object to it, I assure you! You must know that I am a – a stranger to the tenderer emotions. Except,' she added, in a less elevated strain, 'for falling in love with one of the footmen when I was twelve, and that was *not* a lasting passion, besides being quite ineligible, so we need not consider it. Are you acquainted with any wealthy old gentlemen, Adam?'

'I'm afraid not. And if I were I should conceal them from you! I had liefer by far let Fontley go than see you sacrificed to save it, and though you haven't yet been in love there's no saying but what you might be one day, and then what a bore it would be for you to be tied to a wealthy old gentleman!'

'Yes,' she agreed, 'but one ought to be ready to make sacrifices for one's family, I think. And, after all, he might be dead by then!'

'Very true! And if he had survived – though I don't think it at all likely that he would! – we could always finish him off with a phial of some subtle poison.'

This appealed so strongly to Lydia that she went into a peal of laughter, at which inopportune moment the door opened to admit Lady Lynton, trailing yards of crape, mobled with black lace, and leaning on the arm of her elder daughter. She paused on the threshold, saying in a faint, incredulous voice: '*Laughing*, my dear ones?'

Charlotte, who was as kind as she was beautiful, said: 'It was so delightful to hear! Lydia was always able to make dear Adam laugh, even when he was in pain, wasn't she, Mama?'

'I am glad to know that there is anyone at Fontley who is able to laugh at this moment,' said Lady Lynton.

There was nothing in her voice or mien to lend colour to this statement, but none of her dear ones ventured to cavil at it. Having completed the discomfiture of the guilty parties by heaving a mournful sigh she allowed Charlotte to support her to a sofa, and sank down upon it. Charlotte arranged a cushion behind her head, placed a stool under her feet, and retired to a chair on the other side of the wide hearth, directing a look of anxious enquiry at her brother as she sat down. There was a strong resemblance between them. Both favoured their mama, unlike the larger and darker Lydia, who took after her father. Lady Lynton's oft-repeated assertion that Charlotte was the image of what she herself had been strained no one's credulity, for although time had faded the widow's fair beauty, and domestic trials had implanted a peevish expression on her classic countenance, she was still a remarkably handsome woman.

'I collect,' she said, 'that That Man has departed. I might have expected, perhaps, that he would have thought it proper to have taken leave of me. No doubt I must accustom myself to being treated as a person of no account.'

'I'm afraid I must take the blame of that omission on myself, Mama,' said Adam. 'Wimmering was anxious to pay his parting respects to you, but I wouldn't permit it, knowing you to be laid down upon your bed. He charged me with the task of making his apologies.'

'I am only too thankful to have been spared the necessity of seeing him again,' stated her ladyship, somewhat irrationally. 'I never liked him, never! And nothing will convince me that our misfortunes are not due to his management of your poor father's affairs!'

Once again Charlotte intervened. 'May we know how matters stand, Adam? We feel they can't be worse than our conjectures, don't we, Mama? It can scarcely come as a shock to us, even if we are quite ruined.'

'Nothing could be a shock to *me*,' said her parent. 'After all I have undergone I have become inured to disaster. I only wish to know when I must expect to find the roof sold over my head.'

'I won't do that, I promise you, Mama,' Adam replied. 'Indeed, I hope that you at least may be able to live in tolerable comfort, even if we can none of us remain at Fontley.'

Charlotte said in a faltering voice: 'Must Fontley be sold? Can nothing be done to save it?'

He was looking down at the smouldering logs in the hearth, and answered only with a tiny shake of his head. Tears started to her eyes, but before they could spill over Lydia created a diversion by observing dispassionately that she rather thought Mama was suffering a Spasm.

The widow's aspect was certainly alarming, and although she revived sufficiently, when her vinaigrette was held under her nose, to express a desire for hartshorn, it was not until a dose of this cordial had been procured by her younger daughter, and held to her lips by Charlotte, that she was able to raise her head from the cushion, and to utter in brave, but failing accents: 'Thank you, my dear ones! Pray don't regard it! It was nothing – merely the agitation of having the dreadful tidings broken to me in *such* a way – ! You have been for so long a stranger to your home, dearest Adam, that you could not be expected to know how wretchedly worn down are my poor nerves.'

'You must forgive me, Mama: I had really no intention of oversetting you,' said Adam. 'It seemed to me to be cruel to conceal from you what you must learn, sooner or later.'

'No doubt you did as you thought right, my dear son. My first-born!' said the widow, extending to him one frail hand. 'But had your brother been spared to me *he* would have understood how shattering this blow must be to me! Ah, my poor Stephen! always so considerate, so exactly partaking of my sentiments!'

Since the career of her second-born, cut off while he was still up at Oxford, had been distinguished by a sublime disregard for any other considerations than those immediately concerning himself, this ejaculation caused her surviving children to exchange speaking glances.

It was when Adam was struggling to convince her that her jointure and the direst penury were not synonymous terms that Lydia suddenly exclaimed: 'So Dawes was right! I didn't think it in the least, but only see! These odious tradesmen are sending bills for things Papa never bought, Adam!'

He turned his head quickly to discover that she was engaged in studying the accounts he had left on the desk. Before he could intervene she had betrayed an embarrassing gap in her store of worldly knowledge. 'Papa never gave you a necklace of emeralds and diamonds, did he, Mama? But here are Rundell & Bridge demanding the most *outrageous* sum for one! Of all the wicked cheats!'

The effect of this disclosure on the Dowager was galvanic. Reduced to a moribund state by the efforts of her two elder children to portray in attractive colours her future existence, she sat bolt upright, demanding sharply: '*What?*'

'Lydia, put those papers back on my desk!' commanded Adam, a look of vexation on his face.

'But, Adam –'

'Flaunting it under my very nose!' said Lady Lynton. 'I might have known it! At the Opera, and very vulgar I thought it! Exactly what one would have expected of such a Creature! Oh, it's all of a piece! *We* might go in rags, but he would offer a carte blanche to any Cyprian that took his fancy!'

'Good gracious!' exclaimed Lydia, round-eyed with surprise. 'You can't mean that Papa – Papa! – had a –'

'Hold your tongue!' said Adam briefly, taking the bill out of her hand, and thrusting it into one of the drawers in the desk.

Perceiving that he was seriously displeased she at once begged pardon, but she was obviously so much less concerned with her own indiscretion than with the problem of how any female could welcome the attentions of a gentleman so stricken in years as her father, who had had no fewer than two-and-fifty in his dish, that Charlotte, amongst whose excellencies a sense of humour was absent, later felt obliged to point out to Adam that dear Lydia's impenitence argued innocence rather than depravity.

Lady Lynton had accepted her lord's vagaries with well-bred indifference for years, but the emerald necklace, for some cause which her children never discovered, exercised a powerful effect upon her. Indignation brought a flush to her cheeks, and she so far forgot herself as to recall several of his lordship's previous lapses, declaring, however, that those she had been able to condone. The emerald necklace, which she described as bread snatched from his children's mouths to hang round the neck of an abandoned female, was, she asserted, Too Much. It was certainly too much for Lydia, who uttered a choked giggle, and thus reclaimed her afflicted parent to a sense of her company. She was, she said, grieved that any child of hers could be so totally devoid of delicacy, or proper feeling. She seemed to derive some slight comfort from the reflection that Lydia had always been just like her father; but that damsel's imperfections naturally challenged comparison with the infant Maria's virtues, and led the widow to bemoan the cruelty of Fate, which had reft from her the two children who would have supported and consoled her in her hour of need. One thing leading to another, it was not long before Adam found himself convicted of gross insensibility; while as for Charlotte, who was doing her best to soothe her mama, Lady Lynton wondered that she could hold up her head after her wilful refusal to avail herself of the opportunity offered her to restore the fallen fortunes of her family.

'No word of censure will ever pass *my* lips,' she said magnanimously. 'I merely marvel at you, dearest, for anything in the nature of selfishness is wholly foreign to me. Poor child! I wish you may not live to regret that day's work, but, alas, I fear you will find a sad falling-off in young Ryde's attentions now that we are beggared.'

But in this she was wrong. Not twenty-four hours after she had uttered the dismal prophecy Mr Ryde was wringing Adam's hand, and saying: 'By Jove, it's good to see you again, Adam, and looking pretty stout too! But you know how sorry I am for the cause of your being here! What a fellow you must have been thinking me! But I daresay Charlotte told you how it was: I've been away from home – one of my old aunts cut her stick, and I was obliged to post up to Scotland in a hurry. What with the other two clinging to my coat-tails, and all the lawyers' nonsense, I thought I never should be able to break free! But no use to run off before the business was settled: I must have gone back, you know, and *that* I don't mean to do, unless I take Charlotte there on our honeymoon!' He grinned, and added: 'You don't mean to forbid our marriage, do you? You'd better not, I can tell you, old chap!'

Adam laughed, and shook his head. 'I shouldn't dare! But I think you should know that matters are in very bad shape here, Lambert. I shall do what I can to provide Charlotte with some part at least of her dowry, but it won't be what she's entitled to receive, and what you might reasonably expect.'

'No?' retorted Lambert. 'Giving me a chance to cry off? Handsome of you – just like you, indeed! But come now! no more funning! I'm as sorry as I could be, but it's no surprise to me. I don't scruple to own that when Charlotte sent me the news the first thought that entered my head was that now at last we could be riveted! Membury Place don't compare with Fontley, but though my fortune's not handsome it enables me to be sufficiently beforehand with the world to support a wife in comfort – ay, and Lydia too, if she should choose to make her home with us!'

He asked Adam if he would be obliged to sell Fontley; and when Adam replied that he feared so he looked grave, and said that it was a bad business, and that Charlotte would feel it excessively. 'Living so close, you know, and seeing strangers here. I wish I might help you, but it's out of my power. Except,' he added, with his ready laugh, 'by taking Charlotte off your hands!'

It was not to be expected that Lady Lynton would readily allow herself to be reconciled to her daughter's marriage to a mere country squire; but the alternative, which was to provide for Charlotte out of her jointure, won from her a reluctant consent. While reserving to herself the right to deplore the connection she was forced to own that it was not disgraceful: Lambert's birth was not noble, but it was respectable; and his fortune, which had previously seemed paltry, had been changed, in the light of her own miserable circumstances, into a considerable independence. She could never like the match, but she told her son that she must acknowledge that Lambert had behaved with generosity and kindness.

Lydia acknowledged Lambert's kindness too, but told Adam that nothing would prevail upon her to take up residence in his house.

'Well, of course you won't do that,' he replied. 'You will live with Mama.'

'Yes, and though it may seem strange to you I had liefer do so,' she said disconcertingly. 'I hope I value Lambert as I ought, but it would be anguish to be obliged to live in the same house with someone who is always jolly, and laughs so frequently! Depend upon it, if an earthquake engulfed us all he would discover a bright side to the disaster! Doesn't he sometimes set *your* teeth on edge?'

He could not deny it. He had known Lambert since they had been boys together, and liked him well enough; but he was quite as much irritated as Lydia by his unflagging cheerfulness. However, he recognized the worth of his character; and when he saw Charlotte going about in a glow of happiness he was able to look forward to the marriage, if not with enthusiasm, at least with relief. That her future was assured was the one alleviating thought he carried to London with him at the beginning of the following week.

Two

he Lynton town house was situated in Grosvenor Street, and was a spacious mansion, considerably enlarged by its late owner, in the days of his affluence, by the addition of a ballroom, with several handsome apartments over it. It was furnished with old-fashioned elegance; but when Adam visited it he found holland covers on all the chairs, and the mantelpieces swept bare of their ornaments. Almost the only economy the late Viscount had practised had been the closing of his town residence during the winter months. When he had not been invited to stay at Carlton House, he preferred to put up, in the most expensive comfort, at the Clarendon.

Adam put up at an hotel too, but not at the Clarendon. When he was escorted all over his house by the retainer who acted as caretaker he knew that he could dispose of this one of his possessions without a pang. It was associated in his mind with weeks of suffering; he decided that the sooner he was rid of it the better he would be pleased.

The stables at Newmarket were already up for sale, with the hunting-lodge at Melton Mowbray, and the late Viscount's sixteen hunters. Wimmering did not think that any harm would come from selling the racing-stable, but he strongly deprecated putting the hunters up for sale. 'It will create a bad impression, my lord,' he said. 'I cannot like it!' Adam did not like it either, but he was adamant. They were being brought up to Tattersall's this week: Lynton's breakdowns. It was not a pleasant thought, and they wouldn't sell, at the end of the hunting-season, for anything approaching the sums his father had paid for them; but he would be spared the heavy cost of their upkeep. Wimmering was still talking of the need to allay anxiety, but his further researches into the affairs of his late patron had revealed nothing that could encourage Adam to think that he had anything to gain by a postponement of the inevitable; and his reiterated entreaty that the former state of the Deverils should be maintained served only to exasperate an employer whose nerves were already stretched to the limit of their endurance. An engrained courtesy compelled Adam to listen to Wimmering with patience; but no argument which his man of business had as yet advanced caused him to swerve from the line of conduct dictated by his own judgement. He never knew how baffling his courtesy was to Wimmering, or with what relief that harassed man would have greeted an explosion of wrath.

Following his judgement, he had himself interviewed his banker, at Charing Cross. Wimmering begged him to leave such matters in his own, more experienced hands, but Adam said he thought he ought to see Drummond himself. 'My family has always banked with Drummond's,' he said. 'They have always dealt fairly by us, too. I think I should prefer to talk to Drummond myself.'

Mr Wimmering might pull down the corners of his mouth, but it was certain that he could never have achieved the accommodation which old Mr Drummond granted to Adam.

Drummond's was an old-established firm, and amongst its distinguished clients it numbered no less a personage than His Majesty King George; but the name of Deveril figured in its earliest accounts, and it had been with a heavy heart that Mr Charles Drummond had awaited the arrival of the new Lord Lynton. He feared that demands were going to be made which it would be impossible for him to grant. He was not entirely unacquainted with Adam, but he had had no opportunity to form an opinion of his character. He remembered him only as an unassuming young officer, quite unlike his magnificent father; and although that was admittedly a point in his favour it in no

23

way prepared Mr Drummond for a client who not only took him frankly into his confidence, but who said, with a smile that was as charming as it was rueful: 'In these circumstances, sir, it must seem outrageous of me to ask you to let me continue drawing on an account which is already grossly *over*drawn, but I hope I can satisfy you of my ability to pay off the debt. I have worked out, as well as I'm able – but the exact worth of some of my assets must be conjectural – a sort of balance between my debts and my expectations, which, naturally, you will wish to study.'

He had then laid papers before Mr Drummond, who had peered at them with misgiving. By the time he had recovered from the shock of discovering that Adam's expectations were not dependent either upon *a sure thing* at Newmarket, or some speculation calculated to shorten a respectable banker's days, he had made another discovery, which he later imparted to his son.

'The young man's like his grandfather. Same quiet ways, same cool head on his shoulders: he'll do!'

From Charing Cross Adam took a hackney coach to Mount Street, and, with a heart beating uncomfortably fast, trod up the steps to the front door.

He was conducted to Lord Oversley's book-room; and his lordship, exclaiming: 'Adam, my dear boy!' got up from his chair, and came quickly to meet him, grasping his hand, and scanning his face with shrewd, kindly eyes. 'Poor lad, you look hagged to death! No wonder, of course! But you *are* well again, aren't you? I see you limp a trifle: does your leg pain you still?'

'No, indeed, sir: I'm very well. As for looking hagged, that's the fault of my black coat, perhaps.'

Oversley nodded understandingly. He was a pleasant-faced man, rather more than fifty years of age, dressed fashionably but without extravagance, and distinguished by an easy affability. He pulled forward a chair for Adam. 'I don't mean to tell you how sorry I am: you must know how I feel upon this occasion! Your father was one of my oldest cronies, and though our ways fell apart we remained good friends. Now, I'm not going to stand on ceremony with you, Adam: how badly are things left?'

'Very badly, sir,' Adam replied. 'I hope to emerge free of debt, and that, I'm afraid, is the best that can be said.'

'I feared as much. I saw your father in Brooks's, not a sennight before the accident –' He broke off, and after a moment's hesitation said: 'I want to speak to you about that. It caused the deuce of a lot of talk: mere humbug to pretend it didn't! It was bound to do so, and it was bound to bring his creditors down on you like a swarm of locusts.' He cast another of his shrewd glances at Adam. 'Ay, you've been having a devilish time of it. But that's not what I want to say. I've thought about that accident a great deal. He didn't mean it. He may have been all to pieces, but I'm as sure as I sit here that he wasn't riding to break his neck. That's what you've been thinking, isn't it?'

'I don't know!' Adam said. 'I try *not* to think of it!'

'Well, you'll think of it now, my boy!' said Oversley trenchantly. 'If he had meant to put a period to his existence he'd have found a surer way to do it than that! Good God, no man knew better than Bardy Lynton that riding for a fall is no more likely to end in a broken neck than in a broken shoulder! No, no, he never meant it! I knew Bardy! He was too game to cry craven, and too much of a right one, for all his faults, to leave you to stand the roast!' He paused, and laid his hand on Adam's knee, gripping it slightly. 'God knows you've cause enough, but don't think too hardly of him! He came into his inheritance too young. When a lad of his cut is as well-breeched as he was, and has no check on him –'

'Oh, no, no!' Adam said quickly. 'Good God, what right have I –? I didn't know how serious matters were, but I knew it wasn't high water with him: he often said we should soon be under the hatches. I didn't heed him – there always seemed to be enough money – and all I cared for was a pair of colours! If I had thought less of that, and more of Fontley –'

'Now, that's enough!' Oversley interrupted. 'You're not a sapskull, so don't sit there talking sickly balderdash to me! There was nothing you could have done, and if you're thinking Bardy wanted you at home you're out! Let alone that he was proud of

25

you – lord, you should have seen him when you were mentioned in one of the dispatches! – he didn't want you to discover how far he had drifted into Dun territory. Always thought he could make a recover, and set all to rights! And I'm bound to own he had some astonishing runs of luck,' added his lordship reflectively. 'The pity was – But so it always is with your true gamester! Well, well, mum for that! But if you mean to set the blame for this after-clap at any other door than your father's, set it at Stephen's rather than your own! What that young rip cost Bardy, first and last – ! I tell you that, Adam, but we'll say no more about it: the poor lad's accounts are wound up now.'

There was a short silence. Adam broke it. 'I don't know. But there is one matter for which I must blame myself, sir – as much as you do, I daresay.'

Oversley replied with a heartiness assumed to conceal embarrassment: 'No, I don't. I'm not going to pitch any gammon about not knowing what you mean. The round tale is that I ought never to have let you make up to that girl of mine – and so I knew!' He smiled wryly. 'You know, Adam, there's no one I'd liefer have for a son-in-law than you, if the dibs had been in tune, but I knew they weren't, and I ought to have hinted you away as soon as I saw which quarter the wind was in. The fact is I thought it was just a flirtation, and the lord knows you needed something to divert you at that time! I never supposed it would last, once you'd rejoined. And it's my belief it wouldn't have done so – at any rate with Julia! – if it hadn't been for this shocking business, because there's no denying that Julia's a taking little puss, and she don't want for suitors. She's had 'em all dangling after her, ever since she came out, and has had as many silly nick-names foisted on to her as poor William Lamb's wife. Sprite – Sylph – Zephyr – ! Pshaw!' said his lordship, imperfectly disguising his pride. 'Enough to turn the chit's head! Now, I don't say she wasn't cut up when you went back to Spain: she was. In fact, her mother would have it that she'd mope herself into a decline, but that was all flim-flam! A girl who has a dozen posies sent her in a day don't go into a decline! And if you ask me

– and I don't say it to wound you, Adam! – she'd have forgotten that interlude if it hadn't been for some chucklehead calling her the Unattainable. That grassed us, of course. Took to thinking herself pledged to a gallant soldier, and made such a hero of you as would have made the hair rise on your scalp! And then poor Bardy was killed, and there was no keeping it from her that you were in the suds. So now she's declaring that she'll never give you up, which pretty well gaps me – or it would, if I didn't know you too well to think – Damme, Adam, this is a devilish hard thing to say to you, but –'

'You needn't say it, sir!' Adam interrupted, rising, and going with a quick, uneven step to the window. 'Of course it's impossible! I've known that ever since I first saw my father's man of business. I should have come to you immediately – I beg your pardon! I hoped things might not be as bad as Wimmering described. In fact, they are worse. I'm not in a position to offer for anyone. I never dreamed I could say it, but I wish – yes, with all my heart! – that she had forgotten me!' His voice shook; he made a gallant attempt to conceal his emotion, saying: 'I shouldn't then have been obliged to cry off, which I must do – and came here to do.'

Lord Oversley, rising also, and going to him to lay a hand on his shoulder, said: 'I know, my boy, I know! And if I were a rich man –'

He was interrupted. The door opened suddenly; a male voice was heard to exclaim: 'No, dash it, Julia, you can't – !' and he and Adam turned to see that Miss Oversley was standing on the threshold, one hand clasping the door-knob, the other holding her riding-whip and gloves.

For a moment or two she remained there, her lips parted in eagerness, her eyes, almost too large for her little delicate face, full of light. The picture she presented was lovely indeed. She was a slim creature, so fragile that it was easy to understand why her admirers called her Sylph. Even the feathery curls peeping from under a hat like a shako were ethereal; and her severely cut riding-dress seemed merely to emphasize her fairy-like charm.

27

Adam stood gazing at her, his heart in his eyes. She let her whip and gloves fall, and ran forward, uttering in a soft, joyful voice: 'I knew it! You couldn't be so close to me and I *not* know! Adam!'

Entering the room in her wake, her brother Charles interpreted this for his father's ear, saying in an undervoice: 'Saw the hat in the hall, and guessed how it was! Darted off before I knew what she meant to do.'

She would have thrown herself into Adam's arms, but he prevented her, catching her hands in a painful grip, and holding her at a distance. He was very pale, and could not command his voice to speak more than her name. He bent his head to kiss her hands, his own shaking.

Lord Oversley said bracingly: 'A little less in alt, Julia, if you please! We are all glad to see Adam home again, but there is no occasion for these transports. I don't think you and Charlie met when you were last in England, Adam, but I daresay you haven't forgotten each other.'

His heir, nobly seconding this attempt to create a diversion, said immediately: 'Lord, no! That is, *I* remember *you*, Lynton, though you might not remember me. How do you do?'

Adam released Julia's hands. He was still pale, but he replied with tolerable composure: 'Of course I remember you! I own, however, that I might not have recognized you again.'

'No, well, I was only a schoolboy when you first joined. Jupiter, how much I did envy you!'

'Adam!' Julia faltered. 'Oh, what has Papa been saying to you?'

'Now, for heaven's sake, Julia!' interrupted Oversley testily. 'I've said nothing Adam doesn't say himself, so –'

'Oh, *no!*' she exclaimed, turning her brimming eyes towards Adam. 'No, no, I don't believe it! You haven't changed! I know you have not!'

'No – not that, but –'

'For shame, Adam!' she said, showing him an April face. 'Oh, how vexed I am with you! What a scold you deserve! Did you think *I* was fickle? Or that I care a rush for wealth? I think I *will* give you a scold!'

She had stretched out her hands to him again, an enchanting smile trembling on her lips. He took them, but he dared not trust himself to look into her face, and said, keeping his eyes lowered: 'I could never doubt you. But when I – when we – when I had the presumption to ask your father –' He broke off rather hopelessly, and continued after a moment's pause: 'I thought then that I should be able to support you. The ugly truth is that I'm not even able to provide for my sisters. If I were to be thinking of marriage now I should be the greatest villain unhung – and your father as bad, if he so much as considered my suit!' he added, trying for a smile.

She directed an arch look at her parent, and said audaciously: 'Pooh! As though we couldn't bring Papa about our thumbs! *Stoopid!*'

Adam raised his eyes. 'Julia, you haven't understood. Dear love, this is no case of being obliged to live for a time in straitened circumstances. I – I *have* no circumstances. Within a very short space now I shan't even have a home to offer you.'

She stared at him incredulously. 'No home? But – but Fontley – ?'

'I am putting Fontley up for sale.'

There was a shocked silence. Charles Oversley directed a look of astonished enquiry at his father, but Oversley was looking under suddenly frowning brows at Adam. Julia cried, in a throbbing voice: 'Oh, no, no, no!'

Adam did not speak.

She pulled her hands free. 'You cannot mean that! Oh, how can you talk so? Dear, dear Fontley! All its associations – the home of the Deverils throughout the ages!'

'No, hang it, Ju!' expostulated her brother. 'Can't have been! I mean, it's a Priory! That's the same as a monastery, ain't it? Dissolution of the monasteries – well, I don't precisely remember when that was, but the thing is there can't have been any Deverils living there before it – unless, of course – No, that won't fit!' he decided, adding knowledgeably: 'Celibacy of the clergy, you know. So that's a hum!'

In spite of himself Adam laughed. 'Yes, I'm afraid it is. The first Deveril of whom we have any very precise information settled in Leicestershire. There has been a Deveril at Fontley only since 1540 – and a shocking rogue he was, from all I can discover!'

'Very likely,' agreed Mr Oversley sagely. 'Seems to me that most of those old fellows were regular thatchgallows. Well, only think of the Oversley who made *our* fortunes! When he wasn't playing least in sight he was pretty well swimming in lard, wasn't he, Papa?'

'Alas, too true!' said his father, twinkling.

'Oh, don't talk so, don't talk so!' Julia broke in. 'How can you turn everything to jest? Adam, you didn't mean it! Strangers at Fontley? Oh, no! every feeling revolts! The groves and the alleys! The chapel ruins where I've so often sat, feeling the past all about me, so close that I could almost fancy myself a part of it, and see the ghosts of those dead Deverils who lived there!' She paused, looking from one to the other, and cried passionately: 'Ah, you don't understand! Not even you, Adam! How is it possible? Charlie doesn't, I know, but you – ?'

'I should rather think I don't!' said her brother. 'If you ever saw a ghost you'd run screeching for your life! What's more, I remember those ruins quite as well as you do, and very likely better! Whenever we stayed at Fontley we used to play at hide-and-seek amongst 'em, and capital sport it was!'

'There were other days,' Julia said, in a low tone. 'You choose to pretend that you don't care, Adam, but I know you too well to be hoaxed! You were used to partake of all my sentiments: this reserve has been forced on you by Papa!'

Adam replied steadily: 'I do care. It would be absurd to pretend that I didn't. If I seem to you reserved it's because I care too much to talk about it.'

She said, with quick sympathy: 'Oh, how horrid I am! how stupid! I understand you – of course I understand you! We won't speak of it, or even think of it! As for repining, I shan't do so, I promise you! Could you be happy in a cottage? I could! How often I have longed to live in one – with white walls, and a thatched roof, and a neat little garden! We'll have a cow, and I'll learn to milk, and make butter and cheese. And some hens, and a bee-hive, and some pigs. Why, with these, and our books, and a pianoforte, we shall be as rich as nabobs, and want nothing to complete our felicity!'

'Oh, won't you?' struck in her unappreciative brother. 'Well, if you mean to cook the meals Lynton will precious soon want something more! And who's to kill the pigs, and muck out the henhouse?'

This sardonic interpolation went unheeded. Julia was rapt in contemplation of the picture she had conjured up; and Adam, tenderly amused though he was, felt too deeply moved to laugh. He could only shake his head; and it was left to Lord Oversley to bring his daughter down to earth, which he did, by saying briskly: 'Very pretty, my dear, but quite impractical. I hope Adam can find something better to do than to keep pigs. Indeed, I have no doubt he will, and all the more easily without encumbrance! No one is more sorry than I am that things have turned out as they have, but you must be a good girl, and understand that marriage is out of the question. Adam feels this as strongly as I do, so you need not think me a tyrant, puss!'

She listened with whitening cheeks, and turned her eyes imploringly towards Adam. She read the answer in his face, and burst into tears.

'Julia! Oh, don't, my darling, don't!' he begged.

She sank into a chair, burying her face in her hands, her slender form convulsed by deep sobs. Fortunately, since neither her father nor her brother showed the smallest ability to contend with such a situation, Lady Oversley at that moment came into the room.

A very pretty woman, plumper than her daughter, but with the same large blue eyes, and sensitive mouth, she exclaimed distressfully, and hurried forward. 'Oh, dear, oh, dear! No, no, my love! Adam, dear boy! Oh, you *poor* children! There, there, Julia! Now, hush, my dearest! You mustn't cry so: you will make yourself quite ill, and think how painful for poor Adam! Oh, dear, I had no notion you had come in from your ride! Oversley, how *could* you? You must have been perfectly brutal to her!'

'If it is brutal to tell her that she can't live in a thatched cottage, rearing hens and pigs, I have certainly been brutal, and Adam too!' retorted Oversley, with some acerbity.

Lady Oversley, having removed Julia's hat, had clasped her in her arms, and was tenderly wiping the tears from her face, but she looked up at this, and exclaimed: 'Live in a cottage? Oh, no, dearest, you would be very ill-advised to do that! Particularly a thatched one, for I believe thatch harbours rats, though nothing, of course, is more picturesque, and I perfectly understand why you should have a fancy for it! But you would find it sadly uncomfortable: it wouldn't do for you at all, or for Adam either, I daresay, for you have both of you been accustomed to live in such a *very* different style. And as for hens, I would not on any account rear such dispiriting birds! You know how it is whenever an extra number of eggs is needed in the kitchen: the hen-woman is *never* able to supply them, and always says it's because the creatures are broody. Yes, and then they make *sad* noises, which you, my love, with your exquisite sensibility, would find quite insupportable. And pigs,' concluded her ladyship, with a shudder, 'have a *most* unpleasant odour!'

Julia, tearing herself out of that soft embrace, started to her feet, dashing a hand across her eyes. Addressing herself to Adam, standing rigid behind a chair, his hands gripping its back, she said in a voice choked by sobs: 'I could have borne any privation – any discomfort! Remember it!' She laughed hysterically, and hurried to the door. Looking back, as she opened it, she added: '*My* courage did not fail! Remember that too!'

'Well, of all the shabby things to have said!' ejaculated Mr Oversley, as the door slammed behind his sister.

'Hush, Charlie!' commanded his mama. She went to Adam, and warmly embraced him. 'Dear boy, you have done just as you ought – just as we knew you would! My heart *aches* for you! But don't despair! I am persuaded you will come about! Recollect what the poet says! I'm not sure *which* poet, but very likely it was Shakespeare, because it generally is, though why I can't imagine!'

With these obscure but encouraging words she departed, pausing only to recommend Mr Oversley to follow her example. Only too thankful to escape from this painful scene, Mr Oversley took leave of Adam. When he had gone, Adam said: 'I think, sir, that I'll take myself off too.'

'Yes, in a minute!' Oversley said. 'Adam – what you said to Julia – Fontley – You are not serious? Things are not as bad as *that*?'

'I was quite serious, sir.'

'Good God! But you must have ten or twelve thousand acres of good land!'

'Yes, sir. Much of it encumbered, and all of it so neglected that the rent-roll has dwindled to little more than a thousand pounds a year. It could be ten times as much if I had the means –' He stopped. 'Well, I haven't the means, and I can only hope that someone more fortunately circumstanced will perceive how easily farms worth no more than twelve shillings an acre might be valued, five years from now perhaps, at four times that sum. I think we must be fifty years behind the times at Fontley.'

Hardly heeding him, Oversley exclaimed: 'Adam, this must not be! Yes, yes, I know! You're saddled with short tenancies – no proper covenants – open fields – too much flax and mustard being grown – bad drainage – But these ills can be remedied!'

'Not by me,' Adam replied. 'If I had twenty – fifteen – even *ten* thousand pounds at my disposal I think there is a great deal I could do – supposing that I were free of debt, which, unhappily, I am not.'

Looking very much shocked, Oversley began to pace up and down the room. 'I hadn't thought – Good God, what can have possessed – Well, never mind that! Something must be done! Sell Fontley! And what then? Oh, yes, yes! You'll rid yourself of debt, provide for your sisters, but what of yourself? Have you considered that, boy?'

'I daresay I shan't find myself quite destitute, sir. And if I do – why, I shan't be the first officer to live on his pay! I haven't sold out, you know. As soon as I've settled my affairs –'

'Nonsense!' interjected Oversley. 'Don't stand there talking as though selling your birthplace was no more to you than disposing of a horse whose action you don't like!' He resumed his pacing, his brow furrowed. After a few moments, he said over his shoulder: 'Julia's not the wife for you, you know. You don't think it now, but you'll live to be glad of this day's work.' Receiving no answer to this, he repeated: 'Something must be done! I don't scruple to tell you, Adam, that I think it your duty to save Fontley, whatever it may cost you to do it.'

'If I knew how it might be done I don't think I should count the cost,' Adam said, a little wearily. 'Unfortunately, I don't know. Don't tease yourself over my affairs, sir! I shall come about. I'll take my leave of you now.'

'Wait!' said Oversley, emerging briefly from deep cogitations. Adam resigned himself. Silence reigned, while his lordship stood frowning at the carpet. After a long pause he looked up, and said: 'I think I may be able to help you. Oh, don't stiffen up! I'm not offering to frank you, my dear boy! The lord knows I would if I could, but it's all I can do to keep myself above hatches. This curst war! Ay, and if Boney is beaten before the year's out – did you see that Bordeaux has declared for the Bourbons? The latest on-dit is that there's a deputation coming to invite Louis to go back to France. I have it on pretty good authority that they are expecting it, at Hartwell. I don't know how it will answer, and in any event they don't look for any sudden prosperity in the City, whatever be the outcome. Well, that's for tomorrow, and not what I had in mind to say to you. It occurs to me –' He paused, and shook his head. 'No, better I shouldn't disclose to you – I don't suppose for a moment you'd like it, and I'm not even sure that – Still, it might be worth while to throw out a feeler!' He looked undecidedly at Adam. 'Not going back to

Fontley immediately, are you? Where are you staying?'

'At Fenton's, sir. No, I'm not going home for some days yet: there's a great deal of business to be done, and although Wimmering is very good – far more competent than I am, indeed! – things can't be settled without me.'

'Good!' said Oversley. 'Now, there's only one thing I have to say to you at present, Adam! Don't do anything rash until I've seen what I can do! I have a notion in my head, but it might well be that it won't answer, so the least said to you now the better!'

Three

When Adam had left Mount Street Lord Oversley suffered some qualms of conscience, fearing that he had raised hopes that he might presently be obliged to dash to earth. Had he but known it his apprehensions were wasted: Adam's hopes were not at all raised. If, at a moment of severe emotional stress, he had been capable of weighing them, he would have concluded that they were the words of a kindly optimist, for he could imagine no way in which Oversley could rescue him from his embarrassments. He was not so capable. For many hours the ruin of his own hopes drove the larger problems with which he was confronted to the back of his brain. They were not forgotten, but while his lost love's breaking voice still echoed in his ears, and her beautiful face was vivid in his memory, every other ill seemed trivial.

In some detached corner of his mind he knew that his present despair could not, in nature, endure, and ought not to be encouraged, but it was long before he could drag his thoughts from contemplation of what might have been and concentrate them instead on what must be.

It was perhaps fortunate that there was too much business demanding his attention to leave him with much time for reflection. It acted as a counter-irritant rather than a palliative, but it kept him fully occupied.

A diversion, which presented him with an added anxiety, as well as some inevitable amusement, was provided by his younger sister, who sent him a long letter, for which he was obliged to disburse the sum of two shillings. Lydia apologized for this vicarious extravagance, pointing out to him that since he was away from home she had been unable to obtain a frank.

She had abandoned her matrimonial schemes. Charlotte (Adam invoked a silent blessing on her head) was of the opinion that the acquisition of a wealthy and senile husband was not a matter to be accomplished with the speed requisite for the re-establishment of the family fortunes. Recognizing the force of this argument, Lydia wrote to warn Adam not to place any reliance on her former project. In a loving attempt to alleviate the pangs of disappointment she assured him that if she should contrive, at some future date, to achieve her ambition her first care would be to compel her hapless spouse to buy back Fontley, and to bestow it instantly on her dear Adam.

Meanwhile, she was making plans for her own maintenance. She thought it only right to inform Adam that Mama, after calculating ways and means, had come to the conclusion that although no one must doubt her readiness to stuff her last crust into the mouth of a famished daughter she would be wholly incapable of providing for this damsel out of the miserable portion which was her jointure.

With a sinking heart Adam picked up the second sheet of this missive, and discovered that Mama had formed the intention of seeking an asylum in Bath, with her sister, Lady Bridestow. This, Lydia wrote, could never prosper, since Aunt Bridestow was a widow of much longer standing than Mama.

The precise significance of these words eluded Adam, but he gathered that they were ominous. Whatever might be the issue the younger Miss Deveril had realized that she was unlikely to be a comfort to Mama, and had therefore decided to seek her own fortune, since nothing (heavily underscored) would prevail upon her to be a charge on her brother. It was just possible that her new scheme might not win his approbation, but she had no doubt that his commonsense would rapidly enable him to perceive all the advantages attached to it.

In the deepest foreboding he turned the sheet, to discover that his worst fears had been outdistanced: the younger Miss Deveril (but she rather thought she should adopt the name of Lovelace) had formed the intention of leaping to fame and affluence upon the London stage with her brilliant portrayals of all the better known comedy rôles. And let not Adam doubt that she could do this! At Christmas, when a large party had been entertained at Fontley, theatricals had been the order of the day. *Twelfth Night* had been the chosen play; and by the greatest stroke of good fortune the lady selected to enact the part of Maria had been struck down at the eleventh hour by a sudden indisposition and Lydia had taken her place. Everyone had declared her to be a Born Actress. In this unanimous judgement she concurred, but doubted, modestly, whether she would make a hit in the tragic rôles. Comedy was her *forte*, and although this might entail the playing of some breeches-parts she was persuaded that Adam would see no real objection to that, whatever Charlotte might say. In short, she would be very much obliged to him if he would approach whichever of the theatrical managers he thought the most respectable, and represent to this magnate that a rare chance was offered him of engaging the services of a young actress perfectly ready to take the town by storm, and not at all afraid of challenging comparison with such experienced players as Mrs Jordan, or Miss Mellon, or Miss Kelly. He gathered, with a grin, that the appearance on the boards of Miss Lydia Deveril (or Lovelace) would be the signal for these ladies to retire into chagrined obscurity.

He might laugh at his sister's naïve plans, but they added nothing to his peace of mind. It distressed him to know that she was scheming how to support herself when she should have been thinking of her coming-out, and drove to the back of his tired mind his own trouble. He found the time, not to approach a respectable manager, but to write a tactful reply to Lydia; and was engaged on this task when a waiter came up to his private parlour with a visiting-card on a salver, and a note addressed to him in Lord Oversley's hand.

'Gentleman waiting downstairs, my lord.'

Adam picked up the card, and read it with slightly raised brows. It was a rather larger card than was usually carried, and the name on it was inscribed in extremely florid script. *Mr Jonathan Chawleigh* ran the legend. It was followed by an address in Russell Square, and by another in Cornhill. This seemed very odd. Mystified, Adam turned to Lord Oversley's letter. It was brief, merely requesting him to receive *my good friend, Mr Chawleigh*, and to give careful consideration to any proposition which that gentleman might lay before him.

'Desire Mr Chawleigh to step upstairs,' Adam said.

He recognized in the waiter's wooden countenance, and in the utter lack of expression with which he replied: 'Very good, my lord,' profound disapproval. Undismayed, but at a loss to account for Mr Chawleigh's visit, he nodded the waiter away, and awaited events. That Lord Oversley had some scheme in mind for his relief was plain enough, but in what way the unknown Mr Chawleigh could contribute to it he was quite unable to imagine.

In a few minutes the waiter returned, announcing Mr Chawleigh, and into the room stepped a very large, burly man, who halted on the threshold, and favoured Adam with a fierce stare, directed from under a pair of craggy brows.

The stare was at once suspicious and appraising. Adam met it tranquilly enough, but he did not entirely relish it. There was amusement in his face, but a faint hauteur too: what the devil did this fellow, who looked like a tradesman, mean by glaring at him?

Mr Chawleigh was a middle-aged man, whose powerful frame was clad in an old-fashioned suit of snuff-coloured broadcloth. Unlike his host, who wore a close-fitting coat of black superfine, with cutaway tails, pantaloons, and Hessian boots, Mr Chawleigh favoured a mode that had been for many years worn only by respectable tradesmen, and perhaps a few country squires who had no ambition to figure in the world of ton. His coat was full-skirted, and he wore knee-breeches, with stockings, and square-toed shoes embellished with steel buckles. His shirt-points were no more than decently starched, and his neckcloth was tied with more neatness than artistry; but his waistcoat relieved the general drabness of his raiment with broad, alternating stripes of grass-green and gold. The most henhearted member of the dandy-set would have died at the stake rather than have worn such a garment, but it was certainly magnificent. So was the diamond pin stuck into Mr Chawleigh's neckcloth, and the emerald ring on his finger. He was plainly a man of substance, but he reminded Adam of nothing so much as a belligerent bull, with his great, muscular shoulders, his short, thick neck, and the habit he had of champing his jaws, as though chewing the cud of his ruminations.

'Mr Chawleigh?' Adam said.

'That's my name. Jonathan Chawleigh: no more and no less! That ain't to say I couldn't get a handle set to it, if I'd a mind to do it. I'd look as like as ninepence is to nothing, wouldn't I? Nay, Jonathan Chawleigh's good enough for me! Good enough for anyone, come to think of it,' he added ruminatively. 'I'll tell you this, my lord! – you won't find a name that's more honoured in the City, look where you will!' This was uttered in a voice of menacing challenge; but fortunately for Adam, who could think of nothing whatsoever to say, Mr Chawleigh continued abruptly: 'Now, I'm one that likes to be sure of my ground! You *are* the Viscount of Lynton?'

Taken aback, Adam answered: 'I'm Viscount Lynton – yes.'

'No *of*?' said Mr Chawleigh acutely.

'No *of*,' corroborated Adam, with admirable gravity. 'We Viscounts, you know, are a part of what you might call the scaff and raff of the peerage! No one under the rank of an Earl may use of!'

'That's something his lordship *didn't* tell me,' Mr Chawleigh observed. 'I daresay it don't make much odds, but the fact is I did fancy an Earl. Still, a Viscount's better than a Baron. A Baron's no manner of use to me: you won't budge me from *that*!' He directed another of his searching looks at Adam, and chuckled:

'Ay, you're wondering who the devil I am, and what I want with you, ain't you?'

Adam laughed. 'I do wonder what you want with me, but not who you are, sir! You are Lord Oversley's friend. Won't you sit down?'

Mr Chawleigh allowed himself to be shepherded to a chair, but said, keeping his shrewd eyes fixed on Adam's face: 'Told you that, did he? I take that kindly in him. I wouldn't make so bold myself, though I don't deny I've been able to nudge his lordship on to a sure thing now and now, and I've always found him very affable. But I'm no tuft-hunter, prating about my grand friends, Lord This and Lord That, which don't bamboozle any but gapeseeds. You want to remember that!' he added, shooting out a thick finger at Adam. 'You won't find me setting up in Mayfair, all amongst the nobs, for I know well I'd be doing naught but making a bobbing-block of myself.' He refreshed himself with a pinch of snuff. 'That's better!' he announced, wiping his nose with a handkerchief of finest lawn. 'Hardman's 37: nothing to beat it!' He looked at Adam with a twinkle in his eyes. 'So that's all you know about me, is it? A friend of my Lord Oversley!' He brooded over this for a moment or two. 'Didn't tell you more than that, eh?'

'No,' Adam replied, adding, with a smile: 'Having told me that there was no need to tell me more.'

'H'm! Didn't tell you what my business with you is? I thought he would – though he did say he would leave me to lay to you my own way. Damme if he's not a knowing one! Guessed I'd want more than his testimony before I'd come up to the chalk.' He nodded, and cast another penetrating stare at Adam. 'If he had told you what I am he'd have told you that I'm mighty well up in the stirrups. I'm one as likes round dealing – which isn't to say I won't get a point the better of a man in a matter of trading, mark you! But there's no one can say he was clerked by Jonathan Chawleigh! I run no rigs, my lord, because it ain't my nature, and, what's more, a good name's worth a hundred Dutch bargains! I've got that all right and regular, and as for my credit, that's good wherever there's trading done. You'll be wanting to know how I made my blunt – for I didn't come into the world hosed and shod!'

Feeling slightly stunned, Adam was about to disclaim any such desire when his instinct warned him that his overpowering visitor would take this in bad part. He tried, therefore, to look as if he were interested. Mr Chawleigh smiled indulgently, and said: 'I'll wager you wouldn't be much the wiser if I was to tell you, my lord, and that's as it should be: each to his own last! You might say I was an India merchant, which is how I began in trade. I'm that, sure enough, but I'm some other things besides: in fact, I've got a finger in pretty well every pie that was worth the baking.'

'Forgive me,' said Adam, 'but why do you tell me this?'

'It might be,' said Mr Chawleigh, watching him, 'that I'd be willing to stick a finger in your pie, my lord.'

'So I collect,' said Adam. 'But if Lord Oversley has informed you that my pie is worth the baking I think I should tell you that he has misled you.'

'That's as maybe. But I'll tell you to your head, my lord, that the tip of my little finger in your pie would be enough to save your groats. Suppose I was to thrust my whole hand in?'

'You'd find yourself with a bad investment, Mr Chawleigh. I don't know what Lord Oversley may have told you, but since I've no more liking for Dutch bargains than you have I'll make it plain to you at once that my affairs are quite out of frame. I imagine you don't invest your money without seeing at least the chance of a handsome return. I can't offer you that. If, as I suspect, you think of taking up a mortgage –'

'I've got no interest in mortgages,' interrupted Mr Chawleigh. 'Not but what I'd buy up those you've got already, and never ask a penny of you – if we reached an agreement! Nor I don't want to buy that place of yours neither. It's not money I'm looking for, my lord. It's something different I want, and you may take it I'm ready to pay down my dust to get it if I find the right article, which it may be I have done. Setting aside what his lordship says of you, I like the cut of your jib, my lord – no offence meant or taken, I hope!'

'None at all,' responded Adam, as much amused as bewildered. 'I am much obliged to you! But what is it that you do want of me?'

Mr Chawleigh sat champing his jaws for several moments, as though uncertain how to proceed. Finally, he scratched his head, and ejaculated: 'Damme if anyone ever had to urge me to come to the point before in a matter of business! I'm a plain man, my lord, and how to wrap things up in clean linen I don't know, nor don't want to. The fact is, it 'ud have come better from his lordship. However, you've put the question to me downright, and I'll give you a square answer: It's your name I want, my lord.'

'My *name*?'

'Properly speaking,' amended Mr Chawleigh, 'your title. Though an Earl was what I had in mind, supposing I couldn't get a Marquis. A Duke I don't hope for, and never did: you won't find Jonathan Chawleigh casting beyond the moon! Dukes are above my touch, and no need to tell me so!'

'My dear sir, what *are* you talking about?' demanded Adam, in the liveliest astonishment. 'I can't give you my title!'

'Damme, I'm not such a nodcock that I don't know that!' said Mr Chawleigh, with asperity. 'It ain't for myself I want it! It's for my daughter!'

'Your daughter!'

Mr Chawleigh raised an enormous hand in a quelling gesture. 'Easy, now! Don't you go stiffening up till you've heard what I've got to say!'

'Are you acquainted with Wimmering – with my man of business?' demanded Adam.

'I'm not, but I'll be happy to meet him – supposing we should come to an understanding. Not that I wouldn't act as fair by you without any lawyer to oversee the bargain, but I don't think the worse of you for wanting to make sure you ain't being burnt. What's more, I'd as lief settle it with a man of affairs. That way, we'll have it all shipshape and Bristol-fashion.'

'I beg your pardon! I fear I misled you. I asked the question –
oh, for quite another reason!'

'Ay, did you? Well, maybe I can guess what that was,' said Mr
Chawleigh with his rather grim smile. 'Don't you get to thinking
that because I'm a Jack Straw I'm a clodpole besides! I'm as
nacky a man as any in the City: I wouldn't else have made my
fortune! And if, as I'll be bound he did, your man of business told
you that the only way to bring yourself about was to get riveted
to an heiress he told you no more than's true, for all you may not
like it, which I can see you don't.'

Feeling more than a little battered, as much by his visitor's
discursiveness as by his forceful personality, Adam attempted to
stem the flood. 'Mr Chawleigh, pray do not –'

'Now, wait a bit!' interrupted Mr Chawleigh, again raising his
ham-like hand. 'If you don't care for the scheme you can say so,
and no harm done, but I came here to make you an offer –
provided I made up my mind that you'd suit, which I have done
– and I'll go through stitch with it, for that's my way. I don't think
the worse of you for not leaping at it like a cock at a blackberry
– in fact, I'd have bid you good-day, if you had – but it won't hurt
you to hear what I've got to say. And the first thing I've got to
say, so as there'll be no misunderstanding betwixt us, is that I've
a pretty fair notion how badly you're dipped. That don't matter
to me, because it wasn't you that played wily-beguiled with your
fortune, which would have been quite another pair of shoes: I'll
frank no gamester, not if he was a dozen Marquises rolled into
one! His lordship assures me you don't bet nor play more than is
genteel, and that I don't object to, though I'm not a betting-man
myself.' He paused, but Adam, realizing that nothing short of a
brigade of nine-pounders would halt him, had resigned himself
to the inevitable, and offered no comment. This seemed to please
Mr Chawleigh, for he nodded, and smiled affably. 'Well, now!'
he said, settling himself in his chair with all the air of a man about
to hold forth at length. 'You'll be wondering what made me take
such a notion into my head, and I'll tell you, my lord. I've no
other chick nor child, nor never looked to have when Mrs

Chawleigh was carried off. There were plenty that set their caps at me, mark you, for I was a pretty warm man then, but I never could fancy putting anyone in her place. She was a grand lass, my Mary! Sound as a roast, and came of good stock, too: yeoman-stock, and proud of it! She was thought to have married below her station when we got ourselves leg-shackled, but I swore I'd set her up in style before she was much older, and, by God, I did it! She died when Jenny was no more than three years old: died in childbed, and the brat with her – not that I cared for that, though it was a boy, like we'd hoped for. I'll say no more about that, or I'll be falling into the dismals. The thing is, when Jenny was born, Mrs Chawleigh said to me – thinking I'd be disappointed she wasn't a son – "Jonathan," she said, "mark me if we don't live to see her married to a lord! For the way you're rising in the world," she said, "I don't see what's to stop her!" Funning, she was, but the notion took both our fancies, and the long and the short of it is that when she died I made up my mind I'd marry Jenny according to her wish. And when Jonathan Chawleigh makes up his mind, my lord, he's a hard man to baulk!'

Adam found no difficulty in believing this, but he said gently: 'Don't you think, perhaps, that Mrs Chawleigh would have wished to see her daughter married to a man of superior rank, and greater substance than mine?'

'Ay, I don't doubt she would,' replied Mr Chawleigh frankly. 'But she didn't want for sense, and she'd have seen as fast as I did that it was no manner of use thinking of Marquises and Earls for a girl like Jenny. Mind, no expense was spared on her rearing! I'm no muckworm, and I never grudged a groat of the fortune I spent on educating her! And this I will say, I got her turned out in prime style! Every inch a lady she is! She had all the extras: pianoforte, singing, dancing, French and Italian, watercolour painting, use of the backboard – everything! And as for book-learning, why, I often say she's as good as an almanack! I sent her to school in Kensington, you know. She didn't like it above half: wanted to stay at home with me, but I knew better than to let her do that. I could have got governesses for her, and dancing-masters, and the rest, but that wouldn't have helped her to rub shoulders with the nobs, would it? Which is what she has done, make no mistake about it! Ay, I sent her to Miss Satterleigh's Seminary for the Daughters of Gentlemen.' A rumbling laugh shook him. 'If I was to tell you what it cost me, first and last, my lord, you wouldn't credit it! A Bluestocking, that's what that tabby is supposed to be, but what I say is that she should have set up a two-to-one shop instead of a school, for a bigger lickpenny I wish I may never meet! Held up her long nose at my Jenny she did, until I let her know how full of juice I was. After that –' He paused, caressing his chin, and grinning reflectively. 'Well, I've got to own she was a damned knowing one! There's not many can boast of having put the change on Jonathan Chawleigh, but she did it, just as soon as she saw I was ready to pay through the nose for what I wanted. Which I did, I promise you. However, I don't grudge it to her, because, though it didn't answer as well as I'd hoped for, that wasn't her fault.' He sat in ruminative silence for a moment or two, before disclosing, in a burst of confidence: 'You won't find me puffing off my goods above their value, so I don't mean to tell you my Jenny's a beauty, because she ain't. Mind you, she's by no means an antidote: not squinney, nor buttertoothed, nor anything of that kind! I'm bound to own, though, that she don't take. She's quiet, you see, and as shy as be-damned. That's what floored me, and I don't deny there's been times when I was downright vexed with her, for she hasn't lacked for chances to get arm-in-armly with the nobs, if she'd only made a push to do it, instead of shrinking into a corner, and staying dumb as a mouse, so that no one so much as noticed her. Now, if she'd been of Miss Julia's cut – ! There's a beauty for you! *She* don't lack for suitors, I'll warrant you an egg at Easter! Ay, that was the one friendship Jenny struck up at school that *did* make me feel hopeful. The lord knows what made 'em take a fancy to each other, for they ain't a bit alike, setting aside that my Jenny's two years older than Miss Julia. That was how I came to be acquainted with my Lord Oversley. Well, I was able to do him a good turn at a time when he was in bad loaf, which put him, as you might say, under a bit of an obligation. Now, him and me's as different as chalk from cheese, but we got to be pretty friendly. He's a man I like, and one as I can talk to without round-aboutation, which I did, telling him straight what I wanted for my girl. Of course, I wasn't looking to him to find a lord for Jenny, but what I did want, and what I got, was for my Lady Oversley to put her in the way of meeting a lord or two. There's no one could have been kinder: that I *will* say! She had my Jenny to all manner of grand parties, besides inviting her just to spend the day with Miss Julia, the way she'd get acquainted with all the swells that came there paying morning visits, and the like. It ain't her blame that nothing came of it.' He sighed, and shook his head. 'Well, it's not often I've been taken at fault, but I own I was beginning to think myself at a stand when his lordship came to me, to propose I should consider whether a Viscount wouldn't answer the purpose, because if so he rather fancied he might be able to put me in the way of getting next and nigh the very man for my money. Very frank and open he was with me, and a rare good character he gave you, my lord, if you won't take snuff at my saying so. Nor at my telling you that I wasn't by any means mad after the scheme. Letting alone a Viscount's not an Earl, whichever way you look at it, I wouldn't want to rivet my Jenny to anyone that was ready to marry a midden for muck, as the saying is. Nay, you've no need to take an affront into your head, my lord! The first thing my Lord Oversley told me was that the chances were you wouldn't like the notion – which I took leave to doubt, begging your pardon, until he told me who you was. Lord Lynton was what he called you, and, barring that I knew your pa was a member of what they call the Carlton House Set, and a buck of the first cut, by all accounts, I was none the wiser. But, of course, as soon as he disclosed to me that you were Captain Deveril – well, that put a different complexion on the matter!'

'Did it?' said Adam, regarding him with a fascinated eye. 'I can't think why it should, but – but pray continue, sir!'

'Ay, it did,' nodded Mr Chawleigh. 'Not that I'd ever clapped eyes on you myself, but I've always had a strong notion that my Jenny liked you better than any of the sprigs of fashion she was acquainted with.'

Startled, Adam said: 'But have I ever met – ?' He stopped, realizing, too late, the infelicity of this involuntary exclamation.

Mr Chawleigh, to his considerable relief, was unoffended. 'Ay, you've met her,' he replied indulgently. 'Often, you've met her, but it don't surprise me that you shouldn't call her to mind, for that's how it always is: she lets the other girls shine her down. She's no gabster, but when you were in town last year, worn to a bone with what was being done to you by a pack of surgeons, as they call themselves, though to my way of thinking butchers would be nearer the mark, and not one of 'em will I have lay a finger on me, for I'd as lief be put to bed with a shovel and be done with it – well, when you were hobbling about, as blue as megrim,' said Mr Chawleigh, unexpectedly picking up the main thread of his argument, 'she used to speak of you now and now: nothing much, you know, but enough to make me prick up my ears. Seems you weren't so taken up with Miss Julia but what you could find the time to behave civil to Jenny.'

A vague memory of having on several occasions found a strange female visiting Julia flickered in Adam's mind, but as he was quite unable to remember what she had looked like, or what he could conceivably have done to earn her approval, he prudently refrained from any pretended recognition. Mr Chawleigh might be discursive, but no one encountering his shrewd eyes could suppose him to be one whom it would be easy to deceive.

'Well, there it is!' said Mr Chawleigh. 'I don't know that there's much more I've got to say at this present, except that I'm not looking for an answer until you've had time to turn it over in your mind, my lord.'

Adam got up. 'You are very obliging, sir, but –'

'Nay, think it over before you commit yourself!' interrupted Mr Chawleigh. 'Acting hasty is bad business, take my word for it! There's no saying, after all, that my Jenny would be any more willing than you are. You sleep on it! Ay, and have a talk with his lordship, or your man of business. You want to be sure you're not being bobbed, and you've only got my word for it that I'm a man of substance.'

'I am quite sure you are all you say you are, sir, but, indeed –'

'Well, so you may be, but it's only reasonable you should want to make a few enquiries. You won't catch Jonathan Chawleigh buying a pig in a poke, and do as you'd be done by is my motto. If you're satisfied, which you will be, my idea is you should do us the honour of taking your pot-luck with us in Russell Square one evening, and get acquainted with Jenny. There'll be no company: just me, and Jenny, and Mrs Quarley-Bix. She's the good lady I hired to bear Jenny company, and take her into society. And why I call her a good lady I *don't* know, for to my mind she's no great thing. In fact, there are times when I think that I was regularly taken in over her,' said Mr Chawleigh darkly. 'It wouldn't surprise me if I was to discover that she was no more related to these Quarleys of hers than what I am. Or if she is, she's one of the dirty dishes you get in the best of families, according to what his lordship tells me, and which they don't own by more than a common bow in passing. I don't say she hasn't got an air of fashion, but what I *do* say is that you've only to set her up beside my Lady Oversley to see she ain't up to the rig. What's more, the only time I went out driving in the Park with her and Jenny, there was a lot of bowing, and simpering, and waggling of hands, but nobody came up to speak to her. Though that,' he added fairly, 'might have been because I was in the barouche, and no one would take me for a man of mode, not if I was to dress myself up to the nines they wouldn't! Well, well, I'll be mighty interested to know what *you* think, my lord, for you're one as *is* up to the rig – bang-up to it, as I saw at a glance! Mind, that's assuming Jenny's agreeable! I haven't spoken to her yet, but I will.'

Adam, feeling much like a man caught in a tidal wave, made a desperate attempt to battle against an irresistible force. 'Mr

Chawleigh, I beg you most earnestly to do no such thing! I am fully sensible – I assure you I appreciate –'

He was once more checked by that large, upflung hand. 'You think it over!' recommended Mr Chawleigh kindly. 'If you don't like the notion, when you've slept on it, I'll have no more to say, and so I promise you! But think it over carefully! I know you're all to pieces, and trying to bring yourself off honourably, and I think the better of you for it. But if you was to make my Jenny a ladyship – *and* treat her right into the bargain, which I'm pretty sure you would do, and you'd have me to reckon with if you didn't – there'd be no more worriting about debts or mortgages: *that* you can depend on! You could hang it up to any tune you please – and there's my hand on it!'

He held it out as he spoke, saying, as Adam, in a sort of trance, put his own into it: 'I'll bid you good-day now, and that's my last word for the present!'

Four

*A*dam was left to recover from the effects of this shattering visit, which he soon did, passing from revulsion to amusement, and presently banishing the interlude from his mind. It recurred when he sat down to finish his interrupted letter to his sister, and with it the echo of her voice, saying: '*One ought to be ready to make sacrifices for one's family, I think.*' She was certainly ready to do so, but she was too young to know what it meant, and she had not yet been in love. He smiled, recalling the naïve plan she had made for his relief; but the smile was not a happy one, and it soon faded. He wondered what her ultimate fate would be, and tried to picture her living with Lady Lynton in Bath. Not such a dreadful prospect, it might have been thought; but he found himself looking forward to it with misgiving, and thought that besides securing a part at least of her dowry from the wreck of his fortunes he must contrive to provide her with an allowance, for he could not doubt that whatever economies were practised by Lady Lynton would be at Lydia's expense. On the only occasion when he had ventured to suggest various ways of retrenchment to her, such as the substitution of a more modest maid for her staggeringly expensive dresser, she had put him utterly to rout by replying that she had considered this expedient, but that when she had asked herself if Poor Papa would have wished her to make this dismal change she had received an unequivocal answer: he would not have wished it at all.

'And you can't argue about that,' had observed Lydia,

'because it's true! He would merely have said: "Pooh! Non-sense!"'

One of the economies which Adam feared his mother might practise was in the matter of Lydia's coming-out. Lady Lynton's disposition was not social; she had never enjoyed large parties; and it seemed probable that she would make penury an excuse for neglecting this part of her maternal duties. The thought just flickered in Adam's mind that if he were himself married, and in affluent circumstances, his wife would be able to launch Lydia into society.

The thought vanished; he dipped his dry pen in the ink-well, and ended his letter to Lydia rather abruptly, not regaling her, as he had intended, with an account of his interview with Mr Chawleigh.

The afternoon was disagreeably enlivened by a note sent round by hand from Wimmering's place of business. That harassed practitioner had received a disturbing communication disclosing yet another obligation incurred by the late Lord Lynton. He very much feared that it would have to be met. No documents relating to the transaction were in his possession; he wrote in haste to enquire whether the present Viscount had discovered any relevant matter amongst his father's private papers.

Adam, realizing that persons committing suicide were not necessarily insane, set about the task of sifting, yet again, the mass of his volatile parent's papers.

He was engaged on this labour when he received a visit from Lord Oversley.

'I have only a few minutes to spare,' Oversley said, grasping his hand, 'but I felt I ought to make a push to see you, in case you should act hastily, before I'd had a chance to represent to you – You've seen Chawleigh, I know: he came to call on me directly afterwards. He's taken a fancy to you: I thought he might.'

'Much obliged to him!' returned Adam. 'I would I could return the compliment!'

'Ah!' said his lordship. 'That's what I was afraid of. Just as well I decided to snatch a moment to see you!'

'Good God!' exclaimed Adam. 'You can't have supposed – you of all people! – that there was the least chance I should – Why, it's unthinkable!'

'Then I don't scruple to tell you, Adam, that you're not the man I took you for!' said his lordship. 'I'll also tell you that if you whistle down the wind the best chance you'll ever have offered you to save Fontley, provide for your sisters, and bring yourself off clear of debt, I shall think so much the worse of you that I shall be glad, instead of sorry, that you're not my son-in-law!' He saw Adam stiffen, and said in a milder tone: 'I know it's a mighty hard thing to do, and not the match anyone would have chosen for you, but the ugly truth is, boy, that you're in the devil's own mess! I say in all sincerity that you owe it to your name to seize any honourable chance that offers of bringing yourself about.'

'Honourable?' Adam ejaculated. 'Selling myself to a wealthy Cit's daughter? Oh, no! Not myself: my title!'

'Pooh! No need for any Cheltenham tragedies! It's a fair bargain, and one that's being struck more often than you know. Yes, yes, you have formed what you believe to be a lasting passion for Julia! Lord, if we were all to marry our first loves what a plague of ill-assorted marriages there would be! Put her out of your mind! You may believe me when I tell you that she's no more fitted to be the wife of a marching officer than –'

'This is unnecessary, sir!' Adam interposed. 'If I haven't been able to put her out of my mind, you may rest assured that there's no thought of marriage to her there, or to anyone!'

'Now, listen, Adam!' begged Oversley. 'If you're thinking that Miss Chawleigh is like her father, she's not! She's not a beauty, but she always seemed to me an agreeable, well-behaved girl. I see no reason why she shouldn't make you an amiable wife. She's a little shy, to be sure, but perfectly sensible, and will give you no cause to blush for her manners. As for Chawleigh, I don't think he'll embarrass you. He's not encroaching. Yes, I know he has a bee in his brain where his daughter's concerned, but he don't himself wish to be admitted into the ton. You might not believe it, but he's never been across my threshold till today. I'm under a considerable obligation to him, and I did think I might be regularly in for it, but not a bit of it! All he wanted me to do was to put Jenny in the way of meeting what he calls *the nobs*! Refused the only invitation I ever sent him to dine in Mount Street: told me he'd be happy to dine with me in the City, but wouldn't come to my house. There's much in him that I like – and there is no one whose credit stands higher in the City!'

'I'm sure he's a very respectable person,' said Adam, 'but I have no desire to marry his daughter.'

'Come out of the clouds, Adam!' said Oversley sternly. 'They say – and I believe it! – that he's one of the richest men in the country, and that girl of his will inherit his whole fortune! He has a name for driving devilish hard bargains, but he's not a screw, and the more he spends on his Jenny the better pleased he seems to be. Marry her, and you will live as high as a coach-horse for the rest of your life! You will not only be able to hold Fontley: you will be able to bring it back to what it was in your grandfather's day.' He laid his hand on Adam's shoulder, gripping it. 'Listen to me, you young fool! You've no right to refuse the only chance offered you to restore what your father squandered! If you could do the thing by your own exertion I wouldn't urge you to this marriage, but you can't. You talk of rejoining your Regiment, and for anything I know you might achieve the highest rank. But once Fontley has passed out of your hands you will never win it back again. You think that over, boy, and remember that you're the head of your house, and have the power to prevent its falling down – if you choose to exert it!' His grip tightened. 'Don't make a piece of work over it!' he said, with rough kindness. 'It's a fair bargain: no need to feel you're offering false coin! The girl knows you're not in love with her. As for the rest – I wish with all my heart you might have had time to recover before this came upon you, but, believe me, Adam, you *will* recover! Now, that's all I have to say. Good God, look at the time! I must be off!'

A quick handshake, and he was gone, distressed by the drawn look in Adam's face, but not (as he later informed his lady) unhopeful of the issue.

And on the following day, after passing a sleepless night, Adam wrote to accept Mr Chawleigh's invitation. Two days later still he set out in a hackney-coach, to take his pot-luck in Russell Square.

He had been bidden for six o'clock, and warned that the occasion was to be informal, but although he had at first supposed this to mean that morning-dress would be worn, a doubt later shook him, and resulted in his assuming the long-tailed coat, white waistcoat, black pantaloons, and silk stockings which constituted correct evening attire. Possibly he would find himself overdressed, but to be underdressed, he suspected, might be taken as a slight.

It took some time to reach Russell Square, which was of recent date, built on the site of Bedford House, when this ducal mansion had been demolished fourteen years previously. Adam retained a dim memory of having been taken to Bedford House, as a child, but as the hack proceeded on its slow way over the cobbles it seemed to him, in the oppression of his spirits, that he was being carried beyond the realms of gentility. However, when he at last reached his destination he was agreeably surprised by the size and style of the square. It covered a very large area, and was almost surrounded by brick houses which were sufficiently imposing to enable house-agents to advertise them as Desirable Mansions. In the centre was a railed garden, with several trees, shrubberies, and an enormous statue of a man leaning on a plough.

Having paid off the hack, Adam trod up the shallow steps to Mr Chawleigh's front door. It was flung open before he had had time to do more than lift his hand to the massive brass knocker, and he was bowed into the house by what at first glance appeared to him to be a platoon of footmen. There were, in fact, four of them, besides a butler, far more stately than his own at Fontley, who conducted him up the crimson-carpeted stairway to the drawing-room on the first floor, and sonorously announced him.

It was still daylight, but although the curtains had not been drawn across the windows the candles had been lit in the magnificent crystal chandelier that hung from the ceiling, and in all the wall-lustres. A myriad points of light momentarily dazzled Adam. He had a confused impression of glitter, mingled with yellow satin, gilded mirrors, chairs, and picture-frames before his attention was claimed by his host, who surged forward to meet him, his hand out-thrust, and a loquacious welcome on his lips.

'Come in, my lord, come in!' he said hospitably. 'I'm heartily glad to have the honour of receiving you, and on the stroke of the hour, too, which I didn't look for, not after the scold I got from my ladies here for having invited you to dine so early! Well, well, I know it ain't fashionable to dine before eight, but I hope you'll pardon it, for the fact is I get so sharp-set if I'm kept waiting for my dinner that there's no bearing it. But I don't know when I've been so put out! If your lordship didn't drive up in a common hack! Now, if you'd only told me you hadn't brought your carriage up to town I'd have sent my own to fetch you! Well, you'll not go back to Fenton's in a hack, that I promise you! Here, Butterbank! send round to the stables to tell 'em the carriage will be wanted later on!'

'My dear sir, you are very good, but I assure you it is unnecessary!' Adam said. 'Don't turn your coachman out on my account, I beg!'

His protest was swept aside, Mr Chawleigh observing that his servants all seemed to live at rack and manger, and would be the better for some work to do.

Up till this moment, his formidable bulk had obscured the other two occupants of the room from Adam's view, but he now bethought him of his duties as host, and turned to perform the necessary introductions. This he did in a fashion of his own, saying: 'Well, now, here we have Mrs Quarley-Bix, my lord, and that's my daughter!'

An angular female came forward, extending her hand, and

56

uttering, in a voice expressive of disproportionate delight: 'Lord Lynton! *How* do you do? I believe I have not previously had the pleasure of meeting you, but I must have recognized you, I believe, from your resemblance to your amiable mother.'

Adam shook hands, responding with some mechanical civility. He realized, thankfully, that his instinct had not betrayed him when it prompted him to present himself in a swallowtailed coat. Mrs Quarley-Bix was wearing a low-bosomed gown of lilac sarsnet, with a train, and a quantity of ribbon-trimming. A turban was set on her head, kid gloves covered her arms, and as well as her reticule she carried a fan.

Even more richly attired was the young lady who blushed vividly, and dropped a slight curtsy, as Adam's eyes turned towards her, for although a dress of figured French muslin was perfectly proper to her years it was so loaded with lace and silk floss that very little of it could be seen. A row of remarkably fine pearls was clasped round her throat; pearl drops, rather too large for her short neck, hung from her ears; several flashing bracelets adorned each arm; and a brooch composed of rubies and diamonds was stuck into the lace at her bosom. A tinsel shawl, and spangled slippers completed an *ensemble* which only so fond a critic as her father could have thought becoming.

Miss Chawleigh had not inherited her sire's inches. Uncharitable persons had been known to describe hers as a little squab figure. Adam was not a tall man, but her head only just topped his shoulder. There was a suggestion of squareness about her; she was already plump, and would probably become stout in later life. She was certainly not a beauty, but there was nothing in the least objectionable in her countenance. Her eyes were not large, but they were of a clear gray, well-opened (except when she was amused, when they narrowed to twinkling slits), and holding a look of grave reflection; her hair, elaborately crimped and curled, was mouse-coloured; she had a small, determined mouth, a button of a nose, and a complexion which would have been good could she but have overcome an unhappy tendency to blush fierily whenever she was embarrassed.

She was as unlike Miss Oversley as she could be. There was no brilliance in her eyes, no allure in her smile, no music in her flat-toned voice, and not the smallest suggestion of the ethereal either in her person or in her bearing. Where Julia seemed to float, she trod with a firm, brisk step; where Julia could be enchantingly arch she was invariably matter-of-fact. She enjoyed a joke, but did not always perceive that one had been made; and she looked as though she had more sense than sensibility.

No blinding flash of recognition struck Adam, but he was able to identify her with the commonplace girl whom he had too often found in Mount Street a year earlier. He went up to her, saying, with his endearing smile, and easy civility: 'I need no introduction to Miss Chawleigh, sir, for we are old acquaintances. How do you do? What a long time it seems since we last met!'

She gave him her hand, but replied only with a quick, spasmodic smile, and a very fleeting glance up at him. The carnation deepened in her cheeks; he felt sincerely sorry for her embarrassment, and tried to help her over the awkward moment by making some remark about the size of Russell Square: surely the largest in London?

Fortunately, since she remained tongue-tied, he was answered by Mr Chawleigh, who was delighted to tell him the history of the square, the circumstances which had led him to remove to it from Southampton Row, and the price he had paid for his house in it.

'It wouldn't suit me to be peacocking about among the nobs in Mayfair – not but what we see plenty of 'em driving up to No. 65, now that this painting-fellow's come to live there, I can tell you! They come to have their portraits taken, and very fine they are, by all accounts. So they should be, is what I say! You'd hardly credit it, my lord, but he'll chouse you out of eighty or a hundred guineas for a small picture I wouldn't give a hundred shillings for!'

'Oh, you are too satirical, Mr Chawleigh!' protested Mrs Quarley-Bix. 'You must know, Lord Lynton, that we speak of

Mr Lawrence. Such genius! I positively dote on his pictures, and – dare I say it, dear Mr Chawleigh? – have often indulged the wish that you would commission him to take our sweet Miss Chawleigh's likeness.'

'Ay, well, I did have a notion of it, but when he got to talking of four hundred guineas for a full-length, which is what I wanted, because if I have the thing done at all I'll have it done handsomely – well, I was off! Having a touch at me, is what I thought! However, there's no saying but what I may come to it yet – that's to say, if things go the way I want 'em to,' he added significantly.

'*You*, I daresay, Lord Lynton, have been familiar with this quarter of the town when Bedford House was still standing? One can't but deplore its passing! So noble a mansion! so many associations! What a pang it must cause you to see the estate built over!'

'Oh, no!' Adam replied. 'I don't think I ever visited Bedford House above once in my life, and I was so young then that I have only the dimmest recollections of the event.'

'But you are acquainted with the Duke, I need hardly ask? He reminds one so much of his brother, the *late* Duke, whom, of course, you must often have seen. One of your father's friends, was he not? Ardent agriculturists, both of them, you know. You observed the Fifth Duke's statue in the square? One of Westmacott's, and quite in his best manner – if I am any judge of the matter!'

'Well, it's a fine, big statue,' conceded Mr Chawleigh, 'but what a Duke wants with a plough I *don't* see, nor yet with agriculture, which is work for farmers, not for Dukes. Each man to his own last is my motto.'

'Oh, but I assure you, dear sir, agriculture has become quite the thing!' cried Mrs Quarley-Bix. 'I believe it was Mr Coke of Norfolk who made it fashionable, and *he*, you know –'

'Lord, ma'am, how you do run on!' exclaimed Mr Chawleigh impatiently. 'Ah, there's the dinner-bell at last! Jenny, my dear, you'll lead the way downstairs, and we'll hope you've ordered a neat dinner to set before his lordship, even if there wasn't a turtle to be had, not for love or money. But I warned you it would be pot-luck, my lord!' He added, in case Adam should take him too literally, and be dismayed: 'Plain, good, and plentiful is my rule, and nothing ever set on the table which I wouldn't like to offer to a guest, supposing one was to drop in for a bite. I don't know what Jenny has to offer us today, but one thing I *do* know: you'll get no hashes and haricots in Jonathan Chawleigh's house!'

He might have spared his breath. By this time, Adam had formed a fair notion of what lay before him; and he was not in the least surprised at the array of dishes and side-dishes which weighed down the long dining-table, and overflowed on to the sideboard. Since the occasion was informal, only one course had been provided, a circumstance which made Adam feel profoundly thankful. He was not a large eater, and had for several years been accustomed to camp-fare, which, more often than not, consisted of hare soup, and a scraggy chicken, and to do justice even to one course which comprised a dozen dishes was a penance. Mr Chawleigh said, with a wave of his hand: 'You see your dinner, my lord!' and thereafter made few contributions to the conversation, only sparing enough time from the serious business of eating his way through the meal to apologize for the absence of turbot from the board, recommend the sweetbreads, and call for more sauce.

Miss Chawleigh explained with composure that the recent storms had made it impossible to procure any turbot; and Adam, for want of anything better to say, gave her a humorous description of some of the less appetizing meals he had eaten in Spain. She smiled, and said: 'But in one of your billets – I remember that you told us about it – there was always a *penella*, which was very good. Have I that word right?'

'Indeed you have, and it *was* good! A kind of stew, which I never saw off the stove – but what was put into it I didn't discover: a little of everything, I suspect!'

'I don't hold with stews,' remarked Mr Chawleigh. 'Leftovers, that's what they are, and just as well eaten in the kitchen. Allow me to tempt you to a morsel of ham, my lord!'

Adam declined it; and Mrs Quarley-Bix, possibly with the amiable motive of promoting further conversation, began to enumerate all the scions of nobility, at present serving in the Peninsula, whose parents were old acquaintances of hers, or distant relations. She had no doubt at all that they were well-known to his lordship; but as those who were not in Cavalry Regiments were to be found in the 1st Foot Guards, he was unable to respond satisfactorily; and was grateful to his host for creating a diversion, even though he might deprecate the manner of it.

'Hang Lord This, and the Honourable That!' said Mr Chawleigh. 'Try a mouthful of duckling, my lord!'

Adam accepted the duckling; and, while his host carved several slices from the breast, forestalled any further enquiries into his military acquaintances by asking Miss Chawleigh if she had read Lord Byron's last poem. Her answer surprised him, for instead of going into instant raptures, she gave a quick shake of the head, and said: 'No. I don't mean to, either, for it seems to me to be about another barbarous, Eastern person, and quite as full of dripping swords as the *Giaour*, which I thought horrid!'

'Oh, hush, Miss Chawleigh!' cried Mrs Quarley-Bix, throwing up her hands in affected dismay. 'Divine Byron! How can you talk so? The *Bride of Abydos*! The opening lines! – *Know ye the land where the cypress and myrtle Are emblems of deeds that are done in their clime –*'

'Yes, that's very pretty, but I think the next lines nonsensical. The rage of the vulture *may* melt into sorrow, though it seems most improbable, but why the love of the turtle should madden to crime I can't imagine. And, what is more,' she added resolutely, 'I don't believe it!'

'Certainly not!' Adam agreed, considerably entertained by this novel point of view.

'I don't know anything about the love of turtles, and nor does anyone else, if you were to ask me, but the best way of cooking 'em is the West Indian way, with a good pint and a half of

Madeira, and a dozen hard eggs spread over the top, and popped under a salamander,' said Mr Chawleigh.

'Dear Mr Chawleigh, a misapprehension! The poet writes of the turtle-*dove*!'

'Oh! Well, why can't he say so? I don't know that I've ever eaten turtle-doves, but I daresay they're much the same as pigeons. I'm not over and above partial to them myself,' said Mr Chawleigh reflectively, 'but when I was a lad we used to have them cooked in batter. Pigeons in a Hole, they were called.'

'Like Toad in the Hole?' enquired Miss Chawleigh.

'My dear Miss Chawleigh, how can you talk so?' protested Mrs Quarley-Bix. 'Lord Lynton is looking perfectly shocked!'

'Am I?' Adam said. 'My looks belie me, then.' He addressed himself to his hostess, saying, with a slight smile: 'I can't tell you how refreshing it is to encounter a female who doesn't fall into ecstasies at the mere mention of Byron's name!'

'Are you quizzing me?' she asked bluntly.

'Of course I'm not! I'm no great judge of poetry, but surely Lord Byron's verses are extraordinarily over-rated?'

'Well, that's what I think,' she replied. 'But I have for long been aware that, try as I may, I don't appreciate poetry as I should. I did make the greatest effort to read the *Bride of Abydos*, however.'

'Unavailing, I collect?'

She nodded, looking a little conscience-stricken. 'Yes – though I daresay I should have persevered if the library had not sent me a parcel containing two books which I most particularly wanted to read. I found I could no longer concentrate my mind, and so abandoned the attempt. And *one* was perfectly respect-able!' she said defensively, adding, in response to his lifted eyebrows: 'Mr Southey's *Life of Nelson*: has it come in your way?'

'Ah, yes! *That* is a noble work, indeed! Worth all his Thalabas, and Madocs, and Curses! But what, Miss Chawleigh, was the other work – not so respectable! – which lured you away from Abydos?'

'Well, that one was a novel,' she confessed.

'A novel preferred to Lord Byron! Oh, Miss Chawleigh!' exclaimed Mrs Quarley-Bix archly.

'Yes, I *did* prefer it. In fact, I turned to it with the greatest relief, for it is all about quite ordinary, *real* persons, and not about pirate chiefs, or pashas, and nobody kills anyone in it. Besides, it was excessively diverting, just as I guessed it would be.' She glanced shyly at Adam, and said, with a tiny stammer: 'It is by the author of *Sense and Sensibility*, which – b-but I daresay you might not recall! – I liked, but M-Miss Oversley thought too humdrum. I remember that we argued about it one day, when you were present.'

'No, I don't recall the occasion,' he replied, his colour a trifle heightened, 'but I know that Miss Oversley prefers the romantic to the humdrum. She is extremely fond, too, of poetry.'

'Well, each to his own taste,' said Mr Chawleigh, who had come to the end of his repast, 'but I'm bound to say I don't see what's the use of writing poetry, except for children to learn at school, though what good that does 'em I don't know. Still, it was pretty to hear you recite, Jenny, and wonderfully you used to remember your pieces.'

Mrs Quarley-Bix cast a speaking glance at Adam, but he evaded it, and seized the opportunity offered by his host's remark to draw Miss Chawleigh into an interchange of reminiscences of the various poems which they had been compelled as children to learn by heart. Miss Chawleigh became much less self-conscious over this game of odious comparisons: a circumstance which led her parent to observe, when the ladies had left the dining-room, that he could see that she and Adam went along like winking together.

Adam knew himself to be stiffening, and tried to overcome repulsion. He was not quite successful, but Mr Chawleigh did not pursue the subject, deeming it of more immediate importance first to ascertain that his port was being properly appreciated; and, next, to discover whether his noble guest's opinion of Mrs Quarley-Bix tallied with his own. Adam answered this evasively, for while he was by no means

63

enamoured of the lady he thought her situation an uncomfortable one, and so profoundly pitied any person who was obliged to live with Mr Chawleigh that he was reluctant to abuse her.

'Well, to my mind, she's nothing but a show-off,' said that worthy. 'I was hoping you'd give her a set-down, for if there's one thing I can't abide it's sham! No, and I don't like Smithfield bargains either, which is what I've a shrewd notion I got when I hired her to companion Jenny. Mind, I'm not a nip-farthing, but I want value for my blunt, and not a penny do I grudge when I've got it, *that* you may depend on! I daresay you noticed the pearls my Jenny's wearing? I bought 'em at Rundell & Bridge, and paid eighteen thousand for them without so much as a blink – though I brought them down by a couple of thousand before I said Done! of course.'

It was not difficult to persuade him to talk about his possessions. Before he declared that it was time they joined the ladies, Adam had led him on to describe the circumstances under which he had obtained the massive epergne on the table; what he had paid for the various pictures that adorned the walls; how he had had the dinner-service which Adam sincerely admired, straight from the Custom-house; and a great many other pieces of information of the same nature. Despising himself, Adam encouraged him to expatiate on his favourite theme. It was bad; but not so bad as to be asked whether he liked Miss Chawleigh well enough to marry her, which was the question he knew to have been hovering on Mr Chawleigh's tongue.

When they entered the drawing-room, they found the ladies seated by the fire, Miss Chawleigh being engaged with some embroidery. Mrs Quarley-Bix at once drew Adam's attention to this, begging him to marvel with her at the exquisite design, which dear Miss Chawleigh had herself drawn, and to declare if he had ever seen anything so beautiful.

'I am for ever saying that she puts me to the blush, with her industry, and her accomplishments. I flatter myself that I'm not an indifferent needlewoman, but *her* stitches are set so neatly that

I am quite ashamed to let my own work be seen. Her music, too! My dear Miss Chawleigh, I hope you mean to indulge us this evening? Allow me to ring for the footman to open the instrument! *You*, Lord Lynton, I know will be pleased with her performance, which, I venture to say, is most superior.'

He responded at once by saying that he would very much like to hear Miss Chawleigh play, but she excused herself with so much determination that he forbore to press her. Mrs Quarley-Bix appealed for support to Mr Chawleigh, but in vain.

'Ay, she plays very prettily, and I don't deny I'm fond of a good tune now and then, but we don't want any music now,' he said. 'I've promised his lordship a sight of my china, love, so do you come over to the cabinet and show him the best pieces, for you know more about it than I do, as I've told him.'

She obeyed, but as Adam knew too little about china to be able to draw her out, this attempt to promote a good understanding between them was not very successful. Miss Chawleigh's knowledge might be considerable, but she was plainly not an enthusiast. Adam, recalling that her father had told him that she was as good as an almanack, thought that textbook would have been the better simile. She could enlighten his ignorance on soft paste and hard; explain that the Vincennes blue on a bowl which he admired was applied with a brush; tell him that a pair of brilliantly enamelled creatures seated on pedestals were kylins; but when she drew his attention to the beautiful texture of an inkstand of St Cloud porcelain she did so in a flat, dispassionate voice; and her hands, when she displayed a ruby-backed plate of the Yung-Chêng dynasty, were careful, but not the hands of a lover. Adam realized suddenly, and with a flicker of surprise, that it was not she, with her superior knowledge, who really loved all these bowls, beakers, and groups, but her father, who could only say, as he fondled a *famille noire* vase: 'It's the *feel* of it, my lord: you can always tell!'

It seemed so strange that a man who judged the worth of a picture by its size, and furnished his house with vulgar opulence, should not only collect china but distinguish instinctively between the good and the bad, that Adam's interest was caught. He tried to lure Mr Chawleigh on to talk about his hobby, but no sooner did that gentleman perceive that his daughter had retired into the background than he broke off, and said, as he restored to the cabinet a graceful Capo di Monte group: 'Well, I don't know why I've a liking for these things, and that's a fact! It's my Jenny you should talk to, if you want to know about 'em: she's got book-learning, which I never had.'

'I don't think Miss Chawleigh will be offended, sir, if I venture to say that you have something of more worth than book-learning.'

'No, for it is very true,' she said at once. 'I learned about china to please Papa, but I am not myself of an artistic disposition.'

'Oh, Miss Chawleigh, how can you say so?' exclaimed the faithful Mrs Quarley-Bix. 'When I think of the charming sketches you have done, your embroidery, your musical talent –'

'Now, that does put me in mind of something!' interrupted Mr Chawleigh. 'I want to show his lordship the perspective drawing Jenny did of the square! Do you come down to the library, ma'am, and help me to look for it!'

To her credit, Mrs Quarley-Bix did her best to combat this blatant attempt to leave the young couple alone; but not all her assurances that Mr Chawleigh would find the sketch in a certain portfolio availed to turn him from his purpose. His Juggernaut quality came to the fore; and in a very few minutes he had succeeded in sweeping the reluctant lady out of the room, saying, with obvious mendacity, that both she and he would be back in a trice.

The situation was awkward, and was not rendered less so by Miss Chawleigh's embarrassment. It rendered her scarlet-faced and tongue-tied; and when Adam made some light remark to bridge the awkward moment she did not respond, but, raising her eyes to his face in a stricken look, blurted out: 'I'm sorry!' before turning away, her hands pressed to her burning cheeks.

For a moment his only feeling was one of vexation with her for having so little address. She had only to respond to his lead, and

66

the situation could have been carried off. Her look of conscious-
ness, the words she had uttered, even the hasty way she turned
from him, made this impossible. Had she not been so unmistakably distressed he could almost have suspected her of trying to
force his hand.

She had walked away to the fire, and after a struggle to regain
her composure, she said: 'It is – it is the greatest imposition to be
obliged to admire my drawings; and to have them displayed to
visitors – is what I particularly dislike! But Papa – You see,
nothing will deter him! I – I am so sorry!'

He recognized a gallant, if belated, attempt to pass the thing
off, and his vexation died. He hesitated, and then said: 'Miss
Chawleigh, would you prefer me to agree that it is a sore trial to
have one's sketches shown-off, or – or to say, quite frankly, that
I don't think any two persons can ever have found themselves in
such an embarrassing fix as this?'

'Oh, no! so mortifying!' she said, in a stifled voice. 'I didn't
know that – that Papa had the intention – tonight – so soon – !'

'Nor I, indeed! But he has done it, and it would be foolish in
either of us, don't you think? to pretend not to understand why
we have been pitchforked together.' He saw her nod; and
continued, not easily, but with a good deal of earnestness: 'I wish
you will be open with me. Your father is trying to make a match
between us, but you don't like it, do you? You needn't be afraid
of telling me so: how should you like it, when we are barely
acquainted? *My* fear is that you have been compelled to entertain
me tonight against your wish. Believe me, you have only to tell
me that this is so, and the affair shall go no further!'

This frankness steadied her. She had been standing with her
back to him, looking down into the fire, but she turned now, and
replied, in a low tone: 'I wasn't compelled. Papa wouldn't do so.
I know it must appear – and he does like to rule the roast – but
he is too fond of me to constrain me, and – and too kind, even
though he may seem, sometimes, a – little overbearing.'

He smiled. 'Yes, a benevolent despot, which is, perhaps, the
worst sort of tyrant, because the hardest to withstand! Where all

67

is being done with the best of intentions – and by a parent, to whom one must owe obedience – it seems almost monstrous to rebel!'

Her flush had faded; she was even rather pale. 'I should be reluctant to do so, but if it were necessary, in such a matter as this, I – I *should* rebel. That's not the case. He *wishes* me to marry you, my lord: he doesn't *compel* me.'

There was a faint frown on his brow; he regarded her intently, trying to read her face. 'The tyranny of affection?'

She shook her head. 'No. It would grieve me to disappoint him, but I shouldn't hesitate, if – if my affections were already engaged, or I disliked the scheme.' This was spoken calmly, but with an effort. She moved towards a chair, and sat down. 'You asked me to be open with you, my lord. I don't dislike it. If you think – if you feel you could bear –' She checked, and went on after a tiny pause. 'I'm not romantic. I perfectly understand the – the circumstances, and don't expect – You said yourself that we are barely acquainted.'

He was obliged to master an impulse to retreat, and to tell himself that her acceptance of the proposed match was no more coldblooded than his own. He was quite as pale as she, and he replied, in a strained voice: 'Miss Chawleigh, if you feel that *you* could bear it I shall count myself fortunate. I won't offer you false coin. To make the sort of protestations natural to this occasion, would be to insult you, but you may believe me sincere when I say that if you do me the honour to marry me I shall try to make you happy.'

She got up. 'I shall be. Don't think of that! I don't wish you to *try* to – Only to be comfortable! I hope I can make you so: I'll do my best. And you'll tell me what you wish me to do – or if I do something you don't like – won't you?'

He was surprised, and a little touched, but he said, as he took her hand: 'Yes, indeed! Whenever I'm out of temper, or grow tired of being comfortable!'

She stared for a second, saw the quizzical look in his eyes, and laughed suddenly. 'Oh – ! No, I *promise* you I won't get into a miff!'

He kissed her hand, and then, lightly, her cheek. She did not shrink, but she did not look as though she liked it. And since he had no desire to kiss her, he let go her hand, not offended, but relieved.

Five

The engagement was almost immediately announced, and the wedding-day fixed for a month later, on the 20th April. Whether from impatience to see his daughter ennobled, or from fear that Adam might cry off, Mr Chawleigh was anxious to clinch the bargain, and was with difficulty restrained from sending off notices then and there to the *Gazette* and the *Morning Post*. He said in a burst of unendearing frankness that the sooner the news was made public the better it would be for Adam; but he was forced to acknowledge that it would be improper to advertise the marriage before Adam had broken the news of it to his family.

Another set-back was in store for him. In the midst of his plans for a wedding exceeding in magnificence any that had ever preceded it he was pulled up by a gentle reminder that the recent bereavement suffered by his prospective son-in-law put out of count any such schemes: the ceremony, Adam said, must be private, with only the immediate relations and particular friends of both parties invited to attend it. This was a severe blow, and might have led to a battle of wills had not Jenny intervened, saying in her downright way: 'Now, that's enough, Papa! It wouldn't be the thing!'

In other quarters the intelligence was received in widely divergent ways. Lord Oversley said he was damned glad to hear it; and Lady Oversley burst into tears. Wimmering, momentarily stunned, recovered to congratulate his patron, and to beg him to leave all financial arrangements in his hands. Like Mrs

Quarley-Bix he was killed with delight, the only leaven to his joy being Adam's resolve to continue in his plan to sell the town house. To representations that now more than ever would he need a town house he replied that he had the intention of hiring one of more modest dimensions than the mansion in Grosvenor Street; to the warning that a hired place could not be thought creditable, he merely said: 'What nonsense!'

Adam communicated the news of his betrothal to Lady Lynton by letter, making business his excuse for not returning to Fontley. He could not bring himself to face the inevitable astonishment, the questions, and, perhaps, the disapproval that must greet his announcement; and he knew himself to be unequal to the task of describing Mr Chawleigh by word of mouth. He could write that he was a wealthy merchant, with whom Lord Oversley was on terms of friendship; and Lady Lynton would not know, reading of Jenny's quiet manners, superior understanding, and well-formed figure, that these fluent phrases had not tripped readily from his pen. He ended his letter by begging his mother to come to London, to make the acquaintance of her future daughter-in-law, but thought it advisable to send by the same post a brief and much more forthright letter to his elder sister.

'*Charlotte, I depend upon you to bring Mama to town. Represent to her how improper it would be for her to be backward in any attention: the ceremonial visit* must *be made. If she holds by her intention to settle in Bath I should wish her to decide which of the furnishings in Lynton House she desires for her own use, which can't be settled in her absence. Tell her this, if she should fly into one of her ways.*'

Before any letters reached him from Fontley the notice of his engagement had been published, and his circumstances underwent a sudden change. Persons who had been dunning him for payment of their accounts became instantly anxious to obtain his custom. Tailors, haberdashers, jewellers, and coach-makers begged the favour of his patronage; and foremost on the list was the firm of Schweitzer & Davidson, whose unpaid bill for raiment supplied to the Fifth Viscount ran into four figures. Even the elder Drummond permitted himself a smile of quiet triumph when he pointed out the announcement to his heir. 'His lordship, my boy, will draw on Drummond's to whatever tune he pleases,' he said.

'Yes, sir: I should think so!' replied Young Drummond, awed.

This result of his engagement came as a welcome change from the incessant demands with which Adam had previously been assailed, but the knowledge that he owed even the obsequiousness of the management and staff of Fenton's Hotel to Chawleigh-gold could scarcely be expected to gratify him. Nor did a letter from Miss Oversley help to elevate his spirits.

Mama had broken the news to Julia, saying, as she put the fatal copy of the *Gazette* into her hands: 'Julia, my love, you must be brave!' She had been brave, supported by Mama's exquisite understanding, but the notice had for a time quite overpowered her, and she felt that her mind would not soon recover its tone. Tears made it difficult for her to write, but indeed she wished him happy, and had compelled her reluctant hand to pen a note to Miss Chawleigh – '*once, as I believed, my friend.*' She was leaving town to visit her grandmama in Tunbridge Wells: Mama thought it would be wiser to run no risk of a chance encounter with Adam for the present.

The next post brought him a spate of letters from various relations, ranging from a demand from his Aunt Bridestow to know *who* was this Miss Jane Chawleigh? to a sentimental effusion from an elderly spinster cousin, who was persuaded that Miss Chawleigh must be the most amiable girl imaginable: an observation which made Adam realize that he knew nothing about his bride's disposition.

He had to wait several days for letters from Fontley, but they arrived at last: a frantic scrawl from Lydia, who was sure that Jenny must be the horridest girl in the world; and a troubled letter from Charlotte. Dearest Mama, she wrote, had suffered so severe a shock from the discovery that her only surviving son had become engaged to a totally unknown female that her every faculty had been suspended. Alarming spasms had subsequently attacked her; and although this distressing condition had yielded to the remedies prescribed by their good Dr Tilford she was still too knocked-up to attempt the arduous task of writing a letter.

'*Approbation cannot at present be hoped for,*' wrote Charlotte, sounding a warning note, '*but I believe she will exert herself to do all that is proper to this occasion. She struggles to overcome her fidgets, but the intelligence that you mean to sell Lynton House has been productive of some agitating reflections, our dear Brother having been born there . . . Here, Dst. Adam, I was interrupted by my Beloved Lambert. His visit has done Mama a great deal of good, for he has been sitting with her for an hour, representing to her with calm good sense all the advantages of your marriage . . .*'

It seemed that until she had had the benefit of Lambert's calm good sense Mama had declared that her bereavement put it out of the question that she should either stay in a public hotel, or pay morning visits. But Lambert's counsel had prevailed: provided that Adam could procure accommodation in some genteel hostelry placed in a quiet situation Mama would make the painful effort required of her. But *not*, Charlotte wrote, the Clarendon, with its poignant memories of Dearest Papa.

The most welcome letter Adam received came from his father's astringent elder sister. Writing from her lord's seat in Yorkshire Lady Nassington congratulated him on his common sense, and offered him both her house in Hampshire, as a honeymoon resort, and the services of her third son to support him through the wedding ceremony.

Adam was glad to accept the first of these offers, for Mr Chawleigh was showing alarming signs of being more than willing not only to plan the honeymoon, but to pay for it as well; but the second he refused, having provided himself with a groomsman in the lanky person of Timothy Beamish, Viscount Brough, the eldest son of the Earl of Adversane.

His friendship with Brough dated from his first term at Harrow, and had survived both separation and diverging interests. A desultory correspondence had kept them in touch, and the link had been strengthened after a few years by the arrival at the headquarters of the 52nd Regiment of Mr Vernon

Beamish, a raw and bashful subaltern, for whom Brough solicited Adam's patronage. '*If he doesn't fall overboard, or lose himself in the wilds of Portugal, you will shortly be reinforced by my little brother, my dear Dev,*' had scrawled Brough. '*Quite a nice pup, so be kind to him, and don't let him play with the nasty Frogs. . . .*'

Brough had not been in London when Adam returned from France, but two days after the notice of Adam's impending marriage appeared in the *Gazette* he strolled into Fenton's Hotel, and, upon being informed that my Lord Lynton was out, said that he would await his return. An hour later Adam entered his private parlour to find him lounging in a chair by the fire, his very long legs stretched out before him, and the rest of his form hidden behind a copy of the *Courier*. He lowered this, as the door opened, disclosing a cadaverous countenance which wore an expression of settled melancholy.

'*Brough!*' exclaimed Adam joyfully.

'Now, don't say you're glad to see me!' begged his lordship. 'I hate whiskers!'

'Whiskers be damned! I was never more glad to see anyone!'

'Pitching it *too* rum!' sighed Brough, dragging himself out of his chair. 'Or have you but this instant arrived in England? Come along! don't hesitate to try it on rare and thick!'

Adam gripped his bony hand, smiling. 'I've been in England some weeks. Three – but it seems more.'

'Running rather sly, aren't you?' drawled his friend.

'No – upon my honour! I looked for you in Brooks's, but was told you were in Northamptonshire still. I wrote to you yesterday: you can't have received my letter, surely? How did you find me out? What brings you to town?'

'I haven't received your letter; I found you out by enquiring for you in Grosvenor Street; I was brought to town by the notice in the *Gazette*,' replied Brough, ticking off the several questions on his long fingers. 'That, you know, conveyed the intelligence to my powerful mind that you had returned to England. But why I should have taken the notion into my head that you might have some use for me I can't conjecture!'

'Until your powerful mind apprehended that I wanted you for my groomsman!' said Adam, smiling up into his deep-set eyes. 'Will you do that for me, Brough?'

'But of course! With the greatest pleasure on earth, dear boy! I'm not acquainted with Miss Chawleigh, but m'father tells me it's an excellent match. Says you've done just as you ought, and I'm to present you with his felicitations. By the bye, how is my young brother?'

'He was in a capital way when I saw him last. I wish I knew what's been happening since I left! Soult's on the run, but not rompéd yet. What a moment to have been obliged to apply for furlough! Not that it is that, of course. I'm selling out.'

'Well, you'd think it a dead bore to be serving in peacetime,' remarked Brough. 'The on-dit is that the Bourbons will be back before the summer's out. I don't know how much of a set-back that pitiful business at Bergen-op-Zoom will prove to be. Graham seems to have made a rare mull of it.'

Adam nodded, grimacing, but said: 'We shan't be lurched by that. If we can outflank Soult, pin him up against the Pyrenees, cut off from his supplies, see if the whole house of cards don't tumble down! You've no notion what the feeling is in southern France: *we* thought the natives better-disposed towards us than the Spaniards!' He laughed suddenly. 'We pay for what we commandeer, you see, which Boney's army doesn't! Lord, I do wish I knew where we are now! It's nearly a month since Orthes – I suppose we're held up by a mingle-mangle of politicians!'

On the following day, the news of a victory at Tarbes on the 20th March was published. A part of the Light Division had been hotly engaged, but it did not seem as though the 52nd Regiment had taken much part in the action: a circumstance which slightly consoled Adam for his enforced absence. Nor, however, did it seem that Wellington had succeeded in cutting Soult's lines of communication. The Marshal was retiring in good order upon Toulouse.

Matters of more domestic moment claimed Adam's attention. Mr Chawleigh, baulked in his plans for a splendid marriage ceremony, wanted to know whether his Jenny was expected to wait until the following year before being presented at Court. He understood, on the authority of Mrs Quarley-Bix, that she could not go into society until this function had been performed; but while he didn't wish Jenny to do anything not quite the thing, it was plain that he viewed with considerable disfavour any post-ponement of her début. If she was not to appear at any ton-party, it would look as though my lord was ashamed of his bride, and that (said Mr Chawleigh, his jaw pugnaciously out-thrust) was not what he had bargained for.

Adam neither relished the manner of this admonition nor wished to take part in the season's festivities, but he did appreciate Mr Chawleigh's objection. Mr Chawleigh was paying him handsomely to establish Jenny in the ranks of the ton, and although the letter of the bargain might be fulfilled by her elevation to the peerage, the spirit of it demanded that every effort should be made to introduce her into society. There could be little satisfaction in becoming a Viscountess if one was obliged to live for a whole year in seclusion. Moreover, if no presentation took place, and no cards were sent out announcing the bridal couple's readiness to receive visits of ceremony, Adam was afraid that some of the high sticklers whose notice was of the first importance to a lady desirous of entering the exclusive circle to which they belonged might consider that the period of mourning absolved them from any duty to call on Lady Lynton thereafter. It might even be thought that to preserve the strict period of mourning was a tacit signal that the usual civilities were not expected, for it was certainly very odd conduct to interrupt this period for the celebration of nuptials which it would have been more proper to have postponed.

'Ay, but your affairs won't wait, my lord,' said Mr Chawleigh, when Adam tried to explain the difficulty to him. 'I won't tip over the dibs until I see the knot tied, because I'm not one to shell out the nonsense without I've better security than you can offer me. Now, there's no need to nab the rust! I don't doubt you'd stick to the bargain, but who's to say you'd be alive to do it?

Anything could happen to you, and then where would I be? Holding a draft on the Pump at Aldgate!'

This point of view could scarcely be expected to appeal to Adam; but his sense of humour came to his rescue, and, instead of yielding to a reckless impulse to repudiate the betrothal, he sought counsel of Lady Oversley.

She perceived the intricacies of the situation at once, and gave the matter her profound consideration. 'She must be presented,' she decided. 'It would have a very strange appearance if she weren't, because one always is, you know, on the occasion of one's marriage. And there is nothing improper in going to a Drawing-room when in mourning, though *not*, I think, in colour – except lavender, perhaps. Only, who is to present her? In general, one's mother does so, but poor Jenny has no mother, and even if she had – dear me, yes! this is a trifle awkward, because I don't think you *could* ask it of your own mother. Not while she is in such *deep* mourning, I mean! Well, it will have to be me, though I am strongly of the opinion that if we could but hit on a member of your own family it would create a better impression.'

'My Aunt Nassington?' suggested Adam.

'*Would* she?'

'I think she might.'

'Well, if you can coax her into it, do so! No one could answer the purpose better, because she's of the first consequence, and positively famous for the crushing set-downs she gives to perfectly respectable persons! *Her* approval must be of the greatest value. As for the rest, I don't think you should go to balls. Dinner-parties and assemblies, yes! Balls, no! At least, you might attend one, but you shouldn't dance at it.'

'I can't,' Adam pointed out. 'Too lame, ma'am! What a figure I should cut!'

'So you would!' she agreed, brightening perceptibly.

She did not disclose that the recollection of his disability had relieved her mind of a severe anxiety; and if he guessed that she had been racking her brain to think how she could induce the haughty patronesses of Almack's to bestow vouchers on Jenny he did not say so. But he must have known that the right of entry to these chaste Assembly Rooms in King Street conferred on the recipient a greater distinction than a Court presentation, and was far more difficult to obtain. The club was presided over by six great ladies, who imposed rules that were as inflexible as they were arbitrary. Mere rank was no passport to Almack's; and although the disappointed marvelled that anyone should covet a ticket to an assembly where no more stimulating beverage than orgeat could be got, and where nothing was danced but Scotch reels and country dances, such disgruntled animadversions hoaxed no one. It might be more amusing to twirl round a ballroom in the new German waltz, or to embark on the intricacies of the quadrille; and there was not a hostess in London who would have dreamed of regaling her guests on tea and stale bread-and-butter; but no one could pretend that invitations to all the smartest balls of the season conveyed the *cachet* won by a single appearance at Almack's.

Having passed the six hostesses under mental review, Lady Oversley was so much relieved to be spared the task of begging Lady Sefton or Lady Castlereagh, both very good-natured, to bestow vouchers on Jenny that she offered to act as matron of honour at the wedding. This, however, Jenny refused, saying that she had invited a Miss Tiverton to support her on the occasion. She told Adam that Miss Tiverton was perfectly genteel. The remark grated on him, but he said lightly: 'If you like her I'm sure she must be an amiable girl. Your chaperon I cannot like! Will you feel yourself obliged to invite her to your parties?'

'Oh, no! I don't mean to keep up the acquaintance,' she said calmly. 'I dislike her very much.'

There was a hint of her father's ruthlessness in this, which dismayed him. She saw that he was looking grave, and added: 'I don't feel under an obligation to her, you know. She has been handsomely paid, and she has been able to feather her nest in a great many ways. All my wedding-clothes are being made at the most expensive houses, you know, and so of course she receives commissions for having put business in their way.'

'Good God! Surely it is most improper of her to be urging you to extravagance so that she may make a profit? You will indeed be well rid of her!'

'Oh, yes, but I daresay she feels it to be of no consequence, since Papa likes me to shop at all the most expensive places.' She hesitated, and then asked shyly: 'That puts me in mind of something I wish to ask you: must I engage a dresser? Mrs Quarley-Bix says I must, and I'll do what you think right – only I would very much prefer to keep my old maid with me! I *know* a grand dresser would despise me!'

'If all dressers are like my mother's Miss Poolstock she'd hold up her nose at both of us. A more top-lofty female I never encountered!'

'Then may I tell Papa you don't think it necessary?'

'Yes, tell him Miss Poolstock has given me such a hatred of dressers that I won't have one in the house! And, talking of houses, what do you wish me to do about a town house? Wimmering tells me there will be no difficulty in selling the one in Grosvenor Street, so perhaps we should be looking about us for another – if either of us can spare the time, which I doubt! Shall I tell Wimmering to try what he can find for us while we are in Hampshire? then, if he saw any he thought suitable we may inspect them before I take you to Fontley.'

She agreed at once; and asked if they were to go to Fontley immediately after the honeymoon.

'Unless you should dislike it. I want to make you acquainted with it, and with my people.'

'Would you like to remain there? Not come to town at all this season?'

'What, miss *all* the season?' he replied in a rallying tone. 'No, indeed! Have you forgotten that you are to be presented? We ought to make a push to be back in town before the middle of May, which will relegate our stay at Fontley to a very few days.'

'I only thought – since you are in mourning – that perhaps you had liefer not go to parties?'

'On the contrary, I've consulted Lady Oversley, and she assures me that it will be proper for us to do everything but dance. And I don't dance, you know – though I'll engage to escort you to balls next year, and stand, as my sister tells me Byron does, gloomily surveying the company!'

Six

*L*ady Lynton took two days to reach London, since she elected to travel in the family coach, an old-fashioned vehicle which had not been designed for swift progress. It had the advantage of being roomy enough to accommodate Miss Poolstock, as well as herself and Charlotte, but she did not mention this when she explained to Adam why she had lumbered up to town in it. She reminded him instead that one of his first economies had been to dismiss the postilions always kept by his father. 'Whether that was quite wise, dearest, I must leave it to you to decide. I am sure you did what you thought right, and I don't regard the inconvenience to myself.'

'But you could have hired postilions, and come in the post-chaise, Mama!' expostulated Adam.

He would have done better to have held his peace, for he was speedily brought to a sense of his shortcomings. These included a callousness which made it possible for him to contemplate with equanimity all the dangers to which his mother would be subjected were she to entrust herself to hired post-boys.

He had time, while this homily was being delivered, to assimilate the details of her raiment; and as soon as he found himself alone with his sister he demanded to be told whether Mama meant to call in Russell Square rigged out in crimped crape, and with her only ornament a large mourning-brooch, depicting, in *grisaille* on mother-of-pearl, a female drooping miserably over a tomb. 'And why hasn't Lydia come with you?'

Charlotte was obliged to confess that Lydia had not wished to come. 'She is so very much attached to you that she felt she couldn't bear – that is to say, she –'

'I understand you,' he interrupted. 'She is mistaken, however. Miss Chawleigh is a very agreeable girl. I think Lydia will like her. I hope she will, for if she doesn't it must lead to a breach between us, which would grieve me very much indeed.'

She bowed her head, but ventured to say: 'Only let me *once* tell you, my dear brother, how deeply sensible I am of the sacrifice you are making! When I reflect that if I had had your resolution –'

'Charlotte, don't be a goose! You are not assisting at a tragedy! Oh, I know what's in your mind, but *that* was put out of the question whether I married, or stayed single. Don't, I beg of you, make a piece of work of it!' He gave her a slight hug, which told her more than anything he had said. 'Has Mama made up her mind where she wishes to live? Does she remain at Fontley, or does she hold by the Bath scheme?'

'By the Bath scheme, and – oh, Adam, I am in such a worry over it, and can't help feeling that perhaps it is my duty to accompany her! But Lambert thinks that if once I go to Bath Mama will renew all her objections to my marriage. I am in the wretchedest indecision, and wish you will advise me!'

'You'll marry Lambert, of course. Mama will have Lydia to bear her company, and Aunt Bridestow as well. Why should you hesitate?'

'If you don't think it would be wrong – Mama so lately bereaved!' she faltered.

He assured her that he did not, which made her look brighter, and later won him a hearty handshake from Mr Ryde, who told him that the Dowager had been showing disquieting signs of rescinding her consent to the marriage.

'The thing is, old chap, that now you are going to mend matters so handsomely she don't like the match any more than she ever did,' he confided. 'Let her but take Charlotte off to Bath and she'll find first one excuse and then another to keep her there!'

'I see. Well, if my mother insists on going there at once we had best fix the date of your wedding for the week following my – Jenny's and my return from Hampshire.'

This arrangement quite failed to win the Dowager's approval. She said that two such hasty weddings in one family would present a very odd appearance.

'I must own that I think it would be better to postpone Charlotte's marriage for a few months,' Adam agreed. 'If you feel that, don't remove to Bath till the autumn! There is no occasion for you to do so, after all.'

'Dearest, you must not ask too much of me!' countered her ladyship. 'If my remaining at Fontley could benefit you I would stay, exerting my last strength to suppress the painful feelings that must arise from seeing a stranger – and one who I *cannot* believe is worthy of the position she is to fill – set in my place! But there is nothing I could do to help you, my poor boy.'

This did not augur well for the forthcoming visit to Russell Square; but this seemed, from what Adam could gather, to have passed off fairly well. Lady Lynton and Charlotte found Miss Chawleigh and her chaperon at home, but since theirs was a morning-call they did not meet the master of the house. Charlotte thought that Mama had been agreeably surprised by Miss Chawleigh, for although she deplored her lack of countenance, and prophesied that she would be fat before she was forty, she had said, as she and Charlotte drove back to Albemarle Street, that she was thankful at least that she would not have to blush for her daughter-in-law's manners. 'And, indeed, Adam, I thought her very unaffected and pleasant, and I am sure I shall learn to be fond of her,' said Charlotte nobly.

Lady Lynton's severest strictures were reserved for Mrs Quarley-Bix, whom she described as odious and insinuating. She said that a worse trial than to be obliged to endure the company of such a person could not be imagined. But that was before she had made the acquaintance of Mr Chawleigh.

The meeting took place at Lothian's Hotel, and was of an informal character, the task of inviting the Chawleighs to dine quietly there being entrusted to Adam. Lady Lynton, facing this subdued festivity with the courage of a martyr, adjured him to do what he could to exclude Mrs Quarley-Bix from the invitation, but very handsomely exonerated him from future blame by saying that she had no hope of his succeeding, since such Encroaching Females could be depended on to thrust themselves in wherever they were least welcome. However, all was rendered easy by Mr Chawleigh, who, after expressing his gratitude for what he termed her la'ship's condescension, added: 'And mind, now! Not a word to Mrs Q.-B., for I'll be bound her la'ship don't want *her* simpering and writhing all over!'

Only the Chawleighs, therefore, presented themselves at Lothian's Hotel on the appointed evening, and were ushered into Lady Lynton's private parlour. Miss Chawleigh's jewels were rather too magnificent both for her age and the occasion, but there was no fault to be found with her half-robe of lilac silk; and if her parent's knee-breeches and blazing tie-pin were more suited to a Court function than to a family dinner-party this outmoded style did him no disservice in the Dowager's eyes.

Her son might view with dismay the trappings of her woe, but on Mr Chawleigh they exercised an instant effect. He bowed low over the frail hand extended to him, and said that he took it very kindly of her to have invited him to dine. 'Which I'll be bound must have gone against the pluck with your la'ship, when it stands to reason you ain't feeling able for company.'

A sad smile acknowledged this tribute. 'So pleased!' murmured the widow, sinking down into her chair again, and indicating with a movement of her fan that he was to take the one beside hers. While the younger members of the party made rather laborious conversation amongst themselves the widow gave Mr Chawleigh of her best. By the time a waiter came to announce that dinner awaited them in the adjoining parlour Mr Chawleigh knew how many and how grievous were the sufferings she had undergone, and how bravely she had borne up under the bludgeonings of misfortune. He even knew what an effort it had cost her to undertake the journey to London (in circumstances of extreme discomfort), and he was quite as much shocked as she could have wished. He thought it dreadful that a high-born lady of obvious fragility should have been jumbled over bad roads in a cumbersome old coach, and without even one outrider for her protection. He assured her that he would think himself honoured to be permitted to convey her back to Fontley in his own post-chaise. 'None of your yellow bounders, my lady!' he told her. 'It's as well-sprung as any you've ridden in, which it ought to be, when you think what I paid for it. And proper Hounslow-bred postilions, and that you may depend on, for only the best is good enough for Jonathan Chawleigh.'

Over dinner he entered with alarming vigour into her lady-ship's Bath scheme, offering not only to arrange all the details of her journey, but to send immediately to Bath a smart young fellow from his counting-house to discover what houses were for hire in the town. Lady Lynton said in thread-like accents that she should not dream of troubling him; but he assured her that it would be a pleasure to him to save her the fatigue of house-hunting, and no trouble at all. It began to seem as if the poor lady would find herself swept off to Bath and installed willy-nilly in an establishment chosen for her by the smart young fellow from the counting-house; but just as she cast an anguished glance at her son Miss Chawleigh said bluntly: 'Lady Lynton would prefer to choose her own house, Papa.'

'Yes, and her ladyship has two sons to serve her, sir,' chimed in Lambert jovially. 'That is, if I may be allowed so to term myself!'

He cast an arch look at her as he spoke, which had the effect of making her smile graciously at Mr Chawleigh, and say that she was much obliged to him, but believed that Wimmering would manage her affairs for her.

'Ay, so he will!' agreed Mr Chawleigh, adding with a chuckle: 'A regular downy one he is! He'll see you ain't clerked, my lady!' He saw that this remark had produced constraint, and said cheerfully: 'No need to colour up, my lord! You don't want to concern yourself with business either: you leave me and

85

Wimmering to settle things in our own fashion! I warrant we understand one another as you never could!'

Having in this masterly style put the family at their ease, he then turned his attention to Charlotte. His shrewd eyes looked her over with approval, but conversation did not flourish between them. With every will in the world to talk pleasantly to him, an over-delicate refinement made Charlotte regard him with much the same nervous surprise as she would have felt at being addressed by an aboriginal. Mr Chawleigh's manner with young females was jocular and paternal. He was convinced that they liked to be complimented on their looks, and quizzed about their beaux; but his compliments made Charlotte blush; and when he made a sly reference to her approaching nuptials, prophesying that there would be a score of broken hearts when the news was made public, she raised her eyes in astonishment to his face, unable to conceal how little to her taste was this ponderous gallantry. Lambert came to her rescue, responding for her jokingly. His efforts to entertain Mr Chawleigh were praiseworthy, but the attempt to adapt his tone to what he thought would be acceptable caused him to assume something of the manner of a man good-naturedly humouring a child, and soon earned him a set-down.

Miss Chawleigh bore herself throughout with composure, but rather silently: a circumstance on which her father rallied her, as they drove back to Russell Square. She said: 'Well, I like listening better than talking. But I did talk, Papa: to my lord, and to Miss – to Charlotte! She has asked me to call her that.'

'Mighty condescending of her!' he grunted. 'How do you go on with her? Proud sort of a girl, ain't she?'

'Oh, no! She was very kind, and means to like me, which is truly good, I think, because she doesn't wish my lord to marry me. She tried hard to seem pleased. I'd like to tell her that I understand how she must feel, but I don't know her well enough. And perhaps it wouldn't be quite the thing.'

'Now, Jenny, tell me to my head!' commanded Mr Chawleigh, laying his hand on her knee. 'You don't want to draw back, my girl? I'm not forcing you into it, mind!'

'No, I don't want to do that,' she replied uncommunicatively.

He sat back again in his corner of the carriage, saying that he was glad of it. 'Setting aside the position you'll have – not that that's a thing to be lightly done, and don't you think it! – I like his lordship. That's not to say that he's after my cut, or that I'd want to be joined with him in business, but he's my notion of a regular gentleman. As for his family, I'm sure his ma is a sweet lady, poor soul! I didn't take to that sister myself, but if she treats you as she ought, which you say she does, she may be as niffy-naffy as she pleases for aught I care. Taking the fat with the lean, I like his lordship's family better than I thought to do.'

It was unfortunate that his lordship's family did not reciprocate these sentiments. Lady Lynton, bearing the appearance of one prevented from swooning only by frequent recourse to her vinaigrette, begged to be told what she had done to deserve such an infliction as Mr Chawleigh; and Charlotte exclaimed, wringing her hands: 'Oh, my dear Adam, you should have warned us! The shock to poor Mama! We never supposed he could be such a *very* vulgar person!'

'Oh, come now!' Lambert said, laughing. 'It's natural you should think so, but I can tell you there are many worse! Though I must say –' He stopped, encountering Adam's eyes, blinked, and then said rather hastily: 'I beg pardon! One's tongue runs away with one sometimes!'

Adam nodded, and turned away from him. The ladies were not to be so easily silenced, and, after the usual practice of people discussing the faults of the absent, soon discovered in Mr Chawleigh many and more serious shortcomings than had originally been apparent to them. It was useless to defend him; and an attempt to bring the debate to an end merely resulted in Lady Lynton's exclaiming tragically that things had come to a pretty pass when a mother might not speak frankly to her son. She added that she hoped she had too much regard for his feelings to utter one word in disparagement of his future wife. She could only trust that he would be able to prevail upon her not to overload her person with jewels which, besides being ostentatious, were unsuited to her years, and could at no time be worn to advantage by squabby females who had neither air nor countenance to set them off.

Charlotte felt that this was going too far. She said quickly: 'Depend upon it, she only does so because her father wishes it! How thankful we must be that she is not at all like him!'

'Exactly so!' said Lambert. 'A very agreeable girl, and with a good understanding, I daresay. As for her father – well, ma'am, there's no need to think about him, after all! I heard him tell you that he didn't mean to force himself on you.'

'If I could believe he meant it!' sighed the widow.

'You may at least believe, Mama, that I mean it when I tell you that he will at all times be made welcome in my house!' said Adam, rather sternly.

'Oh, Adam, not at Fontley!' Charlotte cried involuntarily.

'Certainly at Fontley! You seem to forget that but for him Fontley must have been sold! Do you imagine that I shan't invite him to visit us there? Handsome of me!'

She turned her face away, saying in a low voice: 'I had forgotten, or perhaps haven't allowed myself to reflect upon a circumstance so mortifying – so impossible to bring oneself to accept! I will say no more.'

'I think enough has been said,' he returned wearily.

This sentiment was not shared by his mother, who declared herself compelled to say that no one had considered *her* feelings. Her sole consolation was that Adam's poor father was not alive to be similarly lacerated.

Charlotte burst into tears, uttering a choked protest; but a rueful smile crept into Adam's eyes. All he said, however, was: 'Very well, Mama. Shall I cry off? Is that what you wish?'

If he expected the Dowager to be confounded by this question he underrated her. She told him that she had no wishes that were not bound up in the happiness of her dear ones. 'Far be it from me to try to influence you!' she said. 'Alas, our natures are so widely opposed, dearest, that I cannot tell what will make you happy! Wealth means nothing to me. It is otherwise with you, and you must judge for yourself. One thing you may be sure of: no word of blame will ever pass your mother's lips!'

On this splendid line she withdrew to her bedchamber, leaning on Charlotte's arm, and denying any expectation of closing her eyes all night.

Happily for her dear ones, her thoughts were given another direction on the following day by the news that Wimmering had received a very handsome offer for Lynton House. Indeed, the prospective purchaser was prepared to pay the high price set on it if he could have immediate possession. Adam closed with this offer; and the pangs which instantly assailed his parent were almost as quickly cured by his telling her that the sale would make it possible for him to provide for Lydia. So Lady Lynton was able to mourn the loss of a house she neither liked nor wanted, and was supplied with a self-sacrificing reason for acquiescing in its sale. She had now only to decide which pieces of furniture she wished to keep for her own use. Adam gave her carte blanche to take what she chose, and left her to Charlotte's management. Since everything the house contained appeared to hold precious, if hitherto unsuspected, memories, it seemed unlikely that much would remain to be put in store.

Seven

The wedding took place on April 20th, a date that coincided with Louis XVIIIth's entry into London, where he was met in state by the Prince Regent. He had been living privately at Hartwell, and this was the first time in his twenty years of exile that he had been publicly acknowledged as King of France. This circumstance did much to reconcile Mr Chawleigh to the quiet function forced on him by Adam's bereavement. 'For it stands to reason,' he said, 'that with all this fuss and to-do over that Frenchy no one would have paid any heed if I'd done the thing twice as handsomely as I'd have wished to!'

Public events were certainly occupying everyone's attention. Adam had returned from a brief visit to Fontley to hear the Tower guns firing in honour of the Allied entry to Paris; a week later came the news of Bonaparte's abdication, to be closely followed by the publication of a dispatch from Lord Wellington, sent from Toulouse on April 12th. It seemed as if his lordship had won his last victory in the war. It had dragged on for so many years that people felt as much incredulity as excitement; there were even those who darkly prophesied that the Allies would yet be taken at fault; and many who thought it madness to allow Bonaparte to retire to Elba.

'Mark me if he don't start up again!' said Mr Chawleigh. 'There's only one thing to be done with him, and that's to make an end of him, for it stands to reason that a fellow that's been rampaging all over won't stay quiet on a bit of an island, which

90

is what I'm told this Elba is. We'll have him breaking out again, sure as a gun!' He added, after chewing the cud of disgruntled reflection, that it seemed as if the only thing that would make people take notice of his Jenny's marriage was for the Grand-duchess of Oldenburg to attend the ceremony.

This lately widowed lady, sister of the Emperor of Russia, had arrived in London some weeks previously, and was staying at the Pulteney, on Piccadilly, having arranged to hire the whole hotel for the accommodation of herself, one of her daughters, two very ugly ladies-in-waiting, and a number of servants. It was generally believed that a match was being planned between her and the Prince Regent; or, if he failed to obtain a divorce from the Princess of Wales, that she might take his brother, the Duke of Clarence, in his stead. She herself said that her visit was one of mere pleasure and sight-seeing; and it hardly seemed that she was taking trouble to make herself agreeable to the Regent. Well-informed persons said that her only matrimonial schemes were vicarious, and that she was meddling in the affairs of the Princess Charlotte of Wales, whose engagement to the Prince of Orange did not seem to be prospering.

'And why anyone should want to gape at her every time she drives out I'm damned if I know!' said Mr Chawleigh. 'To my way of thinking she's an antidote, in spite of the white skin we hear so much about. It's as well for her she *has* got a white skin, because otherwise you'd take her for a negress, with those thick lips of hers!'

It was evident, in spite of these strictures, that if only some member of the Deveril family had been acquainted with the Grandduchess nothing would have deterred him from inviting her to the wedding: not, as he explained to Adam, from any desire to rub shoulders with such exalted persons, but because he had always promised to turn his daughter off in prime style. 'Which it would be,' he pointed out. 'It would have made as big a hit as if I'd got the Lord Mayor to come in his coach.'

Adam replied sympathetically, but was firm in denying the slightest acquaintance with the Grandduchess. He wondered for an unnerving moment if Mr Chawleigh knew of the late Viscount's friendship with the Prince Regent. Mr Chawleigh did, but he said he hoped he knew better than to aim as high as that. 'A foreigner's one thing, but the Prince Regent's quite another. She may be the Emperor of Russia's sister, but who's *he*, when all's said?'

'Who indeed?' agreed Adam. 'Let us not trouble our heads over any Royals! We shall do much better without them!'

He spoke cheerfully, with nothing in his voice or manner to betray the sense of unreality which possessed him. He seemed to himself to be living in a dream. Dreams were without future, and he did not try to discover what his might be, being too tired to force his brain to look forward. He had, indeed, little time for contemplation: he was kept endlessly busy; and, as the wedding-day approached, was harassed by such a multitude of things forgotten and things left undone that he only managed to snatch one brief meeting with Lord William Russell, who had brought home the dispatch from Toulouse. The meeting did him good; and in learning all that had happened since he had left the Army, getting news of his friends, rejoicing in Lord March's miraculous recovery from the wound he had received at Orthes, and laughing at the latest Headquarters' jokes, he found reality again for a short space, and was heartened by it.

He bore himself at his wedding in a manner which Lady Oversley declared to be beyond praise. She was a good deal affected, and told her lord later that she could have wept to see dear Adam concealing what must be his true feelings, only his pallor showing how much the effort cost him.

In fact, there was no effort. Adam, back in his unquiet dream, only obeyed the dictates of his breeding. Good manners demanded a certain line of conduct, and since it was second nature to him to respond to that demand it was with no effort but mechanically that he talked and smiled at the wedding-breakfast.

There were only a dozen persons present, but nothing could have exceeded the display of plate, or the splendour of the refreshments. The regalia on the sideboard of jellies, creams, and pies made Lydia open her eyes; and she afterwards insisted that she had counted eight dishes a side on the table.

Lydia had come to London in subdued spirits, chastened by a homily from Charlotte. When she first saw Jenny, all white satin and lace and diamonds, she thought she looked dreadfully commonplace. White satin did not become Jenny; and, to make matters worse, she was as flushed as Adam was pale. She was quite composed, however, and spoke her responses clearly; but after the ceremony Lydia thought that perhaps she was not as composed as she seemed, for when she believed no one to be looking at her she pressed her hands to her cheeks, as though to force back her high colour.

Lydia felt very low during the unromantic ceremony; but in Russell Square her melancholy vanished. Her surroundings were entirely new to her, and although she had heard a great deal about Mr Chawleigh's taste she had never imagined quite so much opulence. She looked about her with bright-eyed appreciation, drinking it all in, and wishing that she could exchange just one glance with Adam. That was impossible, but Lord Brough did very well as a substitute. Their eyes met fleetingly, and she saw by the lazy twinkle in his that he was enjoying it as much as she was; and she began to feel much more cheerful. It was still tragic that Adam was married to Jenny instead of Julia, but it was impossible to be sad in the middle of such an ill-assorted party. It was even difficult not to laugh when Mrs Quarley-Bix, robed in Berlin silk, and highly rouged, greeted Lady Lynton with the effusive affectation of intimacy, and lost no time in placing herself on equality with her by the employment of such phrases as: 'You and I, dear Lady Lynton . . .' and: 'Persons of quality, as we know, dear Lady Lynton . . .'

Mr Chawleigh, observing the merry look in Lydia's eye, took an instant fancy to her, and bore down on her. She was not as beautiful as her sister, but what he called a big, handsome girl, with no nonsense about her. By way of breaking the ice he told her that he was downright ashamed of himself for having provided no smart beaux for her entertainment. 'There's only

93

my Lord Brough to be split between you and Lizzie Tiverton, and that's what I call a shabby way of doing things. Not but what there won't be much splitting done, if his lordship's got as much sense as I think he has!'

Lydia, who partook far more of her father's robust character than her brother and sister, was not at all offended by this speech. No one like Mr Chawleigh had previously come in her way, but by the time the assembled guests sat down to the Gargantuan meal provided for them he and she were in a fair way to becoming fast friends; and several times her mother was pained to hear her spontaneous, schoolgirl's laugh break from her. Lady Lynton, conducting herself throughout with impeccable, if chilly, civility, later took Lydia to task for laughing at Mr Chawleigh, and read her a lecture on the want of breeding she had shown in wounding his sensibilities.

But Mr Chawleigh's sensibilities were not even grazed. His shrewd eyes twinkled at Lydia; and he presently told Lady Lynton that he didn't know when he had taken more of a liking to a girl. He added, in a confidential undertone, that he had placed Lord Brough beside her at the table. 'Though she tells me she's not out yet, and his lordship ought to be next to Miss Tiverton. But what I say, my lady, is: Hang Lizzie Tiverton! His lordship will be better pleased to talk to Miss Lydia!'

Lady Lynton, though she accepted the compliment politely, was not gratified. On the other hand, Adam, who had noticed, with relief, that Lydia seemed to be on the best of terms with her host, smiled gratefully at her when he met her eyes across the table.

In his lazy, unconcerned way Brough too was proving himself to be a tower of strength. Mr Chawleigh, quick to detect and to resent condescension, thought him a very nice young fellow: of much the same cut as Lord Oversley, who was good-naturedly engaging Mrs Quarley-Bix's attention at one end of the table, while his lady, at the other end, maintained a flow of inconsequent conversation, laughed at all her host's jokes, and delighted him by partaking of all the dishes offered her and declaring that she had never tasted anything so good.

When Jenny went upstairs to change her dress Lydia accompanied her, rescuing her from Mrs Quarley-Bix, whose proffered ministrations were clearly unacceptable to her. Waiting only to be sure that Miss Tiverton, a very shy girl, did not mean to put herself forward, she got up, saying: 'May I come with you? Pray let me!'

'That's right!' approved Mr Chawleigh. 'You go with Miss Lydia, love, and do you sit down again, Mrs Q.-B.! Jenny don't want two of you to help her dress, thanking you all the same!'

Lydia trod beside her new sister up the heavily carpeted stairs, trying to think of something friendly to say. But it was Jenny who first spoke, saying with a stammer: 'Thank you! I'm much obliged to you! I hope you don't dislike it?'

'No, no, of course not!' Lydia replied, flushing. 'If *you* don't!'

'Oh, no! so kind!' Jenny sighed. 'If you knew what Mrs Quarley-Bix has been like all day – !'

Lydia giggled. 'Your papa says she has been capering like a fly in a tar-box! Goodness, is this your bedchamber? Isn't it *huge*?' She stood looking about her in astonishment, presently remarking that there was much to be said for being an only daughter. 'My bedchamber isn't nearly as big, and nor is Charlotte's.' She added, turning her serious gaze upon Jenny: 'I expect you'll think Fontley pretty shabby.'

'Oh, no, I promise you I shan't! *Pray* don't think – Oh, Martha, Miss Lydia Deveril has been so kind as to come and help me! Martha used to be my nurse, Miss Deveril.'

'You should call me Lydia: I wish you will,' Lydia said, sitting down on the end of an elegant day-bed. She smiled at the angular female who was dropping her a stiff curtsy, and said: 'I won't get in the way: I will only watch!'

The abigail's presence did not help to lessen the constraint that tied each young lady's tongue. Conversation was confined to the merest commonplaces, Jenny's contributions to it being largely monosyllabic. It was not until she stood fully attired, and

Martha had left the room, that she seemed to brace herself, and abruptly addressed Lydia. 'You love him, don't you?' she said. 'You needn't tell me: I know you do, and that this isn't what you – or he – wished. I only want to tell you that he'll be comfortable: I'll see to that!' The intensity of her expression was broken by a wintry little smile. 'You don't think that signifies, but it does. Men like to be comfortable. Well – he will be! That's all!'

She ended this speech with a determined nod, and without waiting for a reply went out of the room with a brisk step, leaving Lydia to follow her downstairs to where the assembled company awaited her in the hall.

The leave-takings were not prolonged. Mr Chawleigh, enfolding his daughter in a bear's hug, bade Adam, between jocularity and ferocity, to take good care of his girl; Lady Lynton said mournfully that she hoped Adam would be happy; Charlotte and Lady Oversley shed tears; and Lydia, convulsively embracing Adam, whispered: 'I don't hate her! I *don't*!' and the gentlemen of the party offered bluff congratulations mingled with recommendations not to keep the horses standing.

The posting-chariot, which was one of Mr Chawleigh's wedding-gifts, stood at the door, a team of match-bays harnessed to it, and the Lynton arms emblazoned on the door panels and the rich hammercloth; behind it a fourgon was drawn up, for the accommodation of my lord's valet, my lady's abigail, and all their baggage; and the final touch of grandeur was supplied by a couple of liveried outriders. Adam handed his bride into the chariot, paused only for a word with Brough, and followed her; the steps were put up, the door shut; and as goodbyes were called and handkerchiefs fluttered the carriage moved forward. Since postilions had been chosen for the journey the box seat, under that resplendent hammercloth, was unoccupied. So too was the rumble, Adam having successfully resisted Mr Chawleigh's attempts to foist two footmen on to him.

The equipage swept round the angle of the square; and as the group on the flagway was lost to sight Adam turned away from the window, and smiled at Jenny, saying: 'Well, your father may say what he chooses, but *I* think we had a very handsome wedding, don't you? Are you very tired after it all?'

'Well, I am fagged,' she acknowledged, 'but not as much as you are, I daresay.'

'Nonsense!'

'You're worn to a bone: I know that. You've had far more to do than I have – besides other things. I only hope you may not be sea-sick in this carriage!'

He laughed. 'I hope not indeed! Do you think you will?'

'Well, I think I might. It sways about so much. I daresay I shall grow used to it, but if I don't you mustn't tell Papa, if you please! He would be so disappointed, for he had it specially built.'

'It won't be as bad once we're off the stones. Lean back and shut your eyes! Did you bring your smelling-salts with you?'

'I haven't any. Oh, yes, I have! A horrid vinaigrette, which was Mrs Quarley-Bix's wedding-gift to me. I expect she had it by her, for she couldn't have supposed it would be of the least use to me.'

'Ungrateful girl! Don't tell me you left it behind!'

'Yes, but never mind! I shall soon grow accustomed.'

This seemed to be true, for after remaining for some time with her eyes closed she presently opened them, and turned her head a little to study Adam's profile. He was not at first aware of her scrutiny, his thoughts being remote from her, and his inattentive gaze fixed on the changing landscape; but after some minutes, as though suddenly conscious that he was being watched, he glanced at her.

His vision of ethereal loveliness vanished. Beside him, plump and a little homely, sat reality, in a stylish pelisse, and a hat whose poke-front and curled ostrich feathers made an incongruous frame for a round, rosy face remarkable only for its determination. Revulsion held him speechless for a moment, but as his eyes met Jenny's he saw the anxiety in hers, and his mood changed to one of compassion. Whatever had been her motive for consenting to the bargain struck by her father, she did not look happy. He thought her case to be worse than his own. The benefits accruing to him through marriage were solid; if she sought social advancement, he, born into the ton, and taking for granted the advantages of birth and rank, believed that she would discover her elevation to the peerage to be a worthless thing. If she had been forced into a loveless match by her father's ambition, she was the more to be pitied. He did pity her, and forgot his own aching heart in the need to reassure her. How to do it he did not know; he could only smile at her, and take her gloved hand in his, saying cheerfully: 'That's better! Have you been asleep?'

Her hand trembled momentarily, but she replied in a steady voice: 'No, but I am better now, thank you. I should like to talk to you, if I may.'

Having possessed himself of her hand he could not think what to do with it, or how to be rid of it. She solved the problem for him by quietly withdrawing it. He said quizzically: 'If you *may*? Now, what can you be going to say that needs my permission, goose?'

She smiled perfunctorily. 'Oh, no! Only that you might not wish – I can't tell, but I think we should discuss our – our situation. I have frequently wanted to, but we have so seldom been granted the opportunity. And perhaps you would have thought it improper in me. I can't tell that either, for I am not thoroughly acquainted with you yet, and, though I do try to set a guard on it, I know I have a blunt tongue – I was for ever being scolded for it, at Miss Satterleigh's!'

'You need never guard it when you talk to me: indeed, I hope you won't! But first let me tell you that I'm not blind to the evils of *your* situation. We are barely acquainted, as you have said yourself: it must be uncomfortable for you indeed!' He smiled at her, not lovingly, but very kindly. '*That* evil will soon be remedied. In the meantime, don't be afraid! I won't do anything you don't like.'

She took a moment or two to answer this, her countenance inscrutable. 'You're very obliging,' she said at last. 'I'm not afraid. That wasn't it! I daresay there are many husbands and

98

wives who were no better acquainted at the outset than we are. It wouldn't do for people who have a great deal of sensibility, but I don't think I have much. I mean, there's no need for you to be in a worry over me: I hate fusses and twitters! In general, persons in my walk of life don't deal much in marriages of convenience, but in yours they are pretty common, aren't they?'

'Yes – that is, I believe they do still occur, but I really don't know much about it,' he said, hardly knowing how to reply to so forthright a speech.

'I don't mean to embarrass you,' she said, perceiving that she had done so, 'but there's no sense in shamming it: we both know that I'm not quality-born. The thing is, you might suppose that I don't understand marriages of convenience. Well, I do, so you needn't fear I shall expect you to sit in my pocket. Nor that you'll find me hanging on you, like a bur, wanting to know what you're doing every minute of the day, and why you didn't come home to dinner.' She raised her eyes, giving him a resolute look. 'I shan't interfere with you, my lord, or ask you any questions. You'll not live under the cat's foot, I promise you.'

'Are you giving me permission to embark on a career of profligacy?' he demanded, trying to turn it off lightly. 'Ought I to bestow a similar carte blanche on you? You'll think me very unhandsome, I'm afraid, for I've no such intention! I'm even shabby enough to reserve to myself the right to ask you any number of questions!'

She shook her head, smiling, but lowering her eyes. 'That's a different matter. Not that it's likely you'll have cause to be uneasy: I'm not pretty enough!' She paused, and drew a difficult breath, her colour mounting. 'I'm not the wife you wished for, but I'll do my possible to behave as I should. You'll be wanting an heir, and I hope I shall give you one. I should like to have children, and the sooner the better. But that's for you to decide.' She stopped, tightly folding her lips, and turned away her face, to look out of the window; but after a few moments, during which he tried to think of something, anything, to say to her, she spoke again, saying in a conversational tone: 'This is a new thing for me, you know: to be going to stay in the country. My mother was a countrywoman, but Papa is town-bred, and hasn't any liking for the country, so whenever we have been out of London it has been to Brighton, or to Ramsgate or some such place. Have we far to go before we reach your aunt's house?'

Eight

*T*hey stayed for less than a fortnight in Hampshire, the honeymoon being shortened by Lady Lynton's determination to join her sister in Bath immediately, and Lambert Ryde's equal determination to marry Charlotte before this date. Family affairs called him north again; and he proposed in earnest what he had originally suggested in jest: that he should carry Charlotte to Scotland for their honeymoon. Charlotte could not deny that the prospect filled her with delight, but wrote diffidently to Adam. On the one hand, she dreaded an indefinite postponement of her wedding; on the other, she could not bear the thought of being led to the altar by anyone but her brother.

'Well, I should think not indeed!' exclaimed Jenny, when Charlotte's letter was shown to her. 'Do write to her directly, and tell her that you'll be there! You can see she's quite in a worry, and what difference does it make if we go to Fontley a few days earlier than we intended?'

'As long as you don't dislike it – ?'

She replied, with the commonsense which made her at once an easy and an unexciting companion: 'What are a few days more or less to us? To be sure, I like it here, but now I know that Lady Nassington means to present me at the May Drawing-room we must have gone back to town at the end of a fortnight, because of my Court dress. I ordered one to be made for me, and chose the materials for it, but I must try it on, you know.' Her eyes narrowed to slits as a rueful chuckle overcame her. 'I shall look *dreadfully* in it!' she disclosed. 'Me, in hooped petticoats!

Why, I'll be as broad as I'm high! Let alone not knowing how to manage, which Lady Oversley warned me I must practise before appearing in public in it. Well, I only hope I don't disgrace you!'

'You won't do that. Then I am to tell Charlotte she may settle for Monday, 9th May, as she wishes?'

'Yes, pray do so! We may go to Fontley on the Friday before, so, if we leave here on the Tuesday, that will give me two days in Grosven – in London, to have the Court dress fitted on me, and to buy the feathers, and the rest.'

She ended on a note of constraint, but he gave no sign of noticing either this, or the stumble in her speech, saying merely, in a pleasant tone: 'Very well: I'll write to Charlotte.'

The honeymoon had contained awkward moments that were inevitable in the circumstances, but these had been overcome, thanks largely (Adam acknowledged) to the prosaic attitude adopted by his bride. If their union was devoid of romance, less embarrassment attached to it than he had foreseen. Jenny was sometimes shy, but never shrinking. The trend of her mind was practical; she entered into married life in a business-like way; and almost immediately presented the appearance of a wife of several years' standing. She quickly discovered, and never forgot, his particular fads; she neither demanded nor seemed to desire his constant attendance on herself, but sent him forth to fish the trout stream, greeting him on his return with an enquiry after the sport he had enjoyed, and a placid account of her own activities. Since these included, besides practising on the pianoforte and sketching in the park, hemming, with exquisitely small stitches, a set of handkerchiefs for himself, he was uncomfortably remorse-ful, feeling that she must have been driven to such a dull task by boredom. She assured him, however, that she enjoyed what she called white needlework; and she certainly seemed content with the quiet life she was leading. Rushleigh Manor might have afforded two persons lost in love an ideal honeymoon-resort; but there was nothing very much for the Lyntons to do there. Adam fished, rode or drove with Jenny; and, in the evenings, they played chess, Jenny played the pianoforte, or sat stitching while

Adam read aloud to her. He was much inclined to blame himself for having brought her to Rushleigh, when one of the livelier watering-places would probably have been more to her taste; but when he said so she shook her head, in her decided way, and replied that she would not have liked it half as well. 'I know all about watering-places, but I have never before stayed in a country house,' she said. 'It's quite new to me, and very agreeable. I am learning a great deal besides, which makes me particularly glad we came here. I shan't be quite so ignorant when we go to Fontley. I didn't know how different it would all be from a town house.'

'Now you are exposing *my* ignorance! Is it so different?'

'Oh, yes! In London, you know, one buys, but in the country one makes – or things grow, like cabbages and apples and eggs – Now, don't laugh at me! you know very well what I mean! Pigs, too: fancy curing one's own hams! You'd hardly credit it, but until I came here I had never seen cows milked, or had the least notion how butter was made. I like watching what they do on the farm as well as anything. Have you a farm at Fontley?'

'A home farm? Yes – though not, I'm ashamed to say, such a neat one as this!'

She accepted this without comment, but asked, after a moment, if Fontley were as large as Rushleigh Manor.

Rushleigh was not Lord Nassington's principal seat; and if Adam had been asked to describe it he would have called it a pretty little place in Hampshire. In fact, it was a charming Queen Anne house of mellow red brick, set in a small park; but it bore so little resemblance to Fontley that he was startled into exclaiming: '*Fontley?* But, my dear Jenny – ! There can be no comparison!'

'Do you mean that Fontley is larger?' she said, not, perhaps, dismayed, but certainly awed.

'Yes, of course it is!' He checked himself, and added, with a laugh and a faint flush: 'I can never think any house superior to Fontley, you know. Now you will be expecting a Chatsworth, or a Holkham!'

'No, I shan't. I've never seen either, so how could I? I collect that Fontley is very big?'

'It is bigger than this house, of course, but – well, it is so different! None of the rooms in it is precisely *handsome*, except for the Great Hall, but there are many more of them than there are here. Perhaps you will be disappointed, or say, as my mother does, that it is shockingly inconvenient, with far too many passages, and staircases, and rooms leading one out of the other. You see, it wasn't built to a plan, as this one was. A part of it – all that remains of the original Priory – is very old indeed, but my predecessors added to it, and altered it, each according to his fancy, until it grew to be – I suppose one might say a perfect hotch-potch! Most of it is Elizabethan – but don't be afraid that you'll find yourself in a bedroom with an uneven floor and a ceiling so low that you can touch it! The principal bedrooms are in the wing my grandfather built. I hope you'll like it – and can set your mind at rest on one point at least! – We have no ghost to trouble you, though we *have* got a ruined chapel!'

'I don't believe in ghosts. Is it a real ruin?'

'Very completely. Indeed, hardly anything of it remains standing.'

'I mean, you didn't make it?'

'Make it?' he repeated.

'Build it? One of Papa's acquaintances did that, when everything Gothic was fashionable, and I believe it was much admired.'

'Oh!' he said, rather blankly. 'No, we didn't make ours: that was done for us, by zealots, during the Civil War.'

'Yes, of course: I should have known that was how it must have been,' she said apologetically. 'You wouldn't have any need to build a ruin.'

Such interchanges as this might disconcert him, but they amused him as well. It was not until she broke the news to him that it was her father who had bought the house in Grosvenor Street that any serious rift occurred between them.

He was reading a letter from Wimmering when she came into

the room, holding in her hand a single sheet covered over with Mr Chawleigh's undistinguished scrawl, and exclaiming: 'Oh, Adam, the post brought me a letter from Papa!'

He looked up. 'Did it? I hope he is well?'

'Oh, yes! That is, he doesn't say, but he never ails! The thing is that he has contrived to do what even I thought was impossible, in such a short space of time. I should have known him better! Particularly when he promised me he would, if he had to hire a whole army of workmen, which I should think he must have done. Papa never promises what he can't perform!'

'No, I'm sure he doesn't. What is it that he has done? Something that pleases you very much, I collect!'

'Yes – if *you* are pleased. Your house, Adam! You thought you had sold it to Mr Stickney, but he was only acting for Papa!'

He stared at her. '*Your* father bought *my* house?' he said.

'Yes, and he would have liked to have given you the title-deeds on our wedding-day, only they were not quite prepared, so then he thought he wouldn't tell you till all the painting and papering was done, and the house ready for us to step into. I never thought it would be in so short a time, but he writes to me that –'

'Was this your notion?' he interrupted.

'No, I'm afraid I didn't think of it,' she replied. 'Though it was through my telling Papa that you meant to sell the house that it came about. He said immediately that he would buy it, and give it back to you, if I thought you would like it, so –'

'And you did think so?'

She perceived suddenly that he was very white. Her own colour receded; she faltered: 'Why, yes! I thought –'

'I put the house up for sale as a means of providing for my sisters!'

'Yes, yes, I know! You told me!'

'And you thought I should *like* him to buy it? At a price I always considered to be extortionate, too!'

Her brow cleared; she said, smiling: 'Oh, but you need not think of that! It was nothing to Papa: I promise you he didn't grudge it! Indeed, he laughed about it, and said that you had a

sure card in Wimmering! Papa never dislikes a man for being
what he calls a *deep old file*! And in this case I believe that he didn't
wish to haggle – oh, I *know* he did not!' She hesitated, and then
said: 'You see, when he asked me why you meant to sell the town
house, and I told him, he – he was very much struck. He said that
he honoured you for it, though it was – he thought – nonsensical.
He is very shrewd, you know: he understood immediately that it
would not do for him to tell you – offer to –' Her voice failed; she
lifted a hand to her burning cheek. 'Oh, was I wrong to permit
it? Papa was so pleased to think he might furnish you with – with
what you needed, without hurting your pride –'

'Without – Oh, my God!' he ejaculated. 'So this was to be an
agreeable surprise, was it? You must excuse me: it is intolerable
to me! Don't you understand – No: you don't, and I can't explain
it to you. I can only trust that your father won't suffer too great
a loss over it. I daresay he won't, if he has furbished the house up
smartly. Recommend him to place it on the market again at
once! I shall be happy to learn that he has disposed of it at a
profit!'

He went out of the room as he spoke, with a hasty, limping
step. Her hand flew out involuntarily, but he was not looking at
her. Her hand dropped; she did not speak; and the next instant
the door had shut with a snap behind him.

She did not see him again for several hours. He had a horse
saddled, and rode for miles, at first a prey to fury, but presently,
as rage abated, falling into a despairing mood. He had been
made to feel his golden shackles; he looked into the future, seeing
himself the slave of Mr Chawleigh's benevolence, and wished,
for a dreadful few minutes, that the shot that had lamed him had
found a more vital target.

When he returned to Rushleigh Manor it was already past the
dinner-hour, but the butler told him that my lady had not yet
come downstairs. He found her at her dressing-table, with her
maid clasping her pearls round her neck. Her eyes turned
quickly towards the door. He saw how anxiously she looked at
him; and he smiled at her, saying: 'I'm afraid I'm late! Don't

scold me! I went farther than I knew, but I shan't keep you waiting above a few minutes.'

'Well, as though it mattered a straw!' she replied. 'I thought very likely you might be late, and told them to keep dinner back. Did you have an agreeable ride?'

He waited until Martha had left the room, and said, as the door was closed: 'Not very. I beg your pardon, Jenny! I was uncivil to you, and unkind: forgive me!'

'There's no need for you to beg my pardon,' she replied. 'It was my fault. I should have asked you – not have allowed Papa to buy the house without telling you.'

A gulf yawned between them; as though she saw it, she said, before he could answer her: 'You'll be thinking I ought to have known better without your telling me. Well, I didn't: no use pretending I did! I see now, though not quite the way you do, I daresay. That's because Papa has always been so rich that I don't regard money much – don't think it signifies, in the way you do.'

'You might well wonder why, having accepted so much from your father, I should ride rusty over this. I can't tell you. Don't let us talk about it any more!' He bent over her, and kissed her cheek. 'You are much kinder to me than I deserve,' he told her. 'I must go and change my rig before our dinner is quite spoilt.'

'Never mind that!' she said. 'Tell me what you wish me to do! You said, recommend Papa to put the house up for sale again: if you meant it, I'll try to make him understand, but I shan't be able – I know I shan't!'

'There seems to be no end to my incivilities,' he said ruefully. 'I wish he hadn't done it, but since he has I can't mend it.'

'I need not tell him? Thank you! – he would be so disappointed! He has taken such pains over it! You see, there's nothing he enjoys more than planning delightful surprises, or giving one costly presents, and – and if one doesn't like them – well, he pretends not to care, but one can't but see how cast-down he is! Which is why –'

'My dear, indeed you need say no more! We won't disappoint him.'

He gave her shoulder a pat, and turned away. As he reached the door, she blurted out: 'You won't like it – and I never knew that he meant to – Adam, he writes to me that he has furnished it for us!'

He paused, his hand on the door-knob. 'Has he? Generous of him! I am much obliged to him! I am sure it was all sadly shabby. And my mother took so much from it, didn't she? I expect I shall hardly recognize the house when I see it again.'

He went out of the room as he spoke; and when they met, a little later, he made no reference to the subject, and nor did she. It was never mentioned again until the arrival of Charlotte's letter, when Jenny's tongue tripped over the words *Grosvenor Street*, and she changed them quickly to *London*.

She would have liked to have been able to talk naturally about the house, but dared not. She had discovered that when Adam was angry he retired behind a barrier which was as impenetrable as it was intangible. Accustomed as she was to her father's unrestrained manifestations of wrath, it had surprised her that Adam should have felt that his own mild outburst called for apology. Had he ripped up at her she would have been sorry, but not alarmed; his forbearance set her at a distance, and his unfailing courtesy made her more frightened of offending than a fit of the sullens would have done.

In the end it was he who broached the dangerous topic, asking her if servants had been engaged. She replied nervously: 'Yes – that is, Papa said he would leave it to Mr Wimmering to hire servants, thinking that he would know best – and, of course, only as a temporary thing, so that if you don't like any of them, or –'

'My dear Jenny, no one knows less than I do about such matters! I'm much obliged to your father. The horrifying thought occurred to me that we might return to town to find ourselves stranded, with no one to cook the meals and sweep the rooms but your Martha, and my Kinver – both of whom, I am persuaded, would have taken instant offence, and deserted us.'

'Papa felt that you would not want to be troubled with such matters, when you had so much else to do – besides wishing it to be a surprise.' She recollected that this rider was far from being felicitous, and hurried on: 'The arrangement is a makeshift one, of course: if you consider too few servants have been hired – or too many –'

'Well, that will be for you to decide,' he interposed. 'The house is yours, and I hope you will manage it exactly as seems best to you.'

Her heart sank; she said: 'No – pray don't say that! Papa gives it to you, not to me!'

'Ah, but you are forgetting that I endowed you with all my worldly goods!' he said lightly.

It flashed across her mind that he had not called Fontley hers. Then her thoughts were diverted by his saying: 'Don't forget to ask me for a frank when you write to tell your father that we shall be in town on Tuesday!'

She laughed at that, and protested: 'Now, you know it was only once that I forgot you could give me one! I think I should write to him directly. He will want to see me, you know.'

'You will ask him to dine, of course.'

Her face lit up; she said eagerly: 'May I do so?'

'But, Jenny – !'

'He told me I must not,' she disclosed. 'He said he would visit me now and then, but privately.'

'Well, it would be quite improper in you to beg him not to talk nonsense, so just tell him that we both look forward to seeing him in Grosvenor Street at seven o'clock on – shall we say Wednesday?'

'Thank you! It will please him very much. I'll write to him immediately!'

She hurried away, so that he was not obliged to answer her, which he hardly knew how to do, since they were not upon such terms of intimacy as would have made it possible for him to speak at all frankly.

They reached Grosvenor Street a little before dusk on the 3rd May. Adam was relieved to see only two footmen reinforcing the middle-aged butler; but this alleviation of his worst fears was not of long duration: by the time he had reached the drawing-room on the first floor he would scarcely have noticed it had there been a dozen stalwart lackeys, all arrayed in dazzling livery, in attendance upon him.

He had said that he would not recognize the house, and he now discovered how true was this prophecy. Mr Chawleigh's taste for opulence had been given full rein. Even the dining room had not escaped his transforming hand, for although Lady Lynton had removed none of its furniture, he had given it a new carpet of Turkish origin, and new curtains of a rich red brocade, draped, and looped, and embellished with bright gold cords and tassels. He had also supplemented the illumination cast by four massive candelabra by several girandoles. In the hall, and on the half-landing, his passion for lights had expressed itself in a succession of oil-lamps, concealed in alabaster bowls, and mounted on tall pedestals. At the foot of the staircase, another of these lamps, on a shaft in the form of a triform Egyptian figure supported by sphinxes, was set on the lowest baluster, and afforded the first sign of what was to be abundantly proved when the first pair of stairs had been ascended: Mr Chawleigh had fallen a victim to the fashionable rage for the Egyptian and the classical styles. The Dowager had stripped the drawing-room of almost everything but the large Aubusson carpet, and on its delicately hued pattern were placed couches with crocodile-legs, occasional tables inlaid with marble and wreathed with foliated scrolls, lyre-backed chairs, footstools on lion-legs, and several candelabra on pedestals entwined with lotos and anthemion garlands.

Jenny had never seen the house before, and, treading silently beside Adam, looked about her in doubt, not knowing where the Deveril influence ended and the Chawleigh began. Certain of her doubts were resolved on entering the drawing-room, where the glossy green and gold stripes of the upholstery caused her to say apologetically: 'Papa has always been very partial to green.' A glance at Adam's countenance informed her that he did not share this partiality, and she added cheerfully: 'Well, those stripes won't do in this room, but I'll soon attend to that. I'll start at once to work a set of chair covers, and Papa will see in a flash that the rest must be altered to suit them.'

'But not at his expense, if you please, Jenny.'

'Oh, no! That is –'

'I should have said, at his added expense. He has made a very handsome settlement, you know, besides all else, and I had rather by far endure these stripes than that you should ask him to change them.'

'I won't,' she promised. 'I only meant that he won't wonder at my covering the chairs again when he sees the ones I shall embroider. Pray tell me what you wish, Adam! Must I not accept gifts from Papa?'

'What he chooses to give you for yourself is no concern of mine. But we'll settle our household accounts ourselves.'

'Yes, Adam.' She added, after a thoughtful moment: 'Though it may be a little difficult now and then. You see, whenever he sees some new thing which takes his fancy, like a Patent Lamp, or a washing-machine, I am afraid he will buy it for us, because that's his way. Particularly anything which he thinks ingenious, like the Rumford Roaster, which *would* have for our kitchen in Russell Square. I didn't have to ask you if it was he who set up all those lamps: I knew it was, the instant I clapped eyes on them: lighting is one of the things he is particularly interested in. He was one of the biggest subscribers to Mr Winsor's Light and Heat Company, and now, of course, he has a finger in the Gas Light and Coke Company.'

'Good God, will he try to bring gas-lamps into the house?'

She laughed. 'No, no, he hasn't run as mad as that! Though I've heard him say that the day will come when we *shall* have gas in houses!'

'Not in my house!' said Adam firmly.

'No, indeed!' she agreed.

She scanned the room again, but beyond remarking that it was a droll notion to set sofas on crocodile-legs made no further criticisms. However, when she reached her bedchamber she gave a gasp, and exclaimed: 'Good gracious, does Papa think I'm Cleopatra? Oh, I never saw such a bed in my life! Whatever does he suppose I shall look like in it?'

It was certainly a startling piece of furniture, of mahogany inlaid with silver, the head decorated with carved Isis. Adam was amused; but Martha Pinhoe was unequivocally disapproving. 'Well may you ask, Miss Jenny – my lady, I *should* say! Heathenish, that's what I call it, and I'm sure I don't know what's come over the Master! For there's worse to come!'

'Good God, what?' demanded Jenny.

'You'll see, my lady!' said Miss Pinhoe darkly. 'But *not* before his lordship! Indecent, that's what it is! You wait, that's all!'

'If it's indecent I think I ought to see it, not her ladyship!' interposed Adam. 'Go away, Jenny! Martha is going to disclose the horrid secret to me, so that I may decide whether it's fit for you to see.'

'For shame, my lord!' said Miss Pinhoe, whose first deferential manner towards him had lasted for rather less than a week. Her defences breached by the smile which had won for him so many well-wishers, it had not been many days before she was treating him as though he as well as Jenny had been her nurseling. She now told him, with a severity which only the initiated would have recognized as a sign of doting fondness, that it was no laughing matter. He cocked a quizzical eyebrow at her, but she was adamant, so he went away, to discover what fell changes the hand of Mr Chawleigh had wrought in the bedchamber which had been his father's. He was relieved to find that the only innovation was a shaving-stand of really excellent design. He was exchanging a few words with his valet when the most spontaneous peal of laughter he had yet heard from Jenny gave the lie to Miss Pinhoe's words, and drew him back to his bride's room.

'Oh, my lord, only look!' Jenny besought him, mopping her eyes with one hand, and indicating with the other the door leading into the dressing-room. 'Oh, I shall die! Where *did* Papa come by such a notion?'

Mr Chawleigh, transforming the dressing-room into a bath-room, lined with mirrors and draped with silk curtains, had provided his daughter with a bath in the shape of a shell: a circumstance which prompted Adam to say, after a stunned moment: 'Clearly, from Botticelli – the Birth of Venus!'

'*Oh!*' wailed Jenny, cast into fresh agonies. 'And I'm not even *pretty*!'

'No, and nor you're not an abandoned hussy neither, my lady!' interpolated her outraged handmaiden. 'Now, give over this instant! I'm sure I don't know what his lordship must be thinking of you, laughing yourself into stitches over what a modest young lady would blush to mention!'

'Yes, but it's a most ingenious affair, you know!' said Adam, who was inspecting it in mingled interest and amusement. 'Look, Jenny! The water comes into it through this pipe, from that cylinder – I wonder what fuel is used for heating it?'

'It's no matter what's used, my lord!' said Miss Pinhoe, her eyes snapping. 'While I have charge of her ladyship, she'll have hot water brought up to her bedroom, and take her bath before the fire, like a Christian! As for kindling a fire under that nasty contraption, why, I'd be afraid for my life! The next thing we'd know would be that it had exploded, like the new boiler, which was another of the Master's clever notions, and if you don't remember what a mess that made of everything, Miss Jenny, I do!'

Jenny's bathroom was not Mr Chawleigh's only clever notion. Having cast a critical eye over the sanitary arrangements in Grosvenor Street, he drove his army of plumbers to create, out of the antiquated apartment discreetly tucked under the stair-case, a water-closet which, in his own phrase, was Something Like. When he dined with the young couple on the following evening, he insisted on demonstrating and explaining to Adam the several features which made the new Bramah model superior to the old; and discoursed with so much assurance on valves, sliders, overhead cisterns, and stink-traps that Adam presently said curiously: 'You know a great deal about these things, sir!'

'Ay, you may lay your life I do. You won't find Jonathan Chawleigh investing his blunt in something he don't understand, my lord!' replied Mr Chawleigh.

He enjoyed himself very much that evening, but he warned his daughter not to make a habit of inviting him to her house. 'For I don't expect it, and, what's more, I told his lordship at the outset that there'd be no need for him to fear he'd have me hanging on him like a barnacle. Now, don't look glum, love! I'll visit you now and now, when you're not expecting company, but don't you dish me up to your grand friends, because it wouldn't do – not if you're to cut a figure in society, which I've set my heart on.'

'I know you have, Papa, but if you're thinking I coaxed Adam into letting me invite you tonight you're out! He said I was to do so, and that's how it will always be, I think, because he is – he is most *truly* the gentleman!'

'Ay, so he is,' agreed Mr Chawleigh. 'Well, I'll have to tell him to his head I don't look to be invited to your parties, and that's all there is to it!'

He did this, adding that Adam must dissuade Jenny from visiting Russell Square too frequently. 'I've told her there's no call for her to do so, my lord, but it'll be just as well if you add your word to mine. Coming to see that Mrs Finchley is doing what she ought! Yes, it's likely she wouldn't be, after being my housekeeper these fifteen years! So you tell Jenny to leave me be, and not think I'll be offended, because I won't. She'll heed what *you* say.'

'I hope she would tell me to go to the devil,' answered Adam. He saw that Mr Chawleigh was looking, for once in his life, confounded, and laughed. 'What a very odd notion you have of me, sir!'

'The notion I have, my lord, is that you're a gentleman, and I'm a Cit, and no getting away from it! What's more, I mean my Jenny to be a lady!'

'Then I wonder you should make it hard for her to support that character!' Adam retorted.

'Damme if I know what you mean by that!' confessed Mr Chawleigh, rubbing his nose.

'Women of consideration don't despise their parents, sir.'

'No, but they don't have to fob 'em off on the ton!' said Mr Chawleigh, making a swift recover. 'I take it very kind of you, my lord, but to my way of thinking mushrooms like me aping the Quality don't take: I'd as lief be a Cit as a counter-coxcomb! So don't you go inviting me to your parties, because I won't come!'

Nor would he allow Adam to thank him for having bought his town house. 'Don't give it a thought!' he begged. 'I was glad to do it, for you've behaved mighty handsomely to me, my lord, and that was something I could do for you, over and above what was agreed on. And if there's anything you don't like, you throw it away, and buy what you *do* fancy to take its place, and chalk it up to me! Though I must say,' he added, looking complacently about him, 'that Campbell has made it look slap up to the mark! I chose him because he makes furniture for the Prince Regent, and the Duke of York, so it stands to reason he must know what's up to the knocker. No expense to be spared, I told him, but no trumpery! It's pitch and pay with me, I said, but don't you run off with the notion that I'm easily bobbed, for you'll catch cold at that, and so I warn you! Well, I don't say he didn't try for a touch at me over that set of chairs in your boudoir, Jenny-love – nothing but bamboo they are, japanned! – but he took his oath they were all the kick, so I had 'em – after he'd knocked a bit off the price.' He beamed benevolently upon his hosts. 'You wouldn't credit what it cost, first and last!' he said simply. 'But I don't grudge a penny of it, as long as you're satisfied!'

Nine

*T*ravelling in a light chaise, behind four horses, the Lyntons reached Fontley just before six o'clock. The Priory was screened from the road by the trees in its park, but there was one place from which a long view of the house could be obtained. Adam directed the postilions to pull up there. He said: 'There it is, Jenny!'

She could tell from his voice how much he loved it, and she wanted to say something that would please him. Leaning forward, she was disappointed to find that it lay at too great a distance from the road for her to be able to distinguish any particular features. She could see only an irregular mass of buildings, not lofty, but covering a large expanse of ground; and the only thing that occurred to her to say was: 'It is quite different from Rushleigh! – just as you told me.'

He signed to the postilions to go on. 'Yes, quite different. How does this country strike you?'

She had been thinking how inferior it was to the undulating Hampshire scene; she answered haltingly: 'Well, it is new to me, and not just what I expected, but I am sure I shall grow to like it.'

'I hope you may, but I suspect one has to be born in the fens to love them. We are crossing Deeping Fen now.' He added, as the chaise bumped and lurched: 'I'm sorry: the surface is shocking, isn't it? We call these roads driftways. That was a grip we passed over – a trench cut crossways for drainage.'

It sounded rather primitive. She scanned the expanse of level

116

fields on either side of the unguarded road, and asked with some misgiving if they were often flooded.

'In winter, yes,' he acknowledged. 'Drainage is our chief problem, and the most costly, alas! We get soak, too: that's sea-water coming up through the silt when the drains are full.'

'I thought it must be pretty damp as soon as I saw those great ditches.'

'Droves. Are you afraid of being flooded out at Fontley? You need not be! I hope to be able to improve matters elsewhere too: I think we must be fifty years behind the times here.'

'I don't know anything about country things: I must learn them.'

'I'm ashamed to say that I know very little myself – only what any boy reared on an agricultural estate would be bound to pick up. Here we are: this is the gatehouse – part of the old Priory – and here's Mrs Ridgehill coming out to give you your first welcome! Say something kind to her: she is one of my oldest friends!'

He had noticed at Rushleigh that she was shy of the servants, and too much inclined to hide this under a brusque manner, but she acquitted herself quite creditably on this occasion, respond-ing to the lodgekeeper's salutations and compliments with no more awkwardness than Mrs Ridgehill thought proper in a bride. The chaise moved forward again; and presently, round a bend in the avenue, the one remaining arch and the several crumbling walls and pillars of the ruined chapel came into view; and, beyond, the heterogeneous mass of the Priory itself. Staring at the long, broken frontage of mingled stone and brick Jenny gave utterance to the first thought that came into her head: 'Good gracious! However many servants do you employ to keep it in order?'

He was not obliged to reply to this, for at that moment he caught sight of Charlotte, hurrying across the lawn with an armful of flowers. He directed Jenny's attention to her; and at once she was assailed by a horrid doubt. She exclaimed, her eyes on Charlotte's plain round dress of white cambric: 'Oh, I am

117

dressed too fine! I didn't know – and there was no one to tell me!'

'Nonsense! you look very becoming!' he replied, jumping down from the chaise as his sister came running across the drive. '*Proserpin gathering flowers!* But I trust *gloomy Dis* won't forestall Lambert, Charlotte!'

Charlotte, who was not bookish, paid no heed to this, but exclaimed breathlessly: 'Oh, my dear Adam, we thought you could not be here for another hour, and had put dinner back accordingly! And here I am, only this instant finished cutting a few flowers for Jenny's room, and in this old gown too! You must excuse me, Jenny!'

This speech might have been designed to put Jenny at her ease, but she still felt, as she descended from the chaise, that perhaps a puce silk dress, a velvet pelisse, and a feathered bonnet were a little out of place at Fontley. Charlotte, however, seemed to see nothing amiss, but kissed her, and led her into the house.

Jenny was relieved, and a good deal surprised, to find that there was far less ceremony attached to this homecoming than would have attended their arrival in Russell Square. The only footmen she saw were two young men, who wore dark livery and their own unpowdered hair; and the butler, who was elderly, and a little bent, would have looked insignificant beside Mr Chawleigh's majestic Butterbank.

'I must take you to Mama directly,' Charlotte said. 'She was sitting with my aunt in the Little Drawing-room – oh, Adam, I should have written to warn you that my Aunt Nassington is here, with my uncle, and Osbert too, but there was no time, for they took us quite by surprise! Not that I mean – that is to say, I am very much obliged to her for coming on this occasion, only we never supposed that she would, though Mama invited her, of course.'

'Oh, lord!' said Adam, pulling a grimace. 'Don't let her bully you, Jenny – or look to me for protection! She frightens me to death!'

'For shame, Adam!' Charlotte reproved him, leading Jenny towards the broad oaken stairway. 'You mustn't heed him,

Jenny! My aunt is very outspoken, but she is perfectly good-natured, I promise you!'

Following his wife and sister up the stairs, across an ante-room to the Long Drawing-room, and down this to the Little Drawing-room beyond it, Adam wondered how Jenny would support her introduction to Lady Nassington, and hoped that she would not become tongue-tied. He was afraid that her ladyship's overbearing ways and caustic speech would paralyse her, and was consequently as much surprised as relieved to discover that Jenny, rendered monosyllabic by Lady Lynton, responded to Lady Nassington without embarrassment.

Physically her ladyship resembled her brother. She was a large woman, with aquiline features, and a gaze of lofty unconcern. Like his, her voice was loud and authoritative; and to some extent she shared his disregard for convention. There the resemblance ended. Lord Lynton's free and easy ways had sprung from a jovial nature; his sister's had their roots in a sublime conviction of superiority, and were so incalculable as to have earned for her the reputation of being eccentric. She said and did what she chose on every occasion, and granted a like indulgence to those who had been fortunate enough to win her favour; but she had reared her daughters to a rigid pattern, and would condemn any breach of etiquette committed by persons she disliked.

She had brought with her to Fontley, besides her husband, a spare man of few words and a harassed mien, her third son, the robust sportsman whom she had offered to Adam as his best man. 'Quite right not to have had him!' she told Adam. 'He's such a dolt I dare swear he'd have made a mull of it, or gone to Church stinking of the stables.'

Adam wondered what entertainment could be offered to Osbert during a week at Fontley at this season; but Lady Nassington besought him not to trouble himself, since it was impossible to interest Osbert during the dead months.

'But the poor fellow will be bored to tears!' he protested.

'He can as well be bored here as anywhere else,' replied her ladyship. 'Never mind him! I must tell you, Adam, that I am agreeably surprised by this wife of yours. No countenance, of course, and dresses badly, but she seems a sensible girl, and she don't play off any airs of sham gentility. You might have done a great deal worse for yourself. I don't object to presenting her, and you may bring her to my rout-party on the 20th: that should launch her pretty well. It's a pity your mother has chosen to be thrown into gloom, but just what I expected! She don't like Charlotte's match either: not a great one, I grant, but if a girl flouts the chances she's offered she must be content with a respectable marriage in the end. I fancied myself in love with his father once,' she added reminiscently. 'It wouldn't have answered, but what I didn't consider beneath my touch I'm sure your mother need not! But she always was a wet-goose. Upon my word, I wonder that you should have turned out so well – I do indeed, my dear nephew!'

A laugh escaped him, but he shook his head at her. 'You know it's most improper to say such things to me, ma'am!'

'Oh, I say nothing behind Blanche's back I don't say to her head!' she replied.

When Charlotte brought Jenny into the Little Drawing-room, Lady Nassington had scanned her appraisingly, and commanded, as soon as she had greeted the Dowager: 'Come here, child, and let me take a look at you! H'm! Yes, it's a pity you're not taller, but I'm glad to see you hold yourself up. How did you like Rushleigh? I hope my people made you comfortable?'

'Yes, that they did, ma'am. I liked it excessively, and have been wanting to thank you for lending it to us. It was all so beautiful, and interesting! I had never stayed in the country before.'

'Town-bred, are you?'

'Yes, though my mother was a farmer's daughter, and came from Shropshire, ma'am.'

'Good yeoman stock, I daresay: you have the look of it yourself. Take my advice, and study to dress plainly! Frills don't become you. Are those real pearls you have in your ears? Yes, they would be, of course, and a thousand pities your neck's too short for them. Lynton! Buy a neat little pair of ear-rings for your wife! She can't wear these.'

'Well, I know my neck's too short,' said Jenny, 'but I shall wear them, ma'am, because Papa gave them to me, and I won't hurt his feelings, no matter what!'

'Very proper!' approved her ladyship. 'I'll speak to your father myself.'

Lady Lynton here intervened, and bore Jenny off to her bed-chamber, saying as she led the way through a bewildering series of rooms, galleries, and corridors: 'You must excuse my sister-in-law: her blunt manners are beyond the line of being pleasing.'

'Oh, no!' Jenny said. 'I mean, I didn't dislike anything she said, for it was all in kindness, and – and I like blunt people, ma'am!'

'I have often wished that my own sensibility were less acute,' said her ladyship.

Daunted, Jenny relapsed into silence. Passing through a doorway into a broad corridor Lady Lynton informed her that they were now in the modern wing of the Priory.

'It seems to stretch for miles!' said Jenny.

'Yes, it is most inconvenient,' sighed the Dowager. 'No doubt you will make a great many alterations. Adam's room is here, and that door leads into a dressing-room. The next is yours, quite at the end of the passage, which I hope you won't dislike.'

'Oh, no! How should I? Oh – how pretty it is!'

'I am afraid it is sadly shabby. It should have been done-up before your arrival, but, not knowing your tastes, I thought it best to leave it to you to choose what you like.'

'Thank you – but I shan't! I like it as it is. I don't wish to change anything, ma'am!'

'Don't you, my dear? No doubt it is foolish of me, but I cannot help hoping that you may not. It is so full of memories! Alas, so many years since I too entered it as a bride!'

Dismayed, Jenny stammered: 'Is it your room? Oh, I would never – *Pray* let me have some other!'

But the Dowager, smiling at her with gentle resignation, merely completed her discomfiture by saying that this was the room always occupied by the mistress of the house. She said that Jenny must not be in a worry, since she herself cared nothing either for her comfort or her consequence. As she managed to convey the impression that she was now housed in one of the garrets it was not surprising that when Adam presently came into the room he found Jenny looking rather troubled.

She was standing beside a table in one of the windows, dipping her hand into a bowl filled with pot-pourri, and allowing the dried petals to sift through her fingers. She looked up when Adam came in, and smiled, saying: 'I couldn't think what makes the house smell so sweet, but now I see it must be this.'

'Pot-pourri? Yes, my mother makes it. I believe she had the recipe from some Frenchwoman – one of the emigrées. You must ask her for it, if you like it.'

'I wonder if she will tell me? Adam, you shouldn't have permitted her to make her own room ready for me!'

'I didn't know she meant to. I'm glad she did, however: it was very proper in her.'

'Well, it makes me ready to sink!' she said. 'She told me that it had always belonged to the mistress of Fontley, as though she had been deposed, which I hope you know I'd never do!'

'My dear Jenny, if you are going to take all my mother says to heart –! My grandfather built this wing, so you are only the third mistress of Fontley to occupy the room!'

She was obliged to laugh at this, but she said: 'Well, I'm sure it must be disagreeable for her to see me in it, at all events. Thank goodness I told her I didn't wish to alter anything in it! She had been dreading that, you know, which I can well understand.'

He looked a little quizzical, but said nothing. Lydia, coming to pay her respects to Jenny a few minutes later, was much less reticent. 'What a bouncer!' she exclaimed. 'Why, it was only last year that Mama had the curtains made, and she had meant to have had new ones this year, because these faded so badly, as you may see! She only said that to make you feel horrid!'

'Lydia!'

'Well, it's true, Adam. For my part, I think *someone* ought to explain Mama to Jenny! The thing is, you see, that she positively delights in being ill-used, Jenny, and making us all feel guilty for no reason at all. Don't heed her! I *never* do!'

This frank exposition of her mother-in-law's character startled Jenny, but by the time she had spent two days at Fontley she had begun to see that there was a good deal of truth in it, and began to feel much more at ease.

She had looked forward with shrinking to her introduction to Fontley, and had concealed under a wooden front her dread of offending unknown shibboleths. She had listened to stories of the formal pomp that reigned in several great houses, had been too shy to ask Adam for information, and had thus entered the house feeling sick with apprehension. But although she frequently lost her way in it she was almost immediately conscious of its home-quality; and since the Dowager disliked pomp she found no rigid etiquette to make her nervous. Even the ordeal of the first dinner-party was less severe than she had expected, for no ceremonial attached to it, and all the family talked so much and so naturally that she was able to sit listening and watching, which exactly suited her disposition. Lord Nassington was found to be quite unalarming; and his son, although, at first glance, over-poweringly large and bluff, was a simple creature, who laughed a great deal, and bore with unruffled good-humour all the shafts aimed at him. He sat beside Jenny at the table, and told her that he was the bobbing-block of the family. He seemed to take as much pride in this as in his mother's ruthless tongue. 'Wonderful woman, Mama!' he said. 'Abuses us all like pickpockets! Do you hunt?'

'No, I don't, and it wouldn't be any use pretending I know anything about it, because you'd be bound to find out that I don't,' she replied frankly.

'Now, that's what I call being a sensible woman!' he exclaimed, and instantly began to recount to her various note-worthy incidents of the chase, which were largely unintelligible to her, and might have continued throughout dinner had not Lady Nassington loudly commanded Lydia to 'draw off that imbecile before he bores Jenny to death!'

The week-end passed pleasantly and uneventfully in exploring the house and the gardens, making the acquaintance of the housekeeper, helping Charlotte with the last-moment preparations for her wedding, and in general making herself quietly useful.

'Shall we come back soon?' she asked Adam, when they left Fontley two days after the wedding.

'Why, yes, if you would like it – at the end of the season. Unless you would prefer to go to Brighton?'

'No, that I shouldn't. That is – do you wish to go to Brighton?'

'Not in the least. I don't want you to be bored, however.'

'Well, I shan't be. In fact, I wish we might have remained here.'

'That would mean missing the Drawing-room, and all the parties we shall be invited to attend. You wouldn't like that, would you?'

'No, of course not!' she said quickly. 'Except that I'm stupid at parties, and shall very likely say the wrong things, and – and mortify you!'

'No, you won't,' he responded. 'You'll soon grow accustomed to parties, make a great many friends, and become a noted hostess! You'll be a credit to me, not a mortification!'

She said gruffly: 'I'll try to be, at least.'

She thought that perhaps the fashionable life was what he wanted, and ventured to ask if he had been to many parties in the Peninsula.

'No, very few. I shall be making my début as well as you!'

That seemed to settle the matter. She nodded, and said: 'Well, I hope we shall be invited to all the *best* parties. How pleased Papa would be!'

There was no doubt about this at least. Mr Chawleigh's vicarious ambition had led him to prosecute searching enquiries into matters which had not previously interested him; and consequently he was able to furnish his daughter with a list of the ton's most influential hostesses. He was delighted to hear that she had been invited to Lady Nassington's assembly, a knowledgeable informant having assured him that her ladyship was the pink of gentility; and strongly adjured her to make herself agreeable to all the fine folk she would meet at this function. 'For his lordship's doing his part like a regular Trojan, and it's only right you should do yours, my girl, and not sit mumping in a corner, as if you'd never been in company before!'

He came to see her dressed for the Drawing-room, and was probably the only person to think she was looking her best. Even Martha Pinhoe could not feel that violet satin over a wide hoop and a crape petticoat sewn all over with amethyst beads became her nurseling; but Mr Chawleigh, surveying this splendour with simple pride, said that Jenny looked prime. A closer scrutiny revealed certain deficiencies, however. He had an exact memory for the jewels he had bestowed upon her, and he wanted to know why she was not wearing the rivière of diamonds and rubies, which had been one of his wedding-presents. 'I'm not saying those pearls didn't cost me a fortune, but who's to know they're the real thing, and not mere trumpery, made out of glass and fish-scales? There's no counterfeiting the fire of a diamond or a ruby. You bring me out her ladyship's jewel-box, Martha!'

'I must say, I like a bit of sparkle myself,' admitted Miss Pinhoe, opening a large casket for his inspection.

'I do, too,' said Jenny, looking rather wistfully at the casket. 'And it does seem a pity, on such an occasion – But Lady Nassington told me not to dress too fine, Papa.'

'Oh, she did, did she? Well, if you was to ask me, love, she was jealous, and afraid your jewels would shine hers down! Not that I've the pleasure of her ladyship's acquaintance, but that's the way it looks to me.'

He was to be granted this pleasure five minutes later, when one startled glance at the famous Nassington emeralds was enough to inform him that the formidable lady who sailed into the room had no reason to be envious of Jenny's jewels.

Her entry took everyone by surprise, including the footman, who had attempted to usher her into the drawing-room while he went to inform his mistress of her arrival. It had been arranged that the Lyntons were to have driven to Nassington House, in Berkeley Square, and to have proceeded thence to St James's; and for a moment of almost equal relief and disappointment Jenny thought that some accident must have occurred, and that there was to be no Drawing-room after all. But her ladyship's first words, as much as her attire, dispelled this notion. 'I thought as much!' she said. 'Good God, girl, do you imagine I am going to take you to Court decked out like a jeweller's window?' Her high-nosed stare encountered Mr Chawleigh, and she demanded: 'Who is this?'

'It's my father, ma'am. Papa – this is Lady Nassington!' responded Jenny, inwardly quaking at what she feared might prove to be a battle of Titans.

'Oh! How-de-do?' said her ladyship. 'Those pearls you gave Jenny are too big. She's got too short a neck for them.'

'That's as may be, my lady,' replied Mr Chawleigh, bristling.

'No may be about it. Take off that necklace, Jenny! You can't wear rubies with that dress, child! And those ear-rings! Let me see what you have in this monstrous great box: good God! Enough to furnish a king's ransom!'

'Ay, that's about the worth of them,' said Mr Chawleigh, glowering at her. 'Not that I know anything about kings' ransoms, but I know what I paid for my girl's trinkets, and a pretty penny it was!'

'More money than sense!' observed her ladyship. 'Ah! Here's something much more the thing!'

'*That?*' demanded Mr Chawleigh, looking with disgust at the delicate diamond necklace dangling from Lady Nassington's fingers. 'Why, that's a bit of trumpery I gave Mrs Chawleigh when I was no more than a chicken-nabob!'

'You had better taste then than you have now. Very pretty: exactly what she should wear!'

'Well, she ain't going to wear it!' declared Mr Chawleigh, his choler mounting. 'She'll go to Court slap up to the echo, or I'll know the reason why!'

'Papa!' uttered Jenny imploringly.

'She'll go in a proper mode, or not at all. Lord, man, have you *no* sense? She had as well shout aloud that she's an heiress as go to Court hung all over with jewels! Puffing off her wealth: that's what everyone would say. Is that what you want?'

'No, indeed it isn't!' said Jenny, as her parent, a trifle nonplussed, turned this over in his mind. 'Now, that's enough, Papa! Her ladyship knows better than you or me what's the first style of elegance.'

'Well, there's no need that I know of for you to be ashamed of my fortune!' said Mr Chawleigh, covering his retreat with some sharp fire. 'Going about the town in a paltry necklace that looks as if I couldn't afford to buy the best for you!'

'If that's all that's putting you into the hips, you may be easy!' said Lady Nassington. 'All the ton knows my nephew's married a great heiress, and you may believe that she'll take better if she don't make a parade of her riches. Tell me this! Would you thank me for meddling in your business, whatever it is?'

'Meddling in my business?' repeated Mr Chawleigh, stupefied. 'No, I would not, my lady!'

'Just so! Don't meddle in mine!'

Fortunately, since Mr Chawleigh's complexion was rapidly acquiring a rich purple hue, Adam walked in at that moment, drawn by the fine, penetrating voices of the contestants. He had been engaged in the intricate task of arranging his neckcloth, and so made his appearance in his shirt-sleeves: a circumstance to which his aunt took instant exception. She told him to go away at once, and to take Mr Chawleigh with him, adding a recommendation to him to put on a fresh neckcloth, since the style he was affecting made him look like a demi-beau.

Mr Chawleigh allowed himself to be drawn out of the room. He was a little mollified by the discovery that her nobly-born nephew was not exempt from Lady Nassington's punitive tongue, but he said, as he followed Adam into his dressing-room:

'Well, if she wasn't your lordship's aunt I know what *I'd* say she was!'

'Was she rude to you?' asked Adam. 'You should hear the things she says to my uncle!'

'I'm bound to say she properly set my back up. And she a Countess! There's a leveller for you! Are you going to change that neckcloth?'

'No. What's she doing here? I thought we were to have gone to her.'

'I'll tell you what she's doing,' offered Mr Chawleigh rancorously. 'Stripping the jewels off my Jenny, that's what she's doing, without so much as a by your leave! Came on purpose to do it, what's more!'

He sat brooding over this until Adam, receiving his cloak and his *chapeau bras* from Kinver, announced that he was now ready. 'So let us go downstairs before my aunt sends to discover what the devil I mean by keeping her waiting, sir!'

'I don't know but what I won't shab off home,' said Mr Chawleigh gloomily. 'I wouldn't have come if I'd known her la'ship would be here, and that's a fàct!'

He allowed himself to be persuaded, however, and accompanied Adam to the drawing-room, where they were presently joined by the ladies.

Lady Nassington had been unable to suppress the crimp in Jenny's hair, but she had reduced the number of ostrich feathers she wore to five, exchanged her over-large ear-rings for a pair of diamond drops, and stripped from her arms all but two bracelets. She had not been able to transform Jenny into a beauty, but she had succeeded (as she informed Mr Chawleigh) in turning her out like a woman of quality. 'She'll do!' she said briskly. 'A nice gal: I like her, and I'll do what I can to bring her into fashion.'

Mr Chawleigh was flattered to know that his daughter was liked by a Countess, but he still regretted the rubies, and would have said so had not Lady Nassington brought his audience to an end by suddenly calling across the room to her nephew: 'Lynton!

Did your father ever take you to Court, or is this your first appearance?'

He was talking to Jenny, but he turned his head, saying: 'No, ma'am: my father presented me at a lêvée when I was eighteen.'

'Papa! Lady Nassington!' Jenny blurted out. 'See what Adam has given me!'

Pink with pleasure, she displayed a fan of painted chicken-skin, mounted on carved mother-of-pearl sticks. It was an elegant trifle, but hardly deserving the delight she evidently felt. An unwelcome suspicion flickered in Adam's brain, as he watched her. She met his eyes, and her pink turned to crimson. She looked quickly away, saying hurriedly: 'It is so exactly what I needed – precisely the right colours!'

'Very pretty,' said Lady Nassington, after a cursory glance.

'Ay, it's well enough,' agreed Mr Chawleigh, subjecting it to a longer scrutiny, 'but what have you done with the ivory one I gave you, painted Vernis Martin? I should have thought it would have been just the thing for that dress of yours.'

Her colour still much heightened, she murmured some disjointed excuse. Lady Nassington brought any further discussion to an end by announcing that it was time they were setting forward. Mr Chawleigh accompanied the party downstairs, and was considerably surprised to be given two of Lady Nassington's fingers to shake before she mounted into her stately town chariot. To this piece of condescension, she added a gracious, if vicarious, invitation to him to visit Grosvenor Street on the following day, to learn from Jenny how her presentation had gone off.

It went off very well. The Queen had spoken most kindly to Jenny – 'Only fancy, Papa! after all these years she speaks with the strongest accent!' – and two of the Princesses had stood talking to her in the most amiable way imaginable, so that she had not felt in the least awkward or tongue-tied. Her only disappointment had been that the Princess Charlotte of Wales had not been present: an extraordinary circumstance, people had seemed to think, for she had been betrothed to the Prince of

Orange since December, so surely she must be out? The Prince had not been present either, although he was certainly in London: that had been a pity, for Jenny had hoped to have seen him. Adam, of course, had seen him frequently, because he had been lately a member of Lord – no, the *Duke* of Wellington's staff! One would suppose that a Prince chosen to wed the Heiress of England must be a Nonpareil, but when Jenny had said this to Adam he had burst out laughing, exclaiming: 'Slender Billy? Good God, no!' She was sorry therefore not to have been able to judge for herself of the Prince's quality.

But this was a small matter. What did Papa think of her having been presented to the Prince Regent, at his particular request? Someone must have pointed Adam out to him, for – would Papa believe it? – he had come up to them, and had shaken hands with Adam, saying how happy he was to welcome him to Court, and how deeply he regretted his old friend's death. Then he had expressed his wish to meet Adam's bride, and Adam had immediately drawn her forward, and Papa could have no idea how charmingly the Regent had spoken to her. His manners were beyond anything perfect! He had stayed for several minutes, chatting to Adam about the late war, and displaying (Adam said) an exact knowledge of military matters. And just as he was moving away he had said that he hoped to see them both at Carlton House one day!

Deeply gratified, Mr Chawleigh rubbed his hands together, and said that it beat the Dutch, by God it did! His one regret was that Jenny's mother was not alive to rejoice in her triumph. 'Still, there's no saying but what she knows all about it,' he said cheerfully. 'To think I was of two minds whether I'd make do with a Viscount, or stand out for an Earl! Well, my Lord Oversley pledged me his word I wouldn't regret it, and I'm bound to own he was right. Why, a Duke couldn't have done better by you! Tell me again what the Prince Regent said to you!'

Mr Chawleigh's opinion of the Prince Regent had not previously been high. While he was not (as he frequently asserted) one to concern himself with the nobs, the doings of this

Royal Nob could scarcely have escaped the notice of the most disinterested person. Had he been asked, Mr Chawleigh would have said that he didn't hold with such goings-on as marrying two wives, and behaving scaly to the pair of them, let alone mounting more mistresses than a plain man could remember, and wasting the ready till his debts had to be paid for him by the nation. It was an open secret, too, that he was seeking evidence on which to divorce the unfortunate Princess of Wales; and, without wishing to join the mob in hissing him, Mr Chawleigh considered that he had treated the poor lady downright scurvily. But in face of the Regent's kindness to Jenny that was all forgotten.

Nor did Jenny recall that when she first saw him she suffered a considerable disappointment. At the age of two-and-fifty little trace remained of the handsome Prince Florizel over whose beauty elderly ladies still sighed. Jenny beheld a middle-aged gentleman of corpulent habit, on whose florid countenance dissipation was writ large. He was decidedly overdressed; his corsets creaked audibly; he drenched his person with scent; and, when in repose, his face wore a peevish expression. But whatever good fairy had attended his christening had bestowed upon him a gift which neither time nor excesses would ever cause to wither. He was an undutiful son, and a bad husband, an unkind father, an inconstant lover, and an uncertain friend, but he had a charm which won forgiveness from those whom he had injured, and endeared him to such chance-met persons as Jenny, or some young officer brought to him by Lord Bathurst with an important dispatch. He could disgust his intimates, but in his more public life his bearing was always right; he never said the wrong thing; and never permitted a private vexation to impair his affability. Unmistakably a Prince, he used very little ceremony, his manners, when he moved amongst the ton, being distinguished by a well-bred ease which did not wholly desert him even when, as sometimes happened, he arrived at some party in a sadly inebriated condition. His private manners were not so good; but no one who saw him, as Jenny did, at his mother's Drawing-room, could have believed him capable of lying to his greatest supporter, taking a crony to listen to his father's ravings, treating his only child with boorish roughness, or floundering, like a lachrymose porpoise, at the feet of an embarrassed beauty. Jenny certainly would not have believed such stories; and when she met him again, two days later, at Lady Nassington's assembly, and received a bow from him, and a smile of recognition, she was much inclined to think that extenuating circumstances must attach even to his two marriages and his mountainous debts.

Ten

ew invitations conferred so great a distinction on the social aspirant as one to Nassington House. Lady Nassington's parties were extremely exclusive, for she disliked fashionable squeezes, and was contemptuous of hostesses who rated the success of their entertainments by the number of guests they could cram into their saloons. It spoke volumes for her forceful personality that she had long since convinced the ton that a card of invitation to one of her assemblies was an honour no more to be refused than a Royal Command.

Lady Oversley was amongst the fortunate recipients of these missives. She studied hers with mixed feelings, for Lady Nassington had included the Hon. Julia Oversley in her invitation, and Lady Oversley would have given much to know whether Lord and Lady Lynton had also been invited. On the one hand, it seemed unlikely; on the other, Adam was her ladyship's nephew, and she had presented his bride at Court. With anyone else that would have settled the matter, but with Lady Nassington one never knew: having performed what she believed to be her duty she was quite capable of ignoring thereafter young Lady Lynton's claims upon her notice.

Lady Oversley wrote a formal acceptance, reflecting that unless Julia remained permanently in Tunbridge Wells meetings between her and Adam were inevitable. A letter from her mother-in-law encouraged her to hope that Julia was showing signs of recovery, her grandmama having arrested her decline by arranging a succession of pleasure-parties which no damsel in the possession of her senses could have failed to enjoy. Admirers had not been lacking; the Beauties of Tunbridge Wells had been eclipsed; and to complete her triumph she had lately added to her court no less a personage than that noted connoisseur of female charm and elegance the Marquis of Rockhill. In the Dowager's opinion, that conquest was enough to drive thoughts of young Lynton out of any girl's head. She added that while it would be absurd to suppose that Rockhill nourished serious intentions, he was sufficiently captivated to make Julia the object of his gallantry 'for long enough to serve our turn'.

Julia's mama was not so optimistic. She was flattered to think that her daughter had pleased the Marquis's discriminating taste; but she could not feel that a widower, well into his forties, would prove to be a formidable rival to a young and charming man for whom Julia had formed a violent attachment. She was also inclined to look a trifle askance upon the Marquis's gallantry, but in this, her lord informed her, she showed herself to be a great goose. 'Nonsense!' he said. 'Rockhill's a gentleman!'

'Good God, you don't think he wishes to *marry* her?' she gasped.

'No, no, of course I don't!' he replied testily. 'He found himself in Tunbridge Wells for some cause or another, and began a flirtation with the prettiest girl in the place to save himself from being killed with boredom, that's all! I only wish it may last until she's recovered from the other affair, but I don't depend on it.'

The possibility that Julia, recovering from one abortive love-affair, might fall a victim to a second occurred to Lady Oversley, but she thought it wisest not to suggest this to his lordship. When Julia returned to London she showed no sign of succumbing to Rockhill's charms, merely saying that he was very kind and amusing, which, in Lady Oversley's opinion, was what any girl might be expected to say of a man old enough to be her father. She did not speak of Adam at all; she seemed bent on extracting every ounce of enjoyment from this, her second London Season, laughed to scorn the idea that an endless succession of parties would prove too much for her constitution, and made plans to fill every moment of every day. Her father might think this hopeful: Lady Oversley could not like the glitter in the eyes that seemed too big for Julia's face, or feel that her restlessness betokened a mind at peace. She did not know what to do about it, and could only hope that one of Julia's adorers would succeed in capturing her bruised heart.

Julia received the news that she had been honoured with an invitation to Nassington House with apparent pleasure. Lady Oversley had meant to have warned her that she must be prepared to meet the Lyntons there, but somehow she could not find just the right words; and in the end she said nothing, salving her conscience with the reflection that Julia must know that there was a strong likelihood that they would be present.

At first it seemed as though she had been right to keep her tongue between her teeth. She could not discover the Lyntons in any of the saloons; and Julia, ravishing in palest blue gauze over an underdress of white satin, was in a mood to be pleased. There were a number of young persons present, and she was soon the centre of a group, delighted to be with her particular friends again, and rapidly drawing her usual court about her. Lady Oversley was able to relax her vigilance, and to join a group of her own intimates, who were discussing all the latest on-dits, from the sudden death of the Empress Josephine from a putrid sore throat, to the news that the Allied Sovereigns were coming to London to take part in gigantic Peace Celebrations.

The Lyntons arrived half-an-hour later, and presently made their way across the first saloon to a smaller one beyond it.

There were perhaps twenty people in the room, but Adam saw only one. Julia was standing near the door, and the sound of her laughter made him stop for an instant on the threshold.

'An ice-maiden! Oh, how absurd! – when I am *so* hot!' She turned as she spoke, and saw Adam, gave a sharp gasp, audible to everyone in the saloon, and fainted.

He was standing so close that when he saw her sway he was able to start forward, and to catch her as she crumpled up.

The startled silence was broken by Jenny's matter-of-fact voice. 'That's right: lay her on the sofa, Lynton, and open one of the windows! She never *could* abide a hot room, poor Julia!'

Almost as pale as his fair burden, Adam obeyed. A gentleman whose air and raiment proclaimed the Man of Mode had taken a hasty step forward, but he checked himself, his inscrutable gaze travelling from Adam's face to Jenny's.

Looking up from her task of fanning Julia, Jenny glanced round the circle, and said, with a friendly smile: 'She will be better directly. Pray don't be alarmed! It is only the heat!'

A quiet voice behind her said: 'Take this, Lady Lynton!' and a delicate hand came over Jenny's shoulder with a vinaigrette in it.

'Thank you! That's just what's needed, and I don't possess!' said Jenny, waving it under Julia's nostrils. She added, in a conversational tone: 'I've never fainted myself, but when we were at school together Miss Oversley was for ever doing it.'

'Someone – you, Mr Tollerton, if you will be so good! – find Lady Oversley, and tell her that Miss Oversley is overcome by the heat!' commanded the same quiet voice.

'Yes, and do you procure a glass of water, Lynton, if you please!' said Jenny.

He left the room immediately, and, by the time he returned to it, Julia had come round, and was leaning against her mother's shoulder, murmuring in some agitation that it was nothing – so stupid! – the room so stuffy!

Most of the other guests had discreetly withdrawn from the saloon, but one or two remained; and Adam, handing the glass of water to Jenny, found himself being regarded through a quizzing-glass raised to the faintly smiling eye of the Man of Mode.

The smile touched a pair of thin, satirical lips. 'Lynton, I fancy?' said the gentleman. Adam bowed. 'Just so! I was pretty well-acquainted with your father, and am happy to make *your* acquaintance.' He let his quizzing-glass fall, and held out his hand, saying, as Adam took it: 'You don't resemble him very much, but I felt sure I couldn't be mistaken. Ah – I'm Rockhill, you know!'

Adam, still shaken by the evening's event, replied with mechanical civility. The Marquis said sympathetically: 'Such an unfortunate contretemps, but not, we must trust, a serious matter.' He levelled his quizzing-glass again, this time at Jenny. 'Your wife?'

'Yes, sir,' Adam replied.

'Admirable woman!' sighed his lordship. 'I felicitate you!'

'Thank you! you are very good!' Adam smiled at Jenny, as she came towards him, and held out his hand. He had pulled himself together, and if he still looked pale he was able to say quite easily: 'Is she feeling better? Let me introduce Lord Rockhill to you: he has been complimenting me on your presence of mind!'

'Well, I'm sure I don't know why he should do so,' she answered prosaically. 'There was nothing to be in a fuss about! How do you do? I think we should leave Julia with her mama now, so shall we go into the other room? Then they may slip away quietly, for Julia is not feeling quite the thing.'

She made as if to lay her hand on Adam's arm, but realized that she was still holding the vinaigrette. She exclaimed at her own stupidity, and turned back to restore the crystal phial to its owner, who received it from her with a smile, and a searching look that was at once kind and appraising. 'Thank you! You, I collect, are Lady Lynton. I am Lady Castlereagh. I think I saw you at the Drawing-room, didn't I? Are you fixed in town now? And ready to receive morning visitors? Then I shall hope to further my acquaintance with you. Let me say that you did very well just now – very well indeed!'

She nodded in a friendly way, and moved away before Jenny could speak, which was perhaps as well, since Jenny, who had been warned that this stately lady's favour was hard to win, flushed to the roots of her hair, and uttered something that was as inaudible as it was disjointed.

In spite of her momentary embarrassment, however, the knowledge that she had been approved by one of the Patronesses of Almack's gave her new confidence; and when she presently perceived an acquaintance of her school-days, and received a cordial greeting from her, she began almost to feel at home. She was a little daunted by a cold stare from Mrs Burrell, and some critical ones from several other haughty-looking dames, but before she could be seriously discomposed she saw the lanky form of Lord Brough bearing down upon her, and was immediately at her ease again. She had met him only once before, but he spoke to her as though they had been friends of long standing, saying, as he came up to her: 'How do you do? No need to ask – you look famously – not even bored!'

Her eyes narrowed in amusement. 'No, indeed! Why should I be?'

'Don't you think this is a devilish dull party? I do – wouldn't have come if I hadn't been dragged here! You and Adam are the only people I've met whom I *wished* to meet – never saw so many quizzes and dragons in my life! Always the same at Lady Nassington's parties: I can't think why anyone comes to 'em!'

'For goodness' sake – !' she protested. 'You'll be heard!'

'Oh, no, no! Not in this hubbub! Queer thing, isn't it? – All persons of the first consideration, making a din like lions at feeding-time. Come and be introduced to my mother: she wants to meet you.' He added, with his lazy smile: 'Most amiable creature in the world! You'll like her: I do myself.'

This, though it made her laugh, seemed a very odd thing to say of his mother, but he was perfectly right in thinking that she would like Lady Adversane, a stout and placid lady of unfashionable appearance and a warm heart. Jenny sat beside her on a sofa, and thought how easy her new life would be if all great ladies were as kind and as homely.

Had she but known it, she was meeting with far more kindness than might have been expected. Everyone knew under what circumstances Adam had succeeded to his father's room, and everyone wished him well. Sally Jersey might exclaim to Lady Castlereagh: 'Oh, goodness me! Don't, I *implore* you, give her vouchers for Almack's!' but even she, with a shrug and a pout, said: 'Oh, well, no! – I don't mean to *cut* her! Poor, dear Bardy's son – ! Goodness me, what *would* Bardy have said to such a connection? My heart is positively *wrung* with compassion for that *poor* young man! She presents such a very *off* appearance, doesn't she? But I'll call in Grosvenor Street, and – yes, I'll send her a card for my rout-party next month! *Anything*, short of vouchers for Almack's! Oh, goodness me, one must draw the line *somewhere*! Tell me – you are so much better acquainted with Lady Oversley than I am! – is it true that young Lynton was previously betrothed to Miss Oversley? And that she swooned just now – actually *swooned*! – at the sight of him?'

'She did swoon,' acknowledged Lady Castlereagh, 'but Lady Lynton, whose conduct, I must tell you, was such as to command my respect, informed us that she always does so in overheated rooms.'

'Oh, excellent address – if she knew the true cause! I daresay she doesn't: she looks stupid! I'm persuaded she's not awake upon *any* suit!'

She was mistaken: Jenny was quite awake upon that suit; and under a stolid demeanour she turned it over and over in her mind. Not by so much as the flicker of an eyelid did she betray to Adam how fully alive she was to the implications of Julia's dramatic swoon; nor did she glance for more than an instant at his face, as it was bent over Julia, lying like a broken flower in his arms. In that one instant she had seen all that his chivalry would have wished to conceal from her; and her immediate intervention had sprung from no innate address but from a fierce resolve to protect him from the curiosity of those others who were witnesses of the episode. She had not looked at him again, and she did not mention the matter when, later, they drove back to Grosvenor Street. Neither of them had ever spoken of his previous attachment: it was a tacitly forbidden subject, which she dared not broach, though it lay heavily between them. There was only one thing to be done in such a situation, and that was to talk about something else. So she beguiled the short drive with commonplaces about Brough's droll sayings, his mother's kindness, the Prince Regent's condescension, and her surprise at having a perfectly plainly dressed gentleman pointed out to her as the great Mr Brummell.

It required no great effort to reply suitably to these trivialities; Adam even found them vaguely soothing. Emotional exhaustion had communicated itself to his body: he had never felt more fatigued in all the strenuous years of his service. He had steeled himself to meet his lost love, but not to encounter the heartrending look in her eyes when, for a moment before she fainted, they gazed into his. He had caught her, and had held her in his arms, and the sweet, nostalgic scent she always used agonizingly recalled the past. He hoped he had not uttered the words that had leapt to his tongue: *Julia, my love, my darling!* He thought he had not. Jenny's flat voice had jerked him back to his senses, prosaically directing him to lay Julia on the sofa. He had obeyed, and, as he straightened himself, he had seen the rampant curiosity in a dozen faces, and had realized that he must at all costs command himself. Providence – in the shape of Jenny, desiring him to procure a glass of water – had come to his rescue, granting him a respite. By the time he had been obliged to return to the room he had regained command over himself: enough, at least, to enable him to play his prescribed rôle throughout an interminable evening.

It was not surprising that it should have exhausted him, for it was more complicated than he had foreseen, and he was obliged to play it while labouring under severe spiritual stress. It was his duty, as he saw it, to thrust his bride into the heart of the ton. It never occurred to him that his own charm and address might achieve his object with the expenditure of very little effort. He saw himself as the insignificant son of a man of immense popularity; and he went to Nassington House determined, however distasteful the task might be, to exploit this popularity, and to persuade his father's friends, if he could, to accept Jenny because they liked him well enough not to wish to wound him. This in itself was sufficiently disagreeable to make him look forward to the evening's entertainment with revulsion; when, at the very outset, to this obligation was added the more urgent need to exert himself to the utmost in an effort to shield his love from malicious tongues – and his wife, too, poor little soul! – what had been designed as a party of pleasure became a prolonged ordeal through which he had moved, exchanging light-hearted conversation with his fellow-guests as though nothing had happened to disturb him. Whether he had succeeded in convincing the suspicious he had no idea: he had done his best, and if that proved to be not good enough he was much too tired to consider what more could be done.

So he was grateful to Jenny for her comfortable commonplaces. They might argue a certain insensibility, but they were preferable to the comments and questions he had dreaded – and why, after all, should she show sensibility over an episode which (if she had realized its significance) could scarcely have wounded her, however much it might have mortified her?

Except that she did not mention the matter at all, which was a little surprising, he could have believed that she really did think the heat responsible for Julia's collapse. She was her usual, matter-of-fact self, though rather sleepy; she demanded neither explanation nor reassurance: he could relax at last.

Some hours later, when he saw her over the teacups at the breakfast-table, he thought she looked as though she had not slept very much after all. She had not, but she merely said that she was unused to such late nights.

'You should have stayed in bed. I wish you may not have got up merely to make tea for me?'

It was what she had done, knowing that he was very unhandy with urns and teapots, but she said: 'As though you couldn't make it yourself! No, indeed!'

'I can't,' he confessed ruefully. 'I can never get it as I like it, and if they make it for me downstairs it's worse. Thank you: that is *exactly* as it should be!'

She smiled, but having supplied his wants turned to the perusal of an advertisement which had been sent her through the post, and which adjured her, in the strongest terms, to lose no time in procuring a new and infallible Nostrum for Gout. She had not the smallest use for this commodity, but if she sat with nothing to occupy her she knew that Adam would bestir himself to talk to her, and Adam did not like breakfast-table conversation.

He went away presently; and after sitting for some time, pondering the problem which had kept her awake during what had remained of the night, she got up from the table, and sent a message to the stables. An hour later, having executed a commission in the Strand, she was being driven back, not to Grosvenor Street, but to Lord Oversley's house in Mount Street.

Mr Chawleigh, to Adam's intense but rigorously suppressed annoyance, had visited the stables and the coach-house attached to Lynton House while the bridal pair were in Hampshire, and had condemned out of hand the landaulette which had previously served the ladies of the house. He thought it a very dowdy turn-out; and he replaced it with a glossy barouche, on whose shallow doors he insisted on having the Lynton arms blazoned. The carriage was drawn by a pair of showy chestnuts. Mr Chawleigh had paid a large price for them, but he was not a judge of horseflesh, and when Adam first saw them he ejaculated involuntarily: 'Oh, my God!'

However, Jenny was not a judge of horseflesh either, so she was quite satisfied with her peacocky pair. They might have been bishoped, as John Coachman told Adam he was willing to swear they had been, but they were quite capable of conveying her about the town in dashing style.

She found Lady Oversley at home, and was taken upstairs to the drawing-room, where her ladyship welcomed her with affection but rather nervously. She was looking harassed, and when Jenny disclosed that she had called to enquire how Julia did she answered in a flurry: 'Oh – ! So very kind of you! My dear, I'm afraid I didn't thank you – in the agitation of the moment, you know! But Emily Castlereagh told me how good you were, and indeed I am very much obliged to you! Poor Julia! The rooms *were* hot, weren't they? I was conscious of it myself, and, of course, Julia's constitution is *not* strong. She is not in very high health – in fact, quite out of sorts! – so I have kept her in bed today, and Dr Baillie has given me a composer for her.'

Jenny nodded. 'I was afraid she would fall into one of her hysterical fits,' she remarked. 'I thought about it a great deal, after we had gone home, and it seemed to me as though the best thing would be for me to come to see you, ma'am, because I don't doubt you're in quite a worry. Well, I don't know much about tonnish people yet, but I expect they don't differ greatly from anyone else, and Julia's going off as she did, the instant she clapped eyes on Adam, is bound to set tongues wagging.'

Thankfully abandoning pretence, Lady Oversley said tragically: 'Oh, Jenny, I declare I am worn to a bone! What with Julia, and then Oversley – But she did *not* faint on purpose!'

'No, of course she didn't. I don't understand how people can faint away as she does, but there's no denying that it never needed more than a harsh word to send her off. She used to suffer dreadfully from the vapours, too.'

'Yes,' sighed Lady Oversley. 'And all the doctors could find amiss was that she was too excitable! But she doesn't have the vapours now – at least, not if she is *gently* treated, and not scolded when she is already so much distressed! I don't mean to say that I didn't sympathize with Oversley – heaven knows I could have *murdered* her! In *that* house of all others, and with Emily Cowper in the very room! But what, I ask you, Jenny, is the use of ringing a peal over the poor child, and driving her into hysterics?'

'Well, it isn't any use at all, and never was,' said Jenny. 'Not that one can wonder at his lordship's ripping up at her, for gentlemen don't like scenes, except when they create 'em themselves, like Papa, when the meat's not dressed right. The thing is, what's to be done now?'

'I can't *think*!' said Lady Oversley. 'I am being driven distracted! Oversley is saying that if Julia can't conduct herself with propriety she had best retire to a convent, which is quite absurd, for if she retired anywhere it would be to old Lady Oversley, but I don't *wish* her to! Here she is, in her second season, and how, I ask you, is she to be creditably married, when her father talks such nonsense, and *she* will do nothing but – Oh, dear, how awkward this is! I shouldn't be talking about it to you at all, which just *shows* how much my nerves are overset!'

'There's no need for anyone to be in a worry over me,' replied Jenny stolidly. 'No need for any flummery between us either, ma'am. No one thinks Adam married me for love. Only it's a pity that everyone should know it was Julia he wanted, and she him.' She paused, frowning. 'There's plenty of people who fall in love, and then fall out of it again, so I daresay it doesn't signify, however many of her friends Julia took into her confidence. But it won't do, will it, for her to be showing everyone that she's wearing the willow for him?'

'No, it will *not* do!' agreed her ladyship, with feeling. 'And so disagreeable to you, too, which, I *assure* you, I perfectly understand!'

'That don't signify. It's Adam I'm thinking about – and you too, ma'am, for you've been very kind to me.'

'I shall have to keep Julia out of his way. And how I am to do it, unless I send her back to Tunbridge Wells –'

'Well, you can't, of course, and to my way of thinking it wouldn't answer. Sooner or later they'll be bound to meet, and ten to one we'd be regularly in for it again, because the sight of him would be bound to bring it all back to her. And it won't do to avoid us, because you've always been very friendly with the Deverils, by what Lydia's told me, and so *that* would set people talking. So what I came to say to you, ma'am, was that the best thing is to let the quizzes see that we're all very good friends. There's no sense in putting Julia in Adam's way more than's needful, but if she visits me, and goes out with me now and then, she *will* meet him, and – and grow accustomed to it.'

Lady Oversley, who was regarding her in a good deal of astonishment, said: 'But Jenny, *surely* you cannot wish – I mean, *is* it wise?'

Jenny was silent for a moment. 'Well, I've been wondering that myself. Of course, the best would be if they were never to meet at all, but since that can't be it seems to me better they should meet often enough for it to get to be an ordinary thing than to meet only by accident.'

'If only I had *known*!' exclaimed Lady Oversley, dissolving into tears. 'I ought never to have allowed it, but it seemed so *suitable*! Oh dear, who could have guessed it would end in my cherished Julia breaking her heart? Though of course I should have guessed she would, because she always said he was like Sir Galahad, which I'm sure he is – if Sir Galahad was the one I think he was – Or don't you think so?' she asked, perceiving that Jenny's eyes had narrowed in sudden laughter.

'Well, I don't know, but I shouldn't have thought so. But I was never one for reading those old romances and legends that Julia dotes on,' said Jenny apologetically. 'I *do* know that he likes his eggs boiled for four minutes exactly, and won't touch muffins.'

'Won't touch muffins?' faltered Lady Oversley.

'Can't abide them! And there's nothing frets him more than having his things out of order. He says it comes from living in tents, when there's no bearing it if you don't keep everything just so. I've been obliged to tell my housekeeper that if she can't keep the maids from rearranging the things on his dressing-table she'll have to leave at the term. Mind, for anything I know Sir Galahad may have been pernickety too – though I'd wager you an egg at Easter, as Papa says, that that's not what Julia thinks!'

'No,' said Lady Oversley faintly. 'No, indeed!'

'So, if you're agreeable, ma'am, I'll try if I can't coax Julia to drive with me in the Park tomorrow. And if you and my lord would bring her to dine with us next week, when Adam's mother and Lydia will be with us, we should be very happy. It would be a natural thing for you to do, wouldn't it, with Lady Lynton going off to Bath, as she is, and spending a couple of nights in Grosvenor Street? It won't be a regular party, though I mean to invite Lord Brough as well.'

'Oh, but Julia would never – Oh, dear, I don't know what to say! Of course it would make an excellent impression, if it were known that we had all dined informally with you, but I'm afraid Julia would shrink from such a scheme!'

'I don't doubt she will, but there's no saying but what I may be able to bring her round my thumb. I'll go up to her, if I may.'

Startled, Lady Oversley said: 'No, no! I mean, she is so much overpowered – She won't wish to see you, Jenny!'

'Very likely not, but she won't have any choice. Now, don't be in the fidgets, ma'am! There'll be no harm done, I promise you!'

With these words she got up, and walked briskly out of the room, leaving Lady Oversley feeling helpless and extremely apprehensive.

Eleven

The light in Julia's room was dim, the blinds having been drawn across the windows. Shutting the door, Jenny said cheerfully: 'May I come in? Though that's a silly thing to say when I'm in already!'

She could just perceive Julia, lost in the middle of the large bed. The fair head turned on the pillow. 'You!' Julia uttered.

'That's right,' said Jenny. 'I came to see how you did. You won't mind if I draw the blinds back: I shall be blundering into the furniture if we don't have a bit more light.'

'Have you come to reproach me?' Julia demanded. 'You need not!'

The sunlight flooded the room; Jenny trod over to the bed, saying: 'Now, when did I ever do so, goose?' She bent over Julia, and kissed her cheek. 'Stop fretting yourself to flinders, love!'

Julia shrank, turning her face away. 'I wish you hadn't come! You mean to be kind, I collect, but you don't understand! If you had sensibility –'

'Well, I haven't, so there's no sense expecting me to behave as if I had. And just as well for Adam I haven't,' Jenny added, 'for if I were to carry on as you do, Julia, he'd be driven demented between the pair of us!'

Julia pulled herself up. 'I would not have spoken his name to you, or have uttered a word of what lies between us, if *you* had but refrained!'

'No, I daresay you wouldn't,' agreed Jenny, shaking up her pillows. 'So I haven't refrained. Not that it's an easy thing to talk about, but it makes for awkwardness if we must never mention it. I don't know how to hide my teeth either, so you say what you wish, and don't fear to offend me, because you won't do it.'

The huge eyes gazed wonderingly at her. 'How strange you are!' Julia said. 'I suppose I never understood you. But I thought I did! When they told me – showed me the notice in the *Gazette* – I wouldn't believe it! You were my friend! You *knew*, but you stole Adam from me! How *could* you?'

'That's more than I can tell you, for I didn't steal him, and wouldn't have done so, even if I'd thought I could. What, set myself up as a rival to *you*? Don't talk such nonsense, Julia! Papa made the match, unbeknownst to me.'

'Oh, that's contemptible!' Julia interrupted, flinging up her hand. 'Next you will tell me it was not in your power to refuse!'

'No, I shan't. I *did* refuse, when he first broached it to me – before I knew how things stood – that things had been put an end to between you and Adam. He *couldn't* have married you, Julia! He was all to pieces! I daresay you don't know what his father's debts were, for it's not likely he'd tell you, but Papa knew, and he told me. Adam was selling everything – even Fontley!'

'That at least I knew! And *he* knew it didn't weigh with me! I would have lived in a hovel, and counted myself happy! You may smile, but it's true!'

Jenny begged pardon, but said: 'It weighed with him – I think, more than anything. I don't understand that myself, but I can see what's under my nose. *He* wouldn't have been happy, not if he'd lost Fontley.'

'I would have made him so! Do you think you will? You won't! It's me he loves, not you!' She caught her breath, and said quickly: 'Oh, no, no, I didn't mean to say that! Hateful, hateful – ! Go, Jenny! *pray* go now!'

Jenny paid no heed to this, but answered: 'I know that. There's no pretence of love between him and me: that wasn't part of the bargain.'

'The bargain!' Julia exclaimed, shuddering. 'No, I can never have understood you!'

'Or him,' interpolated Jenny dryly.

Julia stared at her, repeating slowly: 'Or him! No – or him! Ah, but yes, I do understand what forced *him* to do it! But you? For a title? But you never cared for such things! You can't have sold yourself for mere position!'

'Why not? I'm not the first, and I shan't be the last to do so. Easy to despise what you've always had!' replied Jenny, returning the stare doggedly.

'I don't believe it! I *couldn't* have liked you if you had been so mercenary!'

'Well, it doesn't make any odds what you think of me, and the lord knows I've felt badly enough about it. I wouldn't have consented to it if there had been the least chance of his being able to marry you, but there wasn't. He didn't choose between me and you, Julia: it was between me and ruin. You say he won't be happy, but at least he'll be comfortable! What's more, he's got Fontley, and for all you may not think it that matters to him.' She paused. 'Well, there's no more to be said on that head. What brought me here was what happened last night.'

Julia winced. 'Don't! I can't endure any more! Papa – even Mama – ! Good God, do they think – do you think – that I *meant* to betray myself?'

'Well, your mama and I don't think it. I can't answer for his lordship, but I don't suppose he does either – not but what you can't blame him, if he cut up stiff, because there's no denying you did make us all look no-how!'

'Oh, is that all you can think of?' Julia cried bitterly. 'What of *my* mortification? The *agony* of regaining my senses – seeing all those faces – !' She broke off, covering her eyes with her hand.

'Now, don't get into a taking, love! It's not so bad that it can't be mended,' said Jenny soothingly.

Julia's hand fell. 'Jenny, I didn't mean to! I thought I could meet him again just as I ought! I *could* have done so, had he been there at the outset! But he wasn't! I thought – oh, I was so relieved it made me stupid beyond belief! It didn't occur to me that he might come later. But he did, and when I turned, and suddenly saw him, so close to me – Jenny, it was the shock that made me faint!'

'You don't have to tell me that. If it isn't just like you to fret and fume yourself into such a state that you'd swoon off if a mouse ran across the floor! That's pretty well what I told them all – though it wasn't a mouse I set it down to, but the heat.'

'Mama told me how good you were,' Julia said listlessly. 'Thank you! But they won't believe it. They'll watch me, and whisper about me. Perhaps they'll pity me. *Poor girl! He cried off, you know!*'

'Not if I have anything to say in the matter!' interrupted Jenny. 'That's precisely what I mean to nip in the bud, so I'll thank you not to fall into a lethargy when what's wanted is a bit of rumgumption!'

'Why should you care?' said Julia, sighing.

'Have a little sense, Julia, do!' begged Jenny. 'Very agreeable it would be to have people saying that about my husband!'

Julia looked startled. 'But they wouldn't! They know the circumstances – that he couldn't help himself!'

'That won't stop them thinking he must have treated you pretty shabbily, if they see you looking as if you was sunk in affliction! *He* won't look so, whatever he feels, because he's too much the gentleman to let anyone think he don't like being married to me, so the end of it will be that we'll have people saying he's downright heartless, not caring a straw for anything but a fortune, and happy as long as he's rich!'

'You need not be afraid!' Julia said tragically. 'I am going to return to my grandmother, and live retired. I daresay my very existence will be forgotten within a year!'

'More likely they'd have to build another hotel in Tunbridge Wells to take in your admirers,' said Jenny, keeping her temper.

Julia gave a gasp, and a quiver of laughter. 'Oh, how *can* you be so – so *odiously* unfeeling?'

'Well, you know I've got no sensibility. But I haven't windmills in my head either, so I'll tell you what you *will* do, and that's to confound all the spiteful toads who'd be only too ready to crow over you.' She caught the flash in Julia's eyes, and continued: 'Yes, I can just hear them! Pretending to pity you, like you said, but fairly licking their lips, and saying they'd known all along the Sylph would have a downfall. For you can't knock all the other girls into flinders without stirring up a lot of spite and jealousy: that I *do* know!'

Julia sat up. 'But how?' she demanded. 'Papa wouldn't consent to a betrothal, but people knew!'

'What if they did? They won't think it wonderful that a girl that has as many beaux dangling after her as you have fell out of love as easily as she fell into it! Why, you were barely out of the schoolroom! Then you didn't see Adam for months, so what's more natural than that you should find you'd made a mistake?' She ignored a deep sigh from Julia, and began to draw on her gloves. 'So I'll call for you tomorrow, at about four o'clock, and you'll drive in the Park with me, like the good friends we've always been.'

'Oh, no!' Julia exclaimed imploringly. 'No, I can't!'

'Yes, you can. And I don't mind owning that I'll be very much obliged to you if you will, because I don't care to drive alone, and I'm not yet acquainted with people. Two or three bows are the most I'll get, if I go by myself, but if you're sitting beside me the carriage will be mobbed, I daresay.' She got up, as a reluctant laugh escaped Julia. 'And if you could manage to faint the *next* time you go to a party – but not at Lady Bridgewater's assembly, mind, because she said last night she should send us a card, and it won't answer if you do it when Adam's present – !'

'Jenny, you are too detestable!' protested Julia, between tears and laughter. 'As though I could!'

'You could, if you set your mind to it,' said Jenny, with a tight little smile. 'You've only to think you're stifling from the heat, and stifle you will!'

She bestowed a valedictory pat on Julia's shoulder, and went away without giving her time to consider the implication of this remark. She was met on the floor below by Lady Oversley, who looked an anxious question. She replied to it with a nod, and a smile. 'I didn't say anything about her coming to dine with us, but she'll drive out with me tomorrow, never fear! I'll ask her then.'

Lady Oversley embraced her, shedding a few tears of relief. 'Oh, my dear Jenny, I am so very much obliged to you! Was she – was she still in such distress?'

'That's more than I can tell, ma'am,' replied Jenny, in her blunt way. 'There's no saying – at least, I can't say, because we're no more alike than a dock and a daisy, and I don't understand her, and never did. She *thinks* she is, and it has always seemed to me that she's one of those who'd die of the influenza only because she took it into her head it was smallpox!'

This was rather beyond Lady Oversley, but when she presently recounted it to her lord he looked a good deal struck, and said that Jenny was shrewder than he had supposed. 'That daughter of yours, my dear,' he said, 'lives always in alt, and now we see what comes of it!'

She was accustomed to his very unfair habit of disclaiming responsibility for the existence of any of his children who had vexed him, so she let this pass, agreeing that Julia was too imaginative.

'Ay, she takes after you,' said his lordship inexcusably.

Julia remained in her bedchamber all day, but she appeared at the breakfast-table on the following morning. She looked pale, and was obviously in depressed spirits; and when her father, forcibly admonished by Lady Oversley, greeted her with great heartiness, she responded with a wince, and the travesty of a smile. But by a lucky chance a new walking-dress of French cambric, trimmed with frills of broad-lace, was sent home that day, and it was so pretty, particularly when worn with one of the new Oldenburg hats, that Julia was insensibly cheered. It had seemed at one moment as if she meant to refuse to drive with Jenny; but when she had been persuaded to put on the new dress, and her mama, her maid, her two younger sisters, and their governess had all fallen into raptures she changed her mind, and went out perfectly readily when the Lynton barouche drew up before the door.

Jenny, herself expensively but not very becomingly attired in Brunswick gray lustring, admired the dress too, and so, when they reached the Park, did a number of other persons. If the carriage was not mobbed, at least the coachman had to pull up his horses a great many times. It was the hour of the fashionable promenade, and the Park thronged with vehicles, from ladies' barouches to the Corinthians' curricles; with horsemen, mounted on high-bred hacks; and with exquisites, strolling along the path beside the roadway. It seemed to Jenny that every second person bowed or waved to her lovely companion; and since Julia wished to exchange greetings with her friends, and a large number of gentlemen were eager to pay homage to her, Jenny resigned herself to a dawdling progress. She had the satisfaction of receiving several civil acknowledgements herself, but she privately considered this promenade a waste of time, and was rather bored. It was otherwise with Julia, always responsive to atmosphere, and reviving like a thirsty plant under a shower of compliments and gallantries. The colour returned to her cheeks, the sparkle to her eyes, and her pretty laugh was so spontaneous that no one could have supposed her to be nursing a broken heart.

Not all her admirers were youthful. The Marquis of Rockhill, riding with Brough beside him, stayed for longer than any beside the barouche. He was very civil to Jenny, but she saw the warm glint in his eyes when he looked at Julia, and was not deceived into thinking that he had stopped for any other purpose than to talk to her. She thought him an elderly flirt for Julia, but she guessed him to be a notable conquest, and realized that his caressing manner was attractive to Julia. It was plain that he had a *tendre* for her, but he did not try to monopolize her. When Brough claimed her attention he at once began to talk to Jenny, and did not let his eyes stray towards Julia while doing so, which she thought unusually polite. He was apparently well-acquainted with the Deveril family; and when Jenny disclosed that her mother-in-law would be in Grosvenor Street during the following week he said that he must call to pay his respects to her.

'Such a very old friend – almost a cradle-friend, one might say!'

On an impulse, she said abruptly: 'Would you care to dine with us?' She saw his brows lift in surprise, and explained: 'You see, she means to stay only two nights, so I fancy she won't have time for morning visitors. I mean to invite the Oversleys to dine, and to bring Miss Oversley as well, and it would – we should be very happy if you liked to come, and not care for its being an informal party.'

Under their heavy lids his penetrating eyes looked down into hers. A smile crept into them; he said softly: 'But I shall be delighted to come, Lady Lynton! An excellent scheme! Parties composed of such intimate friends as the Deverils and the Oversleys are always better for a little leaven, are they not?' The smile deepened in his eyes as he saw the wary look in hers, but he said no more, only bowing and then turning away to tell Brough that they must not detain the carriage longer.

In another minute the gentlemen had ridden on, and Jenny, as a sudden apprehension smote her, demanded: 'He *is* a bachelor, isn't he?'

'Yes, of course. He's a cousin of Rockhill's, you know. Lady Adversane is Rockhill's –'

'No, no, not Brough! Rockhill!'

'Oh! No, not a bachelor. He –'

'Oh, my goodness!' exclaimed Jenny, dismayed. 'I invited him to dine with us next week! Whatever must he think of me? As though I didn't know better! Oh, dear!'

'Stupid!' Julia said, laughing. 'He's a *widower*!'

'Thank heaven!' said Jenny devoutly.

Julia glanced curiously at her. 'What made you invite him? I didn't know you were acquainted with him.'

'I'm not – well, barely, at all events! He said he hoped to see Lady Lynton when she comes to town, so I asked him to dine. I told him it was to be quite informal. Your papa and mama are coming, and you too, I hope, for Lydia will be there, you know.'

'I?' gasped Julia. 'Oh, *no*! You cannot ask that of me!'

Casting a warning glance at the back of the coachman, Jenny

said: 'Well, I own it won't be a very lively party, but I mean to invite Brough as well, so I trust it won't be such a dead bore as you think! I wish I knew some more gentlemen! But Adam's friends are all in France, so there's only Cousin Osbert, unless – Would your brother come, do you think?'

'Jenny, I won't, I won't!' said Julia, under her breath.

'Well, if that's so Lord Rockhill will think it a regular take-in, for I told him you'd be there, which was why he accepted.'

Except for reiterating that she would not come, Julia said no more, but lapsed into pensive dejection.

At home she was not so forbearing. The only effect Lady Oversley's entreaties had upon her was to cast her into agitation; and a fit of hysterics might have been the outcome had not her father come into the room, demanding to know what the devil was the matter now. Upon being told, he favoured his wife and daughter with a very tolerable impersonation of a Roman parent, announcing with such unusual sternness that Julia would obey him that she positively quailed, and ventured on no more contumacious a response than an imploring: 'Oh, Papa, pray don't make me go!'

'Not another word!' commanded his lordship. 'I am very much displeased with you, Julia, and if you try my patience any further you will be sorry for it!'

At these terrible words both ladies dissolved into tears. His lordship, finding his rôle rather beyond his power to maintain, beat a dignified retreat, frowning heavily enough to lend colour to Lady Oversley's statement that Papa was very, very angry. The thought that she, who had always been Papa's pet, was now in his black books proved to be too much for Julia's fortitude. She settled down to cry in good earnest, and so despairingly that Papa had to be recalled to soothe her with assurances of his continued regard. As soon as she knew herself to be still loved she grew calmer, and when he said that he sympathized with her much more than she guessed she was so passionately grateful that she was ready to promise to do anything he wished.

When the news of the projected dinner-party was broken to

Adam he was almost as much dismayed, but concealed it better. Jenny, at work on the first of a set of chair-covers, asked him placidly if he thought she might invite Mr Oversley, and he replied, in an indifferent voice: 'You may do so, of course, but I should doubt whether he'll come. If I know Charlie, he'll think it by far too slow!'

He was right, but Mr Oversley did grace the party with his reluctant presence, because his father, using none of the diplomacy he found necessary when dealing with his daughter, told him that he must.

'What, drive Tab to the Lyntons? No, dash it, sir – !' protested Mr Oversley, revolted by the thought of this family expedition.

'Nonsense! If Jenny wants you she shall have you! I daresay she needs you to make up her numbers.'

Mr Oversley, who had been upon the strut for over a year, directed a look of pained reproach at his parent, and said: 'Much obliged to her!'

Lord Oversley laughed, but told him not to be a coxcomb. 'The thing is, Charlie, she has hit on this way of bringing your sister about, after that shocking business at Nassington House, and mighty good-natured of her it is!'

'Here, I say!' exclaimed Mr Oversley, alarmed. 'Julia ain't going off into a faint, is she? Because if there's to be any of that kind of bobbery –'

'No, no, she has promised to behave just as she ought!' said his father reassuringly.

Twelve

*T*he dowager, attended by her daughter and her dresser, reached London in excellent time on the day appointed, for she came post, her previous journey having helped her to overcome her dread of strange postilions. Mr Chawleigh would heartily have approved of the cavalcade which set out from Fontley, for two of the grooms rode with the chaise, and it was followed by a coach carrying my lady's footman and a number of trunks and portmanteaux, and also by a fourgon loaded with such movables as the Dowager considered her own and had removed from Fontley.

She arrived in a wilting condition, but Jenny was on the watch, and as soon as she saw the chaise she called to Adam to go down immediately to welcome his mother. He reached the street in time to support her as she totteringly descended on to the flagway. She was gratified by this attention, and uttered: 'Dear one!' as he kissed first her hand and then her cheek. She then, and in less fond accents, said: 'Lydia *dear!*' as that damsel ruthlessly hugged Adam.

Adam led her into the house, where the first object to attract her apprehensive gaze was the Egyptian lamp at the foot of the staircase. She drew in her breath sharply. 'Good heavens! Ah, yes, I see! A female form, with sphinxes. Dear me!'

'It is a lamp, Mama,' said Adam defensively.

'Is it, dearest? No doubt Jenny found the stair ill-lit. I was never conscious of it myself, but – And are those strange alabaster bowls lamps too?'

'Yes, Mama, they are! And here is Jenny, coming to welcome you!'

He was relieved to see that Jenny was more successful than he had been in dealing with his mother. She greeted her with proper solicitude, and said that it was no wonder she should be feeling done-up.

'I am afraid I am a sad, troublesome guest,' sighed the Dowager. 'I am so much pulled by all I have gone through that I am fit for nothing but my bed.'

'Well, then,' said Jenny, 'you shall come up directly, ma'am, and get between sheets, and have your dinner sent to you on a tray.'

'So kind!' murmured the Dowager. 'Just a bowl of soup, perhaps!'

Lydia, who had been listening in strong indignation to these melancholy plans, exclaimed: 'Mama, you can't go to bed the instant you set foot inside the house! Why, you said yourself, when Mrs Mitcham came to Fontley, that nothing was more odious than a visitor who arrived only to be ill, and was for ever wanting glasses of hot water, or thin gruel!'

'Oh, fiddle!' said Jenny. 'It's to be hoped your mama don't think herself a *visitor* in her son's house! She shall do whatever she chooses. Do you come upstairs, ma'am, and be comfortable!'

The Dowager mellowed. She had had the amiable intention of frustrating any festive scheme which might have been devised for her entertainment by retiring to her bedroom in a state of exhaustion; but as soon as she was entreated to do exactly what she liked she began to think that if she rested for an hour she might feel sufficiently restored to join her family at the dinner-table. She allowed Jenny to escort her upstairs; and although it naturally caused her a pang not to be going to her 'own' room, she found that such careful provisions for her comfort had been made in the handsomely furnished apartment allotted to her that her melancholy abated. By the time she had been settled on a cushioned day-bed, and had been revived with tea and toast, she was wonderfully in charity with Jenny, and told her that rather than disappoint her dear ones she would make an effort to overcome her fatigue sufficiently to come downstairs in time for dinner.

Meanwhile, Lydia, having peeped into the dining-room, and exclaimed, in awed accents: 'Goodness, how *rich*!' had gone up to the drawing-room with her brother. She paused on the threshold, and stood at gaze, not saying anything for a full minute. Then she looked doubtfully at Adam. His eyes twinkled. 'Well?'

'May I say what I think, or – or not?'

'You may, but you needn't. I know what you think.'

'It's the *stripes*!' she said. 'It wouldn't be *nearly* as bad if you took them away – though I must own I don't like that very peculiar sofa much. Those horrid little legs look like some sort of an animal.'

'Reptile. They are crocodile-legs.'

'*Crocodile?*' Lydia inspected them more closely, and went into a peal of laughter. 'Yes, they are! I thought you were trying to hoax me. But why? Oh, yes, *I* see! It's the Egyptian mode, isn't it? I know it's all the crack, but I don't think it's very comfortable, do you?'

'I think it's detestable,' he answered, laughing too. 'Wait until you see Jenny's preposterous bed! She didn't choose this stuff, you know: it was her father.'

'Poor Mr Chawleigh! I expect he thinks it's the very first style of elegance. Mama won't, you know. Besides, she doesn't like Mr Chawleigh. I do, even if he is a funny one!' She heaved a sigh. 'Oh, Adam, I wish Mama hadn't settled on Bath! If she had decided on a house in London I could have borne it better, for I should have had you to talk to when I felt quite *desperate*, which, I'm sorry to say, I frequently do.'

'Has she been very trying?' he asked sympathetically.

'Yes. And I find that I *cannot* be a comfort to her. Am I very unnatural, Adam?' He shook his head, smiling. 'Well, Mama says I am, and sometimes I fear I may be, because I am growing to dislike Charlotte as much as I dislike Maria! Would you have believed it possible that I could? *Charlotte!*'

He laughed. 'Poor Charlotte! But you don't really, you know.'

She eyed him somewhat ominously. 'No! But I shall if *you* are going to call her *poor* Charlotte too!'

'I take it back!' he said hastily. 'I never said it!' Her dimples quivered into being, but she said gloomily: 'It's such humbug! Mama talks about her as if she were dead – except that she hasn't *yet* called her her *sainted* Charlotte. And how she can do so, when she *knows* Charlotte is as happy as a grig – ! We have had a letter from her, you know, sent from York, where they were staying for a few days.'

'No, I didn't know, but I'm delighted to hear that she's so happy.'

'Adam,' disclosed Lydia, in an awed voice, 'she says that Lambert partakes of all her ideas and sentiments!'

'Good God! I mean, how – how fortunate!'

'They shared solemn and elevating thoughts in the Cathedral.'

'No, they didn't,' replied Adam instantly. 'Charlotte had solemn and elevating thoughts, and Lambert said: "Ay, very true! By Jove, yes!" Lydia, you wretch, you are making me as bad as you are yourself! Be quiet!'

She chuckled, but had to wink away a tear. 'Oh, if *only* Maria hadn't died! Then I shouldn't have been obliged to be a comfort to Mama, or have gone to Bath, even!'

He gave her a hug. 'I wish you needn't have gone, but I think you must, at any rate for a time. Try to bear it! If Mama doesn't bring you to London herself next spring, would you like to come to us, and let Jenny present you?'

The hug was returned with interest; Lydia cried rapturously: 'Yes, of all things! Aunt Nassington spoke of bringing me out, but I would far prefer to be with you. If Jenny would be agreeable?'

As Jenny, who came into the room at that moment, said at once that nothing would afford her greater pleasure, Lydia's spirits bounded up, and she said, in a burst of confidence, that she hoped Mama would decide to remain in Bath during the spring.

'Outrageous brat! Take her away, Jenny! By the bye, don't neglect to show her your bathroom! She'll like it!'

Lydia, in fact, was entranced by it, and scandalized Martha Pinhoe by declaring her determination to use it. 'You don't mean to tell me you don't, Jenny? Why, it is a beautiful bath! All these mirrors too! You may see yourself whichever way you look while you're in the bath.'

'Well, that wouldn't be my notion of a high treat!' remarked Jenny. 'However, you're welcome to use it if you choose.'

'No, that she is not, my lady!' declared Miss Pinhoe. 'I'm surprised at you, saying such a thing! We all know what kind of creatures they are that sit in their baths with looking-glasses all round! The idea!'

It was evident that Lydia was exempt from this universal knowledge; and as it was also evident that she was going to demand enlightenment of Miss Pinhoe, Jenny hurriedly took her away to her own room. Lydia approved of this too, exclaiming: 'Why, it's all new, except for that chest, and the little chair by the window! I must say, it's a great improvement: it was dreadfully shabby before!'

'Do you like it?' Jenny asked anxiously. 'I haven't very good taste myself – not that I had anything to do with furnishing the house: Papa did it, while we were at Rushleigh, to – to surprise us. Only I'm afraid he made it all rather too – too *grand*!'

'For my part,' said Lydia, 'I shouldn't care a rush for that. How truly splendid to have a father who gives you such sumptuous surprises!' She hesitated, and then said shyly: 'He won't change Fontley, will he? Not *too* much?'

'No, no, I promise you it shan't be changed at all!' Jenny replied, her colour rushing up.

'I don't mean that this house isn't very elegant!' said Lydia hastily. 'Only that it wouldn't suit Fontley so well!'

It was the opinion of the Dowager, when she descended to the drawing-room, that the style favoured by Mr Chawleigh would suit no house; and at the first opportunity she expressed this opinion to Adam with great freedom. He found himself defending even the green stripes. He said doggedly that stripes were of the first stare. 'Such a very *vulgar* shade!' said the Dowager, with a shudder. '*Far* too much bullion on the curtains too! Alas, when I remember how this room once appeared I can't but grieve at such a transformation!'

He was goaded into retorting: 'It could hardly appear the same, ma'am, once you had removed from it everything but the carpet and three of the pictures!'

This unfilial rejoinder wounded her so deeply that not only were the ghosts of Stephen and Maria evoked, but she said, when Jenny told her of the small party arranged for her pleasure, that no doubt dear Jenny had forgotten that she was in deep mourning.

'As though any of us could forget it, when she is positively *dripping* black crape!' said Lydia. 'But don't be in a worry, Jenny! She won't retire to her room, I promise you!'

Jenny was obliged to be satisfied with this assurance, but her anxiety was not really allayed until the Dowager came downstairs just before eight o'clock arrayed in black silk, and with Adam's mantilla pinned over a Spanish comb (also his gift) set in her fair locks.

'Oh, how pretty you look!' Jenny exclaimed involuntarily. 'I beg your pardon! I couldn't resist!'

'Dearest child!' murmured the Dowager indulgently.

'I take great credit to myself for knowing that nothing would become you better than a mantilla,' said Adam. 'Perfect, Mama!'

'Foolish boy!' she said, rapidly mellowing. 'I thought it right to make the effort, since you have invited these people particularly to meet me. I daresay, if you were to mention that I have a fatiguing journey before me tomorrow, they will not stay very late.'

This did not sound propitious, but it was misleading. From the moment that Rockhill, after holding her hand while he gazed admiringly at her countenance, carried it to his lips with old-fashioned courtesy, the Dowager's enjoyment of the party was assured.

The arrival of the Oversleys coincided with that of Brough; and in the confusion of greetings no one noticed that Adam and Julia stood handlocked for longer than was customary, or heard Julia say: 'This was not of my contrivance!'

'Nor of mine,' he returned, in a low voice. 'You know that I cannot, *must* not say to you —' He checked himself, and pressed her hand before releasing it. 'Only tell me that you are better! The anguish of that moment, at my aunt's, will haunt me all my life, I think.'

'Oh, don't let it do so! I shan't mortify you again, I promise you! We shall grow accustomed, they tell me — forget that there was ever anything but friendship between us. I must wish you happy. *Can* you be?' A tiny headshake answered her. She smiled faintly. 'No, your *heart* is not fickle. I'll wish you content only.'

She turned from him as she spoke to meet Lydia, who came up to her, saying: 'I am so glad to see you, Julia! What an age it has been! The things I have to tell you!'

Adam moved away to mingle with his other guests, only a slight rigidity of countenance betraying that he was labouring under stress. Lydia, who had a schoolgirl's admiration of Julia, was chattering away to her, and Julia seemed to be interested and amused. Adam heard her silvery laugh, and was thankful; for joined with the pain of being so close to her was the unacknowledged dread that she might allow her sensibility to overcome her upbringing, and precipitate them all into embarrassment. He wondered if Jenny, placidly talking to Lord Oversley, had any conception of the ordeal to which she had exposed both himself and Julia. She appeared unconscious; and when she chanced to meet his eyes there was no suspicion in hers, but only a little, friendly smile. She seemed to be enjoying herself; and although this set her poles apart from him it relieved another of his anxieties: at his aunt's assembly, and at Lady Bridgewater's, her shyness had made her an awkward guest, but in her own house it was otherwise. There would be no need for him to keep a watchful eye on her, ready to help her over conversational hurdles, or to nudge her into a hostess's duties: she was quiet, but she was quite assured, because she had been mistress of her father's house for years, and was accustomed to entertaining his friends.

The dinner which was presently served was excellent; and since there were several topics of immediate public interest to be discussed conversation did not flag. Chief amongst these was the betrothal of the Princess Charlotte to the Prince of Orange, for so persistent were the rumours that the Princess had cried off that it was naturally a subject of paramount interest. Various reasons for the rupture were suggested; but Rockhill, who, being one of the Carlton House set, was probably better informed than anyone else present, said that he believed that the rift had arisen from the question of domicile: the Prince expected his bride to live in the Low Countries; the Princess, standing as she did in direct succession to the English throne, was determined to remain in her own country. This resolution, after some discussion, was approved; but it remained for Jenny to say that it seemed strange that the Regent should be willing to send his only child packing to foreign parts.

'Yes, indeed!' agreed Lady Oversley. 'It really makes one wonder – But I believe she is excessively like him!' She then realized that her inconsequent tongue had betrayed her, and exclaimed, with even more inconsequence: 'Which reminds me, Adam, that you must take your seat! Oversley was saying only the other day – weren't you, my love? – that he must put you in mind of it.'

'Yes, I must, I suppose,' said Adam. 'My uncle was speaking to me about it the other evening. He says he will go with me, and tell me what I must do when I get there – for I'm ashamed to say I don't know!' He saw that Jenny was at a loss, and he smiled at her, saying: 'In the House: I've a seat there, and must take an oath, or some such thing. I'm not obliged to make a speech, am I, sir?'

'Oh, no!' Oversley reassured him. 'To be sure, Nassington is the man to sponsor you, except that –'

'But he is *not* the man!' protested Brough. 'Have my father, Lynton!'

The Dowager gave this her support. She distinctly recalled having heard the late Viscount deplore Lord Nassington's Toryism, and was consequently sure that he would be much disturbed if he knew that his son was to take his seat under the aegis of a Government supporter. She then recounted a slightly muddled anecdote, told her by her father, about a party given by Mrs Crewe at the time of the great Westminster Election, at which the guests had worn blue and buff favours, which had something to do with General Washington. Or was it Mr Fox? Well, at all events, the toast had been *True Blue*.

'*True Blue and Mrs Crewe*, ma'am,' corrected Brough, well-versed in the annals of Whiggery. 'Often heard m'father tell that tale. The Prince proposed it, and she whipped back with *True Blue and all of you*! Took very well.'

This naturally brought to mind the Prince's sad change of front, now that he had become Regent; and the discussion became extremely animated. Adam took no part in it, but there was a decided twinkle in his eye; and when Brough said: 'Go with m'father, and take care you sit down on the Opposition bench!' he replied in a soft, apologetic voice: 'But I don't think I wish to sit on the Opposition bench!'

Lord Rockhill laughed; but the other three gentlemen, momentarily stunned by this shocking announcement, recovered only to break into protest, even Mr Oversley being moved to say: 'But you can't! What I mean is, must be trying to hoax us!'

Adam shook his head, which made Brough demand to know why he was a member of Brooks's. 'Oh, that was my father's doing, before I knew anything about politics!' he replied.

'You know precious little now!' said Oversley severely.

'Almost nothing,' Adam agreed. 'Only that I'm not drawn to a set of fellows who have made it their business to snap and snarl round old Douro's heels!'

'Oh, Wellington!' Oversley said, shrugging. 'The belief that his victories have been exaggerated doesn't comprise the *whole* of the party's policy, my dear boy!'

The twinkle in Adam's eye disappeared, and a rather dangerous sparkle took its place; but before he could speak Rockhill intervened, giving the conversation an adroit turn, guiding it by way of Brooks's Club to White's, and disclosing that a Grand Masquerade was to be given by the members of White's, at Burlington House, in honour of the foreign visitors. The ladies found this a topic of far more interest than politics, and at once besieged Rockhill with questions. As might have been expected, he seemed to be very well-informed, and was able not only to tell them the names of the various princes and generals who were coming in the trains of the Tsar and the King of Prussia, but also to give them a forecast of what the celebrations would be. Besides the reviews, and the formal parties, there would be illuminations, fireworks, and lavish spectacles in the parks.

'That's true,' corroborated Jenny. 'At least, I know they mean to have illuminations at India House, and the Bank, and some other places as well, for my father was telling me about it only yesterday. And a civic banquet at the Guildhall, too, with all of them going to it in procession. He is going to hire a window for us – that is to say, he can very easily do so if we should wish it!' she added, with an involuntary look down the table at Adam.

'I should rather think you *would*!' exclaimed Lydia enviously.

'You would too, wouldn't you?' said Brough, who was seated beside her. 'Can't it be contrived? I shouldn't go to Bath, if I were you: very dull sort of a place! Full of quizzes and cripples – balls end at eleven – nothing to do all day but drink the waters and parade about the Pump Room – not the style of thing you'll enjoy!'

'I know I shan't,' she sighed. 'I have to go because of Mama. It is my Duty, so of course I don't expect to enjoy it.'

Jenny, who had quick hearing, had caught some part of this interchange. She said nothing then, but a little later, when the ladies had retired to the drawing-room and the Dowager was enjoying a comfortable gossip with Lady Oversley, she moved to where Lydia and Julia were seated side by side on a sofa, and said abruptly: 'I've been thinking it over, and I believe I should ask Papa to procure a large window, or perhaps a room with several windows, so that we may invite our particular friends to share it with us. Would you care for it, Julia? And do you suppose that her ladyship might spare you for a visit to us, Lydia, so that you could see the procession, and all the other sights?'

'Oh, *Jenny*!' Lydia gasped. 'If you truly mean it, and Mama won't let me come, I'll – I'll jump on to the first stage-coach, and come *without* her leave!'

'No, that won't fit: it wouldn't be seemly,' said Jenny. 'There's no reason why she shouldn't be able to spare you, for it won't be for a few weeks yet, and you'll have time enough to settle her into her new house. I'll broach the matter to her now, while my Lady Oversley is here to add her word to mine, which I'll be bound she will do.'

She gave her little characteristic nod, and crossed the room again. Watching her, Lydia said: 'You know, Julia, one can't but like her, however much one means not to! I quite thought she would be detestable, for I was as mad as fire when I knew what Adam had done, but she's not! To be sure, I should have known she couldn't be, because she was *your* friend.'

'I never knew her,' Julia said, in a low tone. 'O God, will this evening never end?'

She got up as she spoke, and took a few hasty steps away before she recollected herself. The Dowager, seeing her standing by the pianoforte, said: 'Dear child! Are you going to indulge us with a little music? Such a treat!'

Julia stared at her for a moment as though she scarcely understood; and then, without answering, threw her fan and her reticule aside, and sat down at the instrument. The Dowager, saying how well she remembered how very superior was dear Julia's performance, resumed her conversation with Lady Oversley.

Amongst a multitude of damsels who numbered pianoforte-playing as one of their laboriously acquired accomplishments, Julia's performance was indeed superior. She did not always play correctly, but she had, besides a great love of music, real talent, and a touch on the keys which Jenny, who seldom played a wrong note, could never rival.

Lady Oversley felt relieved. She had seen how impetuously Julia had sprung up from the sofa, and she had been seized by apprehension. But she knew that once Julia sat down at the pianoforte the chances were that she would forget herself and her surroundings, and become lost in music; and so she was able to relax her strained attention, and to apply herself to the task of persuading the Dowager to look with a kindly eye upon Jenny's scheme for Lydia's entertainment.

Julia was still playing when the gentlemen came into the room. She glanced up, but indifferently, and lowered her eyes again to the keyboard, and kept them so until she had struck the final chord of the sonatina, and Rockhill, moving forward, said: 'Ah, that was very well done! Bravo! Now sing!'

She looked at him, faintly smiling. 'No, how should I? You know my voice is nothing!'

'A little, sweet voice, charmingly produced. Sing a ballad for me!'

But she sang it for Adam, her eyes meeting his, and holding them. It was a trivial thing, a sentimental air which had been all the rage a year before. She sang it softly, and quite simply, but there was always in her singing a nostalgic sadness that tore at the heart-strings, and made people remember the past, and the might-have-been.

For Adam, to whom she had sung it many times before, the song conjured up every banished memory. He was still standing, his hand resting on the back of a chair, and as he listened, unable to drag his eyes from Julia's face, it closed on the gilded wood, gripping it so tightly that his fingers whitened. Lydia noticed it, and, looking upward, saw an unguarded expression in his face which frightened her. She glanced instinctively at Jenny. Jenny was sitting very upright, as she always did, with her hands folded in her lap, and her eyes downcast; but as Lydia watched her her eyelids lifted, and she directed a long look at Adam. Then she looked down again, and there was nothing in her face to show whether she had seen the suffering in his.

Lydia began to feel uncomfortable. The opulent room seemed to be charged with emotions beyond the range of her experience. Scarcely comprehending, she was yet aware of tension. Blighted love and broken hearts were phrases which had tripped readily from her tongue; it had not appeared to her that Adam, laughing at Jenny's bathroom, poking fun at Lambert Ryde, could be unhappy, until she saw the look in his eyes as he watched Julia. It was a dreadful look, she thought, and dreadful for Jenny to see it, even if she had married him only for social advancement.

She stole a surreptitious glance round the circle. No one was looking at Adam. The older members of the party were all watching Julia; Jenny's eyes were downcast; Charles Oversley, plainly bored, was gazing at nothing in particular; and Brough, Lydia discovered, was looking at herself. There was the hint of a smile in his eyes: it drew a response from her; and this encouraged him to change his seat for the vacant space beside her on the sofa, saying under his breath: 'Musical, Miss Deveril?'

She shook her head. '*No!*'

'Good!' he said. 'Nor am I.' Under their heavy lids, his eyes glanced at Adam, and away again, as though he had intruded upon something not meant for him to see.

The song ended. Hardly had the chorus of acclamation abated than Lydia jumped up, saying: 'Jenny, you said we might play a round game! Do let me find the counters for a game of speculation!'

It was *gauche*; it made the Dowager frown; but Brough murmured approvingly, as he dragged himself to his feet: 'Good girl!'

'Speculation? Oh, no!' uttered Julia involuntarily.

Lady Oversley did not hear the words, but she saw the gesture of distaste, and braced herself to intervene. She was rescued by Rockhill, who gently shut the lid of the pianoforte, and said, smiling with amused understanding into those tragic blue eyes: 'But yes, my little wicked one! Come, Miss Mischief, I depend on you to instruct me!'

She smiled too, but reluctantly. 'You? Oh, no! You will play whist!'

'No: my attention would wander too much.' He took her hand, and held it sustainingly, saying softly: 'Put up your chin, my pretty! You can, you know.'

Her fingers clung to his. 'Ah, you understand – don't you?'

'Perfectly!' he said, the amusement deepening in his eyes.

Thirteen

ive days later, Adam left London for Lincoln-shire, promising to return within a week. He did not ask Jenny to accompany him, nor did she suggest it. He told her that he was going on business connected with the estate; and she answered that he must not think himself bound to hurry back to town if it should prove to be inconvenient to do so. He said: 'I won't fail you! Isn't there a rout-party looming, or some such thing?'

'Oh, yes, but it's of no consequence! If you should still be away I can very well go with Lady Oversley.' She added, with a gleam of humour: 'I must learn to go to parties without you, or we shall have people saying that we are quite Gothic. I expect I ought to set up a – what do you call it? – cicisbeo!'

'Not if it would mean my tripping over him every time I entered the house!'

She laughed. 'No fear of that! Though I did once have an admirer. He thought me an excellent housekeeper.'

'A dull fellow! But I must own I think so too.'

She grew instantly pink. 'Do you? I'm glad.'

It seemed to him pathetic that she should be pleased by such a mild tribute; he tried to think of something else to say, but she forestalled him, turning the conversation away from herself by asking if she should send the necessary order to the stables, or if he preferred to do it himself.

'No orders,' he said. 'I'm going down by the Mail.'

'But – When we have our own chaise, and the boys – perfectly idle, too! – and the Mail won't carry you to Fontley itself!'

'No, it will set me down at Market Deeping, where Felpham will meet me with the phaeton. As for the postilions, I must own I think it ridiculous to keep them kicking their heels at your expense. Does your father insist on their employment? Why don't you turn them off?'

'They need not kick their heels,' she said. 'They are not here only to serve me. That's not as Papa meant it to be when he engaged them for us.'

'Well, they will serve me as well as you when I take you to Fontley later on.' He saw her compress her lips, and said, after a moment's hesitation: 'Leave me some little independence, Jenny! I don't question your expenditure, or wish you to forgo any luxury, but you mustn't expect me to waste your father's money on personal extravagance. Don't look so troubled! there's no hardship in travelling by the Mail, I assure you!'

'No, but – Your father did not do so, did he?'

'My father conducted himself as though he were as wealthy as yours. His example is not one I mean to follow – even if I wished to, which, believe me, I don't! It really wouldn't make me happy to live *en prince*, as he did, and as you, I think, would like me to.'

'You must do as you wish,' she said, in a subdued tone.

He did not pursue the subject. The ice was too thin; nor did he feel able to make her understand what he could not explain even to himself. His personal thrift was illogical: to travel in a public conveyance, to drive his father's curricle in preference to the glossy new one provided for him, to make no unnecessary purchases, gave him only the illusion of independence. He knew it, but in the middle of the luxury that surrounded and stifled him he clung obstinately to his economies.

It was a relief to escape from the splendour of the house in Grosvenor Street, to be alone, to be going home; it was even a relief, when he reached Fontley, to see a worn carpet, faded chintz, a chair covered in brocade so old that it would rip at a touch. There were no modern conveniences, no mirrored bathrooms, no Patent Oil Lamps, no Improved Closed Stoves in the kitchen: water was pumped into the scullery, heated in an enormous copper, and carried in cans to the bedchambers; all the rooms, except the kitchen, where an old-fashioned oil-lamp hung, and blackened the ceiling with its fumes, were candle-lit. The house in Grosvenor Street blazed with light, for Mr Chawleigh had installed oil-lamps even in the bedrooms; but at Fontley, unless the candles were lit in all the wall-sconces, there were miles of dim passages, and one carried a single candle up to bed, guarding its flame from the draughts.

The Dowager had tried for years to induce the Fifth Viscount to renovate Fontley, asserting, with truth, that its shabbiness was a disgrace; and when he had returned to it from the Peninsula Adam had heartily agreed with her; but, escaping from the cushioned splendour of the town house, all the inconveniences of Fontley seemed to him admirable, and he would have received with hostility even a suggestion that the frayed rug in which he caught his heel should be replaced. He did not quite acknowledge it, but in his mind was a jealous determination never to allow Chawleigh-hands to touch his home; shabbiness would not destroy its charm; Chawleigh-gold would destroy it overnight.

But his acceptance of decay did not extend to his land. Here he wanted every modern improvement he could get. He might indulge foolish sentiment over a torn rug; he had none to waste on an ill-drained field, an outdated plough, or a labourer's cottage falling to ruin; and had Mr Chawleigh shared his love of the land he might have been willing to admit him into some sort of a partnership, overcoming his pride for the sake of his acres. But Mr Chawleigh, fascinated by mechanical contrivances, had no interest in agriculture. Born in a back-slum, of town-bred ancestry, there was no tradition of farming behind him, and no inherited love of the soil. How anyone could wish to live any-where but in London was a matter passing his comprehension, but he knew that the nobs (as he phrased it) possessed country estates; and since an estate added greatly to a nob's consequence Adam's value in his eyes had been considerably enhanced when he had learned from Lord Oversley that he was the owner of a large one in Lincolnshire, and of a mansion which figured in every Guide Book to the county. Lord Oversley spoke reverently of Fontley. Mr Chawleigh had no great opinion of antiquity, but he knew that the nobs set store by it, so it was obviously desirable that Jenny should become the mistress of an ancient country seat. In his view, this meant a palatial residence, set in extensive gardens, with such embellishments as ornamental water, statuary, and Grecian temples, the whole being surrounded by a park. Had he considered the matter, he would have supposed that a farm to supply the needs of the household would be attached to the mansion; but that the owner should concern himself with its management he would have thought absurd, and even improper. As for the rest of the estate, he knew that in an agricultural district this must consist largely of farms, which were let out to tenants, and from which the overlord drew a large part of his subsistence. In his opinion, it was a poor source of revenue. No one was going to make Mr Chawleigh believe that there were fortunes to be made in farming: as far as he could see, it was as chancy a business as speculating on 'Change. In any event, it was not for the overlord to meddle in such matters: whatever had to be done was done by his agent. 'Gentlemen,' said Mr Chawleigh, like another before him, 'have no right to be farmers.'

William Sidford, bailiff, was not quite sure, either, that he approved of Adam's interest in what had never interested his volatile parent, although he had welcomed the advent of a master who not only listened to what he had to say, but seemed to understand that only ruin could result from wresting every penny it would yield out of the land, and ploughing not one penny back into it. He had felt hopeful, at first, of being able to check the rot he had been deploring for years; but after spending the better part of four days in the Sixth Viscount's company he was attacked by qualms. His new master was chuck-full of modern ideas, which he had got out of books. William Sidford had no time to waste on books, and he approached new theories with extreme caution, since it stood to reason that what had been good enough for his father and his grandfather must be good enough for him. Not that he was an enemy to progress: when my lord talked of road-making, under-draining, and embanking, he was heartily in agreement with him; and he was by no means averse from adopting the Four-Course System. But when my lord began to talk about Tull's drill, and such new crops as swedes and mangel-wurzels, it became apparent to him that it was his duty to check him. Such notions might answer: he didn't say they wouldn't, nor that the Tullian Method wasn't a good one; but one thing he could tell his lordship, and that was that he wouldn't find the Tullian Method in general use amongst those who might be supposed to know their business. Having been accustomed all his life to see fields that were luxuriant in summer barren, and often flooded, in winter, he found it difficult to adjust his mind to my lord's ideas: winter crops were certainly desirable, but it would cost a mint of money to make it possible to grow them; and as for the enclosures my lord talked about, he didn't know, he was sure, but he had heard it said that enclosures made for poor lean people.

'But, according to what I have read,' said Adam, 'it is rather the open field system that does that, because it means winter idleness, with no hedges to plash, ditches to scour, draining to maintain, or drilled crops to keep clean.' He added, as William Sidford looked doubtful: 'You've told me – and I've seen for myself – that there's much distress amongst the farm labourers.'

'That's so, my lord, but it's on account of the low prices. I disremember when the times were so sickly,' Sidford said. 'By what I'm hearing, there's upwards of two hundred country banks have stopped payment – like they did a matter of twenty years ago.'

These last words were charged with significance, and referred, as Adam realized, to the financial crash of '93, in which the Fifth Viscount had been disastrously involved. It was plain that William Sidford thought the time ill-chosen for unnecessary expenditure. He began to grumble about the Corn Laws, and the Property Tax, but to deaf ears. Adam interrupted him suddenly, saying: 'Wasn't my grandfather very friendly with Mr Coke of Norfolk? Would he be willing to advise me, I wonder?'

William Sidford could advance no opinion, but none was expected, the question having been rhetorical. Adam brought the conference to an end, saying, with a smile: 'I'm woefully ignorant, am I not? I must go to school again. In the meantime, set in hand, if you please, the work upon which we *are* agreed.'

William Sidford left him to the task of composing a letter to Mr Coke. Mistrusting the cross-country mails, he sent it by the hand of one of his grooms. It was productive of an instant response: Mr Coke held the Fourth Viscount's memory in affection, and would be happy to advise his present lordship to the best of his ability. He suggested that Adam should honour him with a visit to Holkham, immediately, if that should be convenient to him. Detecting the cordiality underlying the formality of Mr Coke's reply, Adam decided to take him at his word. He dispatched a brief note to Jenny, informing her that his return to town would be a trifle delayed; and set out for Norfolk.

The apprehensions natural to a modest young man thrusting himself upon the notice of his grandfather's old friend were instantly overcome by the warmth of Mr Coke's welcome. Mr Coke, living in the inherited splendour of Holkham, was a shrewd man of simple tastes and forthright disposition. He had succeeded to the property of his noble kinsman, Lord Leicester, on the distaff side; and instead of scheming to get the Earldom revived, he had applied himself to the task of improving and developing a large estate whose rent-roll amounted to no more than two thousand guineas. Today, rather less than forty years later, it more nearly approached the sum of twenty thousand pounds, and the handsome young man of whom no one had heard had for long been a power in the land. He had never made the least push to get the title revived: he was content to be Mr Coke of Norfolk; and neither his wealth nor his unchallenged supremacy in the agricultural world altered his kindly, unpretentious character. He entertained all sorts at Holkham, from Royal Dukes to quite insignificant persons, and treated everyone alike, without ceremony, but with a genuine desire to make his guests comfortable. In this he was ably seconded by his youngest daughter, who kept house for him. Within a very few minutes of having his hand warmly grasped, and a likeness traced in his countenance to his grandfather, Adam felt at home; and by the time he had spent an evening in his host's company he found himself able not only to ask for advice but to take Mr Coke far more deeply into his confidence than he would previously have believed to be possible.

The problems besetting him in the Lincolnshire fens were not precisely those which had confronted Mr Coke in Norfolk, but Mr Coke's knowledge was not confined to the conditions of his own county. He gave Adam wise counsel, conducted him over his own experimental farm, and patiently instructed him in the intricacies of successful agriculture. When Adam left Holkham, he carried with him, besides a sheaf of notes, a head crammed with so much information that he felt slightly dazed. It would take time to assimilate all he had learned: meanwhile, one fact only stood out clearly: to restore his acres to prosperity would entail the expenditure of far more money than he could hope to raise.

He reached London late one evening, and in a conscience-stricken mood, having overstayed what he felt to have been his leave of absence by a full week. He found Jenny in the drawing-room, at work on one of her chair-covers, and paused on the threshold with such an expression of apprehensive guilt on his face that she burst out laughing, and exclaimed: 'Oh, you look just like a naughty little boy found out in mischief! How can you be so absurd?'

He laughed too, but said, as he came across the room to bend over her and kiss her cheek: 'Well, that's precisely what I feel I am! I beg your pardon, Jenny: it was infamous of me! Didn't I promise I'd come home to go with you to some party or another?'

'Yes, but I told you it was of no consequence: I went with Lady Oversley.'

'You are a great deal too forgiving. An agreeable party?'

'Yes, very. Naldi sang, and I met an old acquaintance there – a girl that was at school with me, and is married now to a Mr Usselby.' Her eyes narrowed in amusement. 'I couldn't but laugh inside myself! I've never clapped eyes on her since she left Miss Satterleigh's, but you'd hardly believe how enchanted she was to meet me again, now that I'm Lady Lynton!'

'What an odious female! I hope you gave her a set-down?'

'Oh, no! Why should I? I'm sure it wasn't to be wondered at,' she responded. Her eyelids lifted as the butler came in, bearing the massive silver tea-tray. This was set down on a table before her, and, having satisfied herself that a plate of freshly-made macaroons stood upon it, she nodded dismissal, and began to make the tea.

'How comfortable this is!' Adam remarked, sinking into a chair. 'I thought you must have had tea more than an hour ago, and had quite made up my mind to it that I should get none – for I shouldn't have dared to ask for it, after my abominable perfidy!'

'Well, what a notion to take into your head!' she said. 'As though you might not have tea whenever you chose to call for it in your own house! Oh, you're joking me, are you? I have a very good mind to hide the macaroons from you!'

'Not my favourite macaroons as well?' he exclaimed. 'Jenny, that's coals of fire! What made you think I should arrive tonight? Or is it just a lucky chance?'

She did not tell him that she had given orders for macaroons to be made every day, but only smiled, handing him the plate, and asked him if his business at Fontley had prospered.

'Well, not entirely, perhaps – but never mind that! I went on to Holkham, you know. I wished you had been with me: you'd have liked it, I think. They are the kindest people – just Mr Coke, and his daughter: a very unaffected, intelligent girl. I was charged with all sorts of civil messages for you, and pledged myself to take you there for the Holkham Clippings, in August. Ah! I've had no tea like this since I left town! You don't know how often I've yearned for it! *Exactly* as it should be! Thank you!

Tell me what you have been doing since I left you! Not drudging over that stitchery all the time, I do trust?'

'Oh, dear me, no!' she responded. 'I have been going about a great deal, I promise you, besides receiving more morning-callers than I looked for.' She paused, longing for the courage to ask him what had been engaging his time at Fontley. He enquired, instead, who had been her morning-callers. Her countenance betrayed neither hurt nor chagrin; tacitly accepting his reserve, she began to enumerate her visitors, adding one or two caustic comments which made him laugh.

He was glad to discover from her account of her activities that she seemed to be finding her feet in society. She had attended several parties, visited an exhibition, driven in the Park with one of her new acquaintances, and had even ventured to invite the Adversanes to go with her to the Opera – though not without misgiving. 'But Brough told me they don't rent a box, and it seemed a shame ours should be standing empty, when it was *Alceste*, which Lady Adversane was particularly wishful to hear, so I plucked up my courage, and asked her if she would be so kind as to go with me. She didn't take it amiss, so I was glad I'd done it.'

'I expect she was very much obliged to you. It comes as news to me, however, that we rent a box at the Opera House. What do we pay for it? Or don't we?'

Her colour rushed up; she cast him a wary glance, faltering: 'Papa thought – It was a present to me, because he knows I'm fond of music. I'm sorry!'

'Why should you be? It's I who owe you an apology: I ought to have attended to the matter – but I expect your box would be rather above my touch! I believe one is obliged to pay four hundred guineas for a quite inferior box, which I feel sure yours is not.'

She was silent, her face wearing the wooden look which he had come to recognize as a sign of discomfiture. His own colour rose; ashamed of having allowed his temper to ride him, he said penitently: 'Now I *do* owe you an apology! Forgive me – or give me a trimming! Why don't you? I certainly deserve that you should!' She gave him instead a tiny shake of the head, and a tremulous smile. He said, with quick compassion: 'My poor dear, you're too patient – and will soon have the devil of a husband on your hands if you don't take care! So you went to the Opera, and enjoyed it, I hope. What else?'

It was a moment before she could recover her balance, but she managed to do it, and to respond, with a little chuckle: 'Well, I went with Mrs Usselby to a lecture by the Memory Man!'

'The *what*?'

'Memory Man – I've forgotten his name, but he is all the crack, I promise you! He teaches one how to remember everything, by supposing rooms with compartments – fifty to each room! Someone said he had reached the seventeenth room, but a Mr Frampton, who came up after the lecture to talk to Mrs Usselby, said he would wager he would be in a puzzle if he were asked to say what was in the forty-seventh compartment! I don't think there's anything more to tell you – except about the Peace Celebrations. There's a great deal of what your Aunt Nassington calls *tracasserie* about the White's Club ball, because by some means or another the Princess of Wales has contrived to obtain tickets for it, and the Prince Regent declares he won't go to it if she does. I don't know how it will be, or what the truth is, and I don't believe anyone does, for everyone has a different story to tell about it!' She paused, drew a breath, and said, with a slight effort: 'The civic banquet is fixed for the 18th. I don't know if you recall – if you would wish –'

He came to her rescue, anxious to make amends for his previous ill-humour. 'Yes, to be sure I do. You were so kind as to invite Lydia to town to see all the lions go in procession to be fed. I think you said your father could procure a window for us. Has he done so? Lydia will be thrown into transports!'

'Well, she is!' Jenny disclosed, thankful to have cleared this fence, and speaking in a far more relaxed tone. 'If only your mama will consent to let her come to us! I had a letter from Lydia yesterday. It seems they are pretty well established in the new house, so that there's no reason why Lydia can't be spared for a few weeks – particularly as she says your mama has met an old acquaintance with whom she is so excessively pleased that she talks of inviting her to stay in Camden Place, to bear her company. Apparently, she is living in straitened circumstances, and – and –'

'Toadeats Mama?' he interpolated.

'Well, that's what Lydia says,' Jenny admitted. 'In fact, she says Mrs Papworth is a Mrs Quarley-Bix – but that I don't at all believe.'

'Good God, I hope not! So Lydia comes to us?'

'I do hope she may, but she says that Lady Lynton has certain scruples – not liking the notion of Lydia's travelling without a proper escort, and not being able to spare Miss Poolstock to go with her.'

'I'd give much to read Lydia's account of this!' he commented.

She laughed, but shook her head. 'No, she didn't say I might show it to you, so I shan't. And I'm sure it is very natural that Lady Lynton should be anxious. The thing is, couldn't we send Martha, in our own chaise, to fetch her? Do you think it would answer?'

'What I think is that is nothing more nor less than a piece of fudge!' he replied impatiently. 'As for your sending Martha, nonsense! Pray, why should you be expected to spare *your* dresser?'

'But I'm not expected to,' she argued. 'It's quite my own notion. I perfectly understand your mama's feelings – for the maid that waits on Lydia is far too young to answer the purpose, you know.'

'I don't – and nor do I know why a young maid won't serve as well as an older one for such a simple journey. If Lydia were obliged to spend a night on the road it would be another matter, but it's no such thing. Send your chaise, if you wish (though that's nonsensical too!), but certainly not Martha!'

She said submissively: 'I won't, if you forbid me, but I wish you won't! I'm afraid Lady Lynton won't let Lydia come to us otherwise, and only think how disappointing! I should like so much to have her with me: indeed, I've been making all sorts of schemes!'

He was as much pleased as surprised. 'Do you really wish it? You're sure she won't be a charge on you?'

'A charge on me! I should think not indeed! It will be the most delightful thing imaginable, to have her company, and to take her to see the sights! Do, pray, let me offer to send Martha!'

'If you really wish to, of course – but I think it by far too good-natured of you, and I don't care to see you imposed on in such a way.'

'Well, what a thing to say!' she exclaimed. 'As though your mama would dream of doing so! I'll write to her immediately. She saw Martha when we were at Fontley, so she will know that Lydia will be perfectly safe in her care.'

She was mistaken. The Dowager, replying with the utmost graciousness to her letter, could not reconcile it with her conscience to permit her young and inexperienced daughter to face the hazards of travel without male protection. Only a mother, she added, could enter into her sentiments, or appreciate how much it cost her to be obliged to deny her dearest child the offered treat.

'Upon my word!' exclaimed Adam, handed this missive to read. 'Mama playing off her tricks! Depend upon it, this is nothing more nor less than a determination to keep Lydia dancing attendance on her. It is too bad! Now what's to be done? Am I to go down to Bath to fetch her? Is that what you wish?'

'Would you do so?' Jenny asked diffidently.

'Yes, I suppose so. What a bore! Very well, I'll contrive to go somehow or other – though when I'm to find the time I don't know! I'm to take my seat on Tuesday, and we seem to have a host of engagements besides. Don't tell Mama I mean to fetch Lydia! No doubt it will be best to take her by surprise.'

In the event the Dowager was taken more by surprise than Adam had foreseen. Mr Chawleigh took a hand in the affair.

Mr Chawleigh, according the plan for Lydia's entertainment his approval, had been following the progress of events with great interest. He saw nothing but what was praiseworthy in the Dowager's scruples; and when what seemed to him a very easy way out of the difficulty presented itself he seized upon it, delighted to be given the chance of enacting Providence. Adam came home one afternoon to be confronted by a stricken bride, who raised apprehensive eyes to his face, and faltered: 'Adam, I must tell you! I didn't know — I never meant — I'm afraid you'll be vexed, but indeed I couldn't help it!'

He put up his brows enquiringly. 'Shall I? Try me!'

'It's — it's Papa!' she blurted out. 'He has gone to fetch Lydia from Bath!' She saw the look of astonishment in his face, and hurried on: 'He sent a note round to me by one of his clerks, just as he was leaving town, so I *couldn't* stop him! It seems he has to go to Bristol on business, and he wrote to say you needn't be in a worry how to find time to fetch Lydia, because he means to return by way of Bath, and will bring her up to town himself. He doesn't understand — that is, he only wishes to be helpful, Adam!'

She ended on a note of entreaty, dreading his displeasure. There was a moment's silence, while he struggled with his emotions. They were too strong: he gave a gasp, and burst into laughter.

She had only the dimmest perception of what made him laugh, for she was not quick to perceive the ridiculous, and she was not assailed, as he was, by a vision of Mr Chawleigh's descent upon the house in Camden Place; but she was too thankful that he was amused rather than vexed to care for the cause of his mirth. She smiled doubtfully at him, and said: 'It's one of his surprises. I told you once how he loves to give one splendid surprises, didn't I?'

'You did, Jenny, you did! Oh, if only I were there to see it!'

She considered this, and said quite seriously: 'Do you think her ladyship won't let Lydia go with him?'

'No, my love. From what I know of your father I confidently expect to see Lydia within the week!' he replied, in a shaking voice.

Fourteen

*T*hree evenings later, just as he was sticking a pin in the folds of his neckcloth, Adam was interrupted by sounds unmistakably betokening his sister's arrival. A peal on the front-door bell, accompanied by the vigorous use of the knocker, was shortly followed by the scamper of footsteps on the stairs, and Lydia's voice calling gleefully: 'Adam! Jenny!'

He grinned, and went out on to the landing in his shirt-sleeves.

'Oh, Adam, isn't it famous? Here I am!' cried Lydia, casting herself upon his chest. 'Mr Chawleigh brought me – and in *such* style! Oh, Jenny, there you are! I do think your papa is the kindest person in the world! Mr Chawleigh, Mr Chawleigh, come up, pray! They are both here!'

Released from a hug that had irreparably damaged his freshly-tied neckcloth, Adam endorsed this invitation, saying, as he looked over the banisters: 'Yes, do come up, sir! – if you have strength enough left after a day spent in this hoyden's company! How do you do, sir? I am very much obliged to you!'

Mr Chawleigh, ponderously ascending the last flight, grasped Adam's outstretched hand, and replied, his countenance wreathed in a broad smile: 'Ay, I thought you would be! Well, Jenny-lass, I've brought her to you, all right and tight, you see, and no fear you'll fall into the dismals with *her* about the house! I'll be off now I've seen her safe in your hands.'

'By all means – if you wish to offend us beyond forgiveness!' said Adam. 'Or do you imagine that Jenny holds household in such a nip-cheese way as to be put out by the arrival of a mere couple of unexpected guests? You should know her better!'

'I *told* you so!' interpolated Lydia triumphantly.

'But you've company? Nay, I won't stay!' said Mr Chawleigh.

'No, we haven't, Papa: it's only that we are going, later, to Lady Castlereagh's assembly – and we need not, need we, Adam?'

'We need, but not for a few hours yet. Come into my dressing-room, won't you, sir, while I finish rigging myself out? Fetch up the sherry, Kinver!'

'Nay, I can't sit down to dinner with you in all my dirt!'

'Well, that's a pretty thing to say, when we had it fixed that you would take me to dine at an hotel, if we found no one at home here!' interrupted Lydia indignantly. 'You didn't say you couldn't sit down in all your dirt when it was only me!'

Delighted to be overborne, Mr Chawleigh went with Adam into his dressing-room, chuckling and shaking his head. 'If ever I met such a saucy puss! Well, I don't know when I've taken such a fancy to a girl, and that's a fact!'

'I'm glad. I'm rather partial to her myself, but I own I was afraid you might find her a trifle exhausting!'

'It 'ud take more than Miss Lyddy to exhaust Jonathan Chawleigh. As good as ever twanged, *she* is. You wouldn't credit how quickly the time passed! Ay, and a real pleasure it is to set her down to a nuncheon! *She's* not one to ask for tea and toast when you've fairly bust yourself, ordering what you think she might fancy! Well, we stopped for a bite at the Peacock – and a set of robbers they may be, but I will say this for them: a very tolerable spread they had laid out for us, for I'd bespoken it beforehand, and a private parlour too, of course, which I told her la'ship I'd done, just to set her mind at ease. "No need to fear I'll be letting Miss Lydia set foot inside a common coffee-room," I said, "nor that any pert young jackanapes will come ogling her while Jonathan Chawleigh has her in charge. She'll be taken care of as if she was my own daughter, and fairer than that I can't say." Which she was, as I hope I don't need to tell you.'

'No, indeed you don't. Did you – did you find it hard to persuade my mother?'

'Oh, no!' replied Mr Chawleigh indulgently. 'Mind you, that's not to say she didn't raise a lot of nidging objections: but that was no more than female fiddle-faddle – not meaning any disrespect towards her la'ship! – and soon settled. "Now, don't you tease yourself over her being a trouble to me, ma'am," I said, "because she won't be; and as for her not being ready to go to London I'll warrant she could be ready in five minutes if she chose. So I'll take myself off to the Christopher, where I'm racking up," I said, "and be back first thing in the morning to take Miss Lydia up." So there was no more said, for she saw I wasn't taking no for an answer.'

This account was later amplified by Lydia, who said that however ungenteel Mr Chawleigh might be he was, in her view, a splendid person. 'Adam, he *rolled* Mama out like pastry! There was never anything like it! Though I must own that the lobsters helped.'

'Lobsters?' Adam interjected, fascinated.

'Oh, he brought a couple of live ones from Bristol, and a jar of ginger, for a present to Mama! They were in a rush basket, and one of them kept trying to climb out. Well, you know what Mama is, Adam! She couldn't take her eyes from it, which quite distracted her. And then Mr Chawleigh mended the handle on the drawing-room door. It has been most troublesome, but he said he could set it to rights in a trice, if we had a screwdriver. We hadn't, of course – I think it's a sort of chisel – but he said very likely we had something that would answer as well, and he went off to the kitchen to see what he could find there.' She gave a gurgle of laughter. 'If you could have seen Mama's face! Particularly when he came back, and read her a scold about the damper in the stove. He said it was being quite wrongly used, and told her exactly how it should be. I was nearly in stitches, because poor Mama hadn't the least notion what he was talking about! And this I *will* say: she behaved beautifully, and even invited him to stay to dine with us, which was truly noble

187

of her! However, he wouldn't do so, but said he hadn't come to put her out, and anyway had bespoken his dinner at the Christopher. And though she said nothing would prevail upon her to let me go with him, she did let me, because she was persuaded she would have one of her worst spasms if she had to see him again!'

'But what a scene!' he said, awed by it. 'And I wasn't there! It's too infamous!'

She chuckled. 'Yes, but I daresay you might not have enjoyed it if you had been, on account of having more sensibility than I have, and not wishing Mama to take him in dislike. For my part, I like him, and I don't give a straw for his being a funny one: in fact, we have become the greatest friends, and he is going to take me to the City, and show me all the chief places, *and* let me watch them mint the coins in the Tower, and *everything*!'

It was soon seen that she was making no idle boast. Not only did Mr Chawleigh redeem this promise, but he began to visit Lynton House more frequently, and always with some scheme for Lydia's entertainment. It seemed to him a great piece of nonsense that she could not go with her brother and sister to parties, and he was much inclined to take Jenny to task for not presenting her at Court immediately.

'Well, I wish I might,' she replied, 'but I haven't Lady Lynton's leave to do so, as I've told you a dozen times, Papa! You wouldn't have me behave so improperly as to do it without her leave – now, you know you wouldn't!'

'If only I'd thought to speak to her la'ship about it!' he said. 'I don't doubt I could have talked her over. And if I'd known Miss Lydia would be obliged to sit moping here while you and his lordship go gadding to all manner of grand parties – I'll tell you what, puss! – you and me will drive into the City to see the illuminations, and have a bite of supper at the Piazza afterwards! That is, if his lordship's agreeable!'

'Of course he'll be agreeable!' declared Lydia, delighted with this scheme. 'I should like it better than anything too!'

'Yes, but only if Adam says you may go,' Jenny said firmly, by no means sure that he would approve of his sister's jauntering about the town with her parent.

When she broached the matter to him, however, he merely said: 'How kind of your father! No, I've no objection – if he really wishes to take her, and won't find it a bore.'

'Oh, there's no question of that!' she replied. 'He says it's a pleasure to take her about, because she enjoys herself so much.' She added reflectively: 'She is just the sort of girl he would have liked for his daughter, I think. She has so much *zest*, besides being full of drollery!'

'For my part, I think he is very well satisfied with his own daughter!'

'I know he loves me dearly, but there's no denying I'm often a sad disappointment to him. Well, it can't be helped, but I do wish I was pretty, and spirited, and amusing!'

'I don't – if *spirited* means what I suspect it does. As for amusing, I think you *very* amusing, Jenny!'

'That's polite, but you mean you think me absurd: a very different thing!' she retorted. 'I daresay you won't object either to my taking Lydia to Russell Square one day? She wants to see the Cossack, who stands outside Mr Lawrence's house whenever the Tsar goes there to have his likeness taken! Did you ever? If it isn't just like Papa to tell her that! Butterbank is friendly with Mr Lawrence's man, you know, and so is able to warn Papa when the Tsar is expected. Myself, I don't care a button for the Tsar – or for the King of Prussia, either; though he's very handsome, I own, in spite of looking so melancholy. And I'm sure I don't blame him for that,' she added, 'for the way he and the rest of them can't stir a foot without having crowds gaping at them is enough to throw anyone into gloom!'

'Don't let Lydia tease you into going to Russell Square if you don't care for it!' he said. 'She'll see the foreigners at the Opera, after all.'

'She won't see the Cossack there. Come to think of it, she won't see much of the Kings and Princes either, because our box is on the same side as the Royal box. Still, there will be plenty more to look at, I daresay.'

She spoke more prophetically than she knew: there was far more for Lydia to look at than anyone could have foreseen. Her view of the Regent, with the Tsar on one hand, the King of Prussia on the other, and a bevy of foreign notables grouped behind them, was restricted; but the Lyntons' box was admirably situated for anyone desirous of seeing the Princess of Wales.

She had been excluded from participation in any of the Royal festivities; but she had her revenge on the Regent, sweeping into the box directly opposite his while 'God Save the King' was being sung. She was attired in black velvet, with a black wig on her head, supporting a diamond tiara, and she presented such a striking figure that she attracted the attention of nearly everyone but her Royal husband.

The anthem ended; and as the Grassini, whose rich contralto voice had led it, curtsied deeply to the Royal box, a storm of clapping broke out in the pit. It was directed pointedly at the Princess, but she took her seat without making any acknowledgement, only smiling wryly, and saying something to one of her suite.

The Regent, meanwhile, had been applauding the Grassini, but the prolonged clapping made him turn, and bow graciously – but whether he bowed to the audience or to his wife was a question hotly argued but never decided.

However it may have been, it seemed to Lydia a rare piece of good fortune that anything so startling should have happened at the very first public function she had attended; and it made her forget that the evening had begun none too comfortably.

Jenny had bought her a swansdown tippet for the occasion, and had persuaded her to wear the pearls Lady Nassington had declared to be too large for her own neck; but when Adam had seen his sister he had said quite sharply: 'Where had you that necklace? Surely it is Jenny's?'

'Yes, she has lent it to me just for tonight. Isn't it kind of her?'

His face had stiffened, but he said pleasantly: 'Very kind, but

I had rather you didn't. It's worth a king's ransom, you know – and I'm certain Mama would say it was not the thing for a chit of your age!'

'No, she wouldn't! She says that pearls are the *only* jewels *chits of my age* may wear! And I promise to take the greatest care –'

'Haven't you a necklace of your own?' he interrupted.

'Yes, but mere trumpery! If Jenny chooses to lend her pearls to me I don't see why *you* should object!' Lydia said indignantly.

Jenny laid a hand on her arm, saying in rather a tight voice: 'Perhaps they are not quite the thing. Your own crystals will be better – they are very pretty, after all! Come upstairs quickly, and change the necklace before Brough arrives! *Please*, Lydia!'

Lydia was suddenly aware of tension, and glancing from Adam to Jenny saw that Jenny's face was much flushed. Yielding to the tug at her wrist she went out of the room with her, but demanded as soon as the door was shut: 'But – but *why*?'

Jenny shook her head, and hurried up the stairs. 'I shouldn't have – he is perfectly right: you are too young!'

'But why should he be so vexed? It isn't at all like him!'

Jenny took the pearls from her, and turned away to restore them to her jewel-casket. 'He wasn't vexed with you. Don't heed it!'

'Was he vexed with you, then? But what had you done, pray?'

'It was only that he didn't like to see you wearing my pearls. It was stupid of me! I forgot – it didn't occur to me –'

She broke off, and forced up a smile. 'Are you ready? Shall we go downstairs?'

'Do you mean that he didn't like me to wear pearls that aren't my own?' asked Lydia. 'But I have often worn Charlotte's trinkets!'

'That's different. Adam has scruples – I can't explain! One should take care, if one is very wealthy, not to – not to obtrude it! Well, it was a downright vulgar thing to have done! I didn't mean it so, but that's what it was: tossing my pearls to you like that!'

'It was excessively kind of you!' said Lydia. 'Sisterly! Like buying this tippet for me! I collect Adam would object to that too?'

'Oh, don't tell him!' Jenny begged. 'It's only a trifle, after all, but – Hark! wasn't that the knocker? We must go down. I told them to serve dinner as soon as Brough arrived, because it won't do to be late at the Opera House.'

She left the room, putting an end to further discussion. But Lydia had nothing to say. A curtain had been lifted, allowing her a glimpse behind the scene of what had seemed to her innocence a state of remarkable felicity. Too young to probe beneath the surface, it had not occurred to her that two people who presented to the world an appearance of calm content might not be as happy as they seemed. It was not the first time she had had such a disquieting glimpse, but on the previous occasion Adam had recovered himself so quickly that she had soon been able to forget the incident. He and Jenny seemed to stand on such easy terms that she had not wondered whether there were shoals beneath those placid waters. To his seventeen-year-old sister it was almost impossible to suppose that Adam was still in love with Julia. Sacrifice Lydia could appreciate; a smiling sacrifice was much harder to recognize, and very hard indeed to understand.

It was in a perturbed mood that she followed Jenny down to the drawing-room. There had been more than vexation in Adam's face when he had seen that she was wearing Jenny's pearls: there had been a look of revulsion; and Jenny had recognized it, and had been hurt by it. Between Adam and Jenny there could be no comparison; but it was, nevertheless, unkind of him to have wounded Jenny, who hadn't meant to offend him.

She was relieved to see, as she entered the drawing-room, that he smiled warmly at Jenny. Perhaps, she thought hopefully, as she shook hands with Brough, she had refined too much upon the incident; perhaps Adam really felt that the pearls were too magnificent for a girl to wear.

Had she but known it, he was deeply conscious of having allowed his revulsion to overcome his forbearance. Seizing the opportunity afforded by her being engaged with Brough, he went up to Jenny, saying in a lowered tone: 'Thank you! I shouldn't have enjoyed a minute's peace if you hadn't persuaded her to take it off! What a hare-brained thing to do, to lend your pearls to my romp of a sister!'

She answered only with a constrained smile. He was tempted to leave the subject, but she was wearing her wooden look, always a sign of distress. Infamous to have wounded her, he thought, when she had meant nothing but good! He tried again. 'What's more, it wouldn't be at all the thing for a girl in Lydia's circumstances to go about with a fortune round her neck.'

Her countenance relaxed; she said: 'No, very true! I hadn't considered – I only thought how well the necklace would become her. I'm sorry!'

'Which it certainly did! Poor Lydia! I wish I may not be in disgrace with her!'

She laughed; and Lydia, hearing her, instantly forgave Adam. Perhaps married persons were subject to tiffs; at all events, everything was comfortable again, with Jenny her placid self, and Adam in quite his best spirits. She went down to dinner feeling that it was going to be a good party after all, which, indeed, it was. Nor was there any further sign of misunder-standing between Jenny and Adam, so that she was soon able to banish the incident from her mind, and to think instead of all the excitements in store for her.

The best of these, in her opinion, would be the processions of the Allied Sovereigns to the Guildhall; for Jenny, everything else dwindled to insignificance beside the gilt-edged card which invited Lord and Lady Lynton to attend a Dress Party at Carlton House on Thursday, 21st July, to have the honour of meeting her Majesty the Queen. Jenny's first thought, on receiving this, was that it must be a hoax; her second that it was a thousand pities Lydia could not attend the function. She was astonished to learn that Lydia had no particular desire to attend it; and quite shocked by the discovery that the Regent, in Lydia's view, was a fat old man, who creaked when he moved, and reeked of scent and Diabolino. He had visited Fontley when she was a very little girl, and she had been obliged to endure his pinching her cheek, and calling her sweetheart. 'And the Queen is a snuffy old thing,' she said. 'Watching the processions will be far better sport!'

Besides the four Oversleys, and Brough, Jenny had invited Mr and Mrs Usselby to go with them on this occasion. It was Adam's private conviction that some of the guests would fail to arrive before the Strand was closed to vehicles; but he found that he had underrated Jenny's talent for organization. She invited all the guests to partake of an early breakfast in Grosvenor Street, saying that she had not taken parties to watch the Lord Mayor's Show for years without learning how to arrange such affairs. 'It's my belief that if you invite people to go to a show you must get them together, and *take* them to it, if you don't wish to be in a worry, wondering if they'll arrive in time.'

Thanks to this foresight all went smoothly, the guests assembling at Lynton House for breakfast, and going on afterwards in three carriages to the Strand. They reached their destination without much trouble, but early in the day though it was the street was fast filling with sightseers. Stabling had been arranged; but how long it would be after the processions had passed before the crowds converging upon the route dispersed sufficiently to allow the passage of vehicles was a question which caused Lord Oversley to remark ruefully to Adam that they might think themselves fortunate if they reached their homes again in time for dinner.

Mr Chawleigh, with his customary munificence, had hired the whole building for the accommodation of the party; and, besides ordering a large and varied nuncheon from Gunter's, with several cases of his best champagne, he had sent Butterbank, with two liveried subordinates, to wait on the company. Lady Oversley was quite as much startled as Mrs Usselby at being received by two footmen, but when she had been conducted upstairs to the first floor, and saw that besides the benches set up in the windows the room had been furnished with several comfortable chairs she was easily able to condone this ostentation. Adam found it more difficult, but not by the flicker of an eyelid did he betray that these lavish preparations had been made without his knowledge or approval. The Usselbys might exchange significant glances, but Mr Charles Oversley, forgetful of the indifference befitting a man of mode, ejaculated, as his eyes fell on the table already spread with pies, pâtés, capons, a glazed ham, and fruit, creams, and jellies past counting: 'By Jupiter, this is something like!'

There were some hours to while away before the head of the procession was expected to come into sight, but the time passed more quickly than the more pessimistic members of the party had expected. Lady Oversley sat down to enjoy a cosy chat with Jenny; Lord Oversley fell asleep over the *Morning Post*; and the rest of the party gathered in the two windows, discussing such topics as the breaking-off of the Princess Charlotte's engagement, and the shocking result of Lord Cochrane's trial; and being amused by watching the crowds in the street, and laying bets on which of the females within view would be the next to drop down in a swoon.

Since Brough was devoting himself to Lydia the merest civility must have obliged Adam to sit down beside Julia, but Lady Oversley, stealing more than one apprehensive look towards them, wished that she knew what they were saying to each other. She would scarcely have been reassured had she been able to overhear their conversation, for a chance recollection had led to the exchange of reminiscences, which she must have thought dangerous. Recalling visits to Fontley, Julia said with a sigh: 'I suppose it is all changed now.'

'Nothing has been changed there,' Adam replied.

'I'm glad. Your mama was used to complain that it was become shabby, but it was so beautiful! I loved it, and should weep to see it made smart.' She raised her eyes to his face. 'Is it agreeable to be very wealthy?'

'I am not very wealthy.'

'No? Well, the wealth may be Jenny's, but your life is very

luxurious, isn't it? It must be pleasant to have everything you want, I suppose.'

He stared at her for a moment, but said at last, evenly enough: 'I suppose so – if it were possible.'

She again raised her eyes, and he saw the tears in them. 'Everything that can be bought. They say happiness can be bought. I had not thought so, but I don't know. Are you happy, Adam?'

'How can you ask me such a question?' he said. 'You must know –' He stopped, and looked away from her.

'I want to know. You seem happy. And I wonder if, perhaps –' She broke off, a tiny frown on her brow. 'I may be married myself soon,' she said abruptly. 'Shall you care for that?'

It was like a blow over the heart, but he had schooled himself to withstand it, and he replied: 'Yes. But I shall wish you very happy. There's nothing else left to us but to wish each other well, is there? Who – Or must I not ask?'

'Why not? It's Rockhill, of course.'

'Rockhill?' he repeated incredulously. 'You're not serious? A man old enough to have been your father, and one, moreover, who – You can't mean it!'

She smiled rather mournfully. 'If you could marry a fortune, why should not I?' she asked.

'The case is different! You know why I –' he checked himself.

'Oh, yes, I know! But did you think I had fallen in love? *Could* you think so?'

'Not that! But – O God, I don't know! Only that every feeling revolts – !'

'Does it? Every feeling revolted in me once, but I didn't tell you so.' He could not answer her, and she said in a softer tone: 'Don't mind it! I mean to try if I can't be a little happy. He's charming, you know, and when I'm with him I feel – oh, peaceful! No, not quite that – I can't explain! But he loves me, and I must be loved! I can't live if I'm not loved!'

They were interrupted. Mr Oversley exclaimed that he could hear cheering in the distance, and adjured his parents to come to the window directly. All was bustle at once, and Adam had time to recover himself while everyone's attention was distracted. As he performed his duties, arranging his guests suitably in the windows, no one would have guessed that beneath his smiling calm a tumult of emotion was raging. Julia's words had been knife-thrusts; he winced under them, and was startled to recognize in the medley of rage, jealousy, and hopeless desire, resentment. The thought flashed through his mind that she might have spared him. It was gone in a moment, yielding to remorse, and an aching pity. Though he had been the victim of circumstance he was the author of her unhappiness, and that she was unhappy he could not doubt: she had spoken them in a whisper, but her last words had been a cry; and in her lovely face had been a look that was almost distraught.

'Here they come!' Lydia's voice broke in on his painful thoughts. 'Oh, how dashing! Adam, what are they? Which regiment?'

He was standing behind her, and leaned forward to look down at the escort. 'Light Dragoons,' he replied, adding, as his eyes took in the buff facings on the blue uniforms: 'The Eleventh – the Cherry Pickers!'

She began to demand an explanation of this nickname, but broke off as the first of the seven carriages carrying the officers of the Regent's household followed the escort. In identifying these personages Brough was found to be more knowledgeable than Adam, who was able to relax his attention again. Mrs Usselby was positive she had recognized General Playoff amongst the foreign generals, but admitted, after argument, that she must have been mistaken, since the Tsar's procession, coming from the Pulteney Hotel, would follow the Regent's.

The state carriages bearing the Royal Dukes followed the generals. Adam glanced towards the other window, to be sure that everyone was enjoying a good view. His eyes fell on his wife's face. She was standing, like himself, behind her guests, and never had she looked plainer. There were spots of high colour on her cheekbones, but under them she was sallow, a trifle hagged. He looked away, unable to bear the comparison with Julia, seated quite close to her.

The Speaker's coach had passed, and the carriages bearing the members of the Cabinet. A troop of Horse Guards came next, preceding the Regent's officers of state, and the foreign suites. As these carriages went slowly past a slight movement to his right made Adam turn his head just in time to see Jenny going unobtrusively out of the room, her handkerchief pressed to her lips. He hesitated; and then, remembering that he had several times thought that she was looking dragged and weary, he withdrew quietly from the window, and followed her.

She had gone into the back-parlour, and had sunk into a chair there. Her eyes lifted as he entered; she removed the handkerchief from her mouth to say faintly: 'It's nothing! I shall be better directly – pray go back! Don't say anything about this!'

He shut the door, looking at her in concern. 'You are ill, Jenny: what is it?'

'I was overcome by the heat. Oh, do go back! I shall come in a minute.'

'I'll see if Lady Oversley has any smelling-salts. *You* don't carry them, I know!'

'*No!* I don't need them, and I don't wish anyone to know!'

'But –'

Her chest heaved. 'I don't feel faint. I feel *sick*!'

This unromantic disclosure made him smile, but it was with real compassion that he said: 'My poor dear!'

'It's nothing!' she repeated.

He went back into the other room, to collect a bottle of champagne from the wine-cooler. Nearly all his guests had their attention fixed on the eight cream horses drawing the Regent's state carriage, but Lady Oversley looked round as he came into the room, and came to him, whispering: 'Is Jenny unwell? Shall I go to her?'

He replied beneath his breath: 'Just a trifle overcome by the heat. Don't heed it! She can't bear that anyone should know, and be made uncomfortable.'

She appreciated this. 'To be sure! Tell her she may depend on me to turn it off, if anyone should remark on her absence. Take my salts! You'll fetch me, if you should need me.'

Thus armed, he returned to the other parlour. Jenny was leaning back in her chair with her eyes closed, but she opened them when he held the vinaigrette under her nose, and said angrily: 'Where had you that? I most particularly asked you not to tell anyone!'

'Stop ripping up at me, little shrew! I had it from Lady Oversley, and all I told her was that you were overcome by the heat. I was obliged to do so, because she had seen you slip away.'

She subsided, and took the vinaigrette from him, sniffing, and saying crossly: 'Such stuff! *Me* to be languishing over a bottle of smelling-salts! Now, don't go opening that champagne, for I don't want it! I'm better, and there's no need for any commotion on my account!'

He thought she looked far from well, but he merely said, as he eased the cork out of the bottle and poured the frothing wine into a glass: 'Try if my cordial doesn't make you feel a degree stouter! Come, Jenny! – to please me!'

The coaxing note brought a tinge of colour back into her cheeks; she received the glass from him in a hand that shook slightly, and said in her gruffest voice: 'Thank you! You're very good!'

He waited until she had drunk some of the wine, and had begun to recover her complexion, and then said: 'Now tell me, Jenny, what's the matter? You've been out of sorts lately, haven't you? Have you been trotting too hard?'

'No, of course I haven't!'

'Then what is it?'

She cast him a goaded look. 'If you *must* know, I'm increasing!' she said baldly.

Fifteen

*I*t had not occurred to him that she might be pregnant, and surprise held him silent, just staring at her. She said defensively: 'Well, it was only what was to be expected, after all! I mean I'm breeding, you know.'

His lips quivered. 'Yes, I understand that, but – I beg your pardon, but *really*, Jenny – !'

'I don't see what there is to laugh at,' she said, eyeing him in resentful bewilderment. 'I thought you would be glad!'

'Yes, yes, of course I am! But to fling it at me like that, and at such a moment – !' His voice shook, but he controlled it, saying contritely: 'I'm sorry – don't look so affronted! I won't laugh at you any more! But what's to be done? You goose, to have come on such an expedition as this! How the devil am I to get you home?'

She sat up, replying with something like her usual briskness: 'You'll get me home when the show's over, and not before, thank you! I'm better now. I told you there was no need for you to be in a worry, and nor there is. It's no more than natural I should have sick turns – though I must own it quite takes the edge off one's pleasure!'

He gave a tiny gasp. 'I imagine it must!' he said unsteadily. 'Poor – poor Jenny!'

'Yes, I can see you think it's highly diverting!' she retorted.

'No, I don't – it's *you* I think highly diverting, not your sickness, I promise you! Are you sure you are well enough to remain here? I wish you had told me before ever we arranged this party!'

'Fiddle!' she said, getting up, and straightening her shoulders. 'I'm in a capital way now. For goodness' sake, don't get into a taking, Adam, for there's nothing wrong with me, and if there's one thing I can't bear it's setting people in a bustle, and having them fidgeting round me, as if I was going into a decline! And mind, now! not a word to Papa!'

'But, my dear – !' he exclaimed, considerably startled. 'Surely you don't mean to keep it secret from him?'

'That's just what I do mean to do, while I'm able. I wouldn't have told you either, if I hadn't been obliged to, because it's early days yet, and no sense in boasting of what might not come to pass after all. Now, Adam, you don't know Papa as I do, so you'll be pleased to do as I bid you! The instant he knows I'm in the family way he'll fly into one of his grand fusses, wanting to keep me in cotton, let alone bringing in half the doctors in London to drive me crazy! You may ask Martha, if you don't believe me! She'll tell you the same, and that I'll do better without being cosseted, what's more!'

'Oh, does Martha know?' he asked, rather relieved.

'Well, of course she does! Now, if you'll pour me out a drop more of your cordial, I shall be as right as a trivet again, and we'll go back to watch the rest of the show. And don't think I shall go off in a swoon, or anything of that kind, for I shan't, and so I promise you!'

He was obliged to fall in with these plans, though with considerable misgiving. They rejoined the rest of the party just in time to see the Tsar's procession pass, and to learn that not even the presence in his carriage of the King of Prussia had deterred certain persons in the crowd from hissing the Prince Regent. If their absence had been noticed, no one commented on it. The show being at an end, thoughts turned towards nuncheon. Adam kept a watchful eye on Jenny, but although she ate nothing but a morsel of capon, and two spoonfuls of jelly, she showed no signs of succumbing again to nausea. The fear, however, that the festivities might prove too much for her remained with him, and although he continued to talk to his guests his brain was occupied in trying to decide what to do if she should be taken ill. It was not until he handed her out of the carriage, in Grosvenor Street, that his mind returned to his conversation with Julia, and even then it did not engross his thoughts. It was no more forgotten than a bruise which gave pain whenever it was touched, but Jenny's pregnancy was a matter of greater importance, because she was his wife, and he was responsible for her well-being.

He was uneasily aware of having failed to respond to her announcement with the delight she had expected him to feel. Though she had immediately concealed it under a more than ordinarily matter-of-fact manner, he thought he had seen a look of chagrin in her face. He was sorry for it, but try as he would he was unable to conjure up any more fervent emotion than a detached feeling that an heir to his name would be desirable. He was more concerned for Jenny, who was obviously enduring a good deal of discomfort. She never mentioned the matter, except to reply to enquiry that she was very well; and to one accustomed to the Dowager's demands for sympathy over the most trifling disorders this stoicism appeared to him far more admirable and unusual than, in fact, it was. He wanted her to consult a doctor, but she would not. 'If you mean I should send for Dr Wrangle, who is the only doctor I'm acquainted with, I won't do it! For one thing, he's an old woman, and for another, he'd tell Papa within the hour, because he'd be afraid for his life not to. And if you mean I should see an accoucheur, there's time and to spare for that, for he couldn't advise me better than Martha, and very likely not as well. So just you forget all about it, my dear, or you'll make me sorry I ever told you!'

'That's asking too much of me. Have I no part in this?'

She gave a sudden chuckle. 'To be sure you have, but you've played it, and the rest's my business!'

'Jenny, this want of delicacy in you puts me to the blush!'

'Well, but – Oh, you're laughing at me! Now, Adam, do but leave me to manage for myself! I promise you I'll do just as I ought.'

'But are you doing just as you ought? All this junketing about the town with Lydia – ! Tell me the truth: wouldn't it be best to send her back to Bath? She has seen all the lions, after all!'

'Yes, I can see what *you'd* have me do!' she retorted. 'Lie on a sofa all day, with that nasty vinaigrette which Mrs Quarley-Bix gave me, in my hand!'

'No, indeed! but I do wonder if I ought not to take you out of town while you are feeling so poorly. Cheltenham, perhaps, or Worthing, or –'

'Oh, do you?' she interrupted. 'Well, I'm sure I'm very much obliged to you, my lord, but I've no fancy for any such place! What a notion to take into your head, with the cards sent out already for our own assembly, and the party at Carlton House, not to mention the Thanksgiving at St Paul's –'

'Good God, we're not going to that, are we?' he exclaimed.

'Well, we are if Brough can procure tickets for us, which he says he can easily do, through my Lord Adversane, I collect. Now, don't put on that Friday-face, Adam! I'm as eager as Lydia is to go! As for sending her back to Bath before the Grand Spectacle in the parks, I won't hear of it! What with a balloon ascent in the Green Park, and the battle of Trafalgar to be fought on the Serpentine in the evening, let alone the Temple of Concord to see, and the Chinese Pagoda, and goodness only knows what more besides, it would pretty well break her heart to be obliged to miss it!'

'Jenny, if you imagine that I am so complaisant as to permit you to kill yourself, trudging all over the parks to inspect a collection of gimcrackery –'

'No, it's you that will do that, my lord!' she said, with another of her sudden chuckles. 'Or Brough, more likely. I shall see all I want to from the carriage, and so I promise you!' She hesitated, and then said: 'Lydia is to go back to Bath as soon as that's over, and I should like it if you would take me down to Fontley. To – to stay, I mean.'

'Of course I'll take you there,' he replied. 'To Holkham too, if you should feel able for it. I don't think you'd care for Lincolnshire during the winter months, so –'

'If I gave you my word not to meddle – change anything – any more than if I was a visitor – ?'

He stared at her, so much shocked by these halting words that for a moment he could think of nothing to say. He had been glad to escape to Fontley from the stifling luxury of Lynton House, but he had never acknowledged to himself that he did not want to see Jenny installed there. It was true, however, and she knew it; and the humble note in her voice when she uttered her request, the look that told him she was afraid of a rebuff, shamed him more than any spoken reproach. He thought, in horror: *I take everything, and give nothing.*

'I know you don't wish me to be there, but I shouldn't tease you,' she said simply.

He pulled himself together, forcing into his voice a lightness he was far from feeling. 'Are you trying to give me my own again, for having laughed at you? What if I tell you that of course I don't wish for you, and think myself much more comfortable without you? *That* would make you look no-how, wouldn't it?'

She smiled, but doubtfully. 'I do make you comfortable, don't I?'

'No, not a bit! Now, be serious, Jenny! Is that really what you would like to do? You don't say it because you think it's what *I* wish?'

'Oh, *no!*' she exclaimed, her brow clearing. 'I should like it of all things! Why, you know how much I enjoyed being at Rushleigh!'

'That was in the spring – and in Hampshire. Whether you will like the fens in winter-time is another matter. Well, if you don't, you must tell me so – or if you are bored to tears, which I'm afraid you may be. When is this absurd Grand Spectacle to take place?'

'On August 1st.'

'*August?* My dear girl, we shall find ourselves in a hurly-burly of –'

'Cits?' she suggested, as he broke off abruptly.

A slight flush betrayed him, but he made a quick recover.

'Nothing so respectable! Jackstraws and counter-coxcombs! Does your father know of this project?'

Her eyes narrowed in a sudden smile. 'That was a master-stroke!' she said disconcertingly. 'Lord, do you think I don't know *Cits* was on the tip of your tongue? Yes, Papa knows, and sees no objection. But if you don't care for Lydia to go –'

'What I don't care for is that you should be knocked-up merely to give Lydia pleasure,' he retorted.

'Well, I shan't be.'

'I'll see what Martha has to say on that head.'

Miss Pinhoe, however, when he consulted her, snubbed him severely, giving him to understand that his solicitude was misplaced, and that any attempt to cosset Jenny was to be strongly deprecated. 'We shall have enough of that when the Master gets to hear of it,' she said grimly. 'You leave Miss Jenny to me, my lord!'

He was glad to be able to do so, but he thought that the secret would not be kept for long from Mr Chawleigh. Very little escaped Mr Chawleigh's penetrating eyes, and once he had perceived that Jenny was looking sickly he would certainly demand to know the cause.

But Mr Chawleigh's eyes were dazzled by a vision of vicarious grandeur, and although he did notice that Jenny was not in her best looks he merely recommended her not to wear herself to a bone with gadding about. 'A nice thing it would be, my girl, if you was to knock yourself up before the party at Carlton House!' he said.

Mr Chawleigh could not think of this function without rubbing his hands together gleefully; nor, whenever he visited his daughter, could he resist the temptation to pick up the card of invitation, and to gloat over it, very often reading it aloud.

'To think how close I came to telling my Lord Oversley you'd be no manner of use to me!' he told Adam, in a burst of confidence. 'Why, a Marquis couldn't have done better for my Jenny! Well, it was a great day for me when I saw her go off to Court to be presented, but no more than what I bargained for, after all. But *this* – ! The Lord Chamberlain being commanded by his Royal Highness to invite you and Jenny to a Dress Party, to have the honour of meeting her Majesty the Queen! I don't scruple to own that I never looked for anything as bang-up as that, my lord!'

Adam, who was becoming inured to his father-in-law's frank utterances, laughed, but disclaimed responsibility. 'No bread-and-butter of mine, sir! We owe the invitation to my father, who was one of the Prince's friends, you know. I hope Jenny will enjoy it.'

'Enjoy it! You may lay your life she will! Ay, and I'll enjoy hearing all about it, I can tell you, and thinking how proud Mrs C. would have been, if she'd been spared to see her wish come true.'

'Perhaps she can see it,' suggested Adam.

'Well, I like to think she can,' confessed Mr Chawleigh, 'but there's no saying – and no sense in getting into the dismals either, you'll be telling me.'

'I shan't, but you put me in mind of a crow I have to pull with you, sir: Jenny tells me that you don't mean to come to our rout-party.'

'No, that I don't, and a fine trimming I gave her for sending me a card – not but what I take it very kind in you to invite me! A pretty figure I'd cut, rubbing shoulders with the nobs! Nor I'm not going along with you to St Paul's neither, so let's hear no more of that!' He gave a deep chuckle. 'Eh, the way my Jenny told me she was getting tickets from my Lord Adversane! "Brough's father," was what she called him, to the manner born!'

Adam was slightly mystified by this, so he left it unanswered, reverting instead to the subject of the approaching rout-party. But to all his persuasions Mr Chawleigh remained adamant, saying, with embarrassing candour, that if my lord started to dish him up at his parties he would soon find that his acquaintance had dropped off.

It was soon made apparent that although he would not attend

the party he had every intention of making his presence felt at it, so keen an interest did he take in the arrangements for it, and so determined was he that it should excel in magnificence every other party held during the Season. 'Order everything of the best!' he adjured his daughter. 'I'll stand the nonsense, never you fear! You'll be wanting half-a-dozen footmen: I'll send those fellows of mine along. And no need to trouble yourself about the champagne, because I'll attend to that, and I warrant you'll hear no complaints from your guests!'

'Thank you – we are much obliged to you, but I've already attended to that matter, sir,' said Adam, trying to speak cordially, and not quite succeeding.

'Then I'll be bound you've wasted your blunt, my lord!' responded Mr Chawleigh tartly. 'Beef-witted, that's what I call it – meaning no offence! – for you might ha' known I could buy it cheaper, *and* better, than what you could!'

Baulked on this issue, he veered off on another tack, offering to augment the Lynton silver with his own formidable collection of plate, to make, he explained, more of a show. This suggestion drove Adam from the room, too angry even to excuse himself. He betook himself to his book-room, and here Jenny found him, some time later. He looked at her with alien eyes, and said curtly: 'Jenny, I have no wish to wound your father, but I shall be obliged to you if you will make it plain to him that I want neither his footmen nor his plate, nor, let me add, do I desire him to frank me!'

She replied calmly: 'As though I didn't know it! Now, there's not a bit of need for you to get into a miff! Just keep a still tongue in your head, my dear, and leave me to deal with Papa – which I promise you I can do! There'll be nothing done you don't like, and I've no more intention of letting him frank us than you have. That's what I came to tell you, for I could see Papa put you into a regular flame.'

He relaxed, saying: 'I hope he could not!'

'Well, he did, of course, but that's no matter. He's one that likes to be giving, and he don't always see when people don't want him to butter their bread on both sides. I've told him how it is, so you may be easy.'

'I'm not at all easy,' he confessed. 'I ought to beg his pardon for behaving so churlishly.'

'No such thing! I don't say he enters into your *feelings*, but he doesn't like you any the worse for not wishing to hang on his sleeve. Don't give it another thought!'

If he was unable to follow this advice, at least he took care to conceal from Jenny that Mr Chawleigh's subsequent activities caused him to feel an even greater unease. Mr Chawleigh, prohibited from bringing his daughter's party up to the nines, turned his attention to the question of her personal appearance. His rout by Lady Nassington still rankled in his mind; and his energies were next alarmingly directed to the task of turning Jenny out in what he called prime style, and what Adam shudderingly thought would transform her into a walking advertisement for a jeweller's shop. He never knew by what means she had dissuaded her father from purchasing for her a ruby and diamond tiara which had taken his fancy; and since she agreed to all Mr Chawleigh's suggestions for her embellishment he was agreeably startled by the discovery, on the night of the party, that she was wearing no other jewels than the delicate necklace approved by Lady Nassington, the diamond aigrette which he had himself given her as a wedding-present, one ring, and only two of her many bracelets.

There was another improvement, for which he was indebted to his sister. Lydia, critically studying the fashion-plates in a periodical devoted to current modes, had suddenly exclaimed: 'Jenny, this would become *you*!'

Looking over her shoulder at the sketch of a willowy female clad in a ball-dress of white satin with a three-quarter pelisse of pale blue, Jenny said bluntly: 'Well, it wouldn't. It would make me look more squat than Nature did, you silly girl!'

'Oh, not the *dress*!' Lydia said. 'The hair! No curls, you see, and no crimping, which I think *hideous*, like Mama's crape! Now, if you were to arrange your hair like this, it would be becoming, and not just in the common style, which my Aunt Bridestow says is *most* important, unless, of course, one has the good fortune to be a Beauty.'

Jenny studied the drawing rather doubtfully. To one accustomed to the effect produced by curl-papers and hot irons the willowy lady's smooth braids presented a very odd appearance. 'I'd look like a dowd,' she decided.

'Do but try it!' coaxed Lydia. 'You know you mean to have it washed and curled again for the party: well, when Martha has washed it, let *me* dress it for you! I have often done so for Charlotte, and even Mama owns that I do it better than Miss Poolstock. And if you don't care for it, Martha can curl it for you after all.'

Jenny allowed herself to be persuaded, not without misgiving. But when Lydia's clever fingers had done their work, and she studied her reflection in the mirror she was not displeased. After a prolonged scrutiny, she said: 'It seems queer not to have curls over my ears, but there's no denying my face doesn't look so broad – does it?'

'Exactly so!' said Lydia. 'You must *never* have those bunches of curls again, but always dress your hair close at the sides, and braid it into a coronet on the top of your head. And I wish you will stop sniffing, Martha! Don't you see how well her ladyship looks?'

'It's not a proper mode, miss,' said Miss Pinhoe obstinately. 'Curls are smart, and nothing will make me say different! And what his lordship will say, when he sees what you've done, I'm sure I don't know!'

'Oh, I do hope he won't think I've made a figure of myself!' Jenny said apprehensively. 'Well, if he don't like it, you must curl it for me again, Martha, and that's all there is to it.'

'I'll have the tongs hot inside of ten minutes, my lady,' promised Martha grimly.

But they were not needed, since Adam, after a quick look of surprise, was pleased to approve of the transformation. 'Turning out in new trim, Jenny?' he asked. 'You'll be setting a fashion!'

'Lydia dressed it for me. Do you like it? Pray tell me truthfully!'

'Yes, I do. Quakerish, but elegant. You look charmingly,' he said.

She did not suppose him to be sincere, but the compliment pleased her, nevertheless, and made the ordeal of receiving some sixty or seventy guests of ton seem less daunting. Any lingering doubts were presently banished by Lady Nassington, who ran a critical eye over her, and said: 'Very good! you begin to look like a woman of quality.'

While it did not rank amongst the Season's most fashionable squeezes the Lyntons' first assembly passed off very creditably. Mr Chawleigh would have voted it a shabby affair; but Jenny, warned by Lady Nassington, offered her guests no extraordinary entertainment, or any excuse for the ill-disposed to stigmatize her party as pretentious. She relied for success on the excellence of the refreshments; for, as she sagely observed to Lydia, guests who had been uncommonly well-fed rarely complained of having endured an insipid evening.

Another circumstance helped to make the party agreeable: there was no lack of conversation, for the Princess Charlotte had once more furnished material for gossip by escaping from Warwick House to her mother's residence in Connaught Place. Everyone was agreed that the flight was attributable to the Regent. There seemed to be no doubt that he blamed the Princess's ladies for the rupture of her engagement, and so he had exercised a father's right to dismiss her household and to install a new staff of ladies. No one could censure him for that; but it was generally thought that to descend upon Warwick House at six o'clock in the evening and there and then to effect this sweeping change was conduct calculated to drive a high-spirited girl into revolt. It had apparently done so, and however deplorable the affair might be it came as a blessing to a hostess fearful of seeing her guests smothering yawns before flitting away to other and more amusing parties. Lady Lynton had scored a hit, for she had sent a card of invitation to Miss Mercer

Elphinstone, and Miss Mercer Elphinstone was not only the Princess's close friend: she had actually been at Warwick House when these exciting events took place, and had been one of the several persons dispatched by the Regent during the course of the evening to persuade his daughter to return to her home. The engagement of the great Catalini to sing at it could not have conferred more distinction on the party than Miss Mercer Elphinstone's presence. Everyone wanted to know whether the Princess and her mother had refused admittance to Chancellor Eldon; whether the Duke of York and the Bishop of Salisbury had been made to kick their heels in the dining-room at Connaught House while the Princess deliberated in the drawing-room with her mother's advisers; whether she had been taken back to her father by force; or whether she had yielded on the advice of Brougham and her Uncle Sussex. And what was to be the outcome?

Miss Mercer Elphinstone was unable to satisfy curiosity on this point, but it was learned within a few days that the Princess had been packed off to Cranborne Lodge, a small house in Windsor Park, where she was residing under much the same conditions as might have been thought suitable for a State prisoner.

'Well, I'm sorry it all happened before the Carlton House fête,' said Jenny, 'for it means I shan't see her, and I did hope I might.'

'Whatever for?' demanded Lydia.

'Well, she's going to be Queen one day, isn't she? Stands to reason anyone would want to see her!'

As she had expected, she was denied this treat, but so splendid was the fête that instead of regretting the Princess's absence she forgot all about it.

The fête was held in honour of the Duke of Wellington, whose bust, executed in marble, was placed in a temple erected at the end of a covered walk leading from a huge, polygon room, especially built by Nash in the garden for the occasion. Jenny was a little disappointed at seeing no more of Carlton House than the

Great Hall, with its coved ceiling and yellow porphyry pillars, but this disappointment too was forgotten when she had passed through this vestibule to the polygon room, which was hung with white muslin, with mirrors past counting flinging back the lights of hundreds of candles. She gave a gasp, and told Adam that she had never seen anything so beautiful in her life.

At half-past ten the Royal party entered the room, the Regent leading the procession with the aged Queen on his arm; and after a lavish supper the Princess Mary opened the ball with the Duke of Devonshire for her partner. Since she was nearing her fortieth year and he was no more than four-and-twenty they might have been considered an ill-assorted couple, but only the irreverent indulged this reflection. The Princess Mary was the Beauty of the Family, and the custom of describing her as a remarkably handsome girl was of too long-standing to be readily altered.

It was past four o'clock when the Queen took her departure. Adam bore Jenny away after this, saying, as their carriage moved forward under the colonnade: 'My poor dear, you must be dead from fatigue!'

'I fancy you are more fatigued than I am. Is your leg paining you?'

'Lord, yes! It has been aching like the devil these two hours past. That's nothing: standing for too long is always a penance to me. I was afraid you might faint at any moment. Insufferably hot, wasn't it?'

'Lord Rockhill says the Regent is terrified of draughts. I thought at first that perhaps I *should* faint, but I soon grew accustomed. Oh, Adam, I can't tell how many people spoke to me, and as for the number who bowed and smiled – well, there was never anything like it! I couldn't believe it was me, Jenny Chawleigh, saying how-do-you-do to all those grand people!'

'I'm glad you enjoyed it,' was all he could think of to say.

Her enjoyment, as might have been expected, was as nothing to Mr Chawleigh's. He listened with rapt interest to her account of the festivity, drew deep breaths when she enumerated all the guests of high rank with whom she had exchanged civilities; and sat rubbing his knees, and ejaculating such phrases as: 'Bang-up to the knocker!' and: 'To think I should have lived to see this day!'

A very little of Mr Chawleigh in this mood was enough to drive Adam from the room. His more robust sister might derive affectionate amusement from this display of unabashed vulgarity; Brough, who was present, might regard Mr Chawleigh with a tolerant twinkle, but he could not. Yet less than a week later he suffered a revulsion of feeling when he walked into the drawing-room to find Mr Chawleigh displaying to Jenny a superb *sang de boeuf* bowl he had that very day acquired.

'Oh, how beautiful!' Adam exclaimed involuntarily.

Mr Chawleigh turned a beaming countenance towards him. 'Ain't it just? *Ain't* it?'

'It's K'ang-hsi, Adam,' Jenny informed him. 'The T'sing Dynasty, you know, when the art of Chinese porcelain was at its height.'

'I don't – but I can well believe it! I never saw anything more exquisite!'

'You like it, my lord?'

'I should rather think so, sir!'

Mr Chawleigh gazed lovingly at it for an instant, and then held it out to Adam. 'Take it, then! It's yours!'

'Good God, sir, no!'

'Nay, I mean it! You'll be doing me a favour!'

'Doing you a favour to take such a treasure from you? My dear Mr Chawleigh, I *could* not!'

'Now don't say that!' begged Mr Chawleigh. 'You take it, and I'll know I've hit on something which you *do* like, and that'll give me more pleasure than what putting it into one of my cabinets would, for it's something I was thinking I never would do. You don't drive the curricle I had built for you, nor –'

His cheeks burning, Adam interrupted: 'I – I found my father's curricle, almost new – ! It seemed a pity – and I had a fancy to –'

'Ay, well, no need to colour up! Your taste don't in general

213

jump with mine. Lord, did you think I hadn't twigged that? No, no, a Jack Pudding I may be, but no one's ever called Jonathan Chawleigh a bleater!'

'Certainly *I* have not!' Adam said, trying to hide his discomfiture. 'As for my not liking what you've given me, sir, ask Jenny if I wasn't delighted with the shaving-stand you placed in my room!'

'*That's* nothing! You take this bowl, my lord, and it *will* be something.'

'Thank you. I can't resist – though I know I ought!' Adam said, receiving the bowl from him, and holding it between his hands. 'You are a great deal too good to me, but you need never think I don't value this treasure as I should. You have given my house an heirloom!'

'Well,' said Mr Chawleigh, much gratified, 'I'm sure I didn't look for you to say that, but I don't deny it's as good a piece as you'll find anywhere – and not bought for a song either!'

Jenny said, in a practical tone that betrayed none of the relief she felt: 'Now, where will you have it put, Adam? It ought to be under lock and key, but it won't look well all amongst the Bow China, and I don't care to turn that out of the cabinet, for it belongs to your family, besides being very pretty.'

'Don't trouble your head over it, my dear! I know just where I mean to put it,' Adam said, turning the bowl carefully between his thin fingers. 'What a lustre, sir! How can you bear to part with it? No, Jenny, it would *not* look well amongst the Bow China! It is going to stand alone in the library at Fontley, in the embrasure at present occupied by that very ugly bust of one of my forebears.' He set the bowl down on the table, saying as he did so: 'When you come to visit us, sir, you shall tell me if *you* approve of *my* taste!'

'Nay, I wouldn't want you to put it in your ancestor's place!' said Mr Chawleigh. 'It wouldn't be seemly!'

'My ancestor can remove himself to the gallery. I don't want to look at him, and this I do want to look at. There are wall-sconces on either side of the embrasure, sir, and – But you will see for yourself!'

'Now, don't you run on so fast, my lord!' Mr Chawleigh admonished him. 'It's not by any means a settled thing that I'll be visiting you in the country.'

'You're mistaken, sir. I know you don't care for the country, but you must resign yourself.'

'Well,' said Mr Chawleigh, intensely pleased, 'I don't deny I'd like to see this Fontley of yours, but I told you at the outset you wouldn't find me foisting myself on to you, and no more you will.'

'I hope you'll think better of that decision, sir. I shall be obliged to kidnap you, if you don't. That's a fair warning!'

Mr Chawleigh's formidable bulk was shaken by chuckles. 'Eh, it would puzzle you to do that, lad – my lord, I *should* say!'

'You should not – as I have frequently told you! It wouldn't puzzle me in the least: I should hire a gang of masked bravoes to do the thing. So let us have no more of your flummery, sir!'

Mr Chawleigh thought this an excellent joke, but it was not until he had been assured that he would not arrive at Fontley to find the house full of his son-in-law's grand friends that he could be brought to consent to the scheme.

'A nice thing when I have to beg and pray my father to pay me a visit!' Jenny said severely. 'And well do I know you wouldn't have hesitated, not for a moment, if Lydia had been going with us!'

This sally made Mr Chawleigh laugh heartily. He denied the accusation, but admitted that it seemed to him a great pity Lydia was not to remain in her brother's charge.

In this opinion he met with agreement, but neither Adam nor Jenny could feel that it would be proper to keep her away from the Dowager, whose letters were becoming ever more querulous, and who described herself as counting the moments until her youngest loved one should be restored to her.

So, when the fête in the parks was over, Lydia went regretfully back to Bath, bearing with her a store of rich memories, and renewed theatrical longings. One visit to Drury Lane had been enough to set her on fire. She had sat spellbound throughout a performance of *Hamlet*, her lips eagerly parted, and her wide gaze fixed on the new star that had appeared in the theatrical firmament. So entranced had she been that she had barely uttered a syllable from start to finish; and when she had emerged from this cataleptic state she had begged to be taken home before the farce, since she could not endure to listen to any other actors in the world after having been so ravished by Kean. Subsequent visits (two of which she had coaxed out of Mr Chawleigh) to see Kean play in *Othello*, and *Riches*, had confirmed her in her first opinion of his genius, and had provided her with her only disappointment: that she had come to London too late to see him as Shylock, in which rôle he had taken the town by storm in this, his opening London season. In the first heat of her enthusiasm she could imagine no greater felicity than to play opposite him, and startled Jenny by evolving various schemes for the attainment of this object. These quite scandalized Mr Chawleigh, who begged her not to talk so silly, and nearly promoted a quarrel by saying that he couldn't see what there was in such a miserable little snirp as Kean to send the town mad.

Adam entered gravely into all his sister's plans, and was far more successful than Jenny or Mr Chawleigh in convincing her that they would not answer. He wasted no breath on foolish arguments, but he did suggest that perhaps Kean might not think a lady half a head taller than himself quite the ideal stage partner. These casual words sank in; Lydia became thoughtful; and when it next occurred to her sympathetic elder brother that an actress who excelled in comedy would find too little scope for her genius in the company of one acclaimed for his portrayals of the great tragic rôles, she was most forcibly struck by the truth of this observation. So, although it would have been too much to have said that she no longer cherished hankerings, Adam was reasonably confident, when he put her on the Bath Mail with her maid, that she would not prostrate their fond parent by divulging them to her.

Sixteen

*T*wo days later the Lyntons left London, driving to Fontley by easy stages and in the greatest comfort. Much to Jenny's relief Adam showed no disposition to practise any of his economies, but carried her to Lincolnshire in all the luxury to which she was accustomed.

For her, the journey, in spite of some queasiness, was the most agreeable she had as yet experienced in Adam's company. Their previous expeditions had taken place when they were so barely acquainted that being shut up together for several hours at a stretch had imposed a strain on them, neither knowing whether the other would like to talk, or to remain silent; and each being anxious not to bore or to appear bored. This awkwardness no longer lay between them; and although they spoke of nothing that went far below the surface they talked with the ease of intimacy, and were able to lapse into companionable silences without feeling any compulsion to seek a new topic for conversation.

At Fontley Jenny was glad to be idle for some days. She even admitted that she was a *little* tired, but she assured Adam that the quiet of the country was all that was needed to restore her to high health. He thought, but privately, that it would not be long before she was wishing herself back in London, for however much he might have to occupy him at Fontley he could not imagine what she would find to do.

But Jenny, wandering about the rambling house, peeping into dust-sheeted rooms, discovering treasures in forgotten corners, knew that there was plenty to do. It was work after her own heart, but so morbidly afraid of offending was she that she hardly dared even to alter the position of a chair. When they had entered the Priory Adam had said: 'I daresay you will wish to make changes. My mother, you know, doesn't take much interest in household matters – no such capital housewife as you are, Jenny! Dawes will show you all about, and you must do as you think proper, if you please.'

She did not say: *I am only a guest in your house,* but it was what she thought, for he uttered the speech just stiltedly enough to betray that it had been rehearsed. It was prompted by his courtesy: she appreciated its generosity, but if he had told her not to meddle she would have been less daunted.

Charlotte, driving over from Membury Place, did not help to put her at her ease. She came full of kind intentions; but when she entered the Priory she could not help casting an anxious glance round the Great Hall, which was not lost on Jenny. Charlotte had not seen Lynton House since Mr Chawleigh's hand had fallen heavily upon it, but she knew all about the green stripes, the sphinxes, and the crocodile-legs, and she had dreaded to discover that Fontley had been transformed already into something more nearly resembling Bullock's Museum than a gentleman's country seat. Relieved to detect no change in the Hall, she accompanied Jenny upstairs to the Little Drawing-room, saying as she tucked a hand in her arm: 'Dear Jenny, you must let me thank you for being so kind to Lydia! She wrote to me, you know: one of her pelting letters, crammed with the tale of her doings! Four pages! Lambert said, in his droll way, that he was thankful she was able to get a frank from Adam, for it would otherwise have ruined us to receive it!'

'Well, there's no need to thank me, for I never enjoyed anything half as much as having her with me,' replied Jenny. 'I miss her sadly, I can tell you.'

'Oh, I'm glad! To be sure, I think everyone must like her, for she is the dearest girl, besides being what Lambert calls full of fun and gig!' They had by this time reached the Little Drawing-room, where Charlotte instantly perceived an alteration. She exclaimed: 'Oh, you have taken away the marquetry sewing-table!'

It was mere comment, but it threw Jenny on to the defensive. 'I have only moved it into the library,' she said stiffly. 'Adam told me I might do so.'

'Yes, of course! I didn't mean – It just seemed strange not to see it where it was always used to be! But I know many people dislike marquetry: my cousin Augusta can't bear it!'

'I like it very much,' replied Jenny. 'It is exactly what I need for my silks and threads, so it was wasted in this room. Adam likes to sit in the library in the evening, you know. We have taken up our readings again – he was used to read to me when we were at Rushleigh – and that's why I moved the table, so that I'd have my embroidery ready to my hand.'

'Oh, yes! How cosy! I remember thinking how exquisitely you stitched when Mama and I visited you in Russell Square and so much admired the work you were engaged on. It quite put me to shame – and Mama, of course, was never a needlewoman.'

Jenny could not help wondering how the Dowager had occupied herself at Fontley. Her inspection of the house had given her the poorest opinion of her mother-in-law: besides being no needlewoman she was no housewife either. She had told Jenny that she had been obliged to let the house fall into disrepair, but in her place Jenny would have set stitches to the first split in a brocade curtain; and if her domestic staff had been so much reduced as to have made it impossible for them to keep the furniture polished she would have set about the task herself rather than have allowed wood to grow dull and handles tarnished. She thought that Fontley had suffered as much from a negligent mistress as from an improvident master. The Dowager would have renovated it in excellent taste; but she lacked Jenny's eye for an undusted table, or a corner left unswept, and, in consequence, her servants had grown careless, even Mrs Dawes, the housekeeper, finding it easier to join her mistress in bemoaning the want of extra footmen and chamber-maids than to keep the remaining servants up to their work. Jenny held Mrs Dawes in contempt, and showed it. She did not mean to do so, but she knew nothing of dissimulation, and her blunt tongue betrayed her. When every evidence of neglect was attributed to the want of an adequate staff she grew more and more curt, finally losing her temper when Mrs Dawes said: 'In the old days, my lady, we always had a steward, and a groom of the chambers, and things were different.'

'Well, I should hope they were!' said Jenny. 'Though what a steward has to do with keeping linen in good order I'm sure I don't know!' She saw the housekeeper stiffen, and added, in an attempt at conciliation: 'I can see that more servants are needed, and I'll speak to his lordship about it.'

But the mischief was done. Mrs Dawes was icily civil thereafter, and showed her hostility when Jenny discovered a dinner-service in one of the cupboards, and exclaimed as she inspected it: 'Good gracious, why is this never used, but only that Bristol set, with every plate chipped? Have it all taken out and washed, if you please! It is most elegant!'

'That, my lady, is the Crown Derby china,' responded Mrs Dawes loftily.

'To be sure it is, and with the Chantilly pattern too. Is it quite complete? We will use it instead of the other.'

'Certainly, my lady,' said Mrs Dawes, her eyes downcast, and her hands primly folded. 'If it is his lordship's wish to have the best china used every day I will have it taken out immediately.'

Jenny bit back a tart rejoinder. 'I daresay his lordship won't know one set from t'other, but we'll see!'

She put the question to him as they sat at dinner, saying: 'I find you have the prettiest Crown Derby china stowed away in a cupboard – the French sprig pattern. Mrs Dawes seems to think it must not be used, but should you object to it if we did use it, my lord?'

'*I?*' he said, putting up his brows. 'Of course I should not!'

'No, I thought you would not – or even notice it!' Jenny said, with one of her sudden smiles.

He perfectly understood why the question had been put to him; he said, knowing that his words would spread through the house: 'I daresay I might not. In any event, my dear, I have nothing to say in such matters, and wish you will do as you think best. You are the mistress of Fontley: I shan't dispute with you over *any* changes you may like to make.'

Later, he asked her if she would prefer another housekeeper in Mrs Dawes's place. She said at once: 'Oh, no! Pray don't think – I know she has been here for ever, and didn't mean –'

'Try not to rub against the servants!' he said. 'I should be very reluctant to turn any of the older ones off: Dawes knew Fontley before I did, you know!'

'Oh, no, no! I never meant – Only they despise me so!' she blurted out.

'They won't do so when they know you better.' He hesitated, and then said gently: 'Don't speak to them quite so roughly, Jenny! Most of them are such very old friends of mine!'

'I don't know how to talk to servants,' she confessed. 'You do – but it wouldn't do for me to copy you. I'll try to go on better, but it does vex me so when – Well, never mind! Is the cook an old friend of yours?'

This sudden question made him laugh. 'I don't think I've ever laid eyes on the cook!'

'No, very likely not, for he's only been here a twelvemonth. Now, I told you I wouldn't meddle, but there's no teaching that man his trade, Adam, and to see you pecking at your food as you do is more than I can bear – though I'm sure I don't blame you! So, if you're agreeable, we'll send for Scholes, and then maybe you'll fancy your dinner again.'

'I own it would be pleasant, but how will a French-trained cook relish our old-fashioned kitchens here? I doubt if he'll come into the country, Jenny.'

'He'll come fast enough when he knows it will mean another twenty pounds added to his wages,' said Jenny caustically. 'As for the kitchens, if you don't wish them to be altered, Scholes must make the best of them; but if you would but put in a good closed stove, like the Bodley we have at Lynton House, you'd find it an economy. The fuel this great open range burns – !'

'Does it? I expect we should have had a different stove years ago. Send for what you like! Anything else?'

'No, thank you. I shall be hiring a few more servants, but that needn't concern you, for with Lynton House shut up I'm wonderfully beforehand with the world.'

Mrs Dawes received the news of these forthcoming changes with mixed feelings. Asked to say which of the closed stoves now on the market she considered the best, she preferred to advance no opinion, being, she said, unacquainted with any of them. But this was not true. At Membury Place her dear Miss Charlotte had a closed stove; she had seen and coveted it, and even indulged the hope that his lordship's rich wife would install one at Fontley. She viewed with less favour the importation of a top-lofty town cook, but was considerably softened by Jenny's saying: 'If something's not done we shall have his lordship dwindling to a thread-paper! Well, I don't doubt you know as well as I do that for all he never complains or seems to notice what's set before him he's very nice in his tastes – not to say capricious! – and if the meat's not dressed as he likes it he doesn't eat more of it than would keep a kitten alive.'

The suggestion that his lordship might waste away from lack of sustenance made an instant appeal. Mrs Dawes relented enough to say that he had always been one who had to be tempted to his dinner. Jenny next asked her if she could recall which warehouse had supplied the brocade that covered certain of the chairs. 'For if only I could procure it I'd like to have them recovered,' she said. 'Not changing them, but making them the same as they were before. His lordship wouldn't wish anything to be different, and I wouldn't for the world – Well, I don't mean to turn the house out of doors, but what's worn to shreds must be made new again!'

Mrs Dawes said that she didn't know but what she might be able to recall the name of the warehouse; and, to discourage any idea that she had been won over, brought the interview to an end by saying that she was sorry the second housemaid had given Miss Pinhoe cause for complaint, and also that Miss Pinhoe had not seen fit to mention the matter to her – 'when I should have dealt with it immediately, my lady.'

The haughty Miss Poolstock had been disliked by every member of the household, but her odious air of consequence had marked her as a dresser of the first respectability. Ten minutes spent in Miss Pinhoe's company were enough to inform her fellows that she was not at all the sort of superior female a lady of real quality would employ as her personal maid. A rough tongue had brought her into instant collision with Mrs Dawes, and a feud of promising longevity seemed to be inevitable when a chance word revealed to Mrs Dawes that Miss Pinhoe came from her own county. Frigid enquiry elicited the information that Miss Pinhoe had first seen the light at Church Stretton, not seven miles from Mrs Dawes's birthplace. From that moment the thaw set in, Miss Pinhoe recognizing in the daughter of a well-to-do farmer her social superior, and Mrs Dawes (once this point had been established) admitting Miss Pinhoe into the ranks of her intimates. Neither lady regarded the other with unqualified approval, but to the world they soon presented a solid Salopian front; and bored Dunster and Kinver at every meal in the Room by recalling ancient parochial scandals, and exhaustively pursuing obscure genealogies. Nor was it long before Miss Pinhoe had disclosed an interesting piece of information, which caused Mrs Dawes to regard her mistress with a more tolerant eye. Much would be forgiven to Jenny if she provided Fontley with an heir, but Mrs Dawes suspended final judgement, by no means confident of the issue. In her view, a sickly pregnancy heralded the birth of a daughter: an arrival which would show how unworthy of her position was my lord's vulgar bride.

In fact, Jenny was beginning to overcome her sickness; but although she went briskly about her affairs she felt so far from well that she cried off from the Holkham week. Adam did not press the matter, but went alone, to mingle with the farmers of every degree who flocked to Holkham at this season, and to learn as much as he could from their discussions.

During his absence the new stove was installed; the reliable upholsterers summoned from Lincoln were set to work on the chair-covers; and the entire household was driven into strenuous activity: mending, making, cleaning, and polishing.

Charlotte, visiting her sister-in-law in case she should be lonely while Adam was away from home, exclaimed in astonishment: 'Jenny! Good gracious, how different everything looks! I declare, I hardly recognize dear old Fontley!'

'Oh, *no!*' Jenny uttered imploringly. 'Don't say that! Not different, Charlotte! I have been at such pains – ! You are looking at those curtains, but *indeed* they are *exactly* the same colour as the old ones that were so tattered! The same as they were used to be, before they became faded, I mean. I daresay you have forgotten, but when I unpicked the hems I saw what the colour had been, and was able to match the velvet.'

'To be sure!' Charlotte said hastily. 'My dear sister, I didn't mean the least disparagement! It is all beautiful! How clever you have been! All the furniture positively glowing, too, and the handles on that chest quite dazzling! I thought it had been a new one!'

In her anxiety to convince Jenny that she felt only admiration she praised every improvement rather too enthusiastically, until Jenny said, in a flattened voice: 'You don't like it, do you?'

'Yes, yes, I do! We have all of us so much regretted that poor Papa was unable to keep the house as it should be. I know it was sadly shabby. It is only that at first it seems a little strange – How nonsensical I am! you will laugh at me for missing the dimness, and the faded curtains, but one grows so accustomed – ! We love it so much, you see, that even its shabbiness is dear to us.'

'I don't understand that,' Jenny said. 'Don't you want to see it kept up to the knocker? To my way of thinking, that's no way of loving it.' She added quickly: 'I beg pardon! I shouldn't have spoken so freely.'

'Oh, no! Of course, you are perfectly right! How pleased dear Adam will be, when he sees all that you have done!'

Jenny thought that he would not be pleased; and, remembering that Lydia had once expressed the hope that Fontley would not be changed, wondered if she would ever understand the Deverils.

But Adam neither exclaimed in admiration nor recoiled in dismay when he came home. He reached Fontley some hours later than had been expected, after a tiresome journey. It was past ten o'clock, and the candles had been lit, and the curtains drawn across the tall, Gothic windows. He was tired, and exasperated by a series of mishaps; it did not occur to him that the candle-smoke stains had vanished from the moulded ceiling, or that the furniture shone with beeswax: he only thought that never had his home appeared more mellow or more lovely.

His plump, commonplace little wife came down the stairs to meet him, treading across the hall with her firm step. She was neither beautiful nor graceful; she was even a little incongruous in so gracious a setting; but she was infinitely comfortable. She smiled at him, saying placidly: 'That's nice! Here you are, just in time for supper! We'll have it in the Blue Parlour, to be cosy.'

He had told her that he would return in time for dinner, which was served at six, after the country habit. It occurred to him that no matter how long he kept her waiting she never said: 'How late you are!' or: 'What can have detained you?' He put his arm round her, kissing her cheek. 'My dear, I'm so repentant! But you're quite right not to comb my hair: it has *not* been my fault! First a broken linch-pin, and next one of the wheelers going dead lame! An abominable journey!'

'Oh, how vexatious! And me thinking no more than that you'd put off your start because there was something pleasant offered you to do at Holkham! Well, that's a great deal too bad, but never mind! Supper will be ready as soon as you are.'

'That will be in five minutes.' He gave her a hug, and kissed her again, this time on her firm little mouth. 'You're so kind to me, Jenny! I wish you may not indulge me so much that I become quite detestable!'

Her colour flamed into her cheeks; she said gruffly: 'You'll never be that to me. Now, you let Kinver pull off your boots, and give you a pair of slippers, but never mind rigging yourself out in style! That's the best of living in the country: there's no fear of being surprised by visitors at this hour of night!'

He took her at her word, reappearing presently in a frogged dressing-gown, and regarding her with a provocative twinkle. She chuckled, but said: 'Well, now you can be comfortable, at least! How did you fare at Holkham? Was it an agreeable party?'

'Very – but you were right to cry off, I think. A vast crush, and the talk all of agriculture. I hope I may have profited by the discussions, but I felt as ignorant as when I first went to school! Tell me about yourself! How have you been keeping?'

'Oh, I am perfectly stout!' she asserted. 'Charlotte was so kind as to pay me a visit – and Dr Tilford, too, which, I collect, he did at *your* command, my lord! He's a sensible man, and tells me not to coddle myself.'

'He could have spared his breath! What do you call this excellent chicken-dish? Italian salad, is it? It informs me that Scholes has been restored to us – and thank God for it! Has your new stove arrived? Was it very troublesome to make the change?'

'No worse than what was to be expected,' she replied. 'We had the chimney swept, and the walls and ceiling new white-washed into the bargain, so you'd hardly know it for the same dingy old kitchen.'

She then wished that she had not said this, but Adam merely said: 'I can't conceive how you can have contrived to get dinner cooked while all this was going forward!'

'Oh, quite easily!' she said, not disclosing to his male ignorance that the household had subsisted on picnic meals for three hideous days. She asked him instead to describe the clippings to her.

In general, he took care not to bore her with agricultural talk, but his head was so full of it that he was led on, from the clippings, to tell her about Mr Coke's experimental farm. She listened, watching him, and thinking that he was talking more to himself than to her. When he spoke of stall-feeding, of hurdling sheep over turnips, of trebling livestock for manure, of shorthorns, and of North Devons, she knew that he had his own acres in mind, not Mr Coke's. He sat with the fingers of one hand crooked round the stem of his wineglass, his eyes fixed on the dregs in it; and he answered the few questions she put to him rather abstractedly, until she asked if Mr Coke used the Tullian drill, when he looked up quickly, between surprise and amusement, and replied: 'He has done so for years – but what do you know about the Tullian drill?'

'Only what I've read. It dibbles the soil, and sows the seed – oh, and covers it, too, doesn't it? Is it used here?'

'Not yet. Where did you read about it, Jenny?'

'In one of your books. I have been looking into them, and trying to learn a little from them.'

'My poor girl! Were you reduced so low? I had thought you brought a boxful of books down from London!'

'Oh, I did! But *Mansfield Park* is the only one I've read yet. I kept it by me, and took it up whenever Artificial Manures, and the Four-Course System began to pall. And I must own, Adam, they *do* pall! But that drill seems to me to be an excellent machine, and I think you should adopt it.'

'I mean to, and to induce my tenants to follow my example – I hope! As for manure, we use sticklebacks.'

'*Sticklebacks?*'

'Also pigeon-dung.'

'Oh, you're roasting me!' she exclaimed.

'I'm not. Sticklebacks make the best of all manures. We get them from Boston Haven, at a halfpenny the bushel. Gorse is good for turnips; and in the wolds they spread straw, and burn it.'

'Good gracious! And here have I been trying to learn about lime, and marl, and rape-cake!'

'Poor Jenny! Does it comfort you to know that we use those too? Why should you tease yourself over such dull matters?'

'I like to understand the things that interest you. The home farm isn't large enough to be made experimental, is it? Do you mean to take over one of the others, as Mr Coke did? I know there are some let on short-term leases.'

'Too many,' he said. 'Yes, perhaps I shall do that, one day, but there's so much else to be done first that I'm afraid it won't be for some time to come.'

'Is it very costly, to bring an estate like this into good order?' she ventured to ask.

'Very. I can only do so gradually.'

'I suppose you wouldn't –' She stopped, and then, when he raised his brows enquiringly, blurted out: 'Why don't you sell Lynton House?'

The words had no sooner passed her lips than she wished them unspoken. He answered perfectly pleasantly; he even smiled; but she knew that he had retreated behind his disconcerting barriers. 'Well, you know why I don't,' he said. 'Don't let us fall into a wrangle over that, Jenny!'

'No,' she muttered, her eyes lowered, and her cheeks flaming. 'Only, when I think how much it costs to keep that great house – and how much you need the money *here* – I beg your pardon! I didn't mean to vex you.'

He stretched out his hand to her, and when she laid her own in it, clasped it warmly. 'You haven't vexed me. I think there can be no more generous persons alive than you and your father. Try to understand me! I'm not ungrateful, but there must be a limit set to my indebtedness. I've accepted Lynton House from your father; he holds all the mortgages on my lands, and demands nothing from me in return. To restore those lands to prosperity must be *my* business – and if I can't contrive to do it, the sooner Fontley passes into more worthy hands than mine the better! Can you understand?'

'Yes,' she answered, nothing in her tone betraying the desolation in her heart. 'Fontley is yours, and you will accept no help from Papa in anything that concerns it. Or from me.'

She tried to draw her hand away as she spoke, but his fingers closed round it strongly.

'But for your father I must have sold Fontley,' he said. 'As for –'

'You mean to pay him back, don't you?' she interrupted.

He was startled, but replied almost immediately: 'Yes, I do mean to do that, but *your* services to my house are another matter. If you choose to spend your blunt on new curtains for Fontley – yes, I *have* observed them, and I like them very much! – instead of on all the things I'm persuaded you must have wished to purchase, I'm grateful, but I don't mean to repay you, any more than I mean to thank you for having the furniture polished – which, also, I have observed! The best thing I've yet done for Fontley is to have bestowed on it such a notable housewife: the house begins to look as it should again. You must have been busier than a colony of ants while I was in Norfolk!'

She blushed again, but this time with pleasure. 'Oh, I am so glad you don't dislike the things I've done! I told you I wouldn't meddle, but I thought you might not object to it if I set some things to rights – not changing them, but making them the *same* again! Only Charlotte said that she scarcely recognized the house, and, although she assured me she liked it, I could see she did not, and that put me in a regular quake!'

'Charlotte's a goose!' he said, forgetting that he had dreaded to see even a torn rug replaced. He gave her hand a squeeze, before releasing it, and getting up from the table. 'Let us go to the library! Have you given that smart new curtains as well?'

'No, no, I haven't touched it!' she said quickly. 'I thought, perhaps, that, if you don't dislike it, we might have new curtains made, but none of the colours on the pattern-cards I've yet had sent me are at all like what I *think* these old ones must have been.'

'I fancy they were a sort of mustard,' he said, frowning in an effort of memory. 'Pray don't inflict that on me again! I know I thought them very ugly when my mother first had them hung.'

This cool repudiation of his mother's taste, which she had striven so zealously to copy, almost made her gasp. She suspected him of having said it merely to reassure her; but when they reached the library he looked at the curtains, and pulled a grimace. 'Very dingy! Odd that I shouldn't have noticed it. I suppose one grows accustomed. What shall we hang in their stead?'

Much heartened, she produced her pattern-cards. None of the materials she had thought the most suitable met with more than qualified approval, but when he saw a scrap of red brocade he instantly said: 'That's the one!'

She had expected him to choose a more sober colour, but when he took the brocade over to the corner where the K'ang-hsi bowl had been placed she understood, and applauded his choice. Then she said, knowing that it would please him: 'I give you due warning, though, my lord! – you won't relish the bill! You've chosen the most expensive pattern that's been sent me.'

'Oh, dear, have I? But it's the only one I like! What's the figure?'

'About fifty pounds: I can't tell precisely until I know the measurements.'

'How shocking! But more shocking, don't you think, to dishonour my bowl with anything shoddy? We'll have it.' He gave the pattern back to her, and sank into his favourite chair, stretching out his legs with a sigh of content, and saying: 'How comfortable to be at home again! And not to be obliged to play whist, or take part in a charade. Tell me what has been happening while I was away!'

Seventeen

Three days later Julia came to Fontley. Lord Oversley's seat was situated north of Peterborough, and so within easy distance of Fontley. Julia rode over, accompanied by Rockhill and two of her friends: Miss Kilverley and her brother, an inarticulate and sporting young gentleman who reminded Jenny of Adam's cousin Osbert. Julia explained that the visit was unpremeditated. 'We set out to visit Croyland Abbey,' she said, 'but when Mary – you do remember Mary, don't you? – learned how near we were to Fontley nothing would do for her but to ride on to pay you a visit!'

Jenny, who remembered Miss Kilverley as one of Julia's satellites, somewhat grimly observed this retiring damsel's blush, and look of startled enquiry, but said, as she shook hands: 'Yes, I remember you very well. How do you do?'

'Abominable to have taken you by surprise!' Julia said gaily. 'But I couldn't resist!'

'Why should you?' Jenny returned. 'I'll have a message sent down to Lynton directly: we are getting in the last of the harvest, you know, and he's helping on one of the farms.'

'Helping?' Julia echoed.

'Yes,' said Jenny, with her small, tight smile. 'Dressed up in a smock too, which I can't say becomes him. But that's his notion of enjoyment! I've this instant come back from taking him a nuncheon. Plum cake and beer is what the reapers get at this hour, but beer he can't stomach: it makes him bilious. Now, do you all step this way, and partake of a nuncheon too!'

When Adam came in he found the visitors in the Prior's Parlour, still sitting over the remains of a light repast. He greeted Julia with the ease of long friendship, but he could not keep the warmth from his eyes when they rested on her. She gave him her hand, a smile that was wistful in her own eyes, but a quizzing speech on her lips. 'Your smock, Farmer Giles! Where is it? I am disappointed!'

'Ah, the farmer always puts off his smock when he has company!' he retorted. He shook hands with Rockhill. 'How do you do? And – ?' A lift of the eyebrow put Jenny in mind of her duty; she performed the necessary introduction; and had the satisfaction of seeing him engage the rather shy young couple in a conversation that he soon made general. She had herself no talent for welding ill-assorted persons into one party, and since the Kilverleys were frightened of Rockhill, suspecting him of satire every time he uttered one of his languid remarks, they had been largely silent until Adam's arrival. But in a very few minutes they were chatting happily about the day's expedition, Miss Kilverley joining Julia in rapturous appreciation of the beauties of Croyland, and Mr Kilverley deriving entertainment from Rockhill's disclosure that the Abbey had been founded by King Ethelbald.

Upon Miss Kilverley's expressing the hope that she might be allowed to see a little more of Fontley, Adam replied: 'Why, certainly! But you will be disappointed, I'm afraid. We don't compare with Croyland, you know.'

'Oh – ! That lovely arch!' she protested. 'And is not this room very ancient?'

'Well, it has always been called the Prior's Parlour,' he admitted. 'Part of the outer wall is thought to be original, but the house is more Tudor than mediaeval.'

'Don't disparage it on that account!' Julia said. 'I have sometimes thought that all the ages meet in it, and have indulged the fancy that one might see monks in the gallery that used to be the *dortoire*; a lady in a farthingale vanishing through a doorway; or a cavalier, with his lace and love-locks, going before one down a corridor.'

'Orlando Deveril, for instance?' said Adam, regarding her in tender amusement. 'None of my worthier forebears ever pleased you half as well as that chucklehead!'

She winced. 'How can you talk so? You should be proud of him!' She turned to her friend. 'You will see his portrait presently! the noblest countenance, and with such melancholy eyes – as though he knew himself to be fated! I told you: he is the one who raised a troop, and rode with it to the King's assistance!'

'And subsequently got it cut to pieces in its first engagement,' interpolated Adam. 'The kind of officer, Miss Kilverley, always to be found heroically exposed to the enemy's fire. We suffered under just such an one last year: very gallant – and no general for the Light Bobs!'

She was uncertain whether to laugh or to be shocked; Julia said: 'You are funning, but I don't care for jokes on such a subject!'

'Well,' said Jenny, bringing the discussion to a prosaic end, 'I'm glad to say I haven't seen him, which I'm thankful for, because I shouldn't like it if Fontley was haunted, and you may depend upon it there's not many of the servants would remain above a sennight if they took it into their heads they might come on a monk round a corner.' She rose, saying: 'If we've all finished, we'll go up to the gallery, shall we?'

She nodded to Adam to escort the party, and would have followed had not Rockhill, lingering beside her, said: 'Do you wish to go too? I'm persuaded you'd find it a dead bore – as I should, being perfectly well-acquainted with Fontley's antiquities. Let us leave Lynton to his irreverences, and take a turn about the gardens!'

She was a little surprised, but perfectly willing. As they walked down the vaulted corridor to the Great Hall, she asked him if he were staying with the Oversleys at Beckenhurst.

'No, but in the immediate vicinity,' he replied. 'I am visiting relations – remote, but one should never ignore even the dullest members of one's family, should one? Particularly when they reside precisely where one most wishes to be!'

She cast a quick look up at him, and saw his thin lips curl into the smile which put such innocents as the Kilverleys upon their guard.

'Just so!' he said, answering the enquiry in her eyes. 'You have a great deal of good sense, Lady Lynton, and you are perfectly right in your assumption.'

'I don't know that,' she responded bluntly. 'You'll forgive me if I speak too plainly, my lord, but it looks to me as if you was dangling after Miss Oversley!'

'Yes, and at *my* age too!' he murmured. 'I learn on the highest authority that I am generally held to be indulging a fit of gallantry – senile, I fear.'

'Well, that's nonsense, but it's not to be wondered at that no one should think it more than a flirtation, for there must be twenty years between you, my lord!'

'Rather more,' he confessed wryly, ushering her out into the garden. 'But I'm not, I do assure you, senile, ma'am!'

'No, but, myself, I should never have thought – However, it's no business of mine!'

'No? You disappoint me!'

'I don't know why I should,' she replied defensively.

'No, no, don't fence with me! I'm persuaded we understand one another very well. *You* would naturally be glad to see Miss Oversley married; *I* have every intention of obliging you in the matter!'

She paused at the entrance to the rose-garden, to look frowningly up at him. 'Why do you tell me so?' she demanded.

'Well, do you know, I like you, Lady Lynton,' he replied. 'You compelled both my respect and my gratitude upon the occasion of our first meeting. An awkward – one might almost say a *disastrous* situation, rendered trivial by your admirable presence of mind then, and later by conduct as magnanimous as it was shrewd.'

'Oh, fiddle!' she said roughly, flushing, and walking on into the rose-garden.

He laughed, and followed her. 'If you like! But you must allow me to be grateful – and to pay my debts, if you please! You were a little dismayed, were you not, when you saw who had come to visit you? I fancy you thought me positively beef-witted to have lent myself to the expedition. But I am not at all beef-witted. I am reasonably certain, ma'am, that neither you nor I have anything to fear in regarding our loved ones' meetings with complaisance.'

'You are the strangest creature!' she exclaimed. 'How can you wish to marry Julia, if you know she loves Lynton? You do know it, don't you?'

'But of course! I have been her most sympathetic confidant – perfectly sincerely, too. One remembers one's own first love – with a tiny pang, and such infinite thankfulness! I shan't grudge Julia her deliciously nostalgic memories, or be so abominably gross as to suggest to her that her touching little romance was no more real than a fairy story. She won't indulge them often: only when something has occurred to put her into the hips! And then, poor darling, she will quite forget having made the painful discovery that Lynton really bears very little resemblance to the Prince Charming of her imagination – a creation I find slightly nauseating – but pray don't tell her that I said so!'

She smiled, but said impatiently: 'Oh, Julia knows nothing about Lynton! I don't understand her – never did! I'm sure I hope you may, but it has always seemed to me that she's one who would break her heart over a sparrow she found dead in the gutter as easily as she's done over Lynton. I don't doubt *she'll* recover soon enough, for it's my belief she hoaxed herself into love with Adam, the way I've seen her hoax herself into a high fever, often and often!' She stopped, clipping her lips together, and, after an infinitesimal pause, changed the subject.

He made no attempt to bring her back to it, but talked amusingly to her on a number of idle topics until their stroll through various gardens brought them back to the house again. Voices led them past it to the chapel ruins, where they found the rest of the party. Julia was seated on a fallen block of masonry, her frivolous parasol tilted to protect her complexion from the sun, her gaze fixed in melancholy wonder on Adam, who was standing a few paces away, talking to Mr Kilverley. Miss Kilverley was wandering about the ruins, and occasionally calling out appreciative comments as she discovered a fragment of dog-tooth, or a lichened tomb. Mr Kilverley seemed to have become surprisingly loquacious, and when Jenny and Rockhill drew within earshot such overheard phrases as *ten coombs to the acre*, and *improved rotation*, informed them that Mr Kilverley's knowledge was not confined to horses and hounds: he was an enthusiastic agriculturist.

'Ah, the poor little one!' exclaimed Rockhill, under his breath. 'Own, Lady Lynton, that it is a picture to wring compassion from a heart of stone!'

Julia turned her head, as she heard the approaching footsteps, and smiled. Her smile was always lovely, and just now it held real pleasure, and more than a suggestion of relief. Her soft eyes were raised to Rockhill's face as he went towards her, and when he held out his hand she put one of hers into it, and rose, allowing him to lead her a little away. As they walked slowly round the ruins, Julia's hand in Rockhill's arm, she sighed, and said: 'It is so beautiful, isn't it? Such reflections as these crumbling stones give rise to! I saw it once by moonlight – so still, so mysterious, brooding in silence over the past! How is it possible to look upon these ruins, and to think only that they make a capital ground for playing at hide-and-seek?'

His eyes lit with amusement, but he replied suitably. After a disconsolate pause, she said: 'That's what Charlie says about them, but I didn't think to hear Adam . . .' She did not finish the sentence, but sighed again, and said instead: 'I suppose, being married to Jenny – She is so prosaic! Very kind, and very good, of course, but – oh, I wish she would not change Adam! He was never used to talk so!'

'Perhaps,' suggested his lordship tactfully, 'he was merely setting young Kilverley at his ease.'

'Yes, perhaps – But to call Orlando Deveril a *chucklehead* – !'

'That,' agreed his lordship, 'was certainly very bad, but one

236

must remember that Lynton is a military man, and may regard conduct which to *us* appears in the highest degree noble with rather different eyes.'

They walked slowly on while she digested this. 'Rockhill!' she said suddenly. 'What is a *coomb*?'

'I *believe*,' he replied cautiously, 'that it is some sort of a measure – but pray don't ask me *what* sort, for I haven't the most distant guess!'

'I think it has something to do with wheat,' she said.

'I shouldn't wonder at it at all if you are right: it sounds as if it would have something to do with wheat.'

She looked up into his face at that, laughter brimming in her eyes. 'Oh, Rockhill, you are so absurd – and *such* a comfort to me! I believe you do know: you have farms too, have you not?'

'Several, I fancy, but I am ashamed to confess that I've never concerned myself with their management.'

'You have an agent, like Papa – though Papa does concern himself a little. Not as Adam does! Helping the reapers! Must he do so? It is very dreadful! I had thought, when he married Jenny, he would have a great fortune.'

He smiled at the trouble in her face. 'But it is not at all dreadful, little blossom! Didn't you hear Lady Lynton say that it was *his notion of enjoyment*? I don't doubt it: it's in his blood. Choice, not necessity, takes him out into the fields, I promise you. Coke of Norfolk does the same, and, for anything I know, a dozen others. I'm prepared to wager that before he is much older Lynton will have joined the ranks of the noble farmers – the Russells, the Keppels, Rockingham, Egremont – oh, don't look dismayed! It is most creditable, besides becoming so fashionable that those of us who think it a dead bore will soon find ourselves quite outmoded.'

'I don't think it a bore, precisely,' Julia said. 'I love our farm, at Beckenhurst, and have often thought I should like to be a farmer's wife, with lambs, and calves, and piglets – Papa gave me a lamb once, for a pet, and it was the dearest creature! – but not dull things like crops, except, perhaps, hay.'

'You shall have a little Trianon,' he promised.

'Oh – ! No, no, pray don't talk so! You said you would not! Besides, I know it's nonsensical: one can't have a farm without horrid things like manure, and crops, and swing-ploughs, and turnips! Oh, Rockhill, I can't so easily forget – turn my thoughts, my affections, in another direction!'

'But I have only begged to be allowed to love you, blossom.'

'How *good* you are! No, no, it would be very ill-done of me: I've nothing left to give you, you see.'

'On the contrary! You have beauty to give me. My house needs a mistress, and my daughters a kind mother. I am afraid,' said his lordship, in a tone of deep dejection, 'that they are not happy in their grandmother's charge. An excellent woman, but a trifle over-strict, perhaps.'

'Oh, poor little dears, they have quite *haunted* me since you told me – But hush! here is Jenny coming towards us!'

The Marquis, perfectly well satisfied with the progress he had made, obediently hushed, and presently moved away to talk to his host. With every fibre in his being taut with hostility, Adam still could not dislike him. Rockhill had made many enemies, but when he exerted himself to please no one could be more charming. To Julia he might affect ignorance of farming, but to Adam he chose to disclose a surprising amount of knowledge in one whose enormous revenues derived largely from urban districts. They paced up and down together for a little time, discussing such matters of agricultural interest as the Corn Laws, trunk-drainage, and stall-feeding; and whatever boredom Rockhill felt he concealed admirably.

It was soon time for the visitors to take their leave. There had been no opportunity for Julia to enjoy any private talk with Adam; only at the last did she find herself alone with him for a few minutes. She said then: 'Do you wish I hadn't come? You were not glad to see me, were you?'

'I can't help but be glad to see you. But it's true that I wish you hadn't come. Why did you, Julia? *Here*, where I once thought to –' He checked himself. 'You must know that I can't but find it painful!'

'I, too,' she said mournfully.

'Then why?'

'I wanted to see you, to talk to you. I'm so troubled. I've been lost, you know, ever since that dreadful day in March. Were you ever in a maze? You can't find the way out, though you try every path; and you become frightened, wanting to scream to someone to rescue you, but not doing so, because it would be silly, and' – a bleak smile touched her lips – ' "because you are getting to be a big girl now, Miss Julia, and only babies cry!" '

'I can't help you!' he said, in a shaken voice. 'My love, my love, don't say these things! Don't come here! It would be better that we shouldn't meet, but since we must, let it only be in London, when we find ourselves at the same party! To be together, as we are now – no, no, it won't do! Believe me, Julia, it will be easier for us both if we meet as seldom as may be possible! *This* is torture to us both!'

'I think it need not be. Cannot something be left to us? If your affections had been engaged, or Jenny's, it would be another matter, but yours is a marriage of convenience! *You* did it to save Fontley, *she* to gain social advancement: there has been no pretence of love between you. Jenny could not be *hurt* by anything that passed between you and me, Adam. She knows that you love me – she has always known it! Does she demand that everything should be at an end between us, even friendship? It isn't like her! She has what she desired! Does she demand that you should devote yourself to her, as if you had married her for love?'

It was a moment or two before he answered. Then he said slowly: 'No. Jenny demands nothing of me.'

'Ah, I knew she could not! She's never unreasonable! She's matter-of-fact, too: full of commonsense, without much sensibility, perhaps – she would tell you so herself! – but –'

He interrupted her. 'Yes, she would say that. I don't know how true it may be, but I do know that she can be hurt. You say she has always known that I love you. I've supposed that she must, but she has never spoken of it to me, or betrayed by the least sign that she does know.'

'Why should she care? You've given her so much! She can't grudge me your friendship! Are you thinking of what people would say? But if I were to be married? One's position is then so different!'

He gave a shaken laugh. 'Oh, Julia, my little foolish one! No, I wasn't thinking of your position, but of Jenny's. I couldn't mortify her so. She offered me a carte blanche once, but I knew when I entered into our contract that I was marrying a girl bred in a stricter mould than is general in our order.'

'Oh, yes, yes! Respectability is Jenny's god, but must it be yours?'

He did not answer for a moment, and then he said gently: 'I owe Jenny a great deal, you know. She studies all the time to please me, never herself. Our marriage – isn't always easy, for either of us, but she tries to make it so, and behaves more generously than I do. Given her so much! You know better than to say that, my dear! I had nothing to give her but a title – and I wonder sometimes if she sets any more store by that than you would.'

'Of course she does! I don't blame her: I know what it must have meant to her, situated as she was, to be so elevated! *You* may think it a worthless thing, but how could she? *Easy to despise what you've always had!* Once, she said that to me. I hadn't understood – I was in such distress! – but I did then. She said she wasn't the first and wouldn't be the last to marry for the sake of position.'

'Did she? But position wouldn't compensate her for the humiliation of being pitied, or sneered at, by the ton, because it was seen that I still loved you, Julia.'

'Oh, no, no! But people don't! Think of the Ashcotts! Everyone knows that Ashcott is more than Mrs Porth's *friend*, but no one –'

'It is also pretty freely rumoured that Lady Ashcott has found consolation,' he interrupted. 'But what would Jenny do, if I neglected her? She wasn't born into our set; she hasn't a host of friends and relations, as you have – as Lady Ashcott has; and she's too shy to make her own way. We made a one-sided bargain: it's she who gives, and I who take – but I can at least give her loyalty!'

She caught her breath on a sob. 'I didn't mean – or wish – I wouldn't injure her! But we have been such dear friends, Adam! Must we never meet and talk together, as we were used to do? Jenny wouldn't grudge us such a tiny crumb of comfort!'

'It wouldn't be comfort, Julia. Oh, my love, can't you understand – ?'

'I miss you so,' she said sadly. 'Wouldn't it be a *little* comfort?'

He could only shake his head. She turned away, saying: 'I didn't know we must be wholly estranged. I must be very stupid, I think.'

Eighteen

*I*t was fortunate for Adam that the improvements he had been able to start on the estate kept him too busy to leave him with much time to waste on reflection which he knew to be idle. He could not resent Julia's visit, because his heart still yearned for her; but the sight of her in the house where he had hoped to have installed her as his wife stirred up all his suppressed emotion.

When the visitors had departed he braced himself, glancing at Jenny. But she only said: 'To be sure, it's agreeable to see one's friends, but it's wonderful how they always choose to come when one's busy! I'd meant to have spent the afternoon in the stillroom, but it's too late for that now, and too late for you to go back to your harvesting either.'

Neither of them mentioned the visit again. The next days brought their duties, their small successes, and their annoying failures. There was always something to be done, even if it was only teaching Jenny to drive the chair-back gig she had found in one of the coach-houses; and when no active employment offered there were future plans to be considered, and ways and means to be calculated; so that by the time Mr Chawleigh came to Fontley, midway through September, Adam was too much engrossed in estate business to have much leisure for thinking about the ruin of his hopes, or his lost love's unhappiness.

Mr Chawleigh arrived on a golden afternoon, two hours before he was expected. Neither Jenny nor Adam was at home: a circumstance which disturbed him far less than it disturbed

Dunster, who was thrown off his balance by the size and style of my lady's parent. Before he had time to recover from the first shock he found himself clutching a pineapple, which Mr Chawleigh handed over with a recommendation to him to set it on a plate in the dining-room, out of the cook's way. 'For we don't want it messed up into fritters or ices, mind!' He then turned to admonish his valet, a spindleshanked individual who was climbing down from the chaise with a rush bag in his grasp. 'Bustle about, now!' he ordered. He seized the bag, and thrust that too into Dunster's nerveless hand. 'Now, this you *can* take to the cook, and the sooner the better! It's a turtle, and you may tell him that he's to roast the meat from the blade-bone – and mind this! – it's to be stewed for a couple of minutes first, and then put on a lark-spit, and then brushed over with eggs and breadcrumbs before he ties it to the roasting-spit!'

None of Fontley's guests had ever before handed Dunster a turtle in a rush bag, and he stood dumbfounded until one of the footmen tactfully removed it from his hold, when he recovered himself sufficiently to say: 'Yes, sir!'

'And he can make a soutie of the liver,' added Mr Chawleigh. 'So her la'ship's out, is she? Well, that's no matter: I'll take a turn about the place till she gets back.'

Pulling himself together, Dunster said: 'If you would be pleased to step into the Green Saloon, sir, I will have a message taken to her ladyship directly. No doubt you will be glad of refreshment after your journey, sir.'

'Well, I won't say no to a glass of Madeira, if his lordship has some in his cellar,' replied Mr Chawleigh genially. 'But there's no sense in sending messages to her la'ship: she'll come home soon enough! Do you take that jobbernoll of mine up to the guest-chamber, so that he can unpack my gear while I look around.' He cast a glance round the Great Hall, and added: 'I take it this is the antique part of the house, and very fine too, I daresay, though I've no fancy for stone floors myself, and if that huge fireplace don't give out more smoke than heat you may call me a Jack Adams!' He then waved aside a reiterated offer of escort to the Green Saloon, saying that he would stretch his legs a bit; so there was nothing for Dunster to do but to withdraw. When he returned to the Hall, bringing the Madeira, he found Mr Chawleigh inspecting the staircase. Mr Chawleigh said that it was a handsome piece of carving, but that for his part he would lose no time in laying down a good thick carpet. 'It's a wonder you've none of you broke your necks,' he remarked, taking the glass that was being offered to him. 'What's more, it's to be hoped I don't break mine. Thankee! No need to leave the decanter: I'm as ready to play off my dust as the next man, but I'm not one as has a spark in his throat. Not but what this is a very tolerable Madeira, and you may fill up my glass again before you take yourself off.'

Having disposed of his wine, and dismissed Dunster, he set out on a tour of investigation.

His feelings were mixed. His first view of the Priory had come as a disappointment, for although he had been told that it was a house of great antiquity his informants had not succeeded in ridding his mind of its belief that it must be a Palladian mansion of uniform and stately design. Nor was he favourably impressed by its position. There was no prospect to be obtained from its windows, and he did not like the surrounding country. When he had alighted from his chaise he had perceived that the house was larger than he had first supposed, but he wondered why anyone should admire such a jumble of buildings. There was no elegant façade, and not even a terrace to lend dignity to the irregular frontage. One worn, shallow step led to the porch; and the great oaken door made him feel as if he were entering a Church.

The Great Hall did impress him, however. It was the sort of room anyone could see belonged to a lord. There were two suits of armour flanking the fireplace; various ancient weapons were arranged on the walls; and the Deveril arms were carved in the centre of the stone chimney-piece.

Having taken stock of these embellishments, he wandered off down the vaulted corridor, which led, past a succession of parlours, to a secondary hall, another staircase, and the library.

He thought poorly of the parlours: none of them was large, and most of them were wainscoted, which made them dark. The library pleased him better. It was larger and loftier; and if a new carpet were laid down, and the worn leather covering the chairs renewed it would be a tolerably handsome apartment. He was gratified to see the K'ang-hsi bowl occupying a place of honour. It would have been safer in a cabinet, but it certainly looked very well in the corner embrasure: he would warn Jenny not to let the servants dust it.

By the time Jenny returned to the Priory Mr Chawleigh had explored the better part of the house, and had come to the conclusion that it was a regular rabbit warren, with far too many uneven floors, ill-fitting windows, odd steps, and rooms too small to be of use. He preferred the modern wing, but even this disappointed him, for there was no suite of state apartments, and most of the furniture was so old-fashioned as to be downright shabby.

When Jenny arrived he was standing on the carriage-drive, scanning the gardens. This was unfortunate, for if she had not seen him she would have driven into the stable-yard, and he would have been spared the degrading spectacle of his daughter seated in a paltry gig with a staid cob between the shafts, and no groom beside her to lend her protection or consequence. As it was, she drove up to the house, calling out: 'Papa! Good gracious, have you been here long? And me not here to welcome you! Well, I *am* sorry, but I never thought you could arrive this early!' She leaned down to kiss him. 'I'll just drive the gig into the yard, and be with you directly.'

'I should have thought,' said Mr Chawleigh, in a voice of displeasure, 'that you'd have had a groom to do that for you – even if you don't take one up beside you, like you should! Never did I think to live to see the day when you'd go careering over the country in a dowdy old gig without so much as your maid beside you, and that's a fact! What's more, you ain't dressed as I like to see you: anyone would take you for a farmer's wife!'

'Well, that's just what I am!' she retorted. 'Now, don't put yourself in a fume, Papa! No one dresses fine in the country. And as for me driving alone, if Adam sees no harm in it I'm sure you need not. I've only been to see how the new cottages go on: never off our own land, I promise you!'

'You come down, and tell one of the footmen to take the gig off to the stables!' commanded her parent.

Perceiving that he was seriously vexed, she thought it prudent to obey. She then tucked her hand in his arm, and said: 'Don't be cross, Papa! How nice it is to have you here at last! Do you like Fontley? Have you been about the house at all?'

'It's not what I expected,' he replied. 'I'm bound to say I thought it would be more handsome. From the way my Lord Oversley puffed it off to me – well, it gave me a very different notion of it than what turns out to be the truth!'

Her heart sank; and by the time he had suggested to her various plans for knocking several small rooms into one, carpeting the Grand Staircase, reflooring most of the rooms, and installing a great many modern conveniences, she was so much dismayed that she blurted out: 'Papa! If you say such things to Adam I'll never forgive you!'

'That's a pretty way to talk!' he ejaculated.

'Yes, but you don't understand! Adam is so passionately devoted to Fontley! As if it was a sacred thing! All the Deverils are!'

'You don't say so! Well, there's no accounting for tastes, and I'm sure I've no wish to tread on his lordship's toes – though I'd have thought he'd want to see it brought more up-to-date, if he's so proud of it!'

'It isn't meant to be up-to-date, Papa: it's historical!'

'History's all very well in its place,' said Mr Chawleigh largemindedly, 'but I don't see what anyone wants with it in his home. You can't pretend it's comfortable! And when it comes to having a ruined chapel in your garden, with a couple of mouldy tombs as well – why, it's enough to give anyone a fit of the dismals! If I was his lordship, I'd be rid of it, and set up a few good succession houses instead: there'd be some sense in that!'

246

This did not promise well for the success of the visit; it was not, in fact, at all successful, but neither Mr Chawleigh's strictures on the house, nor his suggestions for its improvement was to blame for this. To Jenny's relief, Adam took these in good part. Mr Chawleigh was powerless to put any of his schemes into execution, so Adam was able to listen to them with amusement. They included the throwing out of several bows and bays, the employment of a landscape gardener to lay out the gardens to better advantage, and the introduction of a herd of deer to the park. Mr Chawleigh argued that deer would make Fontley more the thing, but Adam said: 'If you wish to bestow a herd on me, sir, let it be a herd of short-horns!'

But Mr Chawleigh would have nothing to do with cattle. He told Adam that he had a bee in his head, which made Jenny exclaim: 'Now, that's something *I* want! I've been talking to Wicken – he's our head gardener, Papa! – and we are agreed that a few hives are exactly what we need here. And I for one don't want a grand landscape gardener coming to upset us all! Just as I've started to bring the knot-garden back into order, and have ordered more rose-trees for planting later! No, I thank you!'

'Ay!' said Mr Chawleigh. 'Pottering about a garden is new to you, my girl, but I'll warrant you'll soon tire of it! And as for cows, my lord, you've no call to meddle with such, and you'll get none from me! You leave farming to those as was bred to it, and that's my advice to you!'

His disapproval of Adam's agricultural activities was profound, but this was not what made his visit disastrous. It did not take him more than a day to realize that Jenny was not looking well; and he was so much inclined to set this to the account of Fontley's situation that she told him the truth.

The result was unhappy. His first delight was swiftly followed by wrath; for when he asked when the infant would be born, and learned that it would be in March, he did a rapid sum in his head, and demanded incredulously: 'You've been in a promising way these three months, and never a word to me?'

Neither she nor Martha Pinhoe succeeded in mollifying him;

it was Adam who soothed his rage and his hurt. He said: 'Yes, you have every right to be vexed, sir. I should have insisted on your being told – and also my mother.'

'Oh!' growled Mr Chawleigh. 'So she don't know either?'

'No one knows, except Martha and our doctor here. I don't think *I* should have known if I hadn't seen that she was unwell, and pretty well forced her to tell me.'

'You don't say!' gasped Mr Chawleigh. 'What the devil's got into her? It ain't coming by way of the back door! Well, if ever I knew my Jenny to behave so missish!'

Adam smiled at that, but replied: 'I think her reluctance to tell either you or me was partly due to her dislike of what she calls fuss. And partly to spare you the anxiety she guessed you would feel. She's very much attached to you, you know, sir.'

This diplomacy was not without its effect. Mr Chawleigh pondered for a few moments, champing his powerful jaws. 'A fine way to show she's attached to me!' he said at last, determined not to be won over too easily. 'Her own father, and the last to hear of it!' He went on fulminating for a minute or two, but suddenly said: 'Thought I'd be anxious, did she? Well, she didn't miss her tip! You may lay your life I'm anxious, my lord!'

'I hope you need not be, sir. Our doctor here assures me I need feel no apprehension.'

'And who's he, pray?' said Mr Chawleigh scathingly. 'I'll have no country sawbones attending my Jenny! Croft's the man for her, and Croft she shall have, say what you will!'

'It is you who now have the advantage of me,' said Adam, a little coldly. 'Who, if you please, is Croft?'

'He's an accoucheur – top-of-the-trees! If I could have brought him in to Mrs Chawleigh, him being then what he is now, she might be with me this day – ay, and I might have had a son to my name too!'

'But that's precisely what Jenny has set her face against – to have such a person called in, *driving her crazy*! If I knew of any cause for alarm the case would be different, and I shouldn't hesitate –'

'It ain't what you know, but what I know!' interrupted Mr Chawleigh. 'And if you think you can come the lord over me when it's my Jenny that's in question –' He stopped, controlling himself with a strong effort.

There was just a moment's pause before Adam, recognizing that this outburst sprang from concern, said quietly: 'No, I don't think that. I must have expressed myself very badly if you could suppose –'

'Nay, I didn't mean it!' said Mr Chawleigh roughly. 'You couldn't have treated me more civil if I'd been a Duke, and well I know it! The thing is that it's got me regularly nattered – me knowing what I do know! Now, lookee here, lad! She's the very make of her ma, my Jenny! Three times did Mrs C. miscarry – and the lord only knows how Jenny came to be born hale and hearty! – A son was what Mrs C. wanted – well, so I did too, though I've lived to regret it! She went her full time at the end, and a son it was, but he was stillborn, and Mrs C. was taken from me, like I told you. *She* wouldn't have a fuss made, and that's what came of it! I won't have it happen to my Jenny, no matter what you say, nor she says either!'

'Very well,' Adam said. 'What do you wish me to do? To take her back to London? I will, of course – but she has been in better health since we came to Fontley, and *her* wish is to remain here.'

'Ay!' said Mr Chawleigh, with a bark of laughter. 'Because she knows that's *your* wish, my lord! But she don't bamboozle me! My Jenny wish to be stuck down in the country for months on end? That's a loud one! Moped to death, that's what she'd be!'

'Would she?' Adam said slowly. 'I own, I thought so too, but she isn't moped, you know.'

'She hasn't been here much above a month!' retorted Mr Chawleigh grimly. 'What's more she don't know what it will be like in the winter! I'm no countryman, but don't you tell me that you ain't surrounded by water here, because I wouldn't believe you!'

'You may at least believe me when I tell you that Fontley has never yet been affected by floods!' said Adam, nettled.

249

'Ay, so I may, but you won't tell me you've never had the water come up over the road, and found yourself on an island!'

'If there were any likelihood of that I would bring Jenny to town long before it happened, I promise you. We should have plenty of warning.'

'And I suppose you'll have plenty of warning that there's going to be a heavy fall of snow, such as will block all the roads for a sennight?' said Mr Chawleigh, with heavy sarcasm. 'What if we get a winter like we had last year, with even the Thames so hard-frozen that there was a fair held on it, and the whole country snowbound? A nice thing it would be if Jenny was to be took ill of a sudden! Why, you'd never get the rabbit-catcher here, let alone –' He broke off in confusion, and corrected himself. 'The month-nurse, I *should* say! Yes, you may laugh, my lord, but it wouldn't be a laughing matter!'

'No, of course it wouldn't. But these apprehensions never troubled my mother, sir! Of her five children, four of us were born at Fontley – one of my sisters in November, myself in January.'

'That's got nothing to say to anything. Without meaning any disrespect to her la'ship, she's one of the lean 'uns, and it's my belief they brush through the business a deal more easily than roundabouts like my Jenny.'

Adam was silent for a moment; then he said: 'Very well, sir. It shall be as you think best. But I'm afraid she won't like it.'

This was soon found to be an understatement. When the news was broken to Jenny that she was to return to London, there to await the birth of her child, under the aegis of a fashionable accoucheur, she flew into a towering rage which considerably startled Adam, and reminded him forcibly of her father. That worthy was also surprised. He said that he had never known her to put herself into such a passion, and recommended her not to cut up so stiff. She rounded on him. 'I knew how it would be!' she said. 'Oh, I knew how it would be, the instant I told you I was breeding! I wish I hadn't done so! I wish you'd never come to Fontley! Well, I won't go to London! I won't see Dr Croft! I won't –'

'Don't you think you can talk to me like that, my girl!' interrupted Mr Chawleigh ominously. 'You'll do as you're bid!'

'Oh, no, I will not!' she flashed. 'Not as you bid me, Papa! You've no business to interfere – spoil it all –'

'Jenny.'

Adam had not raised his voice, but it checked her. Her narrowed eyes went swiftly to his face, glaring but arrested. He went to her, and took her hands, holding them closely, and saying, with a faint smile: 'A little beyond the line, Jenny. Ring your peal over me, not over your father!'

She burst into tears.

'Jenny!' ejaculated Mr Chawleigh, aghast. 'Now, give over, love, do! There's no call –' He stopped, encountering his son-in-law's eyes. Their message was unmistakable; so, too, was the tiny jerk of the head towards the door. It was many years since Mr Chawleigh had bowed to authority, and he was quite at a loss, when he found himself outside the room, to account for his submission.

'Adam!' Jenny uttered, tightly gripping his hands. 'Don't heed Papa! I'm very well! I promise you I am! I don't *wish* to leave Fontley! I mean to be so busy – and you know we are to have shooting-parties – and the hunting! You *told* me you were looking forward to that! Adam –'

'My dear, if that's what troubles you there's not the smallest need! I daresay you'll grant me leave of absence now and then! I wish we might have stayed here through the winter, but your father won't hear of it, and – Jenny, think! How *can* I go against him in a matter which concerns *your* well-being?'

She pulled her hands away, saying in a trembling voice: 'You don't wish to go against him. You don't wish me to be here. You never did! You had rather see Fontley fall into ruin than allow me any part of it! You won't even like to see your son here, because he'll be my son too!'

'*Jenny!*'

She gave a strangled sob, and fairly ran out of the room, slamming the door behind her.

For a few minutes he was furiously angry. They had been going on so comfortably together that he had almost forgotten the time when he had not wanted her at Fontley. Her outburst seemed to him unjust; her final words unpardonable. His heart hardened against her. Then his good sense told him that those words at least had been flung at him merely because she was in an ungovernable rage, and could think of nothing worse to say.

He went out presently into the garden. He supposed that he ought to go in search of Jenny, but his anger still smouldered; and because her words had held so much truth he did not know what he could say to reassure her. She was too acute to be deceived by lip-service, and in his present mood of resentment he knew he would find it hard to offer her even as much as that.

He crossed the lawn with his slightly halting step, and passed into the rose-garden. Here Jenny found him some minutes later. He was rather absently nipping off the withered blooms, and when he saw her, hesitating under the arch of the yew hedge, he looked gravely at her, saying nothing.

She had seldom appeared less attractive, for her face was swollen with her tears. She said huskily: 'I beg your pardon! I didn't mean it! Forgive me – pray!'

His heart melted. He moved quickly towards her, not thinking that she was plain and commonplace but only that she was in trouble. He said in a light, caressing tone: 'As though I didn't know that! What a shrew I have married! Scolding like a cut-purse merely because your father and I have more regard for your health than you have!'

'It was very bad,' she muttered. 'I don't know what made me – I think it must be my situation!'

'Oh, indeed?' he said. 'All the fault of this son whom I shall dislike to see here! Well, if he means to make his mama as cross as a cat I certainly shall dislike to see him here, or anywhere else!'

She hung her head, saying imploringly: 'Oh, no, no! How could I say such a wicked thing? I know it wasn't true!'

He patted her shoulder. 'So I should hope! Moreover, Lady

Lynton, if you think that I dislike seeing *you* here you must be even more gooseish than I had supposed – which is not possible!'

She laughed, rather shakily, but said, after a moment's hesitation: 'You don't *wish* to go back to London, do you?'

'No, I don't. I'd thought we were snugly settled here for the winter, and came shockingly near to recommending your papa to go to the devil. But there's no denying that you're not in high health, Jenny, or that Fontley is rather too remote for either your father's peace of mind or mine. It may be that you'll need a more skilled practitioner than old Tilford. It's a great bore, but we'll run no stupid risks, my dear.'

'No,' she said submissively. 'I'll do what you think right. How soon must we go? Not *quite* yet – need we?'

'No, not if you go on fairly prosperously. Next month, before the winter begins to set in. And if this top-of-the-trees doctor of your father's gives you leave, I'll bring you back again. That's a promise!'

She began to look more cheerful, though she said wistfully, as they strolled back to the house, her hand tucked into Adam's arm: 'I wanted him to be born here, where you were born.'

'But for anything we know she might prefer to be born in London,' objected Adam provocatively. 'You were, after all!'

'*She?*' exclaimed Jenny. '*No!*'

'I have a great fancy for a daughter,' said Adam.

'Well, I haven't!' said Jenny, in accents far more like her own. 'Not till we've a son, that is! If I thought – Good gracious, Papa is right! I *will* consult his horrid doctor!'

He gave a shout of laughter; and later, when Mr Chawleigh anxiously asked him if he had persuaded Jenny to behave like a sensible woman, replied promptly: 'Yes, indeed: like a woman of most superior understanding! I had only to hint that she might present me with a daughter to make her perceive instantly the wisdom of putting herself in the hands of an experienced accoucheur!'

'Now, Adam – !' protested Jenny.

'Yes, but it's not a bit of good thinking that he can do anything about *that*,' Mr Chawleigh pointed out.

'Good God! And you said he was top-of-the-trees!'

'I didn't say he was a magician! Yes, I know you're laughing at me, my lord, but it won't do for you to go putting a silly notion like that into Jenny's head. Oh, so now you're in whoops, are you, my girl? Well,' said Mr Chawleigh, regarding his hosts indulgently, 'I was always one for a good laugh myself, so I don't grudge it you.'

When he discovered that the Lyntons had no intention of removing to London until the end of October, he was by no means pleased; but, happily for the peace of the establishment, he was diverted by an accident to the pulley-wheel used in the ice-house. Anything savouring of mechanism immediately claimed his interest; and the rest of his short stay was spent very agreeably by him in overseeing the necessary repair, and devising a rather better arrangement of the sloping door in the passage above the vault.

Nineteen

The Lyntons returned to London at the end of October, in weeping weather. She was putting a good face on it, but it was Jenny who most regretted leaving Fontley. Adam had left his affairs there in as promising a train as his circumstances permitted, and had meant, in any event, to have gone to London for a time in November, when Parliament reassembled. He was looking forward also to seeing his friends again, for although the 52nd Regiment had been in England since the end of July he had as yet met only three of his particular cronies, who had visited Fontley on short furlough. These visits had been much more successful than Mr Chawleigh's. Far from disliking the situation of Fontley, or cavilling at the Priory's many inconveniences, the guests declared it to be the jolliest place imaginable. They enjoyed some excellent partridge shooting; they were extremely well-fed; and their hostess did not expect them to do the pretty. She ministered to their creature comforts, and was apparently pleased if they spent a whole evening in the exchange of Peninsular memories instead of making polite conversation to her. They thought her a capital woman, Captain Langton going so far as to say, with a disarming grin: 'It's a great shame Dev sold out, Lady Lynton! You'd have made a famous wife for a soldier, for nothing ever puts you out! No matter how late he returned to his quarters I'll swear you'd have had a first-rate dinner waiting for him!'

Mr Chawleigh was not present to welcome the Lyntons when they arrived in Grosvenor Street, but he had called there earlier in the day, with a carriage-load of flowers and fruit. Adam could accept such minor tokens of his generosity with equanimity, but it was with tightening lips that he read the note Mr Chawleigh had left for him. Mr Chawleigh had taken it upon himself to request Dr Croft to call at Lynton House on the following day. Adam handed this missive to Jenny without a word. She was so indignant that his own vexation abated, and instead of telling her that he would thank her father to leave him to manage the affairs of his household he found himself excusing that worthy's officiousness, and saying instead that she must not be too provoked, since it sprang only from concern for her welfare.

She was not at all appeased, but said: 'Adam! You'll be pleased to tell Dr Croft that I've changed my mind – don't wish to see him! And *I* will tell Papa that I'll choose my own doctor, or let *you* do so!'

'That would teach him a lesson,' he agreed. 'It would relieve our spleens too, I daresay. The only rub is that we might – when we were cooler – feel a trifle foolish! After all, it was to consult Croft that we came to town, wasn't it?'

'Yes, but –'

'My love,' he said, smiling, 'if ever I enter upon an engagement with your father I'll take care to choose my ground! I don't like this position at all – and I don't like Pyrrhic victories either! I should win nothing but your father's resentment, and an inferior doctor to attend you. I think we'll admit Croft.'

'Oh, very well!' she said crossly. 'But I'm persuaded I shall dislike him excessively!'

In the event, neither of them was drawn to Dr Croft. He was so pompous as to appear opinionated; and he managed to convey the impression that any lady acquiring his services might think herself fortunate. However, his practice was known to be large; and if his manners were too assertive to be generally pleasing he spoke with an authority which engendered confidence in his patients. He was not surprised to learn that Jenny was in poor health, and he did not hesitate to tell her the cause. She was too full-blooded, and too high in flesh: he would prescribe a reducing diet for her, and bleed her once or twice. He explained just how this would benefit her constitution, recounted a few quelling anecdotes relating to ladies of Jenny's habit to whom he had been summoned too late to remedy the harm done by over-eating, and took his leave, promising to visit Jenny again a week later.

She accepted his pronouncement more readily than Adam, saying in a resigned voice that she knew she was too fat. He was doubtful, knowing that she had a hearty appetite; and when he found her lunching on tea and bread-and-butter he protested. 'Jenny, this can't be right! You are always as hungry as a hawk by noon!'

She shook her head. 'I'm not now. I've felt queasy from the start, not fancying my food, and sometimes downright nauseated by the very sight of it, but I'm bound to own I'm better in that respect since I adopted this diet. Now, my dear, just you let the doctor know best, and forget about it!'

He said no more, conscious of his own ignorance; and she, fearful that she might resemble her mother too closely, adhered to her depressing regimen, and tried not to let Adam see that she was in low spirits.

For these, London was more to blame than Dr Croft. The weather was dull, with a good many rainy days, and some foggy ones. Jenny began to hate the gray streets, and could not look out of her windows without wishing herself back at Fontley; or put on her hat, her furred pelisse, and her kid gloves without longing to be able to step out of the house into her own gardens, with none of these elaborate preparations for taking the air. She tried to confide these yearnings to Mr Chawleigh, when he rallied her on being what he called mumpish, but as he could not understand how anyone could hanker after the country he thought she was being fanciful, and ascribed it to her condition. Nor could he understand that the chief cause of her drooping spirits was boredom. Had she complained that she was bored at Fontley it would have been another matter, for as far as he could see there was nothing for her to do there. In London there were endless amusements, such as shops, and theatres, and concerts. He said kindly: 'You don't want to give way to crotchets, love. Not but what it's natural you should get all manner of odd notions into your head just now. Well do I remember your poor ma before *you* were born! Nothing would do for her but to eat dressed crabs, which wasn't a dish she was at all partial to, not in the ordinary way. Well, if I hadn't put my foot down it's my belief you'd have been born with claws, and that's a fact!' He laughed at this recollection, but finding that his joke drew only a slight smile from Jenny said persuasively: 'Now, you know it's all fudge, love! You wasn't bored when you had only me to keep house for, so why should you be bored now, when you've got a husband, and a baby coming and a fine house of your own, and everything you could wish for?'

The thought flashed into her mind that before her marriage she had accepted boredom as the inescapable lot of women, but she said nothing, because she loved him too well to hurt him.

But Jenny owed more to her mother's ancestry than Mr Chawleigh knew, or than she herself had known until Adam had taken her to Rushleigh. She had thought then how much she would enjoy living in a country house of her own, and she had enjoyed it. She took a keen interest in all Adam's schemes for the improvement of his estate; and she had formed a number of schemes of her own for restoring the Priory to its former state. She was practical; and she was a born housewife. Fontley offered her endless scope for her talents; she had looked forward to a winter crammed with employment. The Dowager had left all household matters in the hands of her servants; but Jenny had found a manuscript book in the library which Adam said had been his grandmother's; and its pages revealed that that long-dead Lady Lynton had not disdained to interest herself in such homely matters as *How to Make a Marmalade of Oranges*, and *A Better Way to Pickle Beef*. She had known how to make a *Gargle for a Sore Throat*; and she had stated (in an underlined bracket) that her *Own Mixture of Quicksilver, Venice Turpentine, and Hog's Lard* was the best she had discovered for *Destroying Bugs*.

The winter months would have been all too short for Jenny at Fontley; in London each day was interminable. As her depression grew her placidity diminished. She began to be vexed by trifles, and to fall into a fret of apprehension if Adam came home later than she had expected. She sent him off to Leicestershire for a day's hunting; but when he had gone she spent the time until his return either picturing him lying (like his father) with a broken neck, or indulging an orgy of self-pity, when she first imagined herself to be neglected, and then decided that no one could blame Adam for escaping from so cross a wife as she had become.

From such thoughts as these it was a short step to speculation on the chances of her own death. One gloomy day of fog she occupied herself in drawing up her Will. It seemed a sensible thing to do, even if it did lead her to imagine Adam married to a handsome but heartless female, who would give him muffins for breakfast, and hideously ill-treat her stepson. But when Adam surprised her at this dismal task he was quite unimpressed by her forethought. He put the Will on the fire, and told her she was a goose; and when she said that she would like Lydia to take care of her child he replied that as it was more than likely that Lydia would hold the infant upside-down he thought she had better take care of it herself. That made her laugh, because when he was with her her gloomy imaginings vanished. She was ashamed of yielding to them, afraid that Adam would grow disgusted with an ailing wife; and yet, while she tried to conceal her wretchedness from him, she felt ill-used when he did not appear to notice it. She drove him from her side; but when he had gone away to spend a convivial evening with some of his friends she thought how strange it was that men never saw when one was out of sorts, or said the right thing at the right moment, or understood how miserable it made one to feel always invalidish.

But Adam, who had endured months of real suffering, did understand, and he was deeply troubled for her. He asked her once if she had no relation she would like to have with her to bear her company, but it seemed that she did not know any of her relations. She retained a dim memory of Aunt Eliza Chawleigh, who had died when she was a little girl; but she had no acquaintance with any of her mother's family. They had not liked Mama's marriage to Papa, and there had been a coolness. . . . 'And I don't want anyone to bear me company!' she said. 'Why you should have taken such a notion into your head I'm sure I don't know!'

He said no more; but when he met Lord Oversley in Brooks's, and learned that he had brought his family to London for a few weeks, he called in Mount Street at the first opportunity, and sought counsel of Lady Oversley.

'Oh, poor Jenny!' she exclaimed. 'I know *exactly* how she feels, for I was *never* well in the same situation! I have been meaning to pay her a visit, but there has been so much to do – But you may depend upon it that I shall go to her immediately! My dear Adam, I am persuaded you need not be anxious! If Dr Croft has her in charge you may be sure all will be well!'

'So he tells me,' replied Adam. 'But Jenny is very unlike herself: not as stout, I suspect, as when I brought her to London. Croft takes me out of my depth with his medical talk, but – Ma'am, *can* it be right to keep her on such a low diet, and to bleed her into the bargain?'

He won no support. Lady Oversley begged him not to meddle in matters of which he must be ignorant. The reducing treatment for pregnant ladies was one of the latest discoveries of science: she was only sorry that it had not been in fashion in her day, for she had no doubt she would have derived great benefit from it. 'You know, dear Adam,' she said, 'it is a mistake for husbands to concern themselves too closely in these affairs. Oversley *never* did so, except over my *first* – that was dear Charlie! – when he made me so nervous that I should have become perfectly distracted, had not my dear mother intervened.'

She went on to tell him of the very sensible things her dear mother had said, but he listened only with half an ear. Her comfortable talk about her mother, her sisters, and her innumerable aunts and cousins, served to point the difference between her situation and Jenny's: she had a host of affectionate relations at her back; Jenny had no one but her father and himself.

He was thinking how impossible it was to shirk that heavy responsibility when Julia came into the room. She came quickly forward, holding out her hand, and exclaiming, with a note of joyful surprise in her voice: 'Why – *Adam*!'

He rose at once, and took her hand; but although he smiled and responded to her greeting there was a preoccupied frown in his eyes, and he turned back almost immediately to Lady Oversley, saying: 'I hope you may be right. I don't know – but I'm perfectly ignorant, as you have said.' He held out his hand. 'I must not stay: perhaps, when you have seen Jenny – In any event, your visit will do her good, I know. And you'll tell me then what your opinion is?'

She assented to this, warmly clasping his hand, and patting it. 'To be sure I will! But I'm persuaded there can be no reason for you to be on the fidgets.'

'What is it?' Julia demanded, her eyes searching Adam's face. 'You are in trouble!'

'Indeed I'm not!' he answered, smiling at her. 'Just a little anxious about Jenny, so I came to ask your mama's advice.' He glanced at the clock. 'I must be off! No, don't trouble to pull the bell, ma'am! I'll let myself out. Goodbye, Julia: I'm glad to have had a glimpse of you – and don't ask you how you do, for I can see that you're in great beauty – not in the least dimmed by these abominable fogs!'

A brief handshake, and he was gone, leaving Julia to turn bewildered eyes towards Lady Oversley. 'How strangely he spoke! Anxious about Jenny? Why, Mama? Is she ill?'

'Oh, no, dearest! It's merely that she's in a promising way, and feels a trifle sickly. I daresay it's nothing. I often felt dreadfully low myself.'

'In a promising way!' Julia repeated blankly. 'You can't mean – Oh, Mama, *no*!'

Lady Oversley eyed her uneasily. 'Now, my pet, don't, I

implore you, fly into a taking! It was only to be expected, you know, and a very good thing for them both!'

A convulsive shudder shook Julia; she walked over to the window, and stood staring blindly out. She said, in a queer voice: 'Only to be expected. How – how stupid of me!'

Lady Oversley could think of nothing to say to this; and after a moment or two Julia said, with an effort: 'Is Jenny feeling out of sorts? And Adam is anxious. His mind was full of Jenny.'

'Well, naturally, my love –'

'Naturally, Mama? *Naturally?* When so short a time ago –' Her voice broke; she went swiftly out of the room, leaving her mother in a state of the liveliest apprehension.

Much to Lady Oversley's relief, however, she seemed perfectly calm when she came down to dinner. She even offered to go with her mother to visit Jenny on the following day; but this her ladyship declined, on the excuse of wishing to talk privately to Jenny about her condition.

Jenny was glad to see her, but not communicative. She said that she was very well, and seemed, indeed, to be so much her usual self that Lady Oversley was able to tell Adam that she could find no cause for anxiety. 'To be sure, she looks a little pulled, but you need not refine too much upon that,' she said. 'I daresay she gets moped – and no wonder, in this horrid weather! It is a pity she hasn't a sister to bear her company. Depend upon it, that's all that's amiss: she is too much alone, and so falls into reflection, which is *fatal*, even when one is perfectly stout, because it lowers one's spirits so odiously!'

With this he had to be satisfied; but when Jenny gave him an angry scold for having discussed her situation with Lady Oversley he thought that however cheerful a front she might have presented to that lady she was very far from being her usual self. It was so unlike her to fly into odd rages that he was more perturbed than he allowed her to see. He charmed her out of her tantrum, but while he was promising to refrain in future from troubling himself about her he was turning over in his mind various plans for her well-being.

Three days later he told her that he was going out of town on business, and would be absent for two days. She asked him, rather wistfully, if he was going to Fontley, but he only shook his head, saying: 'No, not to Fontley. I don't expect to be more than one night from home, but I might be a little late – so will you have one of your admirable suppers ready for me on Thursday, *kind* Jenny?'

She could not help smiling, but it was reluctantly, and her voice was decidedly pettish when she said: 'You need not hurry home on my account! Pray don't come on Thursday if it shouldn't be convenient to you!'

'I won't,' he promised, adding, in a soft, provocative voice: 'Crosspatch!'

'I'm not cross! And if you don't choose to tell me where you're going I'm sure I don't care!'

'Now *that*,' he said gravely, 'I am excessively relieved to know, because I *don't* choose to tell you – unless my errand prospers, when I'll make a clean breast of it.'

Her face puckered; she turned it away, saying in a thickened voice: 'I'm sorry! Don't heed me! You must think yourself married to a positive *vixen*!'

'No, just a hedgehog!' he assured her consolingly.

She was appeased, she could even laugh; but when ten o'clock had struck on Thursday evening she abandoned hope, realized that he had callously availed himself of her permission to remain away from home, and sank into gloom. The reflection that she had only her own ill-humour to thank for this miserable state of affairs did nothing to alleviate her woe; but before she had succeeded in convincing herself that he was seeking consolation in the arms of some dazzling bird of paradise she heard a carriage draw up in the street. She listened eagerly, torn between hope and a ridiculous wish not to be deprived of her grievance. But it was Adam. She heard his voice, and hurried out of the drawing-room to look down the well of the staircase. She saw him, and exclaimed: 'It *is* you!'

He looked up, laughing at her. 'Yes, and I've no need at all to tell you what my errand was! *You* shall instead tell *me* if I have brought you an agreeable surprise, ma'am!'

The next instant he was thrust rudely aside, and Lydia came running up the stairs, calling out: 'Jenny, isn't this *capital*? Oh, how happy I am to be here again! Wasn't it a splendid notion for Adam to take into his head? Are you glad to see me? *Please* say you are!'

'Lydia!' gasped Jenny, bursting into tears. 'Oh, *Lydia*!'

She very soon recovered from this most unusual demon-stration, emerging from Lydia's embrace with a transformed countenance, and uttering disjointedly: 'Oh, I was never more glad of anything! How kind of Lady Lynton – Oh, Adam, the idea of your doing such a thing, and never a word to me! I must have your room made ready immediately, love! If I had only known – ! Come into the warm directly: you must be frozen!'

There could be no doubt of her delight; Lydia's arrival acted upon her like a tonic, and within a very few minutes she had lost her weary look, and was chuckling over Lydia's account of her life in Bath, and her description of one Sir Torquil Tregony, whom she insisted on referring to as her Conquest. Jenny, round-eyed with astonishment, gathered, from the graphic word-picture offered her, that this unknown baronet was so stricken in years as to be tottering to the grave; but Adam, more conversant with his sister's notions, assumed (quite correctly) that the dotard was in the region of forty years of age, and slightly afflicted by rheumatism.

'*Fabulously* wealthy!' announced Lydia, helping herself to her third lobster patty. 'Oh, Jenny, you can't think how truly blissful it is to be here again, and to have such sumptuous things to eat! Aren't you going to have one of these delicious patties? You aren't eating anything!'

'I should think not, indeed, when I dined only a couple of hours ago!'

'On a morsel of chicken, and a baked apple?' interpolated Adam.

'Good gracious, are you obliged to starve if you have a baby?'

enquired Lydia. 'I never knew that before! And I must say –'

'Of course I don't starve!' said Jenny. 'Never mind about me! Tell us about this Sir Torquil of yours!'

'Oh, him! Well, Mama thinks him very eligible. In fact, she favours his Suit! Partly because he is very well connected, but mostly because of his wealth. Of course, I see that if I married him I should be able to eat lobster patties every day of my life, but lobster patties, after all, are not everything.'

'Very true!' agreed Adam. 'There is also cold pheasant – though even Sir Torquil's fortune won't enable you to eat that every day of your life. Here you are, snatch-pastry! don't hesitate to tell me if I haven't carved enough for you! Let me tell you, by the way, that Mama says you are inclined to encourage Sir Torquil's – er – Suit!'

'Well, yes,' admitted Lydia. 'But that was only because sitting at home every evening, listening to Mrs Papworth flattering Mama became so intolerable! Sir Torquil wanted to escort us to the Upper Rooms, you see, and I knew Mama would go if *he* invited us.'

'Oh, Lydia, you naughty girl!' Jenny exclaimed, much entertained. 'Of all the wicked flirts – ! And did you enjoy the Bath balls?'

'Not above half. All the Bath quizzes sit round the walls, staring at one – Brough says they are a set of fusty tabbies, and that Bath is the slowest place on earth.'

'Brough?' said Adam, surprised. 'Has he been in Bath? He said nothing to me about it!'

'Yes, he was visiting relations in the neighbourhood. At least, not precisely *visiting* them, because he stayed at the Christopher, but that was what brought him to Bath.'

'Relations living in the neighbourhood? I wonder who they may be? I had thought I was acquainted with most of his relations, but I never heard of any that lived in Somerset.'

'I don't know: he didn't tell us – and I don't think he liked them much, because he didn't seem to go out to see them often.'

By this time Jenny had succeeded in catching Adam's eye,

directing such a dagger-look at him that he blinked. 'Well, that was agreeable,' she said, transferring her attention to Lydia. 'And for how long can Lady Lynton spare you to me? I must write to tell her how very much obliged to her I am.'

'She says I may stay until Charlotte and Lambert go to Bath for Christmas. They mean to spend a night in town, you know, and so they can take me up. Oh, and whatever do you think? – Charlotte is increasing too!'

'No!'

'Yes, she is. Mama had the letter only this week.'

'How pleased she must be!'

'Yes, except that she has a presentiment that Charlotte's baby will take after Lambert. But I must tell you, Jenny, that she didn't say anything like that about your baby. She seems to think it will look just like Stephen, though why it should I can't imagine. However, it has put Mama into *such* a flow of spirits that I took care not to cast a doubt in the way. And I,' said Lydia proudly, 'shall be a *double* aunt!'

Jenny soon learned from Adam that very little persuasion had been needed to induce the Dowager to send her youngest loved one to her. The news that Jenny was soon to provide Fontley with an heir had acted powerfully upon her. As little as Jenny herself did she doubt that the child would be a boy; and so delighted was she that she sent a great many solicitous messages to 'dear little Jenny', and even forbore to censure her for feeling sickly. Adam delivered as many of these as he could remember, when he went into Jenny's room to bid her good night; and as soon as Martha had gone away he demanded to know why he had been glared at in the middle of supper. 'You surely don't think that Brough is dangling after Lydia?' he said incredulously.

'Good gracious, Adam, of course I do!' she exclaimed. 'It's as plain as the nose on your face!'

'But she's only a baby!'

'Fiddle!'

'Good God! Jenny, I'll swear she has no such thought in her head!'

'No, not yet,' she conceded. 'But you won't tell me she hasn't a decided preference for him! As for him, I suppose you think it was for the pleasure of *my* company that he came here so often when Lydia was with us, and escorted us all about! What's more, you've only to let him know that she's here, and mark me if he don't come up to town – to visit some more of his relations, I daresay!'

He laughed, but looked a little dubious. 'I shan't let him know. If you're right, I don't think we should encourage it – not yet, before she's out! I'm positive Mama wouldn't like it.'

'No, very true, but I fancy he knows that, and don't mean to pop the question yet. Something he said to me once makes me pretty sure that he knows you and my lady would say it was too soon. You wouldn't dislike it, would you, Adam, if it did come to pass?'

'Good God, no! I should be delighted.'

'And your mama?' she asked.

'Yes, I should think so. The Adversanes are as poor as Church mice, of course, and at the moment Mama's mind seems to be running on the fabulously wealthy Conquest, but –'

'You don't mean to tell me she really does wish Lydia to marry him? I thought it was just Lydia's nonsense! Well, I hope you'll put your foot down, my lord! The idea! And with a name like that, too!'

'Don't worry! I shan't have to,' he said, laughing. He bent over her to kiss her cheek. 'I must go, or Martha will give me a dressing for keeping you up till what she calls *all hours*. Good night, my dear: sleep well!'

'I know I shall. How comfortable it is to have Lydia with us again! Thank you for bringing her: you're so very kind to me!'

'Am I? Well, you are very kind to me,' he answered.

He left her happier than she had been for a long time. It was delightful to have Lydia again, but the chief source of her contentment sprang from Adam's visit to her room. He was always punctilious in bidding her good night, but he had never before come because he wanted to enjoy a private chat with her.

That was a new intimacy, which seemed to bring her closer to him than she had ever been. He was not her lover, but perhaps, she thought, dropping over the edge of sleep, she could become his friend. Friendship might hold no place in a girl's dreams, but dreams were insubstantial: escapes from reality into the glorious impossible. To consider the likely future was not to dream: it was to look forward; the essence of a dream was to ignore probability and one knew it, even at the height of fancy, when one imagined oneself the beloved of a slim young officer, whose eyes, weary with suffering, held so much kindness, and whose smile was so charming. No thought of friendship had entered plain, plebeian Jenny Chawleigh's quite hopeless dream; but friendship was not to be despised after all: it was a warm thing, perhaps more durable than love, though falling such a long way short of love. One ought never to dream, thought Jenny drowsily. It was better to look forward, and to picture oneself the trusted confidante of one's shining knight rather than the object of his romantic adoration. But he wasn't really a shining knight, she thought, snuggling her cheek into the pillow and sleepily smiling: only her darling Adam, who had to be tempted to his dinner, couldn't bear to have anything in his room disarranged, and disliked breakfast-table conversation.

Twenty

*T*he hope of becoming the repository of Adam's thoughts receded on the following morning. There were some thoughts he would never share with Jenny; and one was brought to light by Lydia, scanning the *Gazette* for items of interest while Jenny made tea, and Adam read what his ladies considered to be a very dull article in the *Morning Post* about the Congress of Vienna. Lydia gave a gasp suddenly, and exclaimed: '*Well!* Oh, no, I don't believe it! But they wouldn't publish it if it weren't true, would they? Well, upon my word!'

Adam paid no heed; but Jenny said: 'What don't you believe, love?'

'Julia Oversley is betrothed! And whoever do you think she is going to marry?'

Adam's eyes had lifted quickly; it was he who answered, saying in a level tone: 'Rockhill, I imagine.'

'Good gracious, did you know, then? But *Julia* – ! Why, he's older than Sir Torquil, I daresay! And Julia, of all people –' She stopped, realizing that she had been surprised into committing a social solecism, and flushed up to the roots of her hair.

'Older, but an even bigger Conquest!' Adam said lightly.

'Yes, I suppose so,' she said, conscience-stricken and subdued.

He retired again behind the *Morning Post*. Jenny broke the awkward silence, asking Lydia what she would like to do that day. Nothing more was said about the engagement until Adam rose from the table, when he said in the pleasant, cool voice which set Jenny beyond his barriers: 'You'll be writing to Julia,

I expect. Say everything from us both that is proper, won't you?'

She assented, and he went out of the room, pausing in the doorway to adjure her, with a faint smile, not to let Lydia wear her to death.

'As though I should!' said Lydia, as the door closed. She looked at Jenny, wanting to discuss the astonishing news, but not quite liking to broach the subject.

'You may say what you choose to me,' Jenny told her, 'but don't talk about it to Adam! He's bound to feel it, even though he may have guessed how it would be.'

'I wasn't perfectly sure that you knew,' Lydia said, rather shyly.

'Oh, yes! I always knew,' Jenny replied, with one of her tight smiles. 'I was very friendly with Julia in those days. I used to watch the way he looked at her. He'd no eyes for anyone else. She told me once I'd stolen him from her: much chance I ever had of doing that! Even had I wished to!'

'Didn't you? No, I don't mean that precisely. Didn't you wish to marry him? I thought –'

'Yes, you thought I wished to marry a man that didn't want me – was head over ears in love with another woman – just for the pleasure of getting a handle to my name!' Jenny broke in fiercely. 'Well, I didn't! I married him because there was nothing else I could do for him!' She caught herself up on a hysterical sob, and gave a gasp, almost immediately saying: 'Oh, I don't know what's come over me, talking like that! Don't heed me! I've grown so twitty and nervous, but I don't mean it! I've been in low spirits, you know, and things upset me that ought not to, like Adam's face just now –' Her voice shook, but she managed to control it. 'It's all nonsense. We go on very comfortably together, I promise you, and – and Adam won't always feel it as he does now, particularly if it's not for ever being stirred up, which it won't be – not if I know Rockhill! I shouldn't wonder if it turned out very well, that marriage, and I'm sure I hope it may. Rockhill's no fool, and he's got very engaging ways – for all you think him in his dotage, love!'

Lydia said slowly: 'She can't have been truly in love with Adam, can she? I mean, if –'

'Goodness knows!' said Jenny, getting up from the table. 'There's no saying – at least, I can't say! You'll not repeat anything I've said, will you? It was nothing but foolishness!'

'To Adam? No,' said Lydia, frowning a little. 'It wouldn't be of any use, would it? Like Mama telling me how deeply attached to me Sir Torquil is, as if that would make me feel a *tendre* for him!'

Jenny smiled rather painfully. 'No. It wouldn't be a bit of use. We'll take a walk to Hookham's presently, shall we? I want to change my books – but I must write to Julia first. I wonder what the Oversleys feel about this?'

She was soon to know, for Lady Oversley came to see how she did, two days later, and was easily persuaded to unbosom herself. Her feelings were mixed. She was but human, and it was impossible for her not to exult at her daughter's triumph; but she was a woman of overflowing sensibility, and it was equally impossible for her not to look on the alliance with dismay. 'If only I could be sure that she will be happy! Because of course it's a splendid match, and when I think of all the caps that have been set at Rockhill I can't help but feel proud! But I wanted Julia to marry for love, just as I did myself, and never have I regretted it, no matter how provoking Oversley may be, which he frequently is, because all men are, particularly when one is married to them! Only one makes allowances – but how, I ask you, Jenny, could one make allowances for a husband one didn't love? When I think of my precious Julia – her sensibility so exquisite, her nerves so delicate, so easily agitated – Oh, Jenny, my heart misgives me!'

'I thought you might not like it very much, ma'am,' Jenny said. 'But it's my belief Rockhill won't wound her sensibility in the way a younger man, without the half of his experience, would be bound to, sooner or later.'

'Yes, I've thought that too, and, as I told Oversley, there are

271

some girls who are happier with *old* husbands, who treat them with fatherly indulgence – if you know what I mean?'

Jenny nodded. 'Rockhill will do that. If you ask me, ma'am, there's little he don't know about handling females!'

'Nothing at all!' said Lady Oversley, with sudden astringency. 'When I think of all the mistresses he's had in keeping, ever since his wife died – and Oversley may believe what he chooses, but what *I* say is, Once a rake, always a rake! Then, too, I think him a very *odd* creature. Would you believe it? he *knows* Julia doesn't love him! For when he asked Oversley's permission to address her, Oversley thought it only right to tell him that she was – that there had been a previous attachment, which she hasn't quite recovered from. And he said, in the coolest way, that he knew all about it! You may imagine how Oversley stared! Julia told him herself, and he seems not to care a button!'

'No, he doesn't,' said Jenny decidedly. 'Well, I don't think he believes she broke her heart over Adam. And he don't care because he understands her, and doesn't set a bit of store by it when she flies into one of her ways. Depend upon it, he'll know how to make her happy!'

'That's what he told Oversley. I don't know, and I *cannot* like his being a widower! Such a *dispiriting* thing, setting aside the children, which, of course, one can't do!'

'Good gracious, has he got children!' exclaimed Jenny.

'Two little girls – though why I say *little*, when the elder is twelve years of age – ! When I think of my poor Julia, scarcely more than a child herself, trying to be a mother to two great stepdaughters, who will very likely detest her –'

'Not they! they'll adore her!' said Jenny. 'Just like all the younger ones did, at Miss Satterleigh's. I'll lay my life they'll be quarrelling over which of them is to have the pleasure of running an errand for her by the time she's been married a month!'

This reflection made Lady Oversley feel rather more cheerful; and she was able, before she left Jenny, to turn her thoughts towards the dress party she was holding in honour of the engagement. It was going to be a splendid function, following a dinner-party to which she was inviting as many of Rockhill's relations as she could squeeze round her table. As these were extremely numerous, she looked forward to seeing her house crammed to bursting-point: a gratifying state of affairs which yet could not quite compensate her for what she called the peculiar nature of the gathering. 'For in general, you know, it is the bridegroom's parents who are the guests of the greatest consequence, but of course Rockhill has none, and when one considers that it is he who is the head of the Edgcott family it is absurd to suppose that one can fall back on his uncle Aubrey! And I must say, Jenny, that although I do his sister Warlingham the justice to own that she has written Julia a very pretty letter, she is *years* older than I am, which is another thing I cannot like!'

The intelligence that all Rockhill's relations were being invited to celebrate his engagement afforded Jenny a satisfaction she did not disclose, and precluded her from feeling any surprise when she received a visit from Brough.

She and Lydia were alone: a circumstance which his lordship bore with noble equanimity. Jenny saw how his lazy eyes lit up when they fell on Lydia, and hoped that in extending a welcome to her husband's friend she might not be held to have encouraged his courtship.

Lydia was unaffectedly glad to see him, exclaiming, as she held out her hand to him: 'Brough! Well, what a surprise! You didn't think to find *me* here, did you? Adam fetched me, to bear Jenny company: isn't it famous?'

Yes, Brough thought it the most famous thing that had ever happened; and although he said nothing that went beyond the line of the strictest propriety it seemed very unlikely that he would post back to Leicestershire quite as soon as had been his original intention.

He had come to town, as Jenny had expected, to attend the Oversleys' party. He was himself related to Rockhill through his mother, but he said that the Edgcotts were nearly all of the opinion that Rockhill had run mad. 'Which is what brought me up to town,' he explained. 'M'mother thought most of 'em would

273

excuse themselves from attending the party: took it into her head that Rock would need support. All humdudgeon! wouldn't dare offend Rock, any of 'em! Though they tell me poor old Aubrey Edgcott is as sulky as a bear: made sure he was going to step into Rock's shoes one day!'

Brough regarded the alliance with a tolerant eye, but said, in a manner very unflattering to the lovely Miss Oversley, that one man's meat was another man's poison. 'Shouldn't like to be married to her myself,' he said.

'Now, you can't deny she'll make a beautiful Marchioness!' expostulated Jenny.

'Oh, lord, no! I daresay she'll cut an excellent dash, but she ain't my notion of a comfortable wife. Never any saying where you'll find her! might leave her up in the attics, and come home to find her in the cellar. None of my business, however. Where's Adam, Lady Lynton? I didn't see him in the club.'

'No, he has gone down to Fontley for a few days,' she replied.

He nodded, making no comment; but when she rather reprehensibly left him alone with Lydia presently, he cocked one mobile eyebrow at that damsel, saying: 'Lynton taking this business ill?'

She heaved a despondent sigh. 'Yes, I think he is. He *said* he had been meaning to go to Fontley this age past, but didn't like to leave Jenny alone, but I think he went because he couldn't bear to hear everyone discussing the betrothal wherever he went.'

'Very sensible thing to do,' said Brough. 'Wouldn't do to say so, of course, but it's my belief he's well out of that affair. Pity he didn't take her ladyship with him, and keep her there! She don't look to be in very plump currant.'

'She isn't, and I wish he *would* take her home, for it's where she wants to be,' said Lydia. 'Only Papa Chawleigh is in one of his grand fusses, and thinks she can't be well anywhere but in London, which, for my part, I think a great piece of nonsense. I told Adam so, but of course he doesn't heed what I say, because he doesn't think I know anything about it. Which,' she added fairly, 'is perfectly true. But I *do* know that Jenny is pining to go back to Fontley.'

Adam might not listen to his sister's advice, but fortunately for Jenny Lady Nassington took a hand in the affair. On her way to spend several weeks with her eldest married daughter in Sussex, she paused in London for a few days, and called at Lynton House one bleak morning to find Jenny recovering from a fainting-fit in the morning-room, with Lydia and Martha Pinhoe in anxious attendance, and the atmosphere redolent of burned feathers and aromatic salts.

'Upon my word!' uttered her ladyship, pausing on the threshold, and surveying the scene with strong displeasure. 'Pray, what is the meaning of this?'

'Good gracious, ma'am, how you startled me!' exclaimed Lydia. 'I didn't know you were in London! Jenny felt very faint suddenly, but she's better now.'

Jenny, pulling herself up, said huskily: 'It's nothing – so stupid – I never did such a thing before! I'm breeding, ma'am!'

'So I perceive,' said her ladyship. 'But as for fainting because of it, nonsense! I collect you've been quacking yourself: I thought you had more commonsense!'

Lydia was inclined to be indignant, but she soon realized that in her formidable aunt she had found a powerful ally. Lady Nassington first administered a dose of hartshorn and water to Jenny, and then demanded to be told why she was racketing about town instead of living peacefully in the country. When she had been put in possession of the facts, she condemned in round terms every person who had been concerned in them, and alarmed Jenny by saying that she would speak to Mr Chawleigh herself. Even Lydia felt that this might be going too far, but after thinking it over in majestic silence for a few moments Lady Nassington decided that before she did anything else it would be proper to consult Adam; so when Adam came in, some time later, it was to be met by the intelligence that his aunt wished him to call at Nassington House on the following morning; and by an entreaty from

Jenny not to allow her to give Mr Chawleigh the promised piece of her mind.

Far from being dismayed by the graphic account of Lady Nassington's visit, supplied by Lydia, his brow lightened, and he said: 'I never thought I should live to be glad Aunt Nassington had come to town! To be sure I'll go to see her!'

'Well, it's only right to warn you, my dearest brother, that she will very likely give *you* a piece of her mind!'

Even that failed to strike terror into his heart; he only laughed, and said that at least she could not eat him, however much she might scold him.

But although she told him that he had been behaving like a gaby, she did not scold, possibly because he said, as soon as he had dutifully kissed her hand: 'You can't think how thankful I am to see you, ma'am! I need advice, as I daresay you've guessed, and I've a notion I shall get better from you than from anyone else. You've seen for yourself how very far from well Jenny is. I don't know whether she told you about the treatment she's undergoing?'

'She did,' responded her ladyship grimly. 'I have no patience with such nonsense! Tea and toast indeed! A fine state of affairs when a healthy young woman is brought so low that she falls into fainting-fits! Between you all, she's begun to fancy herself an invalid. I am not acquainted with Croft, but I have no opinion of him: none at all! I do not approve of newfangled ideas. My advice to you, my dear Lynton, is to remove Jenny to Fontley immediately. Let her busy herself with bringing the Priory back into order, which I judge her to be well capable of doing. That, I assure you, will be very much better for her than to sit moping in Grosvenor Street, with nothing to do but to wonder if she'll die in childbed, like her mother! A pretty notion to have put into her head! When I see her ridiculous father I shall have something to say to him upon that score, I promise you!'

'Yes, ma'am,' he said, smiling a little. 'I don't doubt it! But there will be no occasion for you to see him. If I decide to follow your advice, I'll tell him myself. I own, I'm strongly tempted to do so. I believe Jenny would be better at Fontley. But –' He paused, and then said worriedly: 'I think I ought to get another doctor to her before taking such a step. Croft wishes to keep her under his eye – hints at all manner of complications. I haven't the knowledge to judge the case myself; I can't even say that she was well before we came back to town: she has been unwell from the outset – though I thought she seemed to be going on a degree more prosperously at Fontley. I agree that it was a thousand pities Mr Chawleigh should have alarmed her with his fore-bodings, but how can I brush them aside on nothing but your advice, aunt, and my own wholly unskilled judgement? If she were to be taken suddenly ill – ? If she were to endure a difficult labour – ?'

A just woman, Lady Nassington considered this dispassion-ately. 'Very true,' she said. 'I have frequently observed that you have a great deal of good sense, my dear Lynton. You cannot do better than to call upon Sir William Knighton for his opinion. I give you leave to say that you come to him on my recom-mendation. I have a high opinion of his skill. I venture to think you will be pleased with him.' She added dryly: 'And if you should encounter any objection from Chawleigh, you may inform him that Sir William is one of the Prince Regent's physicians. That, unless I mistake, which is not at all likely, will reconcile him to the change!'

So, three days later, Jenny prepared to receive yet another doctor. Adam brought him up to her room, but he did not stay, as she had made him promise he would. He merely introduced Sir William to her, smiled reassuringly, and withdrew, leaving her with only Martha to protect her from this new ogre.

But Sir William, whom the Prince Regent declared to be the best-mannered doctor he had ever known, was not at all ogreish. Within a very few minutes, Jenny's prickles were laid; and Miss Pinhoe, at first standing, dragon-like, beside her chair, had retired into the background, and was endorsing the doctor's utterances with wise nods. Usually inarticulate, Jenny found herself able to talk quite freely, telling this understanding listener far more about herself than she would have thought possible. When he took his leave, he said with his pleasant smile: 'Well, do you know, Lady Lynton, I think your good father has refined a little too much on your mother's misfortunes. I am going to tell his lordship that in my opinion he should take you into the country, and see to it that you have plenty of fresh milk, and cream, and good country-butter. How much I envy you! a beautiful place, Fontley Priory! I recall that I was once taken to visit it, on a Public Day. Goodbye: I shall hope to hear – indeed, I feel sure I *shall* hear – of your happy delivery, ma'am!'

She held out her hand to him, and when he took it, bowing, held it tightly, saying: 'Thank you! I am so much obliged to you – I can't tell you!' Her feelings choked her; she could only squeeze his hand fervently, and look speakingly up into his face.

Sir William then went downstairs, to talk to Adam, over a glass of sherry. He did not utter one word in disparagement of Dr Croft: indeed, he referred to him as his distinguished colleague. He said that he had the greatest admiration for his skill, and could testify to some of his remarkable achievements in cases thought to be quite hopeless. But it sometimes happened – as no doubt his lordship had noticed in other fields – that men of genius were inclined to run amuck on what he ventured to call pet theories. In short, treatment which was admirable in some cases might well be deleterious in others. Perhaps Dr Croft, relying too much on the information given him by her ladyship's parent, had not sufficiently considered the constitution of his patient's mind. Possibly her ladyship's very deep reserve had made it difficult for her to confide in him. For his part, Sir William believed that it was of paramount importance that ladies in delicate situations should be contented. He could discover no reason for supposing that complications would render her ladyship's confinement perilous; but if my lord felt that the Family Practitioner might need advice and assistance he would be happy to furnish him with the name of an excellent accoucheur, resident in Peterborough.

After that, the two gentlemen enjoyed a pleasant chat about

Spain, which interesting country Sir William had visited in 1809, when, as his medical adviser, he had accompanied Lord Wellesley there; and by the time they shook hands on the door-step Adam entertained quite as good an opinion of Sir William as did his Aunt Nassington.

He went upstairs, to find Jenny radiant, and Lydia triumphant. Jenny stammered: 'He says I am to go home! Not to lower myself any more! He says there's nothing amiss with me but being *blue-devilled*! Oh, I am so much obliged to you for bringing him to see me!'

Only one circumstance marred her joy: she was afraid Papa would be very angry, might even forbid her to leave London: did Adam think that if Papa saw Sir William Knighton *himself* he might consent to let her go?

'Pooh!' said Lydia saucily. 'Only let *me* talk to Papa Chawleigh!'

'Lydia, you shouldn't call him that! I *know* your mama wouldn't like it!' said Jenny.

'Well, that's of no consequence, because she doesn't know anything about it, and I shouldn't think she ever would know. I am *deeply* attached to Papa Chawleigh, and *he* likes it! Shall I go to visit him in the City tomorrow, to tell him what has been decided?'

'No, miss, you shall not!' replied Adam. He smiled at Jenny. 'How soon can you be ready to leave town? Do you want this hoyden to go with us, or shall we send her back to Bath?'

'No, indeed! Of course I want her! But Papa –'

'My dear, stop teasing yourself about your papa! I shall see him tomorrow, and tell him just what Knighton said to me.'

'I don't wish you to quarrel with him!' she blurted out.

'I won't!' he promised.

Knowing her father, she could not be satisfied; she tried to tell him that it would be wiser if she were to break the news to Mr Chawleigh herself; but he only laughed, and recommended her to turn her attention to all the shopping he was persuaded she must want to do before leaving town.

He kept his word to her; and she never knew how great a strain had been imposed upon his temper, any more than the goggling clerks in the counting-house knew how vainly their employer's too-audible fury had expended itself against the barrier of my lord's good-breeding.

When he entered the establishment from which Mr Chawleigh directed his many commercial activities his appearance created a considerable stir. He had never before visited Mr Chawleigh at his place of business, but there was no one within its portals who did not know that Miss Chawleigh had married into the cream of society, and very few who were not agog to obtain a glimpse of her lord.

It was not until he had handed in his visiting card, with a request that it should be taken to Mr Chawleigh, that he attracted any particular attention from the busy clerks in the counting-house, for although he was always dressed with propriety, and a certain military neatness, he flaunted none of the hall-marks of the Dandy, or the Corinthian. But the clerk who received his card contrived to allow one of his fellows a glimpse of it, as he bore it off; and long before Mr Chawleigh had surged out of his private office to greet his son-in-law, the whisper that it was Miss Chawleigh's husband had run round the large room.

'Come in, my lord, come in!' Mr Chawleigh adjured him. 'This is a surprise, and no mistake! And what brings you into the City, I wonder? Nothing amiss, is there?' he added, in a suddenly sharpened voice.

'No, nothing at all, sir. It's merely that I want to talk to you. Are you very busy, or can you spare me a few minutes?'

'Ay, as many as you like! Step into my office, my lord – and see to it I'm not disturbed, Stickney!'

He ushered Adam into his room, shooting a suspicious, side-long glance at him as he did so. He wondered if my lord had run into Dun territory, but it didn't seem likely, for he had no expensive tastes; and, as far as could be discovered, he wasn't a gamester either.

'Now, what can I do for you, my lord?' he asked jovially, having seen Adam comfortably seated, and lowered his own massive form into the chair behind his desk.

'Why, nothing, sir! I've come to talk to you about Jenny.'

'Ay, have you? Well? You said there was naught amiss, so I take it she ain't ill?'

'No – that is to say, no worse than when you saw her last week. On the other hand, she's not at all well, and she grows no better. I've never concealed from you that I don't think Croft's treatment the right one for her –'

'Much you know about it!' growled Mr Chawleigh. 'Now, lookee, my lord! –'

' – and so, yesterday, I brought in Sir William Knighton to see her.'

'Oh, you did, did you? Never thought of consulting *me*, I collect?'

'No,' agreed Adam tranquilly. 'I knew what your opinion was, sir.'

Mr Chawleigh's colour began to rise. 'I'll thank you to tell me what right you've got to go calling in strange doctors to my Jenny without so much as a by your leave!'

Adam regarded him rather quizzically. 'My dear sir, will you not rather tell me what conceivable right anyone *but* me has to do so?'

'I'll tell you fast enough! I have!' declared Mr Chawleigh, glaring at him.

'You're mistaken, sir.'

'Oh, I am, eh? We'll see that! I'll have you remember that I'm her father, my lord!'

'Of course you are, and as her father you have every right to inform me of it, if you think she is not being treated as she should be. But you could hardly call in another doctor to her without first obtaining my permission, could you?' He smiled. 'Come, sir, don't let us quarrel over absurdities! Are you trying to persuade me that if I had told you I meant to call in Knighton you would have objected? You won't do it!'

Mr Chawleigh looked a little taken aback. 'I don't say that, but what I do say is that I don't care for being ridden over rough-shod!'

'Nor do I, Mr Chawleigh,' said Adam gently.

Their eyes met, the one pair rather aloof, the other fierce under their craggy brows. Mr Chawleigh shifted in his chair, clenching one huge hand on its arm. 'Oh! You don't? Well. . . . So you brought in this Knighton – whoever he may be!'

'He is one of the Regent's doctors, and was strongly recommended to me by my Aunt Nassington.'

'Oh, so she's in it, is she? I might ha' guessed as much!' exploded Mr Chawleigh. 'Well, I'd like to give her ladyship a piece of my mind, and that's a fact!'

'And she wishes to give you a piece of hers,' said Adam. He smiled delightfully upon his fulminating father-in-law. 'What a battle of giants it would be! I shouldn't know which of you to lay my blunt on. My aunt was very much shocked, you know, to find Jenny just coming round from a fainting-fit.'

'Fainting? *Jenny?*' Mr Chawleigh said quickly. 'Eh, that won't do! What has Croft to say to it?'

'I didn't inform him of it.'

'*Didn't inform him?* Are you going to tell me that you brought in this other fellow without Croft was there too? And he *came?* If that don't beat the Dutch! Why, it's unheard of! Doctors don't do such – not the bang-up ones! Jenny was Croft's patient, and you should have told Knighton so!'

'I am afraid,' said Adam apologetically, 'that by the time I saw Knighton Jenny had ceased to be Croft's patient. He seemed so much inclined to take umbrage at my wishing for another opinion, and to be so entirely convinced of his own infallibility, that it was really quite useless for Jenny to continue with him, particularly when she didn't like him.'

'*You* didn't like him, my lord!' Mr Chawleigh shot at him.

'No, not at all.'

'Ay! So I knew! If Jenny took against him, I'll be bound it was your doing! I see what it is! You went and picked out a quarrel with him –'

'*Picked out a quarrel with a doctor?*' interrupted Adam, putting up his brows. 'Good God!'

Mr Chawleigh brought his fist down with a crash on the desk. 'You may think to come the lord over me, but you'll catch cold at it! I took care to choose the best for my Jenny, and by God, I'll not have him turned off just because you don't like him! It's him as pays the fiddler that calls the tune, my lord!'

Adam closely gripped his lips together, his eyes narrowed, and very hard. It was a moment or two before he could command himself, but he managed to do it, and to say, quite pleasantly: 'Very true. Did you imagine that you were paying this piper, sir? Let me disabuse your mind of that misapprehension! I have settled Croft's account as I shall settle Knighton's, and the account of any other practitioner who may attend Jenny.'

In a towering passion, Mr Chawleigh flung down his gauntlet. 'Say you so? Well, it was me that engaged Croft, and it's me that'll dismiss him, if I see fit, and until I do see fit he'll continue to attend Jenny, and so I shall tell him!'

'I don't think I should, if I were you, sir,' replied Adam, looking rather amused. 'You'd be making a great cake of yourself, you know. I may not like Croft, but I am quite sure he would not be guilty of the impropriety of attending my wife without my consent. Don't let us dispute on that head! After all, you can't seriously wish Jenny to continue with a doctor who is doing her no good, and whom she dislikes into the bargain! My aunt said that between us all she had become nervous and depressed. That is also Knighton's opinion. He recommends me to take her back to Fontley, and that, sir, is what I am going to do.'

Mr Chawleigh's colour had deepened to an alarming hue. So unaccustomed was he to meeting with opposition that he listened to this speech almost with incredulity. The last words, however, loosened his tongue, and the storm of his anger broke over Adam's head with a violence which reached the ears of the clerks in the counting-house, and caused several of the more nervous individuals there to blench and tremble. No one could distinguish what the old Tartar was saying, but no one could doubt that he was giving my lord a rare trimming; and considerable sympathy was felt for the poor young gentleman.

Adam listened to the tirade with outward calm. When in the grip of passion, it was not Mr Chawleigh's habit to mince his words, nor did he hesitate to utter any insult which occurred to him; but only by the crease between his brows did Adam betray the effort it cost him to keep his own anger under control. There were a number of things it would have given him much pleasure to have said to Mr Chawleigh, but he said none of them. It was wholly beneath him to brangle and brawl with the purple-faced vulgarian hurling abuse at him – and he had promised Jenny that he would not quarrel with her father. So he waited in rigid silence for the storm to blow itself out.

Mr Chawleigh did not expect to meet with retort. On the other hand, to be listened to in unmoved silence was a new and a disconcerting experience. By rights, this wispy son-in-law of his should be shaking in his shoes, possibly trying to stammer out excuses: certainly not sitting there, as cool as a cucumber, and looking for all the world as if he were watching a raree-show which didn't amuse him above half. As his rage abated, something very like bewilderment entered into Mr Chawleigh. Ceasing to rail at Adam, he sat staring at him, breathing heavily, still scowling, but with so much surprise in his eyes that Adam very nearly burst out laughing.

With the tickling of his ready sense of humour, much of Adam's own anger died away. He felt suddenly sorry for this absurd creature, who had clearly supposed that he could browbeat him into submission. He picked up his hat and gloves, and rose, saying, with a lurking smile: 'Will you dine with us tomorrow, sir? We leave town on the day after, but it would distress Jenny very much not to take leave of you.'

The veins swelled afresh in Mr Chawleigh's face. '*Dine* with you?' he uttered, in choked accents. 'Why, you – you –'

'Mr Chawleigh,' interrupted Adam, 'I owe you a great deal, I have a great respect for you – indeed, I have a great regard for you! – but I've not the remotest intention of allowing you to rule my household! If that was what you wanted to do you should have chosen another man to be Jenny's husband. Goodbye: may I tell Jenny to expect you tomorrow?'

Mr Chawleigh strove with himself, finally enunciating ominously: 'Ay! she may expect me all right and tight! But as for dining with you – I'll be damned if I do!'

'As you wish – but she'll be disappointed.' He went to the door, but looked back, with his hand on the knob, to say: 'Don't rip up at her, will you? She's more easily upset just now than you may know. But I don't think you'll wish to when you see how much her spirits have plucked up since Knighton told her she might go back to Fontley.'

He did not wait for a response, but went away, leaving Mr Chawleigh more at a loss than he had been since the days of his boyhood. The clerks eyed Adam covertly as he passed through the counting-house, and were almost as much astonished as their employer. He bore none of the signs of one who had passed through the furnace of the Tartar's fury: his step was firm, his brow serene, and the smile which he bestowed on the youth who leaped to hold open the door for him was perfectly untroubled. *'Well – !'* breathed Mr Stickney. 'I wouldn't have credited it! Not in a hundred years I wouldn't!'

Twenty-one

The Lyntons left London two days later, if not with Mr Chawleigh's blessing at least without any very serious manifestations of his disapproval. His fondness for Jenny restrained him from giving her anything but the mildest of scolds; and he found it impossible, in the face of her glowing looks, to cling to his belief that it was Adam and not she who wished to return to Fontley. What maggot had entered into her head he didn't know; but it was plain that she was as eager to be off as ever she had been to escape from Miss Satterleigh's seminary. He was inclined to take this in bad part, but Lydia was present to coax him out of his ill-humour, and although he was at first a trifle stiff with her it was not long before he was chuckling at her sallies, and telling her with obvious mendacity that she needn't think to come over him with her bamboozling ways.

When Adam presently entered the room, the cloud returned to Mr Chawleigh's brow. He still seethed with resentment, and responded to Adam's greeting with only the curtest of nods, at the same time informing his daughter that he must be off. She begged him to stay, but he said that he had an engagement in the City. He embraced her with great heartiness, and Lydia too; but when he saw that Adam meant to conduct him to his carriage he told him roughly not to trouble himself. However, Adam paid no heed to this rebuff, but followed him downstairs, nodding dismissal to the footman who was waiting to help him to put on his greatcoat, and performing this office himself.

'Much obliged to you, I'm sure!' Mr Chawleigh growled. He hesitated, shooting one of his fiery glances at Adam. 'If any ill comes of this, it'll be on your head!'

'Whatever had been decided must have been on my head, sir,' Adam replied quietly. He held out his hand. 'Forgive me! I know how you must feel, but at least believe that I'm not taking Jenny away to gratify any whim of my own! You may believe too that if it doesn't answer – if there should be the smallest reason for anxiety – I'll bring her back. But I hope there won't be – and you'll bear in mind that Knighton has furnished me with the name of an experienced accoucheur living no farther away from Fontley than Peterborough.'

'Oh, yes, you've got your way, my lord, and so now you think you'll turn me up sweet!' said Mr Chawleigh rancorously. 'I'm not going to do anything that might throw my girl into a taking, but I warn you, when I give my orders I'm used to having 'em obeyed!'

Adam could not help laughing at this. 'Why, yes, so am I! Very promptly, too! But I'm not a clerk in your office, any more than you are a soldier in my company, you know.'

Baffled, Mr Chawleigh strode forth to his carriage.

He drove home in a state of angry frustration, and later conducted himself so morosely at a convivial supper-party at the Piazza that it was generally supposed that one of his many trading enterprises must have failed. It was not until he was about to climb into his bed that he startled his valet by suddenly exclaiming: 'Well, there's not many as 'ud outface Jonathan Chawleigh, that I *will* say! Damme if I don't like him the better for it!' He then recommended the dejected Badger to take himself off, and got into bed, resolved to pay another visit to Grosvenor Street in the morning, to see the party off, so that Adam should see that he bore him no malice.

He arrived to find two travelling chaises and my lord's curricle drawn up outside Lynton House, and the second footman in the very act of placing two hot bricks in the foremost of the chaises. He brought with him a basket of pears, a bottle of his Fine Old Cognac (in case Jenny should feel faint), and a travelling-chessboard, to beguile the tedium of the journey for the ladies (neither of whom cared for the game); and he was very glad he had come, swallowing his pride, because Jenny's face lit up when she saw him, and the hug she gave him did his heart good. He had thought that there might be a little awkwardness between himself and his son-in-law, but there was none at all. No sooner did Adam set eyes on the Fine Old Cognac than he exclaimed: 'You don't mean to shut that precious pair up in a chaise with a whole bottle of brandy, do you, sir? Good God, they'll be as drunk as wheelbarrows before ever we reach Royston!'

This was a joke that kept Mr Chawleigh chuckling for quite some time. He made a joke himself presently, when Adam said: 'By the time you come to visit us, sir, I hope you'll find Jenny much stouter than she is now.'

'Nay, she can't help but be stouter!' retorted Mr Chawleigh.

At the last, when the two chaises bearing the ladies and their maids had moved off, he turned to Adam, and took his outstretched hand in an extremely painful grip. 'Well – you'll take good care of her, my lord!'

'You may be very sure I will, sir.'

'Ay, and you'll let me know how she goes on?'

'That, too. And *you* will come down to spend Christmas with us, remember!'

'Oh, you'll be having your grand friends to stay with you – though I take it very kind in you to invite me!'

'I shan't even be having any of my far from grand friends to stay – more's the pity! There's a pretty strong rumour that my Regiment is going to be ordered to America.'

'Well, I'll think about it,' said Mr Chawleigh. He transferred his grip to Adam's shoulder, slightly shaking him. 'It's time you was off. No hard feeling betwixt us, my lord?'

'None on my side, sir.'

'Well, there ain't any on mine. What's more,' said Mr Chawleigh resolutely, 'if I should have said anything uncivil when we had our turn-up, which maybe I might have done, I ask your pardon!'

Memories of the various offensive things which Mr Chawleigh had said on that occasion flitted through Adam's mind, but he realized that this rough apology represented a heroic sacrifice of dignity, and he responded immediately: 'Good God, sir, what's the world coming to, if you can't give a bear-garden jaw to your son-in-law?'

'Well, well, you're a good lad, lord or no lord!' said Mr Chawleigh. 'Off with you, now!'

He gave Adam a push towards his curricle, waited until he had driven out of sight, and then climbed back into his own carriage, which conveyed him to the head office of the New River Company, where, at a meeting of the principal directors, he more than atoned for any weakness he might have shown in his dealings with his son-in-law.

For Jenny, her mind relieved of its last care, this homecoming was one of almost unalloyed happiness. She reached Fontley in the gloom of a winter dusk; rain was falling, and there was a disagreeably dank chill in the air, but these ills in no way abated her delight. It was the third time Adam had handed her across his threshold, but on neither of the previous occasions had she felt, as she felt now: *This is my home!* Tears sprang to her eyes, and rolled down her cheeks; she saw Dunster and Mrs Dawes through a mist, and could only stammer: 'I'm so happy to be here again!' Then, ashamed of her emotion, she managed to smile, and to say: 'And I've brought Miss Lydia with me – which I know you'll be glad of!'

Little though she knew it, she could have done nothing to establish herself more securely in the regard of her household. Charlotte had told Mrs Dawes how very kind her ladyship had been to Miss Lydia; but it was not until Mrs Dawes had seen with her own eyes on what terms her ladyship stood with Miss Lydia that she realized that dear Miss Charlotte had not been trying, in her sweet way, to reconcile her to my lord's regrettable marriage: like true sisters they were, and who would have credited it that had seen Miss Lydia cry her eyes out when his lordship's engagement had been made known?

At the first opportunity, Lydia visited Charlotte; but although the sisters held one another in mutual affection they were not much akin, and the visit was not wholly successful. Lydia said afterwards that she hoped she valued Charlotte's virtues as she should, but that she had forgotten how dull was her conversation; and Charlotte, while firm in her admiration of her young sister's liveliness, was disturbed to find that instead of having learned a little more conduct Lydia seemed to have even less elegance of mind than when she had but just emerged from the schoolroom.

Unlike Jenny, Charlotte was in radiant health, and seldom had she been in better looks. She was happy in her marriage; she enjoyed being mistress of her own house; and she was looking serenely forward to the birth of the first of what she hoped would be many children. She suffered none of the ills which had attacked Jenny during the first months of her pregnancy; and contemplated without misgiving a long and tedious journey to Bath and back again. Jenny could only marvel at her, for although she was much improved in health by the time the Rydes departed on their visit to the Dowager the mere thought of being obliged to undertake such a journey made her shudder.

Parting from Lydia was a wrench, but it did not cast her into dejection. The lowness and oppression which had grown upon her in London had vanished within a week of her arrival at Fontley, and with the abandonment of her reducing diet her strength began to return, and, with it, her energy. She missed Lydia, but she had a thousand things to do, and took so keen an interest in everything that concerned the estate that her mind was too fully occupied to allow her to feel the want of that gay companionship. She was beginning to know the tenantry too. Knowing how shy she was, Adam had not urged her to perform all the duties which his mother and his grandmother had accepted as a matter of course; but Lydia, discovering her ignorance of her obligations, did not hesitate to instruct her: and so anxious was she to conform to the standard set by her predecessors that she overcame her shrinking, visited the sick, relieved the indigent, and tried her best to be affable. She had none of the Dowager's graciousness; she could never bring her tongue to utter the easy expressions of sympathy which would have won for her an instant popularity; but it was not long before it began to be realized that her brusque tongue concealed a far greater interest in the affairs of her lord's people than the Dowager had ever felt. The sturdy commonsense which made it easy for her to distinguish between the shiftless and the unfortunate might not win universal popularity for her, but it did win respect; she gave freely, but with discrimination; her advice was always practical; and if her blunt strictures were frequently unpalatable they left no one in any doubt that her ladyship was as shrewd as she could hold together.

When Mr Chawleigh arrived, laden with gifts ranging from a tie-pin blazing with diamonds set round a large emerald, which he bestowed upon his stunned son-in-law, to a pound of tea, he found Jenny immersed in preparations for the Christmas dinner it was the custom of the house to give to the farm workers and their families; and he was obliged to own (though grudgingly) that she seemed to be in tolerably good health. He was interested in this particular form of benevolence. He himself (in his own words) always did the handsome thing by his numerous dependants at Christmas; but the country habit of inviting all and sundry to a large party was unknown to him, his gifts taking a monetary form. He had never set eyes on the wives and children of the men he employed; but when he had accompanied Jenny on a visit to a sick woman in the village, he had good-naturedly entertained and astonished the invalid's numerous progeny with conundrums and conjuring tricks, and conceived the notion of adding his mite to the festivities by providing all the children with presents suitable for their various ages and sexes. Armed with the necessary information, he went off to Peterborough, where he ransacked the toyshops to such purpose that Adam told him that his memory would remain green in the district for many years to come.

His visit passed off very well. He was quite unreconciled to country life; he thought the wintry landscape was enough to give one the hips, and could not understand how anyone should prefer to look out upon a vista of gray fields than upon cosy, lamp-lit streets. The night stillness kept him awake; and the sound of cocks crowing at first light inspired him with nothing more than a desire to wring the birds' necks. But when he drove out with Jenny he derived immense gratification from seeing the forelocks which were pulled, and the curtsies that were bobbed whenever they met anyone on the way. That was something that did not happen in London, and it seemed to him to provide one good reason at least for her wish to live in the country. He liked it, too, when she leaned out to ask some woman how little Tom, who had the whooping-cough, did, or whether any tidings had come from Betsy, serving an apprenticeship to a milliner in Lincoln. He could scarcely believe it was his Jenny behaving like a great lady; and he told her, with deep pride, that she did it to the manner born.

She answered seriously: 'No, Papa, that's just what I don't do, and what I never will do, try as I may, because I'm *not* born, and it doesn't come easily to me.'

'Well, no one would believe it, love, so don't talk silly!' he advised her consolingly. 'Beautifully you do it!'

She shook her head. 'I don't. Not as Adam does, and Lydia too. I don't seem to be able to be so easy and friendly, the way they are.'

'To my way of thinking,' said Mr Chawleigh, 'it don't do to be too friendly with servants, and workmen, and such: it leads to them taking liberties.'

'That's what I can't help being afraid of,' she said, in a burst of confidence. 'But there's no one who'd take liberties with Adam, nor with Lydia, because they know just how to talk to people of all sorts, without ever thinking about it, as I do, and – and without its ever entering either of their heads that anyone would be impertinent.'

'Now, if anyone's been giving you back answers, Jenny –'

'Oh, no! No one would. But sometimes I wonder if they would, if I wasn't Adam's wife – when I forget to guard my tongue, and say something sharp.'

He did not quite understand this, but he detected a wistful note in her voice, and asked anxiously: 'You're not unhappy, love, are you?'

'No, no!' she assured him. 'Why, however could you ask me such a question?'

'Well, I don't know,' he said slowly. 'There don't seem to be any reason why you shouldn't be happy, for I've never seen his lordship behave to you other than I'd wish – and you may depend upon it I've kept my eyes open, for there was no saying but what he mightn't have treated you as civil as he does! But sometimes I fall to wondering if you're quite comfortable, my dear.'

'You needn't ever do that. And don't you start wondering if Adam's not every bit as civil to me when you're not by, for he is, and always – *always* so kind! Adam's a great gentleman, Papa.'

'Ay, that's what I thought the first day I clapped eyes on him – but what call you've got to nap your bib about it, my girl, I'm sure I don't know!'

'Well, I'm sure I don't know either,' returned Jenny, blowing her nose, but speaking with reassuring cheerfulness.

So when Mr Chawleigh left Fontley it was with a mind relieved of misgiving. He couldn't for the life of him see why Jenny liked it better there than in London, and it wasn't what he had planned for her, but there was no denying that she did like it, so no use for him to worry his head over what couldn't be mended. And my Lord Oversley, who had ridden over from Beckenhurst one day, had told him, in his jovial way, that he thought they might congratulate themselves on having made up such an excellent match. 'Turning out very well, don't you think?' said his lordship.

Oversley had posted down to Beckenhurst alone, and for a very brief stay. Julia's wedding was to take place early in the New

Year, and Lady Oversley was far too busy with the preparations for it to leave London. So the family remained in Mount Street: a circumstance for which Jenny felt thankful, since the customary exchange of visits between Fontley and Beckenhurst at this season would have been hard to avoid, and painful to maintain.

Adam had not seen Julia since the announcement of her engagement, and he had done his best not to think of her. Jenny was not even sure that he knew the actual date of the wedding, for the subject was never mentioned between them. He did know it, and could not drag his thoughts from it. He could picture Julia, the embodiment of his dreams, walking up the aisle on her father's arm, and he knew that he had reached the end of all dreaming. Whatever the future might hold there would be no enchantment, no glimpses of the isle of Gramarye he had once thought to reach.

It was folly to look back, ridiculous to suppose that Julia was more lost to him today than upon his own wedding-day, fatal to think of her married to Rockhill, whom he could only see as an elderly satyr. Better to count one's blessings, and to remember how much worse off one might have been.

Looking over his water-logged acres, he thought: *I still have Fontley*. Then, as he thought how much it would cost to bring his neglected land to prosperity, depression surged up in him again. He shook it off: it would take time to achieve his ambition; it would be years, perhaps, before he had amassed enough capital to make the cut that would drain the swamped fields he had ridden out to inspect; but with thrift and good management it would one day be done, and the mortgages redeemed. To that end all his schemes were immediately directed. It was no use thinking of the other crying needs: it made him feel rather hopeless to reckon up the farm buildings that needed repair, and the stud-and-mud dwellings which must be replaced by decent brick cottages. Still, he had at least made a start, and very fortunate he was to have been able to build even two new cottages, when less than a year before he had faced the prospect of being forced to sell Fontley. That had seemed to him the worst thing that could befall him; he had thought that no sacrifice would be too great that would save his home. He had been offered the means to do it, and he had accepted the offer of his own will; and to indulge now in nostalgic yearning was foolish and contemptible. One could never have everything one wanted in this world, and he, after all, had been granted a great deal: Fontley, and a wife who desired only to make him happy. His heart would never leap at the sight of Jenny; there was no magic in their dealings; but she was kind, and comfortable, and he had grown to be fond of her – so fond, he realized, that if, by the wave of a wand, he could cause her to disappear he would not wave it. Enchantment had vanished from the world; his life was not romantic, but practical, and Jenny had become a part of it.

He rode slowly back to the Priory, wondering why one derived so little comfort from counting blessings. His mood was as bleak as the January day; he wanted to be alone, but he must go back to Jenny, and try not to let her guess what were his true feelings. He hoped that he would be able to maintain a cheerful front, but he thought that it was going to be as difficult a duty as any he had ever undertaken.

But it was only in epic tragedies that gloom was unrelieved. In real life tragedy and comedy were so intermingled that when one was most wretched ridiculous things happened to make one laugh in spite of oneself.

He came round an angle of the Priory from the stable-yard to find Jenny surveying with every sign of disgust a peacock and hen, who appeared to view both her and their surroundings with suspicion and dislike. The sight was at once so surprising and so comical that it drove his other thoughts out of his head. He exclaimed: 'Where the deuce did they come from?'

'Need you ask?' she said bitterly. 'Papa sent them!'

Amusement sprang to his eyes. 'Oh, no, you don't mean it? Now, why should he – Ah, to smarten us up a trifle! Well, and so they will!'

'Adam! You can't wish for a couple of peacocks!' she said.

'There's no *sense* in them! Now, if Papa had sent me a couple of pigeons I'd have said thank-you, and meant it!'

He knew that her view of the animal creation was strictly practical, but this puzzled him. 'But why? Do you want some pigeons?'

'No, I can't say that I do, but at least they would have been of use. You told me that you use pigeon-dung for manure, so – Now, Adam – !'

He had uttered a shout of laughter. 'Oh, Jenny, you absurd creature! What *will* you say next?'

She smiled, but abstractedly, considering the peacocks. 'I know!' she said suddenly. 'I'll give them to Charlotte! They are just the thing for the terrace at Membury Place! And if Papa asks you what became of them, Adam, you'll say that a fox got them!'

Twenty-two

*J*enny's baby was expected at the end of March, but before she was brought to bed Adam had narrowly escaped being involved in the Corn Law Riots, and an appalling piece of news had burst like a thunder-clap over Europe. On the first day of the month, the ex-Emperor Napoleon, having escaped from Elba and slipped through the British blockade, landed in the south of France with a small force, and issued proclamations calling on the faithful to trample the white cockade underfoot, and to return to their former allegiance.

After the first shock, it was felt by all but the most pessimistic that this attempt to regain command of France would prove abortive. Masséna, from Marseilles, had sent two regiments to cut Bonaparte off on his march to Paris; and it did not seem, according to reports received in London, that the ex-Emperor's return was being greeted with any marked display of enthusiasm. But the news grew steadily more disquieting. Instead of following the main road through unfriendly Provence, Bonaparte chose the mountain road to Grenoble, and Masséna's troops failed to intercept him. At Grasse his reception was chilly; but as he proceeded northward through the Dauphiné men began to flock to his standard.

It was reassuring to learn that in Paris complete calm reigned; and if there were those who doubted the willingness of the Minister of War to take active measures against his old master their suspicions were soon allayed by the news that Marshal

Soult had proposed to the Council to throw a large force into the southern provinces, under the command of Monsieur, the King's brother, with three Marshals to support him. With this force in his front, and Masséna's regiments in his rear, Bonaparte must be trapped.

He met a battalion of Infantry of the Line on the road beyond Gap, and, with his unfailing instinct for the dramatic gesture, dismounted and walked forward alone. An officer shouted an order to fire, but it was not obeyed. 'Men of the Fifth!' said Napoleon, standing squarely before the uneasy troops, 'I am your Emperor! Know me! If there is one of you who would kill his Emperor here I am!'

It was hardly surprising that men who had fought under the Eagles should not have availed themselves of this invitation. Instead, they broke their ranks, yelling *Vive l'Empéreur!* and tearing off their white cockades.

After that the end was certain. The Parisians, enjoying a period of prosperity, due to the influx of wealthy English travellers to their city, were for the most part loyal to the Bourbons; at Vienna the Congress declared Bonaparte to be *hors la loi*; the King maintained his lethargy; and Marshal Ney, quite as dramatic a person as the ex-Emperor, heroically announced his intention of bringing Bonaparte to Paris in an iron cage; but Bonaparte continued to advance, gathering troops all the way, and entering Lyons without opposition. A letter inviting Ney to meet him, and promising that flamboyant gentleman a welcome as warm as after the Moskowa, was enough to persuade Ney, Prince of the Moskowa, to renounce his allegiance, and to take himself and his willing troops over to the ex-Emperor's side. They met at Auxerre, on the 17th March; on the evening of the 19th the King, with his family and his Ministers, left Paris in ignominious haste, with Lord Fitzroy Somerset, the English Chargé d'Affaires during the absence of the Duke of Wellington in Vienna, and a horde of visitors to the capital; and on the 20th Napoleon was carried shoulder-high into the Palace of the Tuileries to begin a new reign.

'What did I tell you?' demanded Mr Chawleigh of his son-in-law, who was in London on a brief visit. 'Didn't I say we'd have him rampaging all over the Continent again before the cat could lick its ear?'

'You did, sir, but I'll lay you handsome odds we don't!'

'I've no wish to rob you, my lord!' said Mr Chawleigh grimly.

Mr Chawleigh was taking the gloomiest view of the entire political situation. He said he didn't know what the country was coming to; and, exacerbated by Adam's cheerful mien, recommended him to look at what had happened to us in America.

The news of the defeat and death of Sir Edward Pakenham at New Orleans, in January, had just reached London, and the reminder did bring a cloud to Adam's brow: not because he doubted the ability of the Army to make a recover, but because no one who had served in the Peninsula could fail to sorrow at Pakenham's death. But he only replied: 'Come out of the dismals, sir! You should meet the fellows in my Regiment! I swear they've never been in better heart!'

The officers and men of the 52nd were indeed in good heart, and rendering thanks to Providence for having spared them the crushing disappointment of being absent from the coming battle *à outrance* with the Frogs. Twice had the Regiment set sail for America, and twice had their transports been driven back to port by contrary winds. They were now preparing with the greatest enthusiasm to embark again, their destination this time being the Low Countries.

Encountering Lord Oversley in Brooks's Club, Adam learned that my Lord and Lady Rockhill, enjoying a protracted honeymoon in Paris, had not been amongst those who had fled in such unseemly haste. The Marquis, a cynic, had placed no dependence whatsoever on the loyalty of King Louis's soldiers; and when the news of Bonaparte's landing reached Paris, he brought his bride home immediately, and without loss of dignity. He said languidly that he was quite unfitted to take part in the helter-skelter flight he foresaw; and had never, at any stage of his career, derived amusement from watching the too-easily predictable behaviour of mobs.

Adam was glad to know that Julia was safe in England, but as he had never doubted Rockhill's ability to take care of her the intelligence relieved his mind of no particular anxiety. Julia, taking Parisian society by storm, winning for herself the title of *La Belle Marquise*, had begun to seem remote. Jenny's approaching confinement, the low prices on the agricultural market, the vexed question of the proposed new Corn Laws, were matters of more pressing moment; and added to these was the inevitable longing to be back with his Regiment, which no duty-officer as keen as Adam could escape. So urgent was this desire that if Jenny had not been so near her time he thought he must, by hedge or by stile, have rejoined, casting every prudent consideration to the winds. His good sense told him that to have done so would have been nothing more than a heroic gesture, but this neither quenched his desire nor alleviated the angry fret in his mind. He tried to conceal it from Jenny, and thought that he had succeeded, until she said, in her gruffest voice, and keeping her eyes lowered: 'You don't mean to volunteer, do you?'

'Good God, no!' he replied.

She glanced fleetingly up at him. 'I know you'd like to, but — I hope you won't.'

'I give you my word I won't. As though Old Hookey couldn't do the thing without Captain Deveril's assistance!'

Towards the end of the month, Mr Chawleigh arrived at Fontley to attend the birth of his grandchild. He found Jenny in good health, calmly awaiting the event, all her preparations made, and her house in order, but this in no way assuaged his too-evident anxiety. Adam thought that it would have been better for Jenny had he remained in London, but he had not had the heart to close his doors to him, and could only hope that he would not make Jenny nervous. But two days before Jenny began to be ill the household was cast into astonishment by the wholly unexpected arrival of the Dowager, who had come (she said) because she felt it to be her duty to support dear little Jenny through her ordeal, and lost no time at all in bringing both Mr Chawleigh and Adam to a sense of their folly, uselessness, and total irrelevance.

Adam greeted her with mixed feelings. He was grateful to her for overcoming her disinclination to exert herself on behalf of a daughter-in-law of whom she disapproved; but he feared that her descent upon Fontley would throw Jenny into disorder. He was mistaken. If the Dowager had a passion, it was for babies. She had doted on all her children during their infancies, and her bosom was now filled with grandmotherly fervour. Jenny's failings were not forgotten, but they were set aside: the Dowager, assuming command of the household, was determined to ensure that nothing should be allowed to endanger the birth of her first grandchild; and nothing could have exceeded the gracious kindness with which she enveloped Jenny, or the indulgent contempt with which she dismissed male apprehensions.

Adam begged Jenny to tell him whether she would prefer to be rid of her mother-in-law, but she replied with unmistakable sincerity that the Dowager was being of the greatest support and comfort to her.

Like many women of invalidish habits, the Dowager had borne her children with perfect ease. She could perceive no reason for supposing that Jenny would suffer complications outside her own experience, and her conviction that the issue would be happy gave Jenny a confidence she had hitherto lacked.

Adam, finding himself reduced to schoolboy status, was much inclined to rebel; but Mr Chawleigh, observing him with a sympathetic eye, said gloomily: 'It's no manner of use nabbing the rust, my lord. You wait till Jenny starts in labour! The way females behave when one of 'em's in the straw you'd think we was no better than a set of lobcocks they'd be very well-pleased to be rid of! And don't you get to thinking *you'd* anything to do with this baby, lad, because all you'll get will be a set-down if you start trying to put yourself forward!'

The arrival of the month-nurse made the female dominion at Fontley absolute, and drew Adam into close alliance with his father-in-law. 'The only female in the whole house who doesn't treat me as if I was only just out of short coats is Jenny herself!' he told Mr Chawleigh wrathfully.

'I know,' nodded that worthy. 'I remember when Mrs C. was brought to bed there wasn't one of the maids, not even the kitchen-girl that wasn't a day more than fourteen, that didn't make me as mad as Bedlam, carrying on as if they was grand-mothers, and me a booberkin!'

When Jenny's labour began the month-nurse warned Adam that she was not going to be quick in her time. A few hours later she said, with a bright cheerfulness which drove the colour from Mr Chawleigh's cheeks, that she would be glad if his lordship would send a message to fetch Dr Purley from Peterborough. Adam had, in fact, sent for both this recommended accoucheur, and for Dr Tilford, as soon as Jenny's pains began; and within a very few minutes Dr Tilford drove up in his gig. In due course he was joined by Dr Purley, who, having been engaged to attend throughout the labour, brought both his night-bag and his servant with him. His air of confidence exercised a beneficial effect upon Mr Chawleigh; but it seemed an alarmingly long time before he redeemed his promise to report to my lady's husband and father what his opinion was of her case. However, when he and Dr Tilford joined the anxious gentlemen in the library he appeared quite untroubled, and assured my lord that although he feared it would be some time before her ladyship was safely delivered neither he nor his colleague (with a courteous bow to Dr Tilford) could discover any cause for undue apprehension. Mr Chawleigh could not like the qualifying epithet, and immediately put Dr Purley in possession of the details of his own wife's several disastrous experiences. Without precisely saying so, Dr Purley managed to convey the impression that the late Mrs Chawleigh had been unfortunate in not having been a patient of his; and he left Mr Chawleigh, if not wholly reassured, at least more inclined to take a hopeful view of the situation.

But midway through the second day, after a sleepless night, Mr Chawleigh, whose nerves had been growing rapidly more disordered, lost his precarious hold over his temper, and tried his best to provoke Adam into a quarrel. Adam entered the room after an absence of an hour to be greeted with a ferocious glare, and a demand to know where he had been.

'Only in the estate-room, sir,' he replied. 'My bailiff has been here with some business needing my attention.'

Mr Chawleigh's jaw worked. His son-in-law's quiet voice, far from acting as a damper, violently irritated him. 'Oh, you have, have you?' he retorted, with bitter sarcasm. 'And as cool as a cucumber, I make no doubt! *Business* needing your attention! Why, you don't know the meaning of the word! You and your piddling farms! Much you care for my Jenny!'

Adam stood rigidly silent.

'Ay, you may look down your nose!' Mr Chawleigh flung at him. 'As proud as a cock on your own dunghill, ain't you, my lord? But if it weren't for me you'd have no dunghill – and what's more, if my Jenny snuffs it, I'll see to it you don't have it, as sure as my name's Jonathan Chawleigh, because it'll be your blame, giving Croft the go-by, like you did – bringing her down here – not caring the snap of your fingers what might come of it! Well, that's where you'll find you've made your mistake! And she not thinking of anything but how to please you, and be worthy of you! *Worthy of you!* She's too good for you, and so I tell you to your head!'

Anger, colder than Mr Chawleigh's, but quite as deadly, had welled up in Adam. As he looked at that coarse red face, he felt for a moment almost sick with loathing. Then he saw that large tears were rolling down Mr Chawleigh's cheeks, and was suddenly sorry for him. He did not know that the things he said were unpardonable, or that self-control in moments of stress was incumbent on him. He had fought his way up in the world with no other weapons than his hard head and his ruthless will. He was brutal but generous, overbearing yet curiously humble, and he gave way to his emotions with the ease of a child.

It was a moment or two before Adam could master himself enough to answer temperately. He limped over to the table on which Dunster had set down decanters and glasses, and said, as he poured out some Madeira: 'Yes, sir: she is much too good for me.'

Mr Chawleigh blew his nose defiantly into a large and lavishly embroidered handkerchief. He took the glass that was being held out to him with a muttered Thankee! and gulped down the wine.

'I do care, you know,' Adam said. 'If anything were to go amiss now, you won't blame me as much as I shall blame myself.'

Mr Chawleigh grabbed his hand. 'Nay, you did what you thought right! I'd no call to fly out at you. It's being regularly worn down with worrying over my girl, and nothing I can do to help. I'm not one to sit kicking my heels, the way you and me have been doing, not without getting into high fidgets. Don't you heed me, my lord, for I promise you I don't mean the rough things I say when I'm in a passion! Well, I don't rightly know what I *do* say, and that's a fact!' He shifted ponderously in his chair, to restore his handkerchief to his pocket, and said, with an apologetic glance up at Adam: 'She's all I've got, you see.'

These simple words went straight to Adam's heart. He said nothing, but laid his hand on Mr Chawleigh's shoulder for a moment. One of Mr Chawleigh's own, ham-like hands came up to pat it clumsily. 'You're a kind lad,' he said gruffly. 'I'll take another glass of wine, for I need something to pluck me up!'

He did not again allow his anxiety to get the better of him, though he paced up and down the floor a good deal, until, as the evening wore slowly on, he perceived that Adam was looking very haggard, and realized that there was one thing at least which he could do. He remembered that Adam had shaken his head at every dish offered him at the dinner-table, and went plunging off in search of Dunster, returning presently with a plate of sandwiches, which he bullied Adam into eating. He then applied himself to the task of convincing him that there was no need to get in a stew, because it stood to reason Dr Tilford wouldn't have shabbed off home if Jenny wasn't going on promisingly.

Just before midnight the Dowager entered the library, with a swathed bundle in her arms, which she held out to Adam, saying in thrilling accents that showed clearly whence Lydia derived her histrionic talent: 'Lynton! I have brought your son to you!'

He had sprung up at the opening of the door, but he did not attempt to take the infant, which was just as well, since the Dowager had no real intention of entrusting so precious a burden to his inexpert handling. 'Jenny?' he said sharply.

'*Quite* comfortable!' replied the Dowager. 'Sadly exhausted, poor little thing, but Dr Purley assures me that we have no need to feel alarm. I must tell you that you are very much obliged to him, my dear Adam: *most* skilled! So gentlemanlike, too!'

'May I see her?' Adam interrupted.

'Yes, for a very few minutes.'

He went towards the door, but was checked. 'Dearest!' said his mother, in pained reproof. 'Have you *no* thought to spare for your son?'

He turned back. 'Yes – of course! Let me see him, Mama!'

'The most beautiful little boy!' she said fondly.

He thought he had never seen anything less beautiful than the red and crumpled countenance of his son, and for a moment suspected her of irony. Fortunately, since he could think of nothing whatsoever to say, Mr Chawleigh, who had been obliged to blow his nose for the second time that day, now surged forward, wreathed in smiles, and diverted the Dowager's attention from her son's deplorable want of enthusiasm by tickling the infant's cheek with the tip of an enormous finger, and uttering sounds which put Adam in mind of one calling hens to be fed.

'Eh, the young rascal!' said Mr Chawleigh, apparently delighted by the infant's lack of response. 'So you won't take notice of your granddad! Top-lofty, ain't you?' He looked at Adam, and chuckled. 'Pluck up, lad!' he advised him. 'I know what you're thinking, but never you fear! Lor', when I first clapped eyes on my Jenny I pretty near suffered a palsy-stroke!'

Adam laughed, but said: 'I must own I don't think him beautiful! How tiny he is! Is he – is he healthy, Mama?'

'*Tiny?*' repeated the Dowager incredulously. 'He is a splendid little fellow! *Aren't* you, my precious?'

Mr Chawleigh winked at Adam, and jerked his thumb towards the door. 'You go on up to Jenny!' he said. 'My dear love to her – and don't go putting it into her head she's got a sickly baby, mind!'

Only too glad to escape from the besotted grandparents, Adam slipped out of the room, to find that he had to run the gauntlet of his household, all lying in wait to felicitate him.

He entered Jenny's room very quietly, and paused for a moment, looking across at her. He saw how white she was, and how wearily she smiled at him. Pity stirred in him, and with it tenderness. He crossed the room, and bent over her, kissing her, and saying softly: 'My poor dear! Better now, Jenny?'

'Oh, yes!' she said in the thread of a voice. 'Just so very tired. But it *is* a son, Adam!'

'A very fine son,' he agreed. '*Clever* Jenny!'

She laughed weakly, but her eyes searched his face. 'Are you pleased?' she asked anxiously.

'Very pleased.'

She gave a little relieved sigh. 'Your mama says he's like your brother. Would you like to have him christened Stephen?'

'No, not at all. We'll have him christened Giles, after my grandfather, and Jonathan, after his,' he replied.

Her eyes lit up. 'Do you mean that? Thank you! Papa will be so pleased and proud! You'll give him my love, won't you, and tell him that I am very well.'

'I will. He sent his love to you – his dear love. I left him making the most peculiar noises to his grandson, who treated them with utter contempt – very understandably, I thought!'

That made her laugh so much that Nurse, who had tactfully joined Martha at the far end of the room, brought Adam's visit to an end, informing him in a voice that in no way matched the respectful curtsy she dropped, that my lady must go to sleep now, and would be glad to see him in the morning.

Twenty-three

When Mr Chawleigh learned from Jenny that his name was to be bestowed upon his grandson, and at Adam's suggestion, he was more than pleased: he was overcome. It was several moments before he was able to utter a word. He sat staring at Jenny, his hands on his knees; and when he did at last speak all he could find to say was: 'Giles Jonathan Deveril! Giles-Jonathan-Deveril!'

Nor was this by any means the last time he uttered the names. Every now and then a look of profound satisfaction was seen to spread over his face; his lips would move; he would rub his hands together, and give a little chuckle; and all who observed these signs knew that he was savouring his grandson's names yet again. He was embarrassingly grateful to Adam, telling him that he hadn't looked to have such a compliment paid him, and assuring him that he meant to do the handsome thing by the boy. Adam had learned to hear such remarks without wincing; but he soon grew extremely bored by the next manifestation of Mr Chawleigh's pride in his grandson. The discovery that the infant had no title was a disappointment that seemed likely to bring a lasting cloud to his horizon, nor was his dissatisfaction eased when Adam, rather amused, told him that when he had occasion to write to Giles he would be able to direct his letter to the Honourable Giles Deveril. Mr Chawleigh had a poor opinion of Honourables. He had seen the word written, but he regarded it with suspicion, because he had never heard anyone called by it.

'No, you wouldn't. It isn't used in speech,' said Adam.

'Well, I don't see the sense of having a title which ain't used,' said Mr Chawleigh. 'Shabby, I call it! Who's to know he's got it?'

'I don't know – and, speaking as one who held the title until very recently, I promise you Giles won't care!'

'I'd have liked him to have been a lord,' said Mr Chawleigh wistfully.

'Well, I've no wish to seem disobliging,' said Adam, tired of the discussion, 'but I don't consider it to be any part of my paternal duty to put a period to my life merely to provide Giles with a title!'

He spoke a little impatiently, and was immediately ashamed, because Mr Chawleigh said he hoped no offence was taken, as none was intended. To make amends, he devoted himself to Mr Chawleigh's entertainment all one afternoon, with the result that he became so inwardly chafed that he found himself looking forward with positive yearning to the date of his well-meaning but disastrously irritating guest's departure. This was not long delayed. Mr Chawleigh remained at Fontley only until he was convinced that there was no danger that Jenny would succumb to puerperal fever, which was another of his bugbears. Satisfied on this point, he was as anxious to be gone as Adam was to see him go: the lord alone knew, he said, what silly mistakes his various subordinates had made during his absence from the City. His worst stroke was left to the last moment, when his chaise was at the door, and he was taking leave of Adam in the porch. His mood was benign: his daughter was safe; he had a lusty grandson; his son-in-law had made him as welcome as if he had been a Duke, even naming the baby after him, and behaving, when he'd come the ugly for no reason at all, as patiently and kindly as if he had been his real son. Mr Chawleigh's heart was full of gratitude and generosity, and, unfortunately, it over-flowed. Shaking Adam warmly by the hand, and looking at him with rough affection, he thanked him for the third time for his hospitality. 'If anyone had told me I'd be happy to stay in the country for more than a sennight I'd have laughed in their faces!' he said. 'But you make me so welcome, my lord, that if you don't take care you'll have me posting down to visit you more often than you bargain for. I've got to feel myself so much at home here that the next thing you know I'll be talking about oats and rye and the like as glib as you do! Which brings me to something I've got to say to you!'

'About oats and rye?' said Adam, smiling. 'No, no, sir! You stick to your trade and I'll stick to mine!'

Mr Chawleigh chuckled at this. 'Ay, that's my motto! No, that ain't it: the thing is, Jenny's been telling me about some farm or other you're mad after, for experiments, she said. Well, I'm sure I don't know what you want with such things, and I don't deny it seems corkbrained to me! But there! If you're set on it, I suppose you'll have to have it, so you tell me how much of the ready you need to set it going, and I'll stand the nonsense!'

'How very kind of you, sir!' Adam said, forcing himself to speak pleasantly. 'But I assure you I'm not mad after any farm! I have quite enough to do without saddling myself with an experimental farm.'

Mr Chawleigh was disappointed, but also relieved. He wished to bestow a handsome present on Adam, but it did seem wicked to squander one's blunt on anything so silly as an experimental farm. So he did not press the matter, but set off for London, cudgelling his brain in an attempt to hit on something which his incomprehensible son-in-law really would like to receive.

Adam was left a prey to bitter hatred of insensitive vulgarians, who could never be made to understand how much their oppressive generosity lacerated the feelings of those cast in finer moulds than themselves.

Yet five minutes later he found himself defending Mr Chawleigh from the Dowager's acid criticisms, even telling her that he held him in affection and esteem, which, at that moment, was far from being the truth.

The Dowager was suffering slightly from reaction. She had risen nobly to an occasion, but the occasion had passed. While it was of paramount importance that her daughter-in-law should be kept in a tranquil state of mind she had found it easy to suppress every critical impulse; but Jenny, though slow to recover her strength, was now out of danger, and the Dowager felt at liberty to unburden herself of a great many criticisms and grievances. Adam, having endured an extremely wearing week, keeping his mother and his father-in-law apart, and, when this was impossible, stepping hastily into every breach created by two such ill-assorted persons, was in no mood to listen to these, and he gave his mother a very improper set-down. A serious rupture threatened, but was averted by the Dowager's recollecting that her younger daughter was shortly to make her début, and that in her own miserably straitened circumstances it was quite impossible for her to provide all the expensive raiment necessary for this event.

It had been decided that since Jenny, confined at the end of March, would be very imprudent to embark on the exigencies of a London season, Lady Nassington should launch Lydia into the ton. The Dowager had, in fact, brought Lydia to London, and had consigned her to her aunt's care. She had, at great personal sacrifice, supplied her with a number of elegant ball-dresses, walking-dresses, and demie-toilettes, but it was quite out of her power to provide her with a Court-dress. The child could certainly not afford to pay for this herself, out of the slender allowance her brother made her, and dear Adam would scarcely wish the charge to fall upon his aunt.

He did not wish it; and even less did he wish the cost of Lydia's presentation to be borne by Jenny. He gave the Dowager a draft on Drummond's, which put her so much in charity with him that instead of shaking the dust of Fontley from her feet she remained there for another week.

She was thus present when Lady Oversley drove over from Beckenhurst on a visit of congratulation, bringing with her Lady Rockhill, and the Ladies Sarah and Elizabeth Edgcott; two very well brought-up and rather mouse-like little girls, who (just as Jenny had prophesied) sat and gazed with shy admiration at their lovely young stepmother.

Lady Oversley had neither meant nor wished to bring Julia to

Fontley, but she had found it impossible to leave her behind. The Rockhills were paying a brief visit to Beckenhurst on their way up to London, where Julia was going to buy much prettier dresses for her stepdaughters than their austere grandmama had considered suitable, show them all the sights, and in general entertain them royally before sending them back to their governess and their books at Rockhill Castle. 'But before we leave you, Mama,' Julia said, 'I must go to Fontley to see how Jenny does, of course.'

Lady Oversley ventured to suggest that a letter of felicitation would perhaps be better than a visit.

'When it's known that I'm here, so close to Fontley?' Julia said. 'Oh, no! How unkind it would be in me not to visit Jenny! I won't have it said that I didn't render her every observance!'

When the visit was paid Jenny was still confined to her room, but the Dowager was able to assure Lady Oversley that she was quite well enough to receive her, and dear Julia too. She conducted them upstairs, leaving the little girls seated primly side by side on a sofa in the Green Saloon, with a book of engravings to look at.

Jenny, who was permitted now to spend some hours on a day-bed, greeted her visitors with pleasure, but it was not long before Lady Oversley judged it to be time to withdraw. Julia, she thought, was talking too much and too animatedly to Jenny, who was obviously languid and invalidish. One might almost have said that Julia was *rattling* on in a way that would probably leave Jenny with a headache. She had kissed her, and felicitated her, and admired the baby, which was perfectly proper, but it would have been better to have kept all her gay reminiscences of Paris for a future date. It could not interest Jenny to know what this person had said to Madame la Marquise, or what that person had said about her. Lady Oversley felt uneasily that had it been anyone but Julia she would have suspected her of flaunting her triumphs and her wedded felicity in front of poor little Jenny. So she got up to take her leave. Julia followed her example, saying: 'But I must have one last peep at your baby,

Jenny! Dear little man! He's like you, I think.' She looked up from the cradle, laughing: 'I'm a Mama too, you know! I've two daughters – such darlings! They ought to hate me, but they spoil me to death!'

When the ladies entered the Green Saloon again they found Adam there, trying to draw out the Ladies Sarah and Elizabeth. Julia gave him her hand, exclaiming: 'Oh, you have made the acquaintance of my daughters already! That's too bad! I'm quite as proud a mama as Jenny, I promise you, and had meant to have presented them to you in form.'

He had dreaded this meeting, but when he looked at Julia, and listened to her, she seemed to be almost a stranger. Even her appearance had altered. She had always been charmingly dressed, but in a style suited to her maiden status; he had never seen her attired in the silks, the velvets, and the jewels of matronhood. He thought she looked very rich and fashionable, with all the curled plumes clustering round the high crown of her hat, the sapphire-drops in her ears, the sable stole flung carelessly over the back of her chair, but she did not look like his Julia. It did not occur to him that she was somewhat over-dressed for the occasion, but it had occurred forcibly to Lady Oversley, who had remonstrated, only to be told that she had nothing else to wear, and that Rockhill liked her to look elegant.

She was telling his mother how nervous she had been when Rockhill had taken her to meet his children, making a droll story of it. The little girls giggled, and uttered protestingly: 'Oh, Mama!' She had been afraid that Rockhill's servants would regard her as a usurper, and that his sisters would disapprove of her. Such an ordeal as it had been! But they were all such dear creatures that they positively killed her with kindness: she was becoming odiously spoilt, and would soon, if they persisted in cosseting her, be the most idle, exacting, and selfish toad imaginable.

'Oh, Mama!'

Listening to this, Adam remembered suddenly the words she had spoken to him once. '*I must be loved! I can't live if I'm not loved!*'

313

The thought flashed into his mind that she was basking in adulation; and he wondered for a shocked moment if the caresses and the treats she bestowed upon Rockhill's daughters sprang from this craving rather than from a wish to make them happy. He was aghast, not at her but at himself; he recalled a thousand instances of her sweetness, her generosity, her quick sympathy, her tender heart; and thought: *Who has a better right to be loved?*

'Dear Julia!' sighed the Dowager, when the visitors had departed. 'No one could marvel at the Edgcotts for liking her so well! Dorothea Oversley has been telling me what a conquest she has made over Rockhill's sisters, but, as I said to Dorothea, I should have been astonished if they had not liked her, for she is always so prettily behaved, and so attentive – so exactly what one would wish one's daughter-in-law to be!'

'Sister-in-law, surely, ma'am?' Adam said, in a dry tone.

'Yes, dear – alas!' she replied mournfully.

'I hope the visit may not have tired Jenny: I must go up to her.'

He escaped from her on this excuse, and did indeed go upstairs, to be greeted, as he entered Jenny's room, by some lusty yells from his son, who appeared to have fallen into a paroxysm of fury. Adam was put unpleasantly in mind of Mr Chawleigh, but thrust the thought away. 'It's a constant source of astonishment to me that anything so small should possess such powerful lungs,' he remarked.

Jenny signed to the nurse to take the baby away. 'Yes, and such a strong will!' she answered. 'He's determined not to be laid down in his cradle: that's all that ails him. But he was very good while Lady Oversley and Julia were with me. It was kind in them to come, wasn't it? Did you see them?'

'Yes, and also the two girls – oppressively well-behaved damsels! Was the post brought up to you? I saw you had a letter from Lydia.'

'Yes, bless her! She says she's still as sulky as a bear because Lady Nassington won't allow her to come to see her godson. I wish she might have come, but it is much too far – and I can't say that he's much to look at yet!' She hesitated, and then said haltingly: 'I had a letter from Papa as well.'

'Did you? I hope he's well?'

She nodded, but she did not speak for a moment or two. She had been unhappily conscious for several days that Adam had withdrawn a little from her, behind his intangible barrier. She had ventured to ask him if she had displeased him, but he had put up his brows, saying: 'Displeased me? Why, what have I said to make you think so?' She could not answer him, because he had said nothing to make her think so, and she could not tell him that her love made her acutely sensitive to every change of mood in him. But she knew now what had caused that subtle withdrawal. Rather flushed, bracing herself, she said: 'Papa tells me that he offered to – to make it possible for you to start the experimental farm you wish for – only that you refused it.'

'Of course I did!' he replied easily. 'And very glad he was that I did! I'm much obliged to him – but I can't imagine why he should offer to do what must go quite against the pluck with him.'

'You thought I had asked him to,' she said, resolutely lifting her eyes to his. 'That's why –' She checked herself, and then went on: 'I didn't – but I did mention it to him, not thinking that you wouldn't wish it, which – which you'll say I should have known.'

'My dear Jenny, I assure you –'

'No, let me explain to you how it came about!' she begged. 'I never meant – You see, Papa doesn't understand! He thinks it's crackbrained nonsense, and not the thing for gentlemen to engage in! I only wished to *make* him understand, and I told him about Mr Coke's farm, and how he had prospered, and how important agriculture is. . . . It was his saying that he supposed *you* would be the next to start such a farm that made me disclose to him that you had that intention, when you could afford to do so. I didn't ask him – but I don't run sly any more than he does, and I'll tell you frankly I did hope that perhaps he might come round to the notion! I didn't know you'd dislike it – you told him once that if he wished to make you a present he might give you a herd of short-horns!'

'Did I? I wasn't in earnest. But there's no need for you to fly into high fidgets, goose! I might wish that you hadn't talked to him of that remote ambition of mine, but I never desired you not to, so how should I be vexed with you because you did?'

'You *are* vexed,' she muttered, her eyes downcast.

'Not so much vexed as blue-devilled!' he retorted. 'Have I seemed to be out of reason cross? Well, I am – though I hoped I hadn't let you perceive it! I dislike it excessively when there's no Jenny to pander outrageously to all my fads and fancies, and that's the truth!'

She did not quite believe him, but she was a little cheered, and was able to smile, and to say: 'I'm glad!'

'Wretch! What I endure at my mother's hands – ! Yes, I know I shouldn't say that, but if you dare to tell me so I shall walk out of the room in a miff! By the bye, have you read the news? It was in the *Morning Post*, which I told Dunster to send up to you: old Douro has arrived in Brussels!'

'Wellington! Yes, indeed! I knew you would be cast into transports by *that*!'

He laughed. 'I shall at all events sleep sounder o' nights! The thought of Slender Billy in command of the Army was enough to give anyone nightmares. We shall do now!'

'Oh, dear, I do hope we may! Papa doesn't think so. He says –'

'I know exactly what he says, my love, and all I have to say is that your Papa doesn't know Douro!'

He spoke confidently, but it was not surprising that Mr Chawleigh, and many others, should be pessimistic. The outlook was not promising. Reports reached London that the Emperor was not the man he had been: he grew easily tired; he fell into sudden rages, or into moods of dejection; he had lost his confidence: but the unpalatable fact remained that France had accepted his reinstatement, if not with universal joy, certainly with complaisance. The Midi might be royalist in sentiment; but hopes that were kindled by the raising of a mixed force at Nîmes by the Duc d'Angoulême were soon quenched by the arrival from Paris of Marshal Grouchy, with orders to crush the insurrection. By the middle of April it was known in London that Angoulême had capitulated, and had set sail for Spain. His wife, the daughter of the martyred King Louis XVIth, and a lady of spirit, had been at Bordeaux when the Emperor had entered Paris, and had done her utmost to rally the diminishing loyalty of the troops there; but her efforts had met with no success, and she had been obliged to allow herself to be borne off to safety in an English sloop.

Meanwhile, a new constitution had been drawn up in Paris, which was to be sworn to in the Champ de Mars, at a grand ceremony to be held on the 1st May. The Emperor hoped to crown his Austrian wife and his infant son on this occasion, but his letters to Marie Louise went unanswered. He postponed the Champ de Mai for a month, still hoping to have his wife restored to him, and to detach his Imperial father-in-law from the coalition formed at Vienna. Failing, he switched his diplomatic attempts to England. These too were unsuccessful, but his machinations made those who believed that his power could and must be broken suffer considerable uneasiness, since among the Opposition were many vociferous members, loud in their condemnation of a renewal of hostilities.

'These damned Whigs!' Adam said savagely. 'Do they imagine that Boney wouldn't overrun Europe the instant he saw his way clear?'

'Lambert says,' observed Jenny dispassionately.

He looked up from the newspaper, his anger yielding to amusement. 'Jenny, if you don't take care, we shall find ourselves in the suds! It was almost bellows to mend with me yesterday, when Charlotte uttered those fatal words!'

Between them, Lambert and Charlotte had unwittingly shown Adam that his wife had a certain dry sense of humour. Lambert, whose understanding was no more than moderate, had always been inclined to dogmatize on any and every subject, and this tendency had not been lessened by his marriage.

Charlotte had no opinions of her own: she had only an unshakable belief in Lambert's superiority, and had quickly acquired the habit of prefixing her contribution to whatever subject was under discussion with the words *Lambert says*, uttered with a finality which made them doubly exasperating. Adam was never more surprised than when Jenny, after several hours spent in Charlotte's company, interrupted him one evening, exclaiming: 'Oh, but, Adam, *Lambert* says – !'

She retorted now: 'Yes, and you'd think I'd be ashamed to poke fun at poor Lambert, who is always so civil and kind to me, wouldn't you? Well, so I am, but if I didn't do that I should very likely be downright rude to him, *and* to Charlotte! For when it comes to Lambert setting you right on military tactics – Well, there! it's better to laugh than to get into a tweak!'

He had retired into the newspaper again, and did not answer; but after a few moments he said: 'I shall have to go up to London. How confoundedly inopportune! They'll be draining the Great Dyke, and I wanted to see whether – However, there's no remedy!'

'A debate?' Jenny asked.

He nodded. 'War or Peace. From what Brough writes, it might be a close-run thing. His father thinks Grenville's wavering: bamboozled by Grey, who is for peace at any cost!'

'You don't think the Jacobins would be able to set up a republic?'

'Lambert says? No, I don't. I think it's moonshine to suppose that Boney would ever consent to it, and they wouldn't dare to try to force it on him. The civil population might turn against him, but the Army won't – and, make no mistake, the Johnny Crapauds understand their trade much too well to be pooh-poohed! I know: I've fought against 'em!'

'Well, then, of course you must cast your vote,' she said. 'I wish I could come to town with you.'

'Why don't you?'

'Now, Adam – ! When you know the baby's not weaned – !'

'You could bring him with you.'

She considered this, but finally shook her head. 'No, because I shouldn't want to open up the house only for a few days, and I don't fancy taking him to a hotel, for you may depend upon it people would complain!'

'He *is* noisy,' agreed Adam.

'Only when he's hungry, or has the wind!' she said. 'But I won't come.'

'Jenny, have you been hoaxing me?' he demanded. 'Did you persuade me to believe that you didn't wish to go to town at all this season because you thought I preferred to remain here?'

She shook her head. 'No, upon my honour! The only time I hoaxed you was when I pretended to enjoy all those dreadful squeezes we went to last year, and I only did so because I thought it was my duty. I was never more thankful than when I discovered you were just as bored as I was! Not but what it will be pleasant to go up now and then, I daresay. Not this time: it was merely that I thought suddenly that I'd like to see Lydia, and Papa – but Lydia's coming to us at the end of the season for a nice, long visit, and I don't doubt Papa will spend a day or two with us as well. No, I won't come: only think what a fuss and botheration it would mean!'

'I do think it would be very fatiguing for you,' he admitted. 'I don't mean to be gone more than a few days, you know.'

'You'll stay as long as you feel inclined. I shan't look for you under a sennight, for you'll want to see Lydia, let alone all your friends.'

When she saw him off to board the mail-coach at Market Deeping it was with the private conviction that it would be at least ten days before he returned, but he took her by surprise only five days later, walking into the nursery, where she sat suckling her baby. Thinking that it was the nurse who had entered the room she did not immediately look up. She was fondly watching the child, and it struck Adam that he had never seen her appear to better advantage. Then she glanced up, and gave a gasp. '*Adam!*'

He went forward, saying mischievously: 'Own that I've astonished you – and retrieved my reputation!'

Her eyes narrowed in one of her sudden smiles. 'Well, it's certainly the first time *I've* ever known you return when you'd said you would!'

'*Before* I said I would!' he reminded her reproachfully, bending over her to kiss her, and then tickling the infant's cheek with one finger. 'Well, sir? It would be civil in you just to *acknowledge* me, you know!'

The Honourable Giles, fearful of interruption, shot him an angry look, and applied himself with renewed vigour to the most important business in life.

'You're as greedy as your aunt Lydia,' Adam informed him, sinking into a chair.

'Well, what a thing to say!' protested Jenny. 'Lydia is *not* greedy!'

'You wouldn't say so if you'd seen her in Russell Square, when I took her to dine with your father!'

'Oh, did you do that? How delighted Papa must have been! But tell me, how did you prosper?'

'Capitally! We carried it in both houses. Granville made a speech in support of the Ministers – no great thing, but Grey's amendment was pretty handsomely defeated. All sorts of on-dits are flying about the town; one doesn't know how many of them to believe, but one thing is certain: the Austrians, the Prussians, and the Russians are putting themselves under arms. My own belief is that we shall be at grips with the Frogs pretty soon – and I don't doubt the issue! Boney's only hope must be to *romper* us, with his Army of the North, before the others in the Coalition can be brought into the game. If he could do it – but he won't!' He laughed, and added: 'Your father croaks that Wellington has never yet been opposed by Boney himself! Very true – and so is the converse!' He was interrupted by his son, who, full to repletion, gave a belch. He said: 'We shall never be able to introduce him into polite circles, shall we? All well here, Jenny?'

She nodded, and said, as she helpfully patted the Honourable Giles: 'Tell me about Lydia! Is she enjoying the season? Does she *take*?'

'According to my aunt, she has made quite a hit. She certainly seems to have acquired a large number of admirers! Don't ask me to describe the dress she wore at her Presentation! I didn't see it, and can only assure you that it was *sumptuous*!'

She chuckled. 'Oh, I can almost hear her saying that! Does she go to a great many parties?'

'She informed me with pride that she had attended no fewer than three during the course of one evening. My aunt must have a constitution of iron! By the bye, what a very pretty bracelet you gave her, Jenny!'

Her colour rushed up; she glanced warily at him, stammering: 'It was only a trifle!'

'You needn't have been afraid to tell me,' he said, faintly smiling. 'Yes, I know why you were afraid: you remembered that I wouldn't permit her to wear your pearls. Well, I still would not – they are quite unsuitable, you know! – but there is a vast difference between lending your pearls to Lydia because she is my sister, and bestowing a charming bracelet upon her because she has become *your* sister. And let me add, my love, that in spite of my odd humours I haven't the smallest desire to come the ugly because your father was so kind as to send her an ivory-brisé fan which I do *not* think he purchased dog-cheap! Was that at your instigation?'

'Well, yes!' she admitted guiltily. 'You know what Papa is, Adam! He's so fond of Lydia that he'd have sent her something you wouldn't have liked at all if I hadn't restrained him a little.' Her eyes twinkled. 'I warn you, however, that I shan't be able to do so when it comes to a wedding-gift!'

'Ah!' Adam said. 'That puts me in mind of a rare tit-bit of news!'

She exclaimed: 'Adam! You don't mean –'

'I have received two offers for my sister's hand,' said Adam, with dignity.

'*No!*'

'I assure you! You can't think how patriarchal I now feel! Or the degree of embarrassment I felt on being applied to by a man at least twelve years my senior!'

She gave a crow of mirth. 'Adam, *not* the Conquest?'

'None other! Would you believe it? – having won Mama's approval, he followed Lydia to town, and has been making an absurd cake of himself with his attentions! She swears there was no hinting him away, try as she would, but I consider that no excuse for fobbing him off on to me, the abominable little wretch! With instructions to inform him that his suit was hopeless: you may imagine with what enthusiasm I faced this task!'

'But you did tell him so?'

'I did, but I was obliged to hint that Lydia's affections were already engaged before I could convince him.' He smiled, seeing the eagerly questioning look in her eyes. 'Yes, the other offer came from Brough, exactly as you foretold. At least, he asked me if I had any objection to his marrying Lydia.' He observed the expression of deep satisfaction on Jenny's face, and continued smoothly: 'I told him, of course, to put any such nonsense out of his head –'

'*Adam!*' she gasped.

He burst out laughing. 'Never did I know a fish that would rise to the fly more readily than you, Jenny! Or see anything more ludicrous than your change of countenance! – No, you goose, I gave him my blessing, and some sage advice. *He* was bent on posting off immediately to Bath – for whatever may be your opinion, my dear, he and I are agreed that Mama's consent as well as mine must be obtained. But I know Mama a great deal better than Brough does, and I'm persuaded nothing could be more fatal than for him to present himself to her hard on the heels of the baffled Conquest. Mama must be given time to recover from her disappointment. So we have decided that nothing shall be disclosed to her until next month, when she means to spend a night with my aunt, before coming down to be with Charlotte. According to my aunt, she will by then have resigned herself to the melancholy prospect of seeing Lydia dwindle into a withered spinster, and so may be thankful to entertain Brough's proposal.'

'Your aunt knows then, and likes it? But it is very hard that Brough shouldn't be able to speak to Lydia yet!'

'My dear Jenny, he spoke to her before ever I arrived in town!' Adam said, amused.

'Oh, I'm glad! And she?'

'Well, she told me that she was *rapturously* happy, and I'd no difficulty in believing her.'

'I wish I might see her! Well, at all events, that settles it!'

'Settles what?'

'We must open Lynton House,' said Jenny decidedly.

'Good God, why?'

'For the party. And don't say *what* party, because you know very well there's always a party held in honour of an engagement, and that's one thing Lady Nassington shall *not* do!'

'But –'

'And don't say *but* either!' interrupted Jenny, getting up to carry her sleeping son back to the nursery. 'The instant I know that your mama has given her consent, I'll set about hiring servants. Though I think I'll take Dunster and Mrs Dawes with me, as well as Scholes, because they've got to know my ways, and you may depend upon it they'd be glad to go. And it's not a bit of use arguing, my lord, for my mind's made up, and if you don't know what's due to your sister I do!'

Twenty-four

These disruptive plans were never put into execution. Lydia had a plan of her own, which was laid before Jenny, partly in a characteristic letter from Lydia herself, and partly by the Dowager, who paused at Fontley on her way to Membury Place, where she was going to preside over the entry into the world of a second grandchild.

She had given her consent to Lydia's marriage, but she was still feeling a trifle dazed. Her mind was not elastic, and since she had first made Brough's acquaintance when he had been an overgrown schoolboy, who frequently came to stay at Fontley, clattering at breakneck speed up and down the stairs, bringing a great deal of mud into the house, and engaging with Adam in a number of exploits which even now she shuddered to remember, she had never looked upon him as anything other than one of Adam's friends from Harrow. Jenny had supposed that his visits to Bath must have enlightened her; but the Dowager had accepted without question the excuse he had offered. She had thought it very proper in him to have called in Camden Place, and very good-natured to have taken Lydia out for drives, and to have stood up with her in the Assembly Rooms. It had never so much as crossed her mind that he was extremely particular in his attentions. When he and Adam had been schoolboys Lydia had not emerged from the nursery, and if she had thought about it at all the Dowager would have concluded that Brough regarded Lydia merely as his friend's little sister, to whom it behoved him to be kind.

It had therefore come as a shock to her when Brough had visited her at Nassington House to beg her permission to pay his addresses to Lydia. She told Adam that although the proposed marriage was not what she would have chosen for dear Lydia Brough had expressed himself so beautifully, and with such delicate consideration, that she had allowed herself to be won over.

(*Brough doing the thing in style*, thought Adam appreciatively.)

In fact, Lady Nassington had been very nearly right. If the Dowager did not go so far as to visualize her strong-minded daughter as an ageing spinster, it seemed more than likely to her that a girl who could wantonly reject so eligible a suitor as Sir Torquil Tregony would be perfectly capable of falling in love with a penniless soldier, or even of eloping with an adventurer. Regarded in this light, Brough took on the attributes of a God-send. The match was not a brilliant one, as Julia Oversley's had been; Brough's fortune did not bear comparison with Sir Torquil Tregony's; but, on the other hand, Brough was heir to an Earldom, and to the Dowager, who had been obliged to see her lovely elder daughter thrown away on an undistinguished country squire, and her only surviving son married to a female with no pretensions whatsoever to gentility, this circumstance brought more satisfaction than she would ever, in happier days, have believed possible. It was pleasant, too, to reflect that *one* of her children was contracting an alliance which would meet with the approval of all her friends.

So it was in an unusually mellow frame of mind that she arrived at Fontley. Her first preoccupation was with her grandson, but after she had hung over him adoringly, marvelled at his growth, and discovered that he was even more like his Uncle Stephen than she had previously thought, she was ready to talk about Lydia's engagement, and to discuss with Adam and Jenny Lydia's plan for the inevitable party.

Lydia wanted it to be held at Fontley. At first glance this did not seem to be a very feasible scheme, but closer inspection showed that it was really the most sensible one that could have been devised. Lydia had no wish for a large gathering of relations, friends, and mere acquaintances: she would prefer an informal affair, at which only her own and Brough's immediate relations would be present; and as it was naturally impossible for Charlotte to come up to London, or for Mama to leave Charlotte at such a moment, the obvious place for the party was Fontley. Furthermore, Fontley was much nearer than London to Lord Adversane's seat, so that as the Adversanes had not come to town this year it would be more convenient for them too. They would have to stay the night, of course, but Lydia hoped Jenny would not object to this. Brough's sister ought to be invited, but only for civility's sake: she lived in Cornwall, and certainly would not come; and his brother was with his Regiment, in Belgium. The only other guests Lydia wished to be invited were the Rockhills.

'. . . *at least, I don't precisely wish it,*' she wrote, in a private letter to Jenny, '*but I know Brough does, tho' he does not press it. The thing is that he is much attached to Rockhill, who has always been particularly kind to him, which makes it awkward and slighting not to invite him. I daresay they will refuse, on account of the distance from town, but for my part I do not think it signifies if they do not, because when Adam accompanied my aunt and me to the Bickertons' party they were present, and Julia in high bloom, but Adam did not appear at all conscious, but was perfectly composed, and greeted her in the most natural way . . .*'

Bless the child, did she expect him to betray himself at a rout-party? Jenny thought, wryly smiling, as she put the letter up, and turned her attention to what the Dowager was saying to Adam.

She was explaining to him, at tedious length, the various circumstances which made June 21st the only really suitable date. The most cogent of these was that both Brough and Lydia had engagements in London during the preceding week, and that to postpone the date beyond the 21st would be to run the risk of coinciding with Charlotte's confinement; and the least that the 21st would be a Wednesday.

'Jenny, are you sure you like this scheme?' Adam asked, when they were alone.

'Yes, that I do!' she replied. 'Don't you?'

'Oh, yes! As long as it won't put you to a great deal of trouble.'

'It won't put me to any trouble at all. But if you had rather –'

'No, there must be a party, of course – or, at any rate, you all think so!'

'Well, it's natural we should, but if you don't wish it –'

'My dear, you are perfectly right, and I do wish it!'

He spoke impatiently, and she said no more, believing that his reluctance sprang from the knowledge that the Rockhills were to be invited. He was not thinking of Julia, although he did not want her to come to Fontley, and had been dismayed when he had heard that she might. He was reluctant because he thought no time could have been more ill-chosen for festivity than the present. He did not say so; his brief sojourn in London had made him realize that between the soldier and the civilian there was a gulf too wide to be bridged. It had been no hardship to cut his visit short. The season was in full swing; the looming struggle across the Channel seemed to be of no more importance to the ton than a threatened scandal, and was less discussed. To a man who had spent nearly all his adult life in hard campaigning it was incomprehensible that people should care so little that they could go on dancing, flirting, and planning entertainments to eclipse those given by their social rivals when the fate of Europe was in the balance. But England had been at war for twenty-two years, and the English had grown accustomed to this state, accepting it in much the same spirit as they accepted a London fog, or a wet summer. In political circles and in the City a different and more serious point of view might be taken, but amongst the vast majority of the population only such families as had a son or a brother in the Army regarded the renewal of hostilities as anything more than an inevitable and foreseeable bore. Except that Napoleon had not abdicated in March of 1802, it was the Peace of Amiens all over again. It was disagreeable, because taxes would remain high, and one would once more be unable to enjoy foreign travel; but it was not disastrous, because whatever he might do on the Continent Napoleon would not overrun

Great Britain. Life would go on, in fact, just as it had for as long as most people could remember.

To Adam, who, until so recently, had had no other real object than to defeat Napoleon's troops, such apathy was as nauseating as it was extraordinary. It increased his secret longing to be back with his Regiment tenfold; it drove him out of London, thinking that although he could not be where his heart was at least he need not remain amongst people who babbled about picnics and balls, or prosed comfortably and ignorantly in the clubs about the strength of the forces under Wellington's command.

No veteran of the Peninsula could visualize without an extreme effort of imagination the possibility of the defeat of an Army under that command; but no one with the smallest military understanding could look upon the force now assembled in Belgium with satisfaction. People talked as if it was the same Army that had fought its way from Lisbon to Toulouse, but it was very far from being that Army. The hard core was composed of seasoned Regiments, but its size, so impressive to the uninstructed, had been swelled by raw battalions, and by dubious foreign troops. Adam had heard pompous and well-fed gentlemen lecturing with what appeared to him to be crass stupidity any who could be persuaded to listen on the strategy and the tactics the Duke would employ in the campaign. To hear them prating about the Dutch-Belgian Army was more than Adam could stomach. They seemed to believe that the Dutch-Belgians would be as valuable as the Portuguese Caçadores, whom Marshal Beresford had trained: they were more likely to be as unreliable as the Spaniards, he thought, remembering how often those volatile, damnably-officered troops had proved a dangerous embarrassment during the war in the Peninsula. He kept his tongue between his teeth, because to spread despondency was a military crime. Heaven knew, too, that there were too many croakers already, shaking their gloomy heads, saying that they had always foreseen how it would be, that it was folly to think Napoleon could ever be beaten. The most woodheaded optimist was preferable to these gentry; so, even, were the fashionables, preoccupied with their balls, their scandals, the newest style of tying a neckcloth, the chances of some pugilist in a forthcoming match. It was unreasonable to be so much irritated by the pleasure-seekers: there was nothing for them to do, after all, but to occupy themselves with their usual pursuits. It was even unreasonable to look with bitter contempt upon the rabid Whigs, who had been declaring for years that Wellington's victories had been grossly exaggerated, that he was nothing but a Sepoy General, and who were now so thankful to know that he was in command: Adam knew that he ought rather to rejoice in their conversion. He could not; and the only thing to do was to remove himself from their vicinity. He would never, perhaps, feel himself a civilian, but he was one, and had as little to do in the present military crisis as the most frivolous member of the ton. So he had gone home to Fontley, where there was so much to do that his inward fret was sensibly allayed. He still wished that he were with his Regiment, but if the work into which he had thrown himself was not military it was at least of enormous importance – whatever might be Mr Chawleigh's opinion of it.

Having agreed to the proposed betrothal party, he thought no more about it. Jenny never bored him with her housewifely schemes, so it was only when he saw his mother that the party was brought to his mind; and since Membury was ten miles distant from Fontley his meetings with the Dowager were infrequent. Nor did Jenny vex him by talking arrant nonsense about the military situation. Lambert did so, and Charlotte, too, acting as Lambert's echo, but he met the Rydes as seldom as he met his mother; and, in any event, Lambert (thanks to Jenny) had become a mere bobbing-block.

Jenny rarely talked about the war at all, but when she did mention it she showed, he thought, a great deal of good sense. It did not occur to him that Jenny, like Charlotte, was her husband's echo.

Out of hearing of all the rumours that flew about London, he regained cheerfulness and confidence. One or two of his old friends wrote from Belgium now and then: the news was growing better. Some of the Peninsular Regiments which had been recalled from America had arrived, and in capital trim; the dauntingly heterogeneous Army had been welded into a workmanlike whole (trust old Hookey!); Blücher's Prussians were present in force, and were credibly reported to be well-disciplined soldiers. The Allied Army, in fact, was now ready to receive Napoleon at any date convenient to him. '*We are all anxious to discover what costume he means to wear for the occasion,*' wrote one of Adam's correspondents, in sardonic allusion to the postponed ceremony at the Champ de Mars, at which the Emperor, as far as could be gathered from the accounts published in the newspapers, had appeared in the vaguely historical raiment suitable for a Covent Garden masquerade.

Meanwhile, Jenny went quietly about the preparations for her first house-party, enthusiastically assisted by Mrs Dawes, who perceived in this small beginning the promise of a return to Fontley's former state.

It came as no surprise to Jenny that the Rockhills accepted the invitation. She thought that for some reason beyond the grasp of her own simplicity Julia could not keep away from Fontley and Adam; and she had no reason to suppose that Rockhill would put any bar in her way. So far as she understood Rockhill, he believed that Julia's love for Adam was a romantic fancy merely, which thrived on imagination, and would dwindle in the face of reality. Jenny hoped he might be right, but resented the strain which this peculiar cure imposed on Adam.

However, it could have been worse. She had felt herself obliged to invite them to come to Fontley on the day before her dinner-party, since it would take them some nine hours or more to reach it, but Julia wrote, very prettily, to decline this: she was bringing her next sister, Susan, to join the nursery-party at Beckenhurst, to be cosseted back to health by old Nurse, after an attack of influenza which had left her with an obstinate cough; and she and Rockhill would spend the night there, driving on to Fontley on the following day.

Brough brought Lydia down on the 17th, a Saturday. There was no need to ask Lydia if she was happy: she was radiant. Mrs Dawes, much moved, said: 'Oh, my lady, it quite brings the tears to one's eyes, the way they look at each other, Miss Lydia and his lordship!'

'Brough, is there any news?' Adam asked, as soon as Jenny had taken Lydia upstairs to see her godson.

Brough shook his head, grimacing. 'Nothing but on-dits. It seems pretty certain that Bonaparte ain't in Paris: that's all I know.'

'If he has left Paris, he's gone to join his Army of the North. There ought to be news any day now: it wouldn't be like him to dawdle! Do you believe all these stories that he's a spent force? Gammon!'

'I'm damned if I know what to believe!' said Brough. 'I've never heard so much slum talked in my life – I can tell you that! It's a queer thing, Adam: you'd think there's no question about it that we're in for it again, but there are plenty of fellows still saying there'll be no war – men better placed than I am to know what's brewing.'

'It's war,' Adam said confidently. 'It *must* be! I've been expecting all the week to hear that we're engaged on the frontier: Boney won't wait to be attacked on two fronts! His only hope of making the game his own is to give *us* a knock-down before the Austrians and the Russians can come up!'

'Think he can do the trick?' asked Brough, cocking an eyebrow at him.

'Good God, no!'

The ladies came back into the room, putting an end to discussion. The war was not mentioned again. It seemed remote from Fontley, drowsing in the late sunshine of a summer's evening; but when the little party sat at dinner it came suddenly closer, with the arrival, in a chaise-and-pair hired in Market Deeping, of one of Mr Chawleigh's junior clerks, bearing a letter from his master.

Dunster brought it to Adam, at the head of the table.

Recognizing the scrawl as he picked the letter up, Adam said, a note of surprise in his voice: 'For me?'

'Yes, my lord. The young man desired me to tell your lordship that it is most urgent. One of Mr Chawleigh's clerks, I apprehend.'

Adam broke the wafer, and spread open the single sheet, frowning as he tried to decipher it. An anxious silence had fallen on his companions, all three of whom sat watching him. His frown deepened; his lips were seen to tighten. Jenny's heart sank, but she said calmly: 'Has Papa met with an accident? Please to tell me, my lord!'

'No, nothing like that.' Adam glanced up at Dunster. 'Where is the young man? Bring him in!' He waited until Dunster had left the room before adding: 'It is difficult to discover what *has* happened. He seems to think it necessary that I should post up to London immediately, and has been so obliging as to warn them at Fenton's that I shall be arriving tomorrow evening.' There was an edge to this; aware of it, he forced up a smile, and passed the letter to Jenny, saying: 'Try what you can make of it, my love!'

'Post up to London?' cried Lydia. 'But you can't! How *could* Papa Chawleigh ask you to do so? He *knows* you can't leave Fontley, for I told him myself about the party!'

Mr Chawleigh had not forgotten the party: in a postscript he told his son-in-law never to mind, since he would be able to post back to Fontley in plenty of time for it.

Jenny, deciphering the letter more easily than Adam, was as far as he from understanding why he should have been sum-moned to town; but she saw at once what had vexed him. At no time distinguished by tact, Mr Chawleigh, writing under the stress of urgency, had given full rein to the Juggernaut within him. Adam was to come to town on the following day, and there was to be no argumentation about Sunday-travel; he was to come post; he was to put up at Fenton's, where he would find a bedchamber and a parlour hired for him; and he was there to await further enlightenment. Mr Chawleigh would come to

Fenton's to tell him what he must do. Finally, he was to do as he was bid, or he would regret it.

By the time Jenny had finished reading the letter Dunster had brought a sharp-faced youth into the room, who disclosed that he had come down by the Mail, with instructions from the Master not to return without his lordship. That was all he knew. The Master had not told him why my lord was wanted in London; he had not heard any news about the war. It was obviously useless to question him further, so Jenny bore him off to introduce him to Mrs Dawes, promising that his lordship would let him know in the morning what he had decided to do.

'Queer start!' Brough said, when Jenny had gone out of the room. 'I wonder what's in the wind? Sounds to me as though the old boy *has* had some news – and none too good either.'

'You heard what the clerk said. If there had been any news from Belgium he must have known it!'

'Might not. There's no doubt the City men do get to hear of important news before the rest of the world.'

'Then why the devil didn't he tell me what it is?' demanded Adam irritably.

'He probably don't like writing letters, or don't want it repeated.'

'Adam!' Lydia burst out. 'If you are not here for my party –'

'Of course I shall be here! I can see not the slightest reason why I should post up to town, whatever Mr Chawleigh may have heard!'

Lydia looked relieved; but when Jenny came back into the room, she said bluntly: 'By what the boy tells me, Papa is in a taking. You'll have to go, Adam.'

'I'll be hanged if I do! If your father wanted me to go chasing up to London, he should have told me why!'

She regarded him seriously. 'Well, writing doesn't come easily to him. But I know Papa, and you may depend upon it he'd never have sent for you like this if he hadn't good reason to. There's something he thinks you should do. It looks to me like some matter of business, and if that's so, you do as he tells you, my lord, for there isn't a shrewder head in the City than his!'

He looked vexed, and rather mulish; but when Brough endorsed this advice, recommending him not to be a clunch, he shrugged, and said: 'Oh, very well!'

He made the journey in his own chaise, taking Kinver and the clerk with him, and arriving in St James's Street a little after six o'clock. A Sunday calm seemed to prevail; and when he entered the hotel he was received with all the usual civilities, untouched by any sign of excitement or alarm. He felt more than ever sceptical, and went up to the parlour set aside for his use in a mood that was far from benign.

He found Mr Chawleigh awaiting him, walking up and down the floor in a fret of impatience. Mr Chawleigh was looking more than ordinarily grim, but his scowl lifted at sight of Adam, and he heaved a huge sigh of relief. 'Eh, but I'm glad to see you, my lord!' he said, grasping Adam's hand. 'Good lad, good lad!'

Adam's brows rose a little. 'How do you do, sir? I hope I haven't kept you waiting long?'

'Nay, it's no matter! There's naught to be done till the morning. I'm sorry to have brought you away from Fontley, all in a rush, but there was no help for it, because it's a matter of damned urgency!'

'Yes, so I understand, sir. One moment, however! Have you bespoken dinner?'

'No, no, I've more to think of than dinner!' said Mr Chawleigh testily.

'But if there's nothing to be done till tomorrow we can surely eat dinner tonight!' said Adam. 'What's your choice, sir?'

'I don't know as I'll be staying – Oh, well, anything you fancy, my lord! The ordinary will do for me.'

Adam began to think that there must be something very wrong, if his father-in-law's appetite had failed. He looked at him for a moment, and then turned to his valet. 'Tell them to send up a neat dinner, Kinver, at seven – and some sherry immediately, if you please!' He smiled at Mr Chawleigh, saying, as Kinver went out of the room: 'I've a mind to give you a scold, sir, for not ordering that for yourself. Now, what is it? Why was it necessary for me to come up to town?'

'It's bad news, my lord,' Mr Chawleigh said heavily. 'It's damned bad news! We've been beat!'

Adam's brows snapped together. 'Who says so? Where did you learn that?'

'Never you mind where I learned it! You'd be none the wiser if I was to tell you, but it ain't a hoax, nor yet a mere rumour. There's those in the City whose business it is to know what's going on abroad, and they've agents all over, ay, and other ways of getting the news before it's known elsewhere! We've been gapped, my lord! Beaten all hollow!'

'Moonshine!' Adam was a little pale, but he gave a scornful laugh. 'Good God, sir, did you bring me all this way just to tell me a Canterbury tale?'

'No, I didn't, and it ain't moonshine either! They've been fighting over there these two days past, let me tell you!'

'That I can well believe,' Adam responded coolly. 'But that we've been beaten all hollow – *no*!'

Mr Chawleigh began to champ his jaws. 'No? Don't believe Boney's sitting in Brussels at this very minute, I daresay? Or that those Prussians were rolled up – finished! – at the very outset? Or that Boney was too quick for your precious Wellington, and took him by surprise? I knew how it would be! Didn't I say from the start we'd have him rampaging all over again?'

The entrance of a waiter checked him. He was obliged to contain himself until the man had gone away again; and when he next spoke it was in a milder tone. 'There's no sense in you and me coming to cuffs, my lord. You've got your notions, and it don't matter what mine may be, because what I'm telling you ain't anyone's notion: it's the truth! It came straight from Ghent, where maybe they know a trifle more than we do here! The town's packed full of refugees, and Antwerp too!'

Adam poured out two glasses of sherry, and handed one to him. 'That might well be, if the Army is on the retreat – which might also be. You say the Prussians suffered a bad reverse. I can believe that, but consider, sir! If Blücher was obliged to fall back, Wellington must have done so too, to maintain his communications with him. Any soldier could tell you that! – and also that Boney's first objective must have been to cut them!' He smiled reassuringly. 'I've taken part in a good few retreats under old Hookey's command, sir, and *you* may believe *me* when I tell you that he's never more masterly than when he retires!'

Mr Chawleigh, swallowing his sherry at a gulp, choked, and ejaculated: 'Retires? For God's sake, boy, can't you understand plain English? It's a damned rout!'

'Apparently I can't!' Adam said, rather mischievously. 'But I've no experience of damned routs, you know – unless you count Salamanca a rout? We rompéd Marmont in prime style, but I shouldn't have called his retreat a *rout*.'

'Marmont! This is *Bonaparte*!'

'Very true, but I still find it impossible to believe in your rout.' He saw that Mr Chawleigh's colour was rising, and said: 'Don't let us argue on that head, sir! Tell me why I'm here! Even if your information were correct, I don't understand why it is of such importance that I should be in London. What the devil can *I* do to mend matters?'

'You can save your bacon!' replied Mr Chawleigh grimly. 'Not all of it, but some, I do trust! Eh, I blame myself! I should have warned you weeks ago – same as I should have pulled out myself, the moment I knew the jobbers had closed their books! I've dropped a tidy penny, my lord, and so I tell you!'

'Have you, sir? I'm excessively sorry to hear it,' said Adam, refilling the glasses. 'How did you come to do that?'

Mr Chawleigh drew an audible breath, eyeing him much as a choleric schoolmaster might have eyed a doltish pupil. Speaking with determined patience, he said: 'Your blunt's invested in the Funds, ain't it? Never mind these rents of yours! I'm talking about your private fortune. Well, I know it is – what was left of it! Me and your man Wimmering went into things pretty thoroughly before you was married to my Jenny. Not to wrap it up in clean linen, your pa played wily beguiled with his blunt, so that what was left don't amount to much, not to my way of thinking. Nor your rents don't either – and don't waste your breath telling me what they *might* bring you in, because it don't signify, not at this moment! The thing is, I wouldn't want you to lose your fortune, my lord. I don't say I ain't ready to stand the nonsense, but well I know it 'ud fairly choke you if you was forced to be obliged to me for every groat you spent! Proud as an apothecary you are, for all you've tried to hide it, which I don't deny you have, let alone behaving to me as affable and as respectful as if you was my own son!' He paused, observing Adam's sudden flush with an indulgent eye. 'No need to colour up, my lord,' he said kindly. 'And no need for any round-aboutation either! They'll tell you in the City that Jonathan Chawleigh's a sure card. Maybe I am, maybe I ain't, but I'm not a nodcock, lad, and well I know why you don't drive the curricle I gave you, nor wouldn't let me set up this farm of yours! You don't choose to be beholden, and I like you the better for it! Which is why I bid you come up to town, for there's naught to be done without you're here to give the word. I've seen Wimmering: he knows what's to be done, but he can't move without he has your authority.'

'Have I any?' Adam interrupted, as pale as he had previously been flushed.

'Don't talk so silly!' begged Mr Chawleigh. 'It stands to reason your man of business can't act without you tell him to!'

'So I had supposed! But I'm sadly ignorant: I had also supposed that my man of business would have shown the door to anyone – even my father-in-law! – who came to tell him what to do with my affairs!'

'Well, so he did, in a manner of speaking!' said Mr Chawleigh, keeping his temper. 'Now, don't fly into your high ropes, my lord! We ain't after anything but your good, Wimmering and me, nor he never had any intention of acting arbitrary. But he's a deep old file, and he knows, if you don't, what's the worth of a nudge from Jonathan Chawleigh, and a mighty poor man of business he'd be if he didn't pay heed to it, and act according!

Why, if I'd waited to drum it into *your* head, without a word spoken to Wimmering, it would have been too late to do anything by the time I'd done it, and you'd told Wimmering – which likely you'd have made a mull of, you having no more understanding of business than a babe unborn!'

Adam's anger cooled a little. 'Very well, and what is it that must be done?'

'Sell, of course! *Sell*, my lord, and at the best price you can get! If it can be done – if it ain't too late already – you'll suffer a loss, same as I have myself, but you'll save yourself from ruin! It'll be bad, and I don't deny it, but see if I don't put you in the way of making a recover presently! But there's no time to be lost: once the news is made known there'll be no selling the stock, not if you was to offer it at a grig! Forty-nine was all I got for mine, and they was standing at fifty-seven and a half when the jobbers closed their books! Eh, it don't bear thinking of! A bubble-merchant, that's what they'll be calling me!'

He sounded so tragic that Adam might have supposed that he was facing ruin had he not had every reason to think that however large a part of his private fortune had been invested in the Funds it represented only a tithe of his enormous wealth. He said: 'I'm afraid I don't perfectly understand, sir. How am I to sell my shares if there's no dealing being done?'

'You leave that to Wimmering!' said Mr Chawleigh. 'He'll know how to do the thing, never you fear! What's more, he's ready and anxious to do it, the moment you say the word. He'll be here to wait on you first thing tomorrow morning, and you'll find he'll advise you the same as I have.' He glanced shrewdly at Adam. 'Well, he did so when that Bonaparte first broke out again, didn't he?'

Adam nodded. Mr Wimmering had written to him in March, venturing to suggest that in view of the uncertain political situation it might be wise for his lordship to consider the advisability of realizing his holding in Government stock; but he had not considered it either advisable or proper to do so, and had replied quite unequivocally.

'Eh, if you'd only listened to him!' mourned Mr Chawleigh, shaking his head.

Adam looked at him thoughtfully. It was plainly a waste of time to attempt to persuade him that a strategic withdrawal was not a rout: civilians were always cast into panic by a retreat, just as they were wildly elated by quite minor victories. So he refrained from telling Mr Chawleigh that his own confidence was unshaken, and tried instead to discover the exact nature of the news which had been whispered in his ear. It was not easy to do this, but by the time the neat dinner had been disposed of, and Mr Chawleigh took his leave, Adam had formed his own conclusions. It was certain that hostilities had begun; it seemed fairly certain that Napoleon, so far from being a spent force, had moved with all his former, disconcerting rapidity. It was possible that Wellington had been taken by surprise, and had been obliged to oppose the enemy with only his advance troops: it sounded like that; and it sounded too as if the action had been fought on ground not of his choosing. In which case, he would certainly retreat; and no doubt the flocks of pleasure-seeking visitors to Brussels would take fright immediately, and make for the coast. It was more difficult to assess the probable extent of the Prussian reverse. Adam had never seen the Prussians in action, but he knew the Hanoverian troops well, and he thought that if the Prussians were at all like the men of the King's German Legion there would be little fear that they would run away, even if they had suffered a repulse. Mr Chawleigh talked as though Napoleon had smashed that army; Adam thought this unlikely, because the Allied Army had also been engaged, which meant that Napoleon must have been fighting on two fronts.

He allowed Mr Chawleigh to leave him in the belief that he meant to follow his advice. It was useless to argue with him; that would only lead to a quarrel. Besides, the poor man was already in a stew of anxiety: probably some of his many trading ventures would be badly affected by a French victory.

Thinking about it, weighing it in his mind, Adam knew that he was not going to try to sell his stock. Mr Chawleigh had done so at a loss, and he seemed to think that the price was rapidly sinking. To sell would be wantonly to diminish his principal; and he would certainly do no such thing: running shy merely because the Allied Army had clashed disadvantageously with the enemy, and had fallen back, perhaps to better ground, almost certainly to maintain communications with the Prussians.

Sipping a last glass of brandy before going to bed, remembering the years of his military service, confidence grew in him. There had been plenty of retreats, but no lost battles under Douro's command: not one!

He thought, regretfully, that it was a pity he hadn't sold his stock at the beginning of March, when Wimmering had advised it. Had he done so, he would now have had a large sum at his disposal, and might have bought again, making a handsome profit.

He set his empty glass down suddenly. The idly reflective expression in his eyes altered; he sat staring intently straight before him, his eyes now bright and hard between slightly narrowed lids. A queer little smile began to play around his mouth; he drew a breath like a sigh, and got up, pouring more brandy into his glass. He stood for quite some time, swirling the brandy round, watching it but not thinking about it. The ghost of a laugh shook him; he tossed off the brandy, set the glass down again, and went off to bed.

Twenty-five

_H_e had just finished breakfast when Mr Wimmering was brought up to the parlour on the following morning. Wimmering was looking grave, but he said that he was very glad to see my lord.

'I'm extremely glad to see you,' replied Adam. 'I need your advice and your services.'

'Your lordship knows that both are at your disposal.'

'I'm obliged to you. Sit down! Now, tell me, Wimmering, what, by your reckoning, am I worth? How much credit will Drummond allow me?'

Mr Wimmering's jaw dropped; he gazed blankly at Adam, and said feebly: 'Credit? Drummond?'

'I don't want to go to the Jews unless I must.'

'Go to the – But, my lord – ! You cannot have run into debt? I beg your pardon! But I had not the smallest suspicion –'

'No, no, I haven't run into debt!' Adam said. 'But I'm in urgent need of ready money – as large a sum as I can contrive to raise! Immediately!'

Wimmering felt a little faint. At any other hour of the day he would have concluded that his client had been imbibing too freely, and was half-sprung. He wondered if Mr Chawleigh's news had temporarily turned his brain. He bore no appearance of being either drunk or unhinged, but it had struck Wimmering as soon as he had entered the room that he was looking unlike himself. There was a tautness about him Wimmering had never before noticed; his eyes, usually so cool, were strangely bright;

and the smile hovering at the corners of his mouth held a disquieting hint of recklessness. Wimmering was at a loss to interpret these signs, never having been privileged to see his noble client in command of a Forlorn Hope.

'Well?' Adam said impatiently.

Wimmering pulled himself together, saying firmly: 'My lord, before I enter upon that question, may I respectfully remind you that there is a far more urgent matter awaiting your attention? If you have seen Mr Chawleigh it must be unnecessary for me to tell you that there is no time to be lost in empowering me to dispose of your stock.'

'Oh, I'm not selling!' Adam said cheerfully. 'I beg pardon! Of course you supposed that that was why I needed you! No, I'm buying.'

'*Buying?*' gasped Wimmering, turning quite pale. 'You're not serious, my lord?'

'I'm perfectly serious – and perfectly sane as well, I promise you. No, don't repeat Mr Chawleigh's Banbury story to me! I've heard it once, and I don't wish to hear it again! My father-in-law is an excellent man, but he has not the smallest understanding of military matters. As far as I can discover, word of a retreat has reached the City, brought by some agent, who had heard that the Prussians had been cut up a trifle, that we had retired, and who no doubt saw the refugees pouring into Antwerp, or Ghent, or wherever he chanced to be, and out of this built up a lurid tale of disaster! My dear Wimmering, do you really imagine that if the Army was in headlong flight not one hint of it would appear in today's journals?'

Mr Wimmering looked rather struck. He said: 'I must own that one would have supposed –' He stopped, as a thought occurred to him, and asked hopefully: 'Have *you*, perhaps, received news from Belgium, my lord?'

'I've received a good deal of news during the past weeks,' Adam replied coolly. 'I won't deceive you, however: I haven't any secret source of information, and I've heard nothing that confirms or refutes my father-in-law's story.' He paused; the disturbing smile grew more marked. 'Have there been moments in your life, Wimmering, when you have felt, *within* yourself, a strong – oh, an overwhelming compulsion to do something that perhaps your reason tells you is imprudent – even dangerous? When you don't hesitate to stake your last groat, because you *know* the dice are going to fall your way?' He saw the look of horror in Wimmering's face, and laughed. 'No, you don't understand, do you? Well, never mind!'

But Mr Wimmering was unable to follow this advice. In a flash of enlightenment he had recognized his late patron in the present Viscount, and his heart sank like a plummet. He shuddered to recall the number of times the Fifth Viscount had yielded to the compulsion of an inner and too often lying voice, how many times he had been confident that his luck had changed. He sank into despair, knowing from bitter experience how useless it would be to attempt to bring his lordship to reason. There was nothing he could do to restrain him, but he did utter an anguished protest when Adam, enumerating his tangible assets, said: 'Then there's Fontley. You know as well as I do how much land I have left unmortgaged – unsettled too! My father blamed himself for that, didn't he? I wish he could know how thankful I am today that the estate never was resettled!'

Mr Wimmering was obliged to draw what comfort he could from the hope that my lord's intangible asset would rescue him from penury. It would certainly weigh more heavily in his favour in the mind of Mr Drummond than any security he could offer – provided the banker did not discover that he was acting in defiance of Mr Chawleigh's advice.

'He won't,' said Adam. 'My father-in-law banks with Hoare's.'

'My lord!' said Wimmering desperately, 'have you thought – have you considered – what would be your position if this – this *gamble* of yours should fail?'

'It won't fail,' replied Adam, with so much calm confidence that Wimmering was impressed in spite of himself.

But he begged Adam not to command him to carry to

Drummond's proposals of which he wholly disapproved. A very faint hope that these words might give his lordship pause was of brief duration.

'Not I!' said Adam, impish laughter in his eyes. 'If Drummond were to catch sight of that Friday-face you're wearing, my tale would be told! He wouldn't lend me as much as a coach-wheel!' Laughter faded; he looked at Wimmering for a minute without speaking, and then said perfectly seriously: 'I don't think Providence holds out chance upon chance to one. I think – if I were to refuse this – I should never be offered another. It means a great deal to me. Can't you understand?'

Mr Wimmering nodded, and answered mournfully: 'Yes, my lord. I have for long been aware, alas –' He left the sentence unfinished, only sighing heavily.

'Don't mistake me!' Adam said quickly. 'It's some quirk in me – an odd kick in my gallop, my father would have said! – no fault of Mr Chawleigh's! I've received nothing but kindness from him. Indeed, I hold him in considerable affection!'

Mr Wimmering knew that there was no more to be said. He was well enough acquainted with Mr Chawleigh to feel a profound sympathy for anyone who lay within his power; but he still could not repress a hope that Mr Drummond would prove less accommodating than my lord anticipated. But no sooner did he entertain this hope than it was shattered by a macabre vision of my lord caught in the toils of some blood-sucking money-lender, which so much appalled him that when he presently climbed into a hack the jarvey had to ask him twice where he wanted to go before he could collect himself sufficiently to utter the address of his office in the City.

He had offered to await the result of his client's visit to the bank at Fenton's, but Adam (looking alarmingly like a school-boy bent on mischief) said that he was not going to return to the hotel until late at night, because he meant to take good care to keep out of his father-in-law's way, and it was well within the bounds of probability that Mr Chawleigh might call there to make certain that his advice was being followed. 'I should be obliged to tell him the truth, and that wouldn't do at all,' Adam said. 'I'll come to your place of business, and very likely remain there. I shouldn't think he would call there, would you? He will suppose you to be running all about the City, trying to dispose of my stock. In any event, we will warn your clerk! Is there a cupboard I can slip into, in case of need?'

Jolting over the cobbles in the aged and malodorous hack, Mr Wimmering reflected that with all his faults the Fifth Viscount had never demanded of his man of business a cupboard in which he could hide.

Arrived at his office, he had some time to wait before he heard Adam's halting step on the dusty stairs. He got up from behind his desk, as Adam was ushered into his room, but he had no need to ask how my lord had fared: the answer was plain to see in his smile. Wimmering had had time to recover his usual composure, and he said, in a tone of mere respectful enquiry: 'Your lordship has prospered in your errand?'

Adam nodded. 'Yes, of course! Did you think I should not? Fifty thousand – can you buy up to that figure?'

'*Fifty thousand*?' echoed Wimmering. 'Drummond will lend you fifty-thousand-pounds, my lord?'

'But why not? Consider! I've something in the region of twenty thousand invested in the Funds already; I have Fontley, with the demesne lands; and besides that there are the three farms which –'

'Did he *know* for what purpose you wanted such a sum, my lord?'

'Certainly! *He* doesn't think I've run mad! Nor is he shaking like a blancmanger because we may have suffered a reverse. We had a long talk together: he's a sensible man – really a great gun!' He regarded Wimmering with a decided twinkle, and said reproachfully: 'No, no, you are *quite* mistaken!'

'My lord?' said Wimmering, startled.

'I told him, at the outset, that I wished to impress upon him most particularly that what I had to propose to him had *nothing* whatsoever to do with my father-in-law.'

Wimmering opened his mouth, and shut it again. He could well imagine what the effect of this warning must have been. He began to suspect that he had underrated his lordship, but all he said was: 'Just so, my lord. Very proper!'

Adam laughed. 'Well, he can't say I didn't tell him the exact truth, at all events! Now, listen, Wimmering! Mr Chawleigh assured me that you would know how to sell my stock, so I trust you may know how to buy more for me.'

'There will be no difficulty about that, my lord,' replied Wimmering, at his dryest.

'Good! I don't know how low the price may sink, but I think I ought not to run any risks, so buy *now*, if you please!'

Mr Wimmering closed his eyes for an anguished moment. 'Run any risks . . . !' he repeated faintly.

'If I delayed, in the hope of buying cheaper still, I might miss my tip. At any moment now we may expect to get news from Headquarters, which will put an end to the panic in the City. Drummond warns me not to look for any startling rise immediately. He considers that it's unlikely that the price will go beyond what it was when the books were closed, so do the best you can for me, Wimmering! I know you will.'

'I should prefer to say that I shall obey your orders, my lord,' Wimmering replied.

Though he set about his task with extreme reluctance, he performed it to his patron's entire satisfaction. 'As low as that!' Adam exclaimed, still in that mood of alarming elation. 'You're a wizard, Wimmering! how the devil did you contrive to do it? I wish you will try to look a little more cheerful!'

'My lord,' said Wimmering, 'had I found it impossible to buy at so low a figure I should *feel* more cheerful!'

Adam went off to Brooks's, where he dined, and spent the evening. There were a large number of members present, and for a time he was kept tolerably well-entertained, talking to friends, and listening with amusement to the ridiculous theories being put forward about the progress of the war; but as the evening wore on he ceased to be amused. He began to be

346

irritated, and several times responded to remarks addressed to him with a shortness which bordered on incivility. He moved away presently, wondering why the pessimists should be so much more numerous and vociferous than the optimists. He was a little surprised to find that absurdities could make him angry; but he thought that those who spread ominous stories, which were invariably vouched for as having emanated from trustworthy sources, deserved to be given a sharp set-down. Only fools placed the slightest credence in reports repeated by prattleboxes who had heard them from a friend to whom they had been told by someone who had met a man just arrived from Belgium, but when everyone must be feeling a considerable degree of anxiety it was really criminal to disseminate rumours that could only serve to encourage despondency. He removed himself out of earshot of the war-group, and sat down to glance through the latest issue of the *Gentleman's Magazine*. There was nothing in it of interest; he tried to read one article, but found his mind wandering, perhaps because two elderly gentlemen distracted him by arguing hotly on the respective merits of Turner and Claude. Fragments of other conversations reached his ears: the Panorama in Leicester Fields, somebody's latest witticism, somebody's run of luck at macao: it was incredible that people could be absorbed in such fripperies at such a moment!

His head had begun to ache; he felt depressed, and realized that he was very tired. That accounted for his inability to concentrate his mind on a dull article. It was time he went to bed. He left the club, and walked up the street to his hotel, telling himself that a good night's sleep was all that was needed to restore him to that mood of supreme confidence which had possessed him all day.

He had expected to drop asleep immediately, but no sooner had he closed his eyes than his brain became active, thinking of the day's transactions, speculating on what might have happened across the Channel. He tried to drag it away from the war, and to fix it instead on the schemes he had made for the improvement of his estate, but it was too strong for him. His body ached with fatigue, but whatever position he adopted was uncomfortable within a very few minutes, and the wearier he became the livelier grew his brain. He told himself that his diminishing confidence was a mere reaction from his previous elation, remembering how often, after a hard-won battle, a fit of dejection had succeeded the mood of triumph and rejoicing; but the endless argument in his head went on and on. Doubt shook him; defeat, which had seemed the remotest of possibilities, became probable; far larger in his brain than the memories of Talavera, Salamanca, Vittoria loomed the thought that Wellington had never before faced Napoleon himself. He had laughed at the people who had said that to him, but it was true: Masséna had been the best of the Marshals sent against Wellington: a good general, but not a Napoleon. It was also true, of course, that Wellington had never lost a battle, but that could be said of any general before his first defeat. Struggling against this creeping conviction of disaster, he thought of all the splendid fellows who had made up the Peninsular Army: drunken rascals, perhaps, but more than a match for three times their number of Frogs, as they had proved again and again. All very well in attack, Johnny Crapaud, but when it came to a dogged stand there were no soldiers in the world that bore comparison with the British.

The flicker of confidence flared high for a moment, and sank. There were too many foreigners in this new Army of Wellington's, too many raw battalions. The recruit who had never been shot over might perform prodigies of valour, but it was only the seasoned soldier who could be trusted to maintain his ground in the face of determined attack. The Allied Army was not the Peninsular Army: it was a polyglot force, stiffened certainly by veteran Regiments, but its ranks swelled by such unknown quantities as the Dutch-Belgians, the Brunswickers (many of whom, Major Rowan wrote, were mere children), and Hanoverian Landwehr battalions.

In the small hours of the morning the realization came to Adam that he had acted like a madman; and until a restless, nightmare-ridden sleep overcame him he endured worse agonies than any he had suffered under the surgeons' hands.

When Kinver drew back the blinds in his room, and he awoke, the more lurid of his imaginings seemed absurd; but he got up feeling more jaded than when he had retired to bed, and not much more hopeful.

He was never afterwards able to recall what he had done during that interminable day. When the newspapers appeared they contained the first accounts of actions fought on the 16th and the 17th June. Making every allowance for exaggerations and misapprehensions, they did not afford very reassuring reading. There was no official dispatch: a sure sign that the actions at Ligny and Quatre-Bras had been the prelude merely to the main battle, of which no news had yet reached London.

A nasty business, Quatre-Bras: that much was evident. Boney *had* taken the Duke by surprise: the miracle was that Ney did not seem to have pressed home his attack on a force he must have known to be numerically far inferior to his own. Forgetting his personal anxieties, Adam thought that they must have stood like heroes, the fellows who held the ground until Picton brought up the Reserve, midway through the afternoon. Dutch-Belgians, too: well, that was cheering, at all events! But Picton had been badly cut up, and there was no mention of any British cavalry. A scrambling, desperate fight it must have been, attended by big losses, but mercifully inconclusive. The cavalry skirmishes at Genappe on the 17th furnished exciting material for the journalists' pens, but were relatively unimportant. The worst news was that the Prussians seemed to have been shockingly mauled, and flung back in disarray. There was even a rumour that Blücher had been killed; and where the Prussians were now, whether re-forming, or retreating, no one knew. It might be a serious business, Adam thought, if their officers failed to get them together again.

Trying to build up a picture of the situation from unreliable reports was not easy, but for a short time Adam felt more hopeful, taking comfort from the reflection that although the

349

Reserve must be terribly weakened Wellington had been able to withdraw his troops in good order, and, apparently, without being much harassed by the enemy.

There was no more published news, but as the day dragged on more and more ominous rumours reached London, and were passed from mouth to mouth. The Allied Army had endured a crushing defeat; the remnants of it had fallen back in disorder on Brussels, and had been seen defiling out through the Antwerp gate; deserters from the battlefield had been encountered as far away as Ghent and Antwerp, telling of an unprecedented bombardment, overwhelming attacks by enormous forces of cavalry, hideous carnage.

Adam recognized the falsity of much that he heard, but it was impossible to maintain optimism under the cumulative weight of reported disaster. When not one scrap of reassuring news was received one could no longer laugh rumour to scorn: even if the stories were grossly exaggerated they must be founded on truth; and one was forced, at last, to confront, not the possibility of defeat, but the incredible certainty of it. The confidence which had burned like a flame in Adam all the previous day, sunk to embers during the night, and then flickered fitfully but with diminishing strength with his efforts to keep it alive, was not quite dead when he walked down the street to Brooks's that evening. It still smouldered, but with such a tiny glow that he was barely conscious of it. He felt rather numb, as though he had been battered into insensibility. He tried to realize that the Army had been beaten, but the words conveyed nothing to his brain: they were as meaningless as gibberish. It was easier to realize that he had completed the work of bringing his house to ruin. In the throes of reaction, he had uttered aloud: 'My God, what have I done?' in horror at what then seemed an act of madness; but he had still been able to cherish the hope that his gamble would yet prove successful. The little spark of hope that lurked beneath despair and self-blame was no more based on reason than the disbelief that flashed into his brain when some fresh tale of ignoble rout was forced on him. He knew that when he had staked everything he possessed, even Fontley, he had not thought it a gamble, but he could not recapture the confidence that had then prompted him, or understand how he could have been so crassly, so wickedly stupid as to fly in the face of Mr Chawleigh's advice, and of Wimmering's entreaties.

The club was crowded, and, for once, very few of its members were in the card-room. Everyone was talking about the reports from Belgium, but there was no fresh news, not a hint that any word had been received at the Horse Guards from the Duke's Headquarters. In the large room overlooking St James's Street Lord Grey was proving to the apparent satisfaction of a numerous audience that Napoleon was established in Brussels at that moment. Napoleon had two hundred thousand men across the Sambre, which set the question beyond argument. Nobody attempted to argue; Sir Robert Wilson began to read aloud a letter which confirmed the rumour that what was left of the Army had evacuated Brussels, and was retreating to the coast.

An elderly stranger, standing beside Adam before one of the windows, said in an angry undervoice: 'Gammon! Pernicious humdudgeon! I don't believe a word of it, do you?'

'No,' Adam replied.

The babel of voices rose; peace terms were being discussed. The noise stopped suddenly as someone said sharply: 'Listen!'

The sound of cheering could be heard in the distance. It drew nearer. Adam's unknown companion thrust his head out of the window, peering up the street in the failing light. He said: 'It's a chaise, I think. Yes, but – here, sir, your eyes are younger than mine! What are those things sticking out of the windows?'

Adam had taken a quick, limping step to the window. He said in a queer voice: 'Eagles!'

Twenty-six

*P*andemonium broke out; there was a rush to the windows; as the post-chaise passed staid gentlemen leaned out, waving and cheering; persons who had never been on more than nodding terms clapped one another on the back; and even the most rabid opponents of the war huzzaed with the best.

Adam stood leaning against the wall, so dizzy that he was obliged to shut his eyes. The room was spinning round; waves of alternate hot and cold swept over him; but he managed to remain on his feet, and to overcome his faintness.

Waiters were sent scurrying for champagne; corks began to pop; and someone called out a toast to Wellington. Everyone drank it; Adam saw that the proposer was one of the Duke's bitterest critics, and grinned inwardly. The Duke had no critics tonight, only fervent supporters. Adam thought that the enthusiasm would not last for long; but he could not foresee that within three days several of those who were acclaiming Wellington as the country's saviour would be saying that the battle was rather a defeat than a victory.

Adam did not remain for long in the club, but slipped away presently, and went back to Fenton's. Kinver was waiting for him, a broad grin on his face. Adam smiled at him with an effort. 'Did you see the chaise, Kinver?'

'I should think I did, my lord! With the Eagles sticking out of the windows! Three of them!'

Adam sank wearily into the chair before the dressing-table,

and put up a hand to drag the pin out of his neckcloth. Kinver said: 'I hope you'll sleep tonight, my lord.'

'I think I could sleep the clock round,' Adam said.

He was asleep almost before his head touched the pillow. Kinver thought he had never seen him look more exhausted.

He would have liked to have drawn the curtains round the bed, to guard him from the sunlight that would filter in a few hours through the window-blinds, but he dared not do it: his lordship, accustomed for years to camp-beds, declared himself unable to sleep if snugly curtained from draughts.

But although his room faced east he did sleep the clock round, deeply and dreamlessly, hardly stirring. When he woke at last, the room was full of golden light, subdued by the blinds that Kinver had drawn so closely across the windows. He yawned, and stretched luxuriously, not fully conscious, but aware of a sense of well-being. As he remembered the cause of this, his first thought was one of rejoicing in the victory. Then he realized, as he had scarcely been able to do before, that he was not ruined, but probably richer than he had ever been.

The door creaked; he saw Kinver peeping cautiously at him, and said lazily: 'I'm awake. What's the time?'

'Just gone eleven, my lord,' Kinver answered, pulling back the blinds.

'Good God, have I slept as long as that? I must get up!' He swung his feet to the floor, and stood up, slipping his arms into the sleeves of the dressing-gown Kinver was holding for him. 'Tell 'em to send up breakfast directly, will you? I'm as hungry as a hawk! Have the newspapers come?'

'Yes, my lord, they're laid out for you in the parlour. It looks like Bonaparte's been sent to grass all right and regular this time.'

He went off to order breakfast, and Adam walked into the adjoining parlour, and opened the *Gazette*, sitting down at the table to read the Waterloo Dispatch. He had just come to the end of it when his breakfast was brought in. He was looking grave, which made Kinver say, as the waiter withdrew: 'He is beat, isn't he, my lord?'

'To flinders, I should suppose. But, my God! twelve hours of it! I'm afraid our losses must have been enormous.' He laid the *Gazette* aside, and as he did so caught sight of the date on it. He stared at it incredulously, exclaiming: 'Wednesday, 21st June? Oh, my God!' He saw that Kinver was looking bewildered, and said: 'The dinner-party for Miss Lydia's engagement! Now I *am* in the basket! Why the devil didn't you wake me hours ago?'

'I'm sure I'm very sorry, my lord!' Kinver said, much dismayed. 'What with all the excitement – and you saying you'd like to sleep the clock round – it went clean out of my head!'

'Out of mine too. Can it really be Wednesday? Surely –' He passed a hand over his brow, trying to reckon the days. 'Yes, I suppose it must be. Oh, lord!'

'Do you eat your breakfast, my lord, and I'll send to warn the boys that you'll be needing the chaise in an hour's time!' suggested Kinver. 'We'll be at Fontley by nine, maybe earlier.'

Adam hesitated, and then shook his head. 'No, it won't do. I must see Wimmering before I leave town. Warn the boys to be ready to set forward, however – at about two, perhaps. I'm surprised Wimmering hasn't been here to see me.'

'Well, my lord, Mr Wimmering *did* call,' disclosed Kinver guiltily. 'But when I told him you was abed and asleep, he wouldn't have you wakened, but said he would call again this afternoon.'

'I see. I expect you meant it for the best, but I'm not going to sit kicking my heels here: I shall have to drive into the City.' He then thought that it would be as well to see Drummond too, and smiled at his chagrined valet. 'Never mind! I must have gone to Drummond's in any event.'

His call at the bank lasted for longer than he had anticipated, for Mr Drummond considered the occasion worthy of his very special sherry. Civility compelled Adam to conceal his impatience to be gone; so that it was already two o'clock when he reached Wimmering's place of business.

Wimmering had been on the point of setting out for Fenton's, and exclaimed in disapproval: 'My lord! You should not have put yourself to the inconvenience of coming to me! I left word with your man that I would call again!'

'I know, but I'm in the devil of a hurry!' Adam said. 'There's a dinner-party being held at Fontley tonight, in honour of my sister's engagement, and I swore I'd return in time for it. I shan't, of course, but I might arrive in time to bid the guests farewell, don't you think? I shall be in black disgrace – and deserve to be!'

Mr Wimmering smiled primly. 'I fancy, when the cause of your absence is known, you will be forgiven, my lord. And may I, before I enter upon any business, beg that *I* may be forgiven? Your lordship's head is better than mine. I must confess that I regarded your far-sighted venture with deep foreboding. Indeed, I was so filled with apprehension all yesterday that I found myself unable to swallow as much as a morsel of toast. I blush to own it, but so it was!'

'You need not!' Adam said. 'Don't speak of yesterday! What *I* endured – ! Do you know, I even wondered if I ought not to be in Bedlam? I shall never do such a thing again: I haven't enough bottom for speculation!'

When he presently left Wimmering he was just about to summon up a hack from a nearby stand when he remembered that there was a third call it behoved him to make. He hesitated for a moment, and then resigned himself, and proceeded on foot in the direction of Cornhill. It was going to make him devilishly late, but there was no help for it: the barest courtesy made it necessary for him to visit his father-in-law.

He found Mr Chawleigh alone, and entered his room unannounced, pausing a moment, his hand still grasping the door-knob, looking across at him in sudden concern. Mr Chawleigh was seated at his desk, but he did not seem to be at work. Something about his posture, the sag of his great shoulders, the settled gloom in his countenance made Adam fear that the loss he had suffered must be much larger than he had disclosed. He said in a tone of real concern: 'Sir – !'

Mr Chawleigh's expression did not change. He said heavily: 'You haven't gone home then, my lord.'

'Not yet. I'm leaving today, however. It's Lydia's party, you know, but I wanted to see you before I left town.'

'I know,' Mr Chawleigh said. He got up, and stood leaning his knuckles on his desk. 'You've no need to tell me,' he said. 'No need for you to blame me either, for you couldn't blame me more than I blame myself. Eh, it's taken all the pleasure out of knowing we've beaten Bonaparte! The first time I ever advised anyone against his advantage, and I have to do it to you! Well, I don't know when I've been sorrier for anything, and that's a fact!'

Adam put his hat and gloves down rather quickly on a chair, and limped forward. 'My dear sir – !' he said, a good deal moved. 'No, no, I assure you – !'

'Nay, don't say it, lad!' Mr Chawleigh interrupted. 'It's like you not to ride grub, but I've done mighty ill by you, and it don't make a ha'p'orth of difference that I never meant it to turn out like it has! Now –'

'Mr Chawleigh –'

'Nay, you listen to what I've got to say, my lord!' said Mr Chawleigh, coming round the corner of the desk, and laying a hand on Adam's shoulder. 'If it hadn't been for me, you wouldn't have thought of selling out, would you?'

'No, but –'

' – so it's my blame, and it's for me to make it good, which I will do, and there's my hand on it! Now, we don't want any argumentation, so –'

'You know, sir, you are a great deal too kind to me,' Adam interposed, his slender hand lost in that enormous paw. He smiled at his father-in-law. 'But I didn't come here to reproach you. I came to tell you that I've made my fortune!'

'You've done *what?*' ejaculated Mr Chawleigh, staring at him under suddenly knit brows.

'Well, I daresay you won't think it a fortune,' said Adam, 'but I assure you it seems one to me! I hope you'll forgive me: I didn't follow your advice!'

The grip on his shoulder tightened. 'You didn't sell?' Mr Chawleigh demanded.

'No, sir: I bought!'

'You – Well, I'll be damned!' said Mr Chawleigh, apparently stunned. 'With me and Wimmering telling you – Well, if ever I thought you had it in you – !' A delighted smile spread over his countenance; he released Adam's shoulder to pat him on the back. 'Good lad, good lad!' he said. '*Bought* – ! And what's your profit?'

'I don't know yet, but Drummond thinks it will be somewhere in the region of twenty thousand, sir.'

'Twenty – How did you come by the blunt to buy to that tune?'

'I borrowed it from Drummond – on my own securities.'

'Oh, you did, did you?' said Mr Chawleigh. 'And I suppose he didn't get a notion that *I* was one of your securities?'

'I told him,' said Adam blandly, 'that he was on no account to think that you were in any way concerned.'

Mr Chawleigh regarded him with a fulminating but not unadmiring eye. 'If you wasn't a lord,' he said, 'I'd call you a young rascal!'

Adam laughed. 'Oh, no, would you? It was perfectly true! You were *not* concerned!'

'Yes, it's likely I'd let my daughter's husband be rolled-up, ain't it?' retorted Mr Chawleigh, with asperity. 'Well, well, to think you'd so much rumgumption! Twenty thousand pounds!' He chuckled; but all at once his expression changed, and he directed one of his searching stares at Adam. 'I take it you'll be wanting to redeem the mortgages?' he said belligerently.

There was a long pause. To redeem the mortgages, to make Fontley his own again, independent of Chawleigh-gold, and free from even the shadow of a threat of Chawleigh-interference, had been Adam's only motive for plunging into a speculation which he now regarded as the craziest act of his life. Even when he had been most horrified at what he had risked the thought had persisted that the object was worth any risk. The gamble had succeeded; and now, as he gave back his father-in-law's stare, he realized, in some bewilderment, that having the power to redeem the mortgages he had lost the desire to do it. Almost from the day of his marriage it had been his fixed goal: it should have been his first thought on waking that morning, but he had not thought of it until Mr Chawleigh himself recalled it to his mind. He had thought instead of drainage, and new cottages, and of the experimental farm he had now the means to run. His old obsession suddenly seemed foolish. Mr Chawleigh giving rein to the Juggernaut within him might infuriate him, but he was perfectly capable of handling Mr Chawleigh. And, to do Mr Chawleigh justice, he had never shown the least disposition to interfere in the affairs of Fontley. He had once, in the grip of passion, threatened to foreclose, but Adam had known, even in the heat of the moment, that there was no intention behind the threat, or any comprehension of the effect so brutal a display of power would have on one of finer sensibility than his own. His vulgarity made him sometimes extremely trying, but under it there was much that was admirable, and a softer heart than his fierce aspect would have led anyone to suppose. Looking at him now, Adam knew that he was scowling because he was afraid he was going to be hurt. Well, he shouldn't be: certainly not by the son-in-law who owed him so much and of whom he was so unmistakably fond.

'I'll redeem them if you wish it, sir – of course!' Adam said.

The scowl lifted a little. 'Why should I wish it? I'd a notion you couldn't bear to think I'd aught to do with that place of yours – nor wouldn't rest easy in your bed till you'd paid me back every penny you've had of me!'

'Good God, sir, I hope you don't expect that of me?' countered Adam. 'I could never repay all I owe you!'

'Don't talk so silly!' growled Mr Chawleigh. 'You know I don't!'

'Yes, of course I do – and also that nothing pleases you more than to shower expensive luxuries on me,' Adam said, affection as well as amusement in his eyes. 'As for Fontley, if you mean that I won't let you carpet the Grand Stairway, or fill the park with deer, you are perfectly right! But I give you warning that I have every intention of trying if I can't persuade you to dip that little finger of yours into a project I have in mind. I've no time to go into that now, however. About the mortgages – I have a much better scheme than to waste my money on redeeming them from you: I should infinitely prefer it if you will settle them on Giles.'

The scowl had entirely vanished. 'Now, that *is* a good scheme!' exclaimed Mr Chawleigh, rubbing his hands together. 'Ay, I'll do that, bless him! I'll have it drawn up legally, all shipshape and Bristol fashion, never fear!' A thought occurred to him; he said: 'If you was to do something handsome by the Government you could get yourself made an Earl, couldn't you?'

'To add to Giles's consequence? Not for the world! He's by far too top-lofty already – believes himself to be of the first importance!'

'Young varmint!' said Mr Chawleigh fondly. 'I'd like him to have a proper title, though. Ay, and I'd like to see you made an Earl, my lord, and I don't deny it.'

'If you set such store by titles, sir, why don't you get one for yourself? *I* think you should be an alderman!'

He spoke at random, merely to divert Mr Chawleigh's mind, but he instantly perceived that he had unwittingly hit the mark. Mr Chawleigh stared at him very hard, and said: 'Now, where did you come by that notion, my lord?'

'Ah!'

'Well, maybe I *will* be an alderman before I'm much older,' admitted Mr Chawleigh. 'But don't you go blabbing about it, my lord, because it ain't certain, mind! I'm not saying anything but that there is a vacancy, which everyone knows, now that poor old Ned Quarm's stuck his spoon in the wall, and it *might* be that I'll be voted for.'

'I won't breathe a word to a soul,' promised Adam. 'Alderman Chawleigh! I must say, I like it!'

'You think it sounds well, my lord?' asked Mr Chawleigh anxiously.

'*Very* well! I can fancy myself saying *my father-in-law, the alderman*, too. We shall be all odious pretension – and quite insufferable when you become Lord Mayor!'

Mr Chawleigh was so much delighted by this sally that he was still chuckling when Adam took leave of him.

It was four o'clock when Adam reached Fenton's again, and, in his valet's opinion, much too late to set out on his journey. 'For we shan't be at Fontley before two or three in the morning, my lord, not travelling by night, and everyone will be abed and asleep!'

'Yes, but if I put off the start until tomorrow my guests will have left before my arrival, and I shall never be forgiven,' argued Adam. 'But if they know that I travelled all night to make my apologies in person they will look on me with much more kindness – I hope! Good God! They won't have heard the news! Oh, that quite settles it! I shall be instantly absolved! And, in any event, I want to go home!'

Twenty-seven

*I*t was a little before nine o'clock on the following morning when Jenny called Come-in! to a knock on her door. She was seated at her dressing-table, while Martha Pinhoe set the final pins in her smooth braids, and it was in the looking-glass that she met her errant husband's guilty but laughing eyes. Her own twinkled in spite of herself, but she said severely, as she turned in her chair to face him: '*Well!* A pretty way to use me, my lord!'

'I know, I know!' he said penitently, coming across the room to kiss her. 'But even if I'd remembered what the date was, which I own I didn't, I *couldn't* have come! Have you heard the news?'

She put up a hand to clasp his shoulder for a moment. 'I should think everyone in the house has heard it by now. When did you arrive?'

'Just before three. I drove into the yard, so that I shouldn't rouse you all. My dear, I do beg your pardon! Infamous of me to have abandoned you! Did you desire Lambert to take my place?'

'He wasn't here,' she replied. '*Or* Charlotte, *or* your mama!'

'Oh, good God!' he exclaimed, aghast. 'You don't mean to say that Charlotte is confined already?'

'That's just what I do mean to say. And not a word of warning to me – not that I blame her for that, because she was in the very act of stepping into the carriage when she felt her pains begin. Lambert sent over one of the grooms directly, of course, but there we all were, sitting in the Long Drawing-room, and expecting every minute to see the Membury Place party walk in.

And the end of it was poor Lydia hadn't *one* member of her own family at her engagement party!'

'Except you!'

'That's different. Well, it was a sad disappointment to her, but she behaved beautifully – except for saying, right in front of everyone, that it would have been worse if Charlotte had had the baby in the middle of the party! Did you ever? We must send over to find out how Charlotte does. Why did Papa wish you to go to town, Adam?'

He glanced over his shoulder, to be sure that Martha had left the room. 'He wanted me to sell my Consols. There was something of a panic in the City, you see. He and Wimmering were in the deuce of a pucker!'

Her eyes searched his face. 'I'd a notion it might be that. I'll be bound you didn't sell, however, not feeling as you did!'

'No.' He laughed suddenly. 'Though I didn't feel very confident on Tuesday! Jenny, I have *such* a piece of news for you! It was as much as I could do not to wake you up when I came in, to tell you! I *bought* stock, and I *think* we shall find ourselves richer by twenty thousand, or near it! *Now* am I forgiven?'

'Good gracious!' she ejaculated. 'Oh, my goodness, no wonder I thought you looked as if you was in high croak!'

They were interrupted by an impetuous footstep on the corridor, and by the entrance of Lydia, hard upon a perfunctory knock. 'May I come in? Oh, so my dear brother is here, is he? How delightful! And how *very* obliging of you to have come in time to say goodbye to your guests, *dearest* Lynton!'

'Now, I won't have him scolded!' interposed Jenny. 'Didn't I tell you he wouldn't have failed if he hadn't had good reason to? Well, he's been making his fortune on 'Change, love!'

'Making his *fortune*? Adam, you're cutting a wheedle!'

'I'm not, but don't cry it from the housetops! And where did you learn that excessively vulgar expression?'

'From Brough!' she replied, making a face at him. 'Well, I'm *very* glad, even though I can't help detesting you! Oh, Adam, it was the shabbiest party! You can have no notion! I don't mean

362

that the Adversanes are not the greatest dears, but to have only them, and the Rockhills – ! And to make it worse Julia behaved in the most odious manner!'

'She had the headache, love.'

'Having the headache is no excuse for saying you have a premonition of disaster at a betrothal-party!' retorted Lydia. 'Particularly when she must have known Brough's brother was engaged in the war, and the Adversanes dreadfully anxious, though *they* never spoke of it! And for my part I don't believe she had the headache at all! People who have the headache don't sit down at the pianoforte and play dreary tunes.'

'It *does* seem to have been a dismal party!' said Adam. 'Indeed, I'm very sorry, but do you think my presence would have enlivened it? And I wasn't responsible for the absence of the others!'

'No, but – Oh, well, I daresay it doesn't signify, and at all events Brough and I laughed ourselves into stitches over it! Jenny, shall you object to it if I go away with Lady Adversane? The thing is that Lord Adversane and Brough mean to post up to London immediately, to see if they can come by any news of Vernon at the Horse Guards, but they don't care to leave poor Lady Adversane alone at such a time, so of course I asked her if I might go with her to bear her company, and she said she would be very glad to have me, but only if you could spare me – which I told her I knew you would.'

'Yes, to be sure I will,' Jenny answered, getting up. 'Is Lady Adversane down already? Adam, we must go downstairs at once! Oh, dear, as if it wasn't bad enough that you weren't here yesterday without me not being in the breakfast-parlour before the visitors!'

'Well, she isn't down yet,' said Lydia. 'She soon will be, however, because she was very nearly dressed when I went to her room. And Julia is having tea and toast in bed, which I'm heartily glad of. The gentlemen are all in the parlour, but they are reading the newspapers Adam brought from London, so you needn't trouble your head about *them*. I'll go and tell Anna to pack up my clothes.'

She hurried away. Jenny, snatching up the handkerchief laid out on the dressing-table, and thrusting it into her reticule, said: 'Well, I only hope her ladyship don't think this the most ramshackle house she ever was in! We've to breakfast early because she was wishful to be at home by noon, you know. Where are my keys? Oh, never mind! For goodness' sake, my lord, go down to the parlour!'

The gentlemen were still eagerly reading the London journals when Adam joined them. He made his apologies, but was assured he had no need to make them. 'My dear Lynton, it would have been rather too much to have expected you to leave London before the result of this battle was published!' Adversane said. 'We are very much obliged to you for having posted down to bring us the news so quickly. A great victory, is it not?' He smiled understandingly, and added: 'You have been wishing yourself with the Regiment. We have searched for mention of it in the dispatch, but the Duke merely commends Major-General Adam, amongst the other generals. You knew that the 52nd was a part of his Brigade, of course?'

'Yes, sir, I knew that, but very little more, I'm afraid. We were certainly not engaged on the 16th or the 17th. What part we played, or any of Clinton's Division, at Waterloo I can't discover – though I have a feeling that Hill's Corps was not in the thick of the fighting. The centre was held by the 1st Corps, the Prince of Orange's: I don't think there can be any doubt of that.'

'Enlighten our ignorance!' Rockhill said. 'Mine, I blush to confess, is profound. Why is there no doubt?'

'Well, didn't you notice that the names that *are* mentioned in the dispatch all belong to the 1st Corps? I don't mean the list of commendations, but in the Duke's account of the action? And I can't but think it significant that amongst the list of generals who were killed or wounded there's not one from Hill's Corps. Old Picton killed; Orange, Cooke, Alten, Halkett all wounded! That tells its own tale: *they* were standing the shock, not Hill's people.'

Lord Adversane began to look rather more hopeful. The ladies came in, and in the general exchange of greetings, and comment on the news, Brough seized the opportunity to draw Adam a little aside, and to say, in his lazy way: 'Very soothing, dear boy: I'm obliged to you. Did you mean it?'

'Yes, I promise you I did.'

'Pretty heavy, our losses, ain't they? Ever known so many generals to be hit? Looks bad to me.'

'Of course it's bad! Douro calls our losses *immense*, and if *he* uses such language as that —' Adam broke off. 'Well, we shall see when the lists are published!'

Brough nodded. 'Just so! All well with you, Dev?'

'More than well. I've been repairing my fortune: I'll tell you about it later.'

'Chawleigh nudge you on to a sure thing?'

'No, far otherwise! I flew in the face of his advice, and nicked the nick!'

'You don't mean it? Well done, dear boy!' Brough gripped his arm for an instant above the elbow, giving it an eloquent squeeze. 'Couldn't be better pleased if I'd made my own fortune! Used to count you the unluckiest fellow of my acquaintance, Dev, but I've been thinking lately that you ain't.'

'Good God, I never was! They used to say of me that I'd as many lucky escapes as Harry Smith!'

'Shouldn't be at all surprised: I've seen one of 'em myself,' Brough said cryptically. He continued, almost without a check: 'No objection to Lydia's going off with m'mother, have you? Mama don't show it, but she's devilish anxious, you know.'

'Of course I've no objection, you gudgeon!'

'Taken a great fancy to Lydia,' said Brough, his eyes turning towards that damsel involuntarily. 'Won't get a fit of blue devils if she has her with her — no one could! Made a hit with m'father too: he told me last night she was as sound as a roast! Myself, I think he's a shocking old flirt.'

There could be no doubt that the Adversanes approved of Brough's engagement. Adam thought that Lydia, never a

365

comfort to the Dowager, was already a comfort to her mother-in-law, and would soon become more a Beamish than a Deveril. Once, her overriding ambition had been to restore the fortunes of the Deverils: he recognized, a little ruefully, that she was more concerned today with the fate of her future brother-in-law than with her own brother's affairs.

As though she had read his thought, Jenny said, later, when she stood beside him, waving farewell to Lydia: 'Well, one can't help but feel moped, and that's a fact, as Papa would say! but she's going to be as happy as a grig. What's more, we won't lose her, as we might have done if she'd got herself riveted to someone you weren't acquainted with, and maybe wouldn't have liked above half. How comfortable it will be! Not that we don't go on very well with Charlotte and Lambert, but – Oh, my goodness! Charlotte! If I hadn't forgotten all about it! Well, what a topsy-turvy day this is, to be sure! I must –' She stopped, for they had walked back into the house together, and she saw that Julia was coming down the stairs. She said immediately, in her most prosaic voice: 'Good-morning, Julia! I do hope you slept well? You are just too late to say goodbye to Lady Adversane and Lydia, but they left all kinds of messages for you. Brough and his father set out for London half-an-hour ago, to try if they can learn any more news of the battle, you know.'

Julia, standing with one hand on the baluster-rail, lifted the other to her brow. 'The battle – the battle – the battle! No one can talk of anything else!'

'Well, it's natural the Adversanes should be anxious,' Jenny said. 'Adam, do you take Julia into the Green Saloon! I must scribble a note for Twitcham to carry to Membury Place.'

She went away, as she spoke, walking down the vaulted corridor with a brisk step. In strong contrast, Julia came slowly down into the hall, seeming almost to float over the stairs.

Adam stood, looking up at her, struck, as he always was, by her exquisite beauty and the grace of her every movement.

Her eyes were fixed on his face; she said: 'You should not have returned so soon. I'm still here, you see. But I shall soon be gone.'

He moved towards her, saying: 'I'm very glad that you *are* still here. I hoped you might be, so that I could beg your pardon. An infamous host, am I not? I promise you, I'm very conscious of it, and don't at all think I deserve to be forgiven – for I can tell you won't accept the battle as an excuse!'

'Did you think I should? I know you too well! You didn't wish me to come to Fontley, did you? You should have told me so.'

'My dear Julia – ! No, no, you are quite mistaken!'

'Ah, don't talk like that!' she said impulsively. 'Not to me! Not to me, Adam!'

He was considerably taken aback. The throbbing note in Julia's voice indicated, even to his inexperienced ears, that she was dangerously wrought up. He remembered having been told by Lady Oversley that her sensibility made her subject to hysterical fits, and he devoutly hoped that one of these was not imminent. With a lively dread of being precipitated into a dramatic scene in the most public place in the house, he said: 'Come into the saloon! We can't talk here.'

She shrugged, but allowed him to shepherd her into the saloon. He shut the door, and said: 'Now, what is it, Julia? You can't suppose that I fled from Fontley because you were coming to visit us!'

'You can't bear to see me here! You once told me so –'

'Surely not!' he expostulated.

'You said it was painful: is it still so painful? Why did you allow Jenny to invite me? How could I know –'

'Julia, for God's sake – ! You're talking nonsense, my dear – indeed, you are! I left Fontley because Mr Chawleigh sent me a most urgent message, and for no other reason. I had thought to be back again in good time for Lydia's party, but circumstances intervened which made it impossible. It was very bad of me – and I am deep in disgrace with Lydia! Poor girl! she was set on having all of us at her party, and in the end not one of us was present!'

'Lydia! *She* was not mortified by your absence! No one thought you had stayed away because *she* was here! I would not have believed that you would offer me such a slight! You might

367

have written to me – one line only, telling me not to come, and I should have understood, and made an excuse to remain in town! But to go away as you did – You might as well have declared to everyone that you preferred not to meet me! Lady Adversane is not so stupid that she didn't guess. She was delighted, I daresay! They don't like me, either of them. They made that plain enough! And Brough has always detested me! Nothing could have been more marked than their attentions to Lydia, and their incivility to me. Jenny and I were left quite out in the cold – until Rockhill took pity on Jenny, and talked insipidities to her. There was nothing for me to do but to occupy myself at the pianoforte, which I was able to do without fear of interrupting conversation, since no one paid the least heed.'

He had listened to her first in astonishment, and then in amusement, as it dawned on him that the real cause of her tantrum was not his defection but the attentions paid to Lydia. He did not for a moment suppose that the Adversanes had been uncivil, or even that Julia was jealous of Lydia. If she had been made much of, she would almost certainly have insisted that Lydia, celebrating her betrothal, must be first in consequence. She never tried to shine down her friends; Adam knew how prettily she would coax a shy girl out of her shell, and he guessed that had she found a vacant throne awaiting her at Fontley she would have handed Lydia on to it, with enchanting grace. The trouble had been that she had found Lydia already established on the throne. She had not stepped down from it; nobody had considered that she had any right to it. It was unlikely, too, that she had been accorded the admiration which she quite unconsciously expected. Brough had never been one of her court, and the Adversanes were naturally far more interested in their future daughter-in-law than in Rockhill's wife. She had obviously spent a miserable evening, feeling herself neglected, and was now in a mood to pick out any grievance that offered, and to magnify it into a tragedy.

Adam had never before seen her in a pet, or imagined that she could behave like a spoiled child. He was not in the least angry with her, but he did think that she was being silly and tiresome. He wondered whether she often indulged in dramatic tantrums, and found himself feeling sorry for Rockhill.

'I shall never come to Fontley again,' Julia said.

'Yes, you will,' he replied, smiling at her. 'You'll come to Lydia's wedding, in September, and see what a good host I can be!'

'I never thought that you would wound me – and laugh!' she said, turning her face away, her mouth trembling.

He was conscious, not of a burning desire to fold her in his arms and kiss away her melancholy, but of irritation. 'Oh, Julia, *not* at this hour!' he begged. He took her hand, and raised it to his lips, as she stared at him in amazement. 'My dear, I beg your pardon, but you are being quite absurd! You know very well I didn't run away because I didn't wish to meet you!'

'Ah, no! Not that, but because it's painful to be reminded of the past, and the hopes we cherished! Was it that, Adam?'

'No, Julia, it was *not* that,' he replied firmly. 'I wasn't even thinking of you – in fact, I entirely forgot Lydia's party!'

'*Forgot?*' she repeated, drawing her hand away, and almost shrinking from him. 'How could you do so? It's not possible!'

'I found it very possible. I was engaged on an affair of so much more importance that it drove everything else out of my head. Shocking, wasn't it? But I think you will understand, when I tell you that I had Fontley in my mind. You have always loved it, so you must be glad to know that I've managed to turn my small principal into quite a respectable fortune – large enough, at all events, to enable me to bring Fontley back to what it once was – oh, better than ever it was, I hope!'

'Oh, no, no, don't spoil it!' she cried.

'*Spoil* it?' he said, thunderstruck.

'You said once that I should find everything the same, but it's not the same! Don't make it smart, and new! Don't let Jenny do so!'

He regarded her with a queer little smile. 'I see. When you talk of Fontley, you think of the ruins, and the portrait of my

369

stupid Cavalier ancestor, don't you? But that's not what I think of. The Priory is only a part of Fontley, you know, and not the most important part, either.'

'What then?' she demanded, bewildered.

'My acres, of course.'

'Oh, how much you have changed!' she exclaimed bitterly. 'You had nobler ambitions once!'

'Well, it was certainly my ambition to command the Regiment one day,' he admitted, 'but I don't think I was ever as romantic as you believed me to be. Perhaps we never had time to learn to know each other very well, Julia.'

She did not answer. Footsteps were approaching, and a moment later the door opened, and Jenny came in, a letter in her hand. She said cheerfully: 'I don't mean to interrupt you, but one of Lambert's servants has this instant rid over, and you'll want to know the news, Adam. Charlotte was safely delivered at eight o'clock this morning, and it's a boy! Isn't that capital? He'll be able to play with Giles! Lambert says —' She stopped, meeting Adam's eyes, which were brimful of laughter, gave a gasp, and said unsteadily: 'Now, Adam, for goodness' sake — !' She saw that Julia was looking blankly from her to Adam, and said apologetically: 'I beg pardon! It's just a silly joke — not worth repeating! Charlotte is feeling perfectly stout, and the baby is to be christened Charles Lambert Stephen Bardolph!'

'*What?*' Adam exclaimed. 'Jenny, you made that up!'

She chuckled, handing him the letter. 'See if I did!'

'Good God!' he uttered, scanning the missive. 'And why not Adam as well? Pretty shabby of them to leave me out, don't you think? I shan't send a christening gift. Did you ever hear such a collection of names, Julia?'

'I suppose they will call him Charles,' she replied. 'Pray tell Charlotte how happy I am to hear that she has a son, and how sorry I was not to have seen her! I must run away now, and put on my hat, or Rockhill will give me a scold.'

She smiled brightly upon them both, and went swiftly out of the room. At the head of the staircase she met Rockhill, just about to come down. He smiled at her, saying softly: 'What, my lovely one?'

Her face puckered, she clung to him suddenly, saying in a choked, passionate voice: 'Take me away, Rock! I wish we hadn't come! It's dull and detestable! Please take me away!'

'With the greatest pleasure on earth, my Sylph! I was coming in search of you to suggest that very thing. What a bore that we pledged ourselves to go on to stay with the Rossetts! I shan't have you to myself for as long as five minutes: you will be swept from me, and wholly surrounded by tiresome admirers.'

She gave a tiny laugh. 'Oh, no! How can you, Rock?'

He turned up her face, and kissed her. 'Beautiful baggage!' he remarked. 'Go and put your hat on, my love!'

He sauntered on down the stairs, and was talking to his host and hostess when Julia presently joined him. She was looking quite ravishing, and had recovered her spirits sufficiently to be able to kiss Jenny, thanking her for an enjoyable visit, before turning to offer her hand to Adam, rallying him, with rather glittering drollery, on his haycocks, and adjuring him not to bury poor Jenny alive in the fens.

He answered in kind, escorting her out to where the chaise stood waiting. Standing just within the hall, Rockhill retained Jenny's hand for a minute, saying softly: 'A delightful visit, ma'am! I am so much in your debt! Pray believe that you may command my services at any time!'

'I'm afraid it was dreadfully dull and flat,' she replied.

'Dear Lady Lynton, I assure you it couldn't have been better! Do you know, I fancy we have nothing more to worry us? Goodbye – and a thousand thanks!'

He kissed her hand, and was gone before she was put to the necessity of replying. She went out into the porch to see the chaise drive off, and as soon as it had passed out of sight Adam turned, and came to join her, saying: 'Thank God we have the house to ourselves again!'

Her eyes twinkled. 'Well, *you* didn't see so very much of the visitors!'

'Very true. Poor Jenny, was it quite abominable? I think it must have been.'

'Oh, well! It might have been worse,' she said philosophically. 'Brough took your place, and Lord and Lady Adversane are so kind and easy, you know, that they made it seem as if your not being at home was quite commonplace. Which I'll take good care it don't become!'

He laughed. 'No, no, I swear I will never do so again! Come into the library! I want to tell you how I made my fortune!'

'Adam, did you say it was *twenty thousand*?'

'More or less, I think, if Consols recover to the extent Drummond believes they must. I staked everything I had, and still don't know how I found the courage to do it. *What* a crazy gamble!'

'I don't see that it was that,' she objected. 'You always knew we should beat Bonaparte!'

He said wryly: 'I wasn't so pot-sure when I'd committed myself. Wimmering wanted me to sell as much as your father did.'

She listened in silence to the account of his three days in London, and at the end said slowly: 'You will be able to do all the things you want to, then.'

'Well, hardly that! Not immediately. But I can do enough to set Fontley on its feet, and once that's accomplished I don't fear for the future.' He smiled at her. 'Who knows? By the time Giles comes of age we may be as rich as Mr Coke! By the bye, your father is going to settle the mortgages on Giles.'

'You don't mean to redeem them?' she said, surprised.

'No. He doesn't wish it, and – Oh, I don't know how it comes about, but I found, when I might have done it, that I didn't want to!'

'I'm glad. He wouldn't have liked it.'

'No, I know he wouldn't. I mean to try instead if I can't persuade him to invest some of his wealth in my cut – only, if I *can* bring him round my finger we'll make it a canal. You know, Jenny, that's what's needed in this district, not only for drainage, but for transport. I'm pretty sure it would pay handsome dividends. Do you think he might be interested?'

'Well, there's no saying, but I should think he might. He likes engineering and water-works. But – when you wouldn't let him help you to the farm you want – !'

'This is different. *That* would have been a gift – and I have accepted too many from him; *this* will be a business partnership.' He looked at her, his brows a little raised, a question in his eyes. 'You don't like it, Jenny?'

'Oh, yes! Of course I do!' she said, colouring.

'But you don't. Why are you looking so grave? What troubles you?'

'I'm not troubled. I'm glad, if you are!'

'If I am!'

'If it's not too late!' she blurted out.

He was puzzled for a moment; then he said: 'No. It's not too late.'

She smiled waveringly. 'It's like you to say that. But if this had happened last year . . .'

'I should have married Julia? I doubt it. I suppose I might have contrived to compound with the creditors, but I hardly think Oversley would have consented to such a poor match for Julia. He told me once that he didn't think we were well-suited. In fact, we should have been very ill-suited. *She* would have discovered me to be a dead bore, poor girl, and I am much better off with my Jenny.'

She blushed fierily. 'Oh, no – you don't mean that! I do try to make you comfortable, but I'm not beautiful or accomplished, like she is!'

'No, but on the other hand you don't enact me Cheltenham tragedies when I've barely swallowed my breakfast!' he said. He took her face between his hands, turning it up, and looking down at her for a moment before he kissed her. 'I do love you, Jenny,' he said gently. 'Very much indeed – and I couldn't do without you. You are a part of my life. Julia was never that – only a boy's impractical dream!'

A little pang smote her; she wanted to ask him: '*Do you love me as much as you loved her?*' She was too inarticulate to be able to utter the words; and, in a minute, knew that it would be foolish to do so. Searching his eyes, she saw warmth in them, and tenderness, but not the ardent flame that had once kindled them when he had looked at Julia. She hid her face in his shoulder, thinking that she too had had an impractical dream. But she had always known that she was too commonplace and matter-of-fact to inspire him with the passionate adoration he had felt for Julia. Probably Adam would always carry Julia in some corner of his heart. She had been tiresome today, putting him out of love with her; but Jenny did not think that this revulsion would last. Julia stood for his youth, and the high hopes he had cherished; and although he might no longer yearn to possess her she would remain nostalgically dear to him while life endured.

Yet, after all, Jenny thought that she had been granted more than she had hoped for when she had married him. He did love her: differently, but perhaps more enduringly; and he had grown to depend on her. She thought that they would have many years of quiet content: never reaching the heights, but living together in comfort and deepening friendship. *Well, you can't have it both ways*, she thought, *and I couldn't live in alt all the time, so I daresay I'm better off as things are.*

She felt his hand lightly stroking her hair, and lifted her head. He was looking gravely at her, aware that she was troubled, yet not wholly understanding the cause. She gave him a hug, smiling reassuringly at him. She thought, and was comforted, that though she was not the wife of his dreams it was with her, not with Julia, that he shared life's little, foolish jokes. Her eyes narrowed, twinkling, as she disclosed the latest of these to him.

'I wouldn't tell you till we were alone, but your mama writes that it is *exactly* as she foretold!'

The hint of anxiety in his face disappeared. Amusement took its place; he exclaimed appreciatively: 'Charlotte's child favours Lambert!'

She nodded, chuckling. 'Yes, and she says the poor little thing is positively gross, and quite undistinguished, besides having, *already*, a – a decided air of self-consequence!'

He gave a shout of laughter; and the pain in her heart was eased. After all, life was not made up of moments of exaltation, but of quite ordinary, everyday things. The vision of the shining, inaccessible peaks vanished; Jenny remembered two pieces of domestic news, and told Adam about them. They were not very romantic, but they were really much more important than grand passions or blighted loves: Giles Jonathan had cut his first tooth, and Adam's best cow had given birth to a fine heifer-calf.

ALSO AVAILABLE IN ARROW BY GEORGETTE HEYER

Sprig Muslin

Finding so young and pretty a girl as Amanda wandering unattended, Sir Gareth Ludlow knows it is his duty as a man of honour to restore her to her family. But it is to prove no easy task for the Corinthian. His captive in sprig muslin has more than her rapturous good looks and bandboxes to aid her – she is also possessed of a runaway imagination . . .

April Lady

When the new Lady Cardross begins to fill her days with fashion and frivolity, the Earl has to wonder whether she did really only marry him for his money, as his family so helpfully suggests. And now Nell doesn't dare tell him the truth . . . What with the concern over his wife's heart and pocket, sorting out her brother's scrapes and trying to prevent his own half sister from eloping, it is no wonder that the much-tried Earl almost misses the opportunity to smooth the path of true love in his marriage . . .

The Spanish Bride

Shot-proof, fever-proof and a veteran campaigner at the age of twenty-five, Brigade-major Harry Smith is reputed to be the luckiest man in Lord Wellington's army. Yet at the siege of Badajos, his friends foretell the ruin of his career. When Harry meets the defenceless Juana, a fiery passion consumes him. Under the banner of honour and with the selfsame ardour he so frequently displays in battle, he dives headlong into marriage. In his beautiful child-bride, he finds a kindred spirit, and a temper to match. But for Juana, a long year of war must follow.

arrow books

ALSO AVAILABLE IN WILLIAM HEINEMANN

Georgette Heyer's Regency World

Jennifer Kloester

**A unique and beautifully illustrated companion to
Georgette Heyer's Regency Novels**

A bestselling novelist since 1921, Georgette Heyer is known across the world for her historical romances set in Regency England. Millions of readers love the period for its fashion, famous people and events, and its elegant and often outrageous mayfly upper-class. It was Georgette Heyer who created the Regency genre of historical fiction in the 1930s and 40s with books such as *Regency Buck* and *Friday's Child*. Since then, in many minds, Georgette Heyer and the Regency have become synonymous.

Not a dry history book, but the ultimate, definitive guide to Georgette Heyer's world: her heroines, her villains and dashing heroes, the shops, clubs and towns they frequented, the parties and seasons they celebrated, how they ate, drank, dressed, socialised, voted, shopped and drove. An utterly delightful and fun read for any Heyer fan.

'An invaluable guide to the world of the *bon ton*. No lover of Georgette Heyer's novels should be without it.'
Katie Fforde

WILLIAM HEINEMANN : LONDON